THE
ABBE MOURET'S SIN

In this novel Zola studies the problem of male chastity. How does the Roman Catholic priest, vowed to celibacy, learn to keep unbroken such complete denial of the flesh?

With amazing delicacy but also unflinching courage, he tells the story of young Serge Mouret, Vicar of Artaud, in southern France, victim of the conflict between the world which has made sex evil and the natural impulses which seem to him — when he loves a young girl — virginally pure.

This work of the great Frenchman is also of immense interest from the formal literary standpoint. Zola has gone the whole hog in evolving form to fit the exigencies of the tale. The result is a fascinating combination of stylised realism and sheer poetry.

In shape the novel is rather like the classical three-movement symphony. In the first part the situation is realistically and logically developed. In the second, in meditative mood, we seem to have the perfect poetry of young love. But the classical mould proves inadequate to express the tragedy of life, and in the third part, instead of a gay rondo, we see the more sordid truth which our western world has made of sex.

Here translated with great sympathy, unabridged and in its full vigour by Alec Brown, we have one of world literature's most Ariel-like love stories and an honest examination of a fundamental problem of the Christian ethic.

D1283096

THE ABBE MOURET'S SIN

THE
ABBE MOURET'S SIN

EMILE ZOLA

Translated from the French by
ALEC BROWN

LONDON
ELEK BOOKS

PZ
3
.Z74f
1957

Printed in Great Britain by
HARDING & CURTIS LTD.
Bath, Somerset

INTRODUCTORY NOTE

by ALEC BROWN

I HAVE in my title of this translation emphasised the notion of sin which lies behind *La Faute de l'Abbé Mouret*, because I am writing in 1956, not 1875. It is not merely one minor sin among many that is involved, but precisely the basic sin of sex. To Zola's world I think this was perhaps more clear than to ours. Three-quarters of a century have gone by since this poetic masterpiece was published, and it is now being offered to a reading-public which is not only not predominately Catholic (as France was when Zola wrote), but, (despite reactionary setbacks in some middle-class milieux), also healthily on the way to a new paganism in morals.

This of course does not mean that our children will easily win through to a totally clean attitude towards sex.* The obscurantist forces of religion are restlessly active. Here and there, taking advantage of the flabbiness of thought and betrayal of many scientists, they have latterly even made some advance. The problems of sex and of the allied questions of continence and chastity, are still with us. They are indeed unresolved not only in the average mind of the 'christian' west, but also in its counterpart, the realm created by one-time seminarist Stalin (which is after all only natural, since owing to the backwardness of Russia, all the bolsheviks were able to achieve was the establishment of an ultra-bourgeois state capitalism.)

But let us turn to our book.

Zola's story of the celibate priest who lapsed into earthly love will come rather as a shock to many readers, not because it deals with love, but because the hue and cry raised against the great moralist who wrote it has led them to believe that Zola's principal characteristic is to call a spade sometimes a spade, sometimes a b—— spade. Here however he presents his problem with almost no direct physical details, and largely through the symbolism of words used poetically.

It has indeed been said that in this essay the great advocate of 'naturalism' went too far from nature. Undoubtedly, the lyrical 'middle movement' of the book, in which the awakening of love in adolescence is interpreted through the flowers, shrubs and trees of

*We ourselves are still very far off it.

5

a vast expansive garden run wild, does—if read carelessly—seem over lush. So many are the luscious flowers blooming at the same time that to the disrepectful it might suggest a nursery-man's nightmare catalogue, till one recalls that it takes place in what is almost a sub-tropical climate, where such rampant behaviour is more comprehensible.

Besides, if one reads the book properly—that is, rather slowly, tasting every word carefully while allowing Zola's fantasy to carry one's own freely forward—one cannot but marvel at the author's mastery of sheer organisation and construction. Never once is there a repetition, never once a false note. The fugue is worked out to the full. (Of course, there are some who do not like fugal argument). Certainly the aptness of the imagery, the resources of vocabulary, the virtuoso orchestration of the mere words, and the never-interrupted sense that behind it all there is the inevitable development of a reality at first idyllic, then tragic—a sense emphasised by the matter-of-factness and realism of every word spoken by Albine— (the imaginative trueness of Zola's dialogue is always superb!)—all this constitutes a real *tour de force*.

But before we examine the subject of the novel, first a word about its general position. In the total corpus of Zola's work it is supreme. In no other of his works is there concentrated with such purity either his lofty idealism or his poetic quality. It is the highest evidence of the lofty social and human ethic which always inspired him. To our very existence, for inescapable biological reasons, sex is of cardinal, even prime importance. Hence it is but logical that Zola's greatest poetic creation is all about sex.

Zola, in fact, is in all his work worried about the way European civilisation regulates the basic force of our lives. He is one of the very few first-rank novelists who have dealt with sex as a problem— a very different matter from using it as the subject of their fiction, as a motive-force regarded as entertaining, yet unessential to some 'larger' theme. Other sex-problem novelists who spring to mind at once are Flaubert, Lawrence, Maupassant, Anatole France and de Montherlant. Many others, of course, do at times envisage the problem (Schnitzler, for instance), but not so supremely as this mainly French little group. Those great novel-writers, the Russians, here prove a rather muddle-headed, unanalytical people, always concerned with what they consider the totality of social behaviour, never getting near the real subject, (or, if they do, becoming so clinical as to be distasteful). Dostoyevski clearly scents original sin in sex, but will insist on mixing the sexual union up with other

6

phenomena of human behaviour, which, though no doubt originally rooted in sex, overtly have nothing to do with it. Moreover, he ignores, or is ignorant of (the result is the same), the sexual mainspring in other passions, and is not so much pre-Freudian, as anti-Freudian. In distinction, Zola, though chronologically pre-Freudian, often anticipates the great analyst and writes as if he had studied under him. As for Lev Tolstoy (despite his Kreutzer Sonata and reams of tosh), that great figure, alas, remains in sexual matters merely a sometime roué with a moral hang-over. Carping cries of *verboten*, all puritans forget, do not constitute the analysis which might help us to handle our impulses.

Any true work of art functions by isolating some feature of our reality from the total flux in which we live. It elaborates and intensifies what it isolates, so that we may perceive, experience, even understand it more vividly. In his story of the Reverend Mouret, Zola examines certain social results of the conflict between adolescent love in all its purity and the cruder aspects of the coupling of the sexes and procreation of the species. Now, though no doubt there are here elements which are of universal validity, in the main what Zola treats of are specifically features of our European world misshapen by nearly two thousand years of organised Christianity. In Zola's story, the basic impulses and needs of sex are represented in two ways—in the courtship and marriage of the younger generation of the Provençal village of Artaud (near the author's native Aix-en-Provence) and in the general scene of nature in the background (from the farmyard pets of the young Vicar's simple-minded sister, to the sparrows in the church eaves and all vegetation, this particularly emphasised by the intensity of growth of the great park gardens which have run wild).

At the 'civilised' extreme are two other modes of sex life. There is utter negation, the body-renouncing celibacy of the priesthood of the Catholic church, magnified for emphasis in the intimate picture of a powerfully-built, passionate young priest's inturned struggle to maintain sexual continence. And there is christian civilisation's general response to that negation, shown in the change which takes place in the Reverend Mouret when he is, so to speak, born again, after a serious illness. This negation of negation is romantic love, a hyperconscious, unhealthy hypertrophied idealisation of the sexual relationship. For worship of the abstract Virgin of the Immaculate Conception (the supposed virgin mother of God herself reputed born of a virgin mother!), there is substituted an equally diseased worship of the sexual partner.

To say much more than this about the details of all this would be to retell the whole progression of Zola's story, to its marvellous culmination when old Jeanbernat slices off one of the Friar's ears,* and to do that would be most unfair, robbing every new reader of that most precious gift, the sense of development obtained on first reading a book. For this reason, it is perhaps in a foreword like this pardonable to sum up without giving the detailed items which should be learned by reading the book. And if then anyone asks *where* Zola's enquiry into the problem *gets us*, and what his conclusion is, the answer I think is that, though it is not necessarily the work of art's job to include its own balance-sheet (that surely, is the task of the critic, hence indeed these very words), yet there are of course implied conclusions, even those which are involuntary, implicit in the very nature of the story. Obviously, Zola could not depict the unhappy nature of certain accepted social attitudes and ideals without something with which to contrast them. And, this being so, without inventing utterly unreal people and purely imaginary types of relationship, he clearly had to seek his 'preferable' or 'more healthy' types in the real world about him. We find his true ideal lies somewhere between the crude but less emotionally diseased Artaud peasants, to whom marriage is basically an economic matter and sex both an unavoidable but unquestioned biological urge and unreproved physical pleasure, and the more delicate, but as yet untutored, conjugal realism of Albine, the girl of both fine nurture and natural 'pre-civilisation' living, uncontaminated by religion. One puts Zola's story down convinced that, had the priest but been strong enough to overcome both his own negation and that counter over-affirmation of sex (the two extremes of our western concept of sex, for the sexless way of living of the public-school ideal and of the dedicated priest on the one hand and the romantic promiscuity of the dedicated film-star of our day on the other are merely two sides of the same coin), little Albine would have coped very well with practical life and with a fine sense of balance would have both been a great lover and have reared a healthy family. But the necessary condition for her strength (here, the novel's main weakness, Zola makes her a typification rather than an individual person), is the co-operation of her chosen mate, and when Mouret fails her, she is quick, instinctively, to perceive the unviability of their love.

*A symbolic, possibly phallic act, which a few years later had disastrous consequences not many miles from Artaud in the sex-tormented mind of that poor fellow, Vincent van Gogh the painter.

It is due to the exigencies of Zola's poetisation of reality here that Albine, in her 'natural' death amid autumnal flowers, should also, in her own way, have to deny herself entirely, while with cruel irony the wretched priest carries on, an undying symbol of the evil of negation, gloating in the church eternal (as he thinks it).

There is little doubt where Zola's sympathies lie. But the giants of fiction achieve their vision fairly and impregnate us with a breadth which is all-understanding, and Zola is no exception. Mouret is drawn with greater insight, fairness, and love than Albine, and even the loathsome friar is depicted with sympathy. I doubt if any adherent of Christianity, of whatever brand, has ever so comprehendingly described the aspiration for purity, or its cost to a healthy, otherwise normal man, as Zola in this story.

So much for the substance of the book. Now a word about its manner. There is a totally different aspect of *The Abbé Mouret's Sin* in which the reader may find tremendous enjoyment. It is in its language. Now, it has been suggested that this is far too elaborate and ornate for the taste of us English, a very revealing assertion, since as a nation we both produced Shakespeare and are on the whole highly appreciative of *his* garishly-coloured, overloaded language. Yet, just as we are uncritically greedy for Tudor rhetoric (and its imitations—witness the popularity of Dylan Thomas's poetry), we are equally outstandingly picksome about poetic prose, which the French love. Witness our national attitude towards Oscar Wilde! Perhaps in his lovely prose Wilde was more French than English, and this disagreement arises from a basic difference between the French and English languages. Since this has a crucial bearing on appreciating Zola's prose, it may help the reader to formulate this difference.

Whereas, (despite popular belief), French falls very far short of English as a logical language, being less perfect an instrument in the grammatical machinery of logical sentence construction, we are shockingly indifferent to precision of meaning in our substantive words, our nouns and adjectives. These we tend to use whimsically, wilfully, 'instinctively', emotionally, erratically. We have no *Academy* dictionary to standardise connotations, as the French have. The big Oxford dictionary merely records meanings, it does not really prescribe them, it is an aid to understanding, not to writing, and Webster's big dictionary deals with American, not English.*

*Both an increasing divergence of the meaning of substantive words, plus great imprecision of use of the grammatical structure in American speech and writing.

Even in the 'exact' sciences it is to be observed in English that no sooner is a new work coined, or given a special meaning, a definite function, then another scientist collars it, to use it loosely for an entirely different purpose, while there is among scientists an amazing propensity (as any issue of the weekly *Nature* will show) for inventing new special words where already a perfectly adequate ordinary one exists.

French, on the other hand—and here Zola is indeed a master—tends to allot words precise ambits of meaning. This applies even to those with purely emotive force. This precision of the substantive in French prompts an author to use his words more intellectually, his feeling controlled by thought. He does not indulge so much in hit-or-miss poetic effects, but orchestrates deliberately. Coldly, indeed. All his words are treated as if of equal value—all jewels, in fact. We of course have our jewels too, but we tend to value only the more sterling ones and treat the rest as if they were solder in which to set the diamonds.

Put the difference like this: the 'Shakespearian' way is to toss the jewels into the dun mass, rather as sultanas or 'cherries' into a cake, to be enraptured later when the eye spots one and the thumb can get it out. French prose, when poetic, as Zola's here, is ornate, not to be pretty, not to offer us plums, however luscious, not to be evocative, but to pursue a logical argument or a preconceived course of development, as in music.

Such prose calls for great elasticity in translation. At one moment, bald word for word English would fail to convey all the aroma of the original and one has to seek an approximating evocative paraphrase, while at others one is obliged to avoid the literal word in English for the very opposite reason, in case, lacking its French precision of emotive tone, it should prove too evocative. In such cases one has to seek safety in understatement.

This leads me to my parting word, on how to read such prose. For, even supposing, as of course I do, that in the main this English version, made with loving and admiring care, does Zola justice, one must never forget that, just as different pictures need looking at, different music listening to, in different ways, so books need to be read appropriately. If one sets out to read this novel in what might be termed the 'anglo-saxon' way (the way suited to the English middle-class novel of entertainment from the mid-nineteenth-century on, Thackeray, Dickens, Galsworthy and suchlike), looking primarily for 'the facts', or 'the story'—meaning, of course, facts or story in a crude material sense alone,—one is doomed to be

10

disappointed. One must here read with painstaking tread, savouring all the words, in order to appreciate all the situations and events, material, mental, emotional, both individual, social and biological, with equal intensity.

For in such a novel it is easy to miss the key to understanding. There are events—church services, interviews between priests and parishioners, the development of love between Mouret and Albine, the marriage of the young peasants, the de-auriculation of the friar— which are as real as any others reported in the newspapers. But there are others—the young man's longing for chastity, the monstrous growth of such continence, the spring rise of sap, the influence of the whole pulsation of vegetable life in its diurnal and annual rhythms, the practical basis of a young girl's nascent love, and the poorly co-ordinated urges of the male—which no modern newspaper would treat as news or court of law accept as admissible evidence, but it is the poet-novelist's triumph to set on paper, for those who care to read them, for they are an essential part of his argument. To read about Mouret thus is an effort well worth making. It aids one, incidentally, to appreciate many aspects of life which in an urban civilisation we tend to forget.

ALEC BROWN.

Tarrant Gunville, July 31st, 1956.

BOOK ONE

CHAPTER I

As SHE came in, Teuse dumped her besom and feather-brush against the altar. She was a bit late because she had been soaking-in her six months' big wash. She went straight across the church to toll the *angelus*. Hurrying accentuated her limp. She bumped against benches. The bell rope dangled down from the ceiling near the confessional box, a plain hemp rope, well frayed, with a big knot at the end, black from greasy hands. Teuse weighed down on it with all her ponderous bulk, then got going, and swayed rhythmically, a mass of petticoats, her bonnet askew, her beefy cheeks suffused with blood.

At last, quite out of breath, she straightened her bonnet with one pat and went to sweep up a bit just in front of the altar. The planking of the altar platform did not fit too well, the dust would collect in the cracks. Accompanied by an undercurrent of muttering, her birch-besom fudged out the corners. Then she took off the altar-cloths, noticing with much annoyance that the big top one, which was already patched in a score of places, had worn right through again in the centre, showing the under cloth, which was folded in two and so threadbare, so transparent, that through it you could see the sacred stone in its wooden framing. She gave the age-darkened linen a good dusting, swept her feather-brush along the gradine and put the altar-cards back in place. Then she mounted a chair, to get the yellow cotton loose covers off the cross and the two candle-sticks. There were patches of tarnish all over the brass.

'They do want a rub-up and no mistake,' muttered Teuse, to herself, 'I must get m' powder.'

Next, lurching and jerking her game leg along ponderously enough to crack the stone flags, she went to the sacristy for the mass book, which, without opening it, she put beside the Gospel on the lectern, the pages turned in to the altar. She then lit the two candles. Now taking up her besom, she surveyed the little church to make sure that she had done the Almighty as he should be done. Everything was still, only the bell-rope beside the confessional still swaying with long, supple waves from vaulting to stone floor.

Her clergyman, the Reverend Serge Mouret, had that instant entered the sacristy, a chilly little room which only a short corridor divided from the vicarage dining-room.

'*Bonjour, monsieur le Curé*,' said Teuse, as she made to withdraw,

15

then: 'Oh! Aren't you a lazy one this morning! Do you know it is a quarter after six already?' And, without giving the smiling young priest time to reply, she ran on: 'I've got a bone to pick with you. That altar-cloth! It's got another hole in it. It simply won't do you know, drifting on like this, we've only one other and I've been wearing m' sight out these past three days a-patching at that, if you carry on like this much longer, our poor Lord's table will be as bare as . . .'

But, still smiling, here Serge Mouret cheerfully interrupted: 'My dear Teuse,' he said, 'Jesus does not really need all these trappings. He is always warm and those who love him will always give him a royal welcome.'

He walked across towards a small cistern of water. 'Is my sister up?' he asked. 'I have seen nothing of her.'

'Miss Désirée,' replied Mouret's housekeeper, 'has been down a long time.' Teuse was kneeling now, at a discarded kitchen side-board they used to keep the priest's robes of office in. 'She's already out among her hens and her rabbits . . . She thought her chicks were going to hatch out yesterday, but they haven't, and you can imagine if she's worked up about it.' Then she broke off to ask: 'It'll be the gold chasuble today, won't it?'

Withdrawn into himself, his hands cleansed, muttering a prayer, the Reverend Mouret merely nodded *yes*. Artaud church possessed only three chasubles, one violet, one black and one gold, so the latter, worn on those days for which white, red or green is prescribed, got an unusual lot of wear. With great devotion, Teuse took it from the blue paper-lined shelf where she put it away after every service, cautiously removed the cambric which protected its patterning, and placed it on the sideboard: in the gold part, a lamb was depicted, asleep on a cross of gold, with heavy gold rays all round it. Particularly worn away wherever it jutted out, the metal was tending to flake off and had in places the relief completely disappeared. Indeed, this chasuble was a continual worry to the vicarage, this steady flaking away being viewed with heartfelt anxiety. But the Vicar had to wear it nearly every day. And when the last strands of gilt thread were worn out, however was it to be replaced, not to speak of purchasing the three chasubles for which this one served?

Over the chasuble Teuse now lay out the stole, then maniple, girdle, alb and amice, but as she painstakingly arranged the maniple in cruciform shape on the stole and twisted the rope into the revered initial of Mary's holy name she still continued to nag: 'This girdle ain't worth much either,' she muttered, 'you'll have to bring yourself

16

to buy another, Vicar ... That won't break you. Why, if only I had the hemp, I'd weave you one myself.'

The Reverend Mouret made no response. On a small side table he made ready the chalice. It was a large old silver-gilt one on a bronze pedestal. Drawing it out of the depths of the deal cupboard which contained all the consecrated vessels and vestments, the oils and missals, the candlesticks and the crosses, he lay over it a clean communion cloth and on this the silver-gilt paten with the host, all of which he further covered with a small linen chalice-cover. He was just covering the chalice by pinching up the two folds in the gold-cloth veil matching the chasuble, when Teuse's voice broke in: 'Hold hard, Vicar, there ain't any corporal in the burse ... I took out all the communion cloths and the chalice-covers and the dirty corporals to boil 'em white ... separate, of course, not with the rest of the wash ... But I hadn't told you, had I? I soaked the wash in just now and high time, I can tell you, it was filthy, but it'll come out cleaner than last time.'

And while the priest slipped a corporal into the burse and lay this on the veil with its gold cross on a gold background, she still ran on: 'By the way, Vicar, I quite forgot, that young rascal Vincent hasn't turned up, shall I be your server this morning, eh?'

Mouret shot her a stern glance.

'Get away,' she cried, ' there's nothing wrong in that.' Her broad face beamed. 'I did it once in the Reverend Caffin's day. What's more, I can serve better than those young scoundrels, laughing, the little heathens, if only so much as a blue-bottle flies into church ... Get away with you, Vicar, no matter if I do wear a bonnet and am sixty and my hoops tight as a barrel, I've more respect for the Almighty than any of your wicked little boys, why, only the other day what did I find them doing behind the altar, but playing leap-frog.'

Still shaking his head, Mouret continued to stare at her.

'Out-of-the-way hole, this village is,' she groused away. 'Not a hundred and fifty souls all told in it ... There are days like today when you won't find a living person in Artaud, they even take the babes up into the vineyards, believe me. Think, vines growing out of all them stones, dry as thistles too, they are. Godforsaken hole, miles off the road ... Well, unless an angel comes down from Heaven, Vicar, you won't have nobody to serve mass for you today but me, Vicar, or, begging your pardon, one of Miss Désirée's rabbits!'

However, at this very juncture, who should enter the church but

17

the Brichets' youngest boy Vincent. Softly, he opened the sacristy door and stood there, and his tousled head of carroty hair and bright little grey eyes infuriated Teuse.

'Ah! You young rapscallion!' she cried. 'You've been up to some mischief, I'll bet . . . Come you here, you little villain, hurry up, M. Mouret thinks my hands might contaminate our dear Lord!'

Seeing the boy, the Vicar took up the amice. Kissing the cross embroidered in the centre of the piece of linen, he lay it on his head for a moment, then, folding it back on to the collar of his cassock, crossed the cords and tied them, the right crossing over the left. He then drew on the alba, symbol of purity, putting his right arm in first. Vincent, who had squatted down when he came in, now got up and moved round his Vicar, adjusting the alba, to make sure that it fell evenly all round to within two fingers of the floor. He then handed the girdle to the priest, who tied it very tightly about him, to symbolise the bonds worn by Our Saviour during the Passion.

Meanwhile, Teuse stood by, sore and jealous, but trying to hold her tongue. It was an unequal struggle, and a moment later she suddenly cried: 'Friar Archangias looked in. There wasn't a child in school today. He went off like the wind into the vineyards to tweak the little wretches' ears for them . . . You ought to have seen him. I believe he has something to tell you.'

With a gesture, the Vicar silenced her. All this time he had not opened his lips. Taking the maniple, he intoned the prescribed prayers as he kissed it before laying it across his left forearm to signify the performance of good deeds and then, first kissing this too, crossed the stole over his breast, to symbolise dignity and power. When it came to the chasuble, Teuse had to help Vincent to tie it by its thin little cords, to prevent it falling back.

'Holy Virgin,' she cried suddenly, 'if I haven't forgotten the altar-cruets,' and she hurried to the cupboard. 'Here, you young rascal, quick!'

Vincent filled the cruets, small flasks of coarse glass, with water and wine, while Teuse rummaged hastily in a drawer to find a clean towel. Holding the chalice in his left hand by the knot, the finger-tips of his right hand on the offertory-bag, the Reverend Serge, without removing his biretta, made a deep inclination before a wooden Crucifix hanging on the wall above the sideboard. The boy bowed like him, then led the way out, the altar vessels in his hands under their towel, the priest following, with downcast eyes, in profound devotion.

CHAPTER II

THERE was not a soul in the white-walled church this May morning. The rope dangling by the confessional was motionless again. On the right-hand side of the tabernacle along one wall there was a holy-lamp of tinted glass burning steadily, a patch of red colour. When he had put the altar-cruets on the credence table, Vincent went back to the left, to kneel at the foot of the altar steps, while the Vicar, genuflecting to the flags in reverence of the Holy Sacrament, mounted the steps, spread out the corporal and placed the chalice in the middle of it. Then opening the missal, he came down again. Again a genuflection bent him in two. Making the sign of the cross, his hands together on his breast and in loud, clear tones, his cheeks bloodless from devotion and love, he began the great drama of Almighty God.

'*Introibo ad altare Dei.*'

And little Vincent mumbled back: '*Ad Deum que laetificat juventutem meam,*' gabbling through the responses of the litany and the psalm. But when it came to the last he got badly behind, because he had his eyes on Teuse, who was roving about the church. She had in fact been uneasily watching one of the candles and her agitation seemed to increase when once again the Vicar put his hands together and recited the *Confiteor*. At this point she halted just where the prayer happened to overtake her, but though she lowered her glance and her hand got busy touching her bosom just as the Vicar had done his, her eye was still on the offending wick.

For a few moments more the solemn tones of the priest and the mutterings of his assistant alternated.

'*Dominus vobiscum.*'

'*Et cum spiritu tuo.*'

The man of God here spread his hands wide, then brought them together again and with a gravity tense with emotion cried:

'*Oremus . . .*'

Here Teuse's patience ran out. Slipping behind the altar, she reached that candle and with the tip of her scissors snipped it clean, for it was guttering, there were already two huge tears of lost wax trickling down its sides. By the time she got back and begun to straighten the benches and make sure that there was enough holy water in all the stoups, the Reverend Serge had gone up to the altar

19

where, standing with hands resting on the edge of the cloth, he prayed softly. Then he lay his lips to the altar.

At his back the morning light still flooded the chancel with its palour. The sun had not yet topped the roofs. It might have been a low-pitched, lime-washed stable, the rafters roughly plastered, through which time and again quivered the *Kyrie eleisons* of the service. On either side three tall plain-glass windows, with many panes cracked and some entirely missing, let in light of chalky harshness. Fresh air wafted straight in, and all the poverty of this lost hamlet was laid bare. At the far end, above the main door, which was never opened, the threshold overgrown with grass, there was a gallery of rough-hewn planking from one wall to the other up to which led a miller's ladder. On festival days this erection groaned under heavy peasant clogs. The confessional, an erection gaping at the joints, painted yellow, was near these steps. Opposite, beside the smaller door, was the font, which was of some age, and stood on a stone-built pedestal. Finally, on right and left, in the centre of the wall, were two small, fenced-in altars. That on the left was dedicated to the Virgin. It contained a large gilded plaster Mother-of-God, a regal gilded crown firmly planted on her chestnut hair. Seated on her left arm was a smiling naked Jesus, whose little hand held the radiant globe which is our earth. She was treading the clouds, with winged angels underfoot. The right-hand altar, at which masses for the dead were served, bore a coloured cardboard Christ to match the Virgin. This representation of Jesus, of about the size of a ten-year-old, was undergoing frightful death throes, the head flung back, the sides bleeding, the abdomen ripped open, the limbs contorted and blood-splashed. In the church, there was also a pulpit with five steps up to it, opposite a large grandmother clock in walnut case with tick so loud it could be heard all over the church, just as if there were a big heart beating somewhere under the flagstones. All down the nave were the fourteen stations of the cross, fourteen crudely coloured pictures in black framing, blotching the uncouth white of the walls with the yellow, blue and red of the Passion.

'*Deo gratias*,' stammered Vincent, when the lesson ended.

Preparations for the mystic rite of the immolation of the holy victim now began. The server took the missal and carried it to the left, on the gospel side, taking care not to touch the pages of the book. Every time that he passed in front of the tabernacle he made a sideways genuflection which put his little body all askew. Then, coming back to the right-hand side again, he stood with arms crossed while the gospel was read. The priest now made the sign of the cross, first on the missal, then on his own forehead, to indicate that he would never be ashamed of holy writ, then on his lips, to show his constant readiness to profess his faith, and finally on his heart, to indicate that this was the Lord's and only the Lord's.

'*Dominus vobiscum*,' he intoned, turning round, and when he faced all that whiteness of the little church, his features were obliterated. For a moment he held the paten with the host at chest-level, offering it to God on behalf of himself, his congregation, and all the faithful, living and dead. Then sliding to the edge of the corporal, but without his fingers touching it, he took the chalice and wiped it painstakingly with the chalice-cloth. Vincent had meanwhile crossed to the credence for the altar-cruets, which he now presented, first that with the wine, then that with the water. Next, for the benefit of the whole world, the Vicar offered the empty church the half-full chalice, afterwards returning it to the centre of the corporal. He carefully avoided touching it with his fingers and covered it again with the cloth. After another prayer, he continued his rite, pouring a little trickle of water over thumb and index-finger tips first on one hand, then the other, to wash from them the faintest contamination of sin. And when he had wiped his fingers dry with the manutergium, Teuse, who was waiting at hand, took the dish and emptied it out into a zinc bucket she kept for the purpose at the corner of the altar.

'*Orate, fratres*,' resumed the priest, out loud, facing the empty pews, his hands spread wide in the gesture of prayer, as he invited all men of goodwill to join with him. And then he turned back again to the altar and continued in a lower voice. Vincent mumbled a long Latin sentence in which he got lost. At that moment, golden flames flooded in through the windows. Responding to the priest's call, the sunshine had come to mass. It lit up large golden patches of the left-hand wall, the confessional, the altar to the Virgin, and the clumsy clock. The wood of the confessional snapped sharply. Transfigured by the dazzling light of her crown and golden cloak, the painted lips of the Mother of God smiled down tenderly on the child Jesus. Growing warmer now, the clock ticked away time at a more lively pace. The tiny lime-washed stable of a church now seemed full of warm crowds. Outside, tiny sounds of the happy awakening of the countryside became audible, the blades of grass sighing luxuriously at ease, the leaves brushing the warmth away from themselves, the birds preening and essaying their wings. The world of nature even entered the church in the wake of the sun. At one window, the lofty branches of a mountain-ash thrust in

21

through the broken panes, reaching out its buds as if to peer inside, and through the cracks in the main door blades of grass could be seen thrusting, as if threatening to invade the nave. Amid all this upsurge of life only the large crucifix insisted on death, with the agony of its ochre-blotched, lacquer-plastered flesh lurking in the shadows. For an instant, a sparrow poised on the edge of a hole in a window, peeped in, then flew away again, but almost at once with one silent rush of flight was back, to swoop down among the pews, opposite the altar of the Virgin. A second followed and soon there were sparrows fluttering in from every branch of the ash to promenade with little hops at their ease up and down the flags.

'*Sanctus, Sanctus, Sanctus, Dominus, Deus, Sabaoth,*' came the muttered words of the priest, his shoulders slightly hunched. Vincent jingled his little sanctus bell thrice, and then, scared by that sudden tintinnabulation, the sparrows all flew off together with such a noise of wings that Teuse, who had just vanished into the sacristy, came out again, grumbling away.

'Little wretches, they'll make the whole place filthy . . . I'll bet my life on it, Miss Désirée's been putting crumbs out for them again.'

The awesome moment drew near, the body and the blood of a God were on the point of coming down upon this altar. The priest kissed the altar-cloth and joined his hands in prayer, repeatedly making the sign of the cross over host and chalice. Every single word now of the canon of the mass left his lips ecstatically in his absolute abandonment to humility and gratitude. Each pose, each gesture, each inflexion of his voice, was eloquent of his own littleness and the emotion he felt at being elected for so great a task. Vincent came to kneel at his heels. The boy took the chasuble in his left hand, held it lightly up, and made ready his little bell, while Mouret, elbows resting on the edge of the communion table, the host held between thumb and index finger of both hands, pronounced above it the words of consecration: *Hoc est enim corpus meum.* Then, genuflecting once, he rose slowly to his full height, never taking his eyes off the body, while the boy assisting him crouched prostrate and again jingled the sanctus bell thrice. Next he consecrated the wine: *His est enim calix,* elbows again on the altar, bowing, raising the ciborium, following this now with his eyes, his right hand clutching the knot of the stem, the left supporting the base, till the boy had given the final three rings of the bell, and yet once again the beloved blood was shed, and the great mystery of the Redemption renewed.

'You just wait, you just wait!' threatened Teuse, brandishing her fist in an attempt to scare off the sparrows.

But the little birds were without fear. They had flown back while the bell was actually still jingling, impudent things, fluttering up on to the backs of the pews. Indeed, that repetitive bell-music made them quite exuberant and they responded with bright little voices, interrupting the words of Latin with the pearly laughter of unfettered urchins. The sunshine warmed their plumage, while the gentle poverty of this church was an enchantment to them. Here they were at home, as if in a barn with a skylight left open, and they swarmed and squabbled in a huddle of feathers over the crumbs to be found on the floor. One of them suddenly perched on the gold veiling of that smiling Virgin, another ventured to reconnoitre under Teuse's spread of petticoats, an act of impudence which made her furious.

But at the altar the priest heard nothing of this invasion of the nave of his church. His eyes fastened on the sacred host, his thumb and index finger joined, he knew nothing of this warm early May morning, this rising flood of sunlight, greenery, and birds, lapping to the very feet of that crucifix where nature was doomed to the agonies of a painful death.

'*Per omnia saecula saeculorum,*' he declared.

'*Amen,*' mumbled Vincent.

Finishing the Lord's Prayer, the priest held the host over the ciborium and broke it in two. Thereupon from one half he broke a small fragment which he let fall into the priceless blood, to signalise the intimate union which through this communion he was about to make with Lord God. Out loud, he recited the *Ecce Agnus Dei*, then in low tones pronounced the three orisons prescribed for the occasion and performed the act of his own unworthiness. Then, elbows on the altar, paten under his chin, he jointly communicated the two parts of the host. After this, putting his hands together on a level with his face, in fervid meditation, with the aid of the paten he brought together the consecrated fragments of the host and placed them in the chalice. A morsel stuck to his thumb. With his fore-finger, he crumbed it off. Then, making the sign of the cross with the chalice and placing the paten under his chin again, he took the priceless blood in three gulps, without his lips once leaving the edge of the vessel, thus imbibing the divine Sacrifice to the last drop.

Vincent had now just got to his feet to go back to the sideboard for the altar-cruets, when the door of the corridor which led from the vicarage was suddenly flung wide open, banging against the wall, to permit the passage of a lovely girl of twenty-two. There was an innocent childishness in her bearing. She carried something hidden in her apron.

'Thirteen!' she cried, loudly. 'Every single egg was good!' And she held her apron open to reveal a swarming brood of young chicks with beady black eyes and their first down. 'But just look at them, aren't they pets? The darlings! Oh, look at that little white one getting on the backs of the others! And that one, the speckly, look, it's flapping its wings already! They were jolly good eggs, weren't they? Not one unfertile!'

Teuse, beginning to play a part in the service in spite of whatever the Vicar had said, now quickly handed the cruets to Vincent for ablution, then turned and said loudly: 'Do please be quiet, Miss Désirée! Surely you can see we haven't finished yet!'

Through the open door a powerful farmyard odour, like a sudden burst of fermentation, forced its way into the church and impregnated the sunlight, which by now had reached the altar. For some time Désirée stood still, rapt in the little world she bore, but also gazing at Vincent pouring out the wine of purification, and her brother drinking it down, to ensure that no trace of the sacred substance of Christ's body should remain between his lips. In fact, she was still standing there, transfixed, when he returned, the chalice in his two hands, to have the wine and the water of ablution poured over thumb and index-finger, and drink this too down. But by then the broodie hen, all flurry and anxiety, had caught up with the girl in search of her chicks, and fought to get into the church, so, babbling baby-talk to the chicks, Désirée withdrew, just as, after having laid the purificator to his lips, the young priest wiped the brim and the interior of the chalice with it.

The acts of grace rendered to God, this was the end. For the last time the acolyte went for the missal and brought it to the right. Together with paten and chalice-cover, the priest replaced the communion cloth on the chalice, then, again pressing together the two large folds in the veil, he put down the burse, in which he had folded the corporal-cloth. His whole person embodied intense gratitude. He craved Heaven for remission of his sins, for the grace of a holy life and to deserve eternal life. He was utterly lost now in this miracle of love, the unending sacrifice which day by day fed him with the body and blood of his Saviour. Reading the orisons, he turned and pronounced the words: '*Ite, missa est.*'

'*Deo gratias,*' came the response from Vincent.

Turning now to kiss the altar, he at last made his way back, his left hand under his bosom, his right extended, blessing the church, which was full of the merry-making of the sun's rays and the sparrows' chitter-chatter.

'*Benedicat vos omnipotens Deus, Pater et Filius, et Spiritus Sanctus.*'

'*Amen,*' murmured the server, making the sign of the cross.

The sun was high now and the sparrows had grown bold. While the priest read from the left-hand card the Gospel of St. John, declaring the eternity of the Word, the sun set fire to the altar, whitening the blocks of imitation marble, and engulfing the light given by the two candles, whose short wicks now turned to sombre patches. The triumphant orb brought cross, candlesticks, chasuble, and chalice veil into the ambit of its glory, till all the gilt of them gleamed white under the hot rays. And when, taking the chalice and genuflecting, the priest, head covered, had left the altar to go to the sacristy, before him the boy taking back the altar-cruets and the towel, it was the sun itself who remained behind, sole master of this church. Now it was *his* turn to rest on the altar cloth, set the tabernacle door afire with glory, and laud the fecund rites of the month of May. From the flagstones, warmth began to rise. Through the limewashed walls, through the big Virgin, through even the big Christ, now surged the shudder of rising sap, as if the eternal youth of our world had indeed vanquished death.

CHAPTER III

TEUSE lost no time in putting out the candles. But before she left she simply had to get those sparrows out. So when she took the missal back to the sacristy, the Vicar had gone, after having laid out the holy regalia and washed his hands. He was already in the dining-room, breakfasting standing, off a glass of milk.

'Vicar,' she cried, as she entered, 'you ought to put a stop to your sister throwing crumbs down in the church! A fine game. She started that last winter, said the sparrows were pure gold and our dear Lord would feed them . . . If you don't look out, she'll have us all sleeping in the pen together with her hens and her rabbits.'

'We should be a bit warmer, shouldn't we?' laughed the young Vicar. 'Teuse dear, you're always a-grumbling. Do let our poor dear Désirée enjoy her love of God's creatures. The innocent child knows no other pleasure.'

A-straddle in the centre of the room, Teuse cried: 'Oh, if you had your way, you would even let the magpies build their nests in the church. You just don't see things. You think everything is perfect. Your sister was very lucky indeed to have you take charge of her when you came out of your seminary. I should just like to know who else would let her mess about in a farmyard as you do.'

Then, suddenly changing her tone, in gentler manner, she added: 'True enough, it would be a pity to say the poor lass nay, she doesn't mean no harm. Though she's healthy in body as there's few like her about, she's only like a child of ten, isn't she? Do you know, I still put her to bed every night and have to tell her tales like my babe, to get her to sleep.'

Mouret was still standing, finishing his cup of milk, his fingers rather red from the chill air of the dining-room. It was quite large, with a tiled floor and grey painted walls, and furnished sparsely with table and dining-chairs. Teuse stripped off the serviette she had spread for breakfast on one corner of the table.

'Can't say you dirty much linen,' she muttered. 'Anyone'd think you had an impediment so you just couldn't sit down. You're always like a man just off on a long journey . . . Oh, if only you'd known the Reverend Caffin who was here before you! Poor dear man, may his soul rest in peace, now he was a molly-coddle, if ever there was one, he would have got the indigestion if he'd eaten standing like you . . He was a Norman, he was, from Canteleu. Like myself. And I can tell you, I won't say thank-you to him for bringing me to this out-of-the-way hole. We were miserable, I can tell you, he and I, when we first came here. Poor dear man, he'd got himself into bit of a trouble in our parts, you see. He . . . Why, gracious me, Vicar, don't tell me you've no sugar in your milk? Look, there's your two lumps, untouched.'

Mouret put down the cup.

'Oh yes,' he said, 'I must have forgotten.'

The good housekeeper just stared blankly at him, then shrugged her shoulders. She took the slice of wholemeal bread and butter, which he had also not touched, and wrapped it up. The priest was about to leave the room, but she rushed up to him, and with a cry of 'Just a moment!' dropped to her knees. 'It's only your shoe-laces,' she said, 'you haven't done them up . . . Vicar, I simply don't understand how your feet can bear it in these rough clod-hopper boots you will wear, and you such a fine young man, anyone

26

can see you grew up spoiled! . . . Upon my word, the Bishop must have sized you up mighty well to give you the poorest living in the whole department.'

You're very cross with the world this morning, my dear Teuse.

'No, be fair,' said Mouret, again smiling, 'Artaud was *my* choice . . . Are we not happy here? We have all we need. Why we live in paradaisal peace.'

This silenced her complaints. She too now laughed. 'Dear Vicar,' she murmured. 'You are such an unworldly man . . . But now, just you come and have a peep, how well I've lathered in my wash, that would be far better than you and I squabbling.'

He had no other course but to obey, for she threatened not to let him go at all unless he praised her laundry. As he left the dining-room, he stumbled against a heap of plaster in the corridor.

'Whatever is this?' he demanded.

'Oh! that's nothing,' she replied, in her fiercest manner, 'only your vicarage falling down about your head. But you're all right, of course, you've got all you need . . . Heavens alive, as if the place was not slivered in pieces! Just you look at that ceiling and tell me if it's not got enough cracks for you! If we don't get buried alive one of these days, we'll certainly owe our guardian angels a good fat candle. But that's all right, so long as it suits you. Just like in the church too, for the last two years there's a number of panes have wanted making good. Lord God himself freezes in there in winter. Besides, it would keep those sparrows out. In the end you'll see me plaster them up with paper, I warn you.'

'Hm,' said the priest, 'not a bad idea, that, sticking paper . . . But those walls, you know, are far more substantial than you think. In my room the floor's only come away just under the window. This house will outlast our time.'

When they reached the lean-to, near the kitchen, just to please her he became lavish in his praise of the qualities of her wash. He even had to stick his fingers in the suds and feel them. Then, delighted, the old woman became quite motherly, stopped grousing, and hurried away to fetch a clothes-brush, saying: 'You don't think you're going out with yesterday's mud on your cassock, do you? If only you'd left it on the banisters, it would have been clean ready for you . . . It's quite good, this cassock is. Only do please lift up the skirts when you go through the fields, the thistles tear everything.'

She made him turn about like a child while with violent blows of the brush she cleaned the garment from top to toe.

27

'Ah no, now, now, that'll do,' he cried, making good his escape. 'You will keep an eye on Désirée, won't you? I'll run round now and tell her that I'm going out.'

But just as he said this, there was a ringing voice crying his name and his sister came running up, flushed with happiness, bare-headed, her heavy head of black hair richly bunched at her nape, but her arms filthy to the elbows. She was cleaning out her hen-house. When she saw her brother was on the point of going out, breviary under his arm, she laughed still more heartily, kissing him full on the lips, with her hands held behind her back, so as not to touch him.

'No, no,' she babbled. 'I would make you dirty . . . Oh, what a time I am having! You shall see my farmyard when you get back.'

And off she raced again. Mouret told Teuse he would be back about eleven for lunch. He was a few paces from the vicarage when Teuse, who had accompanied him to the threshold, started yelling after him, her final injunctions.

'Friar Archangias. Don't forget to see him! . . . Go and see the Brichets, too. Old Mother Brichet came round yesterday about the wedding . . . Vicar, please, just a moment . . . listen! I happened to see Rosalie myself, yesterday. The girl can't think of anything better in the world than to marry that big lout Fortuné. You have a word with his father. Perhaps Bambousse will pay some attention to you . . . And don't you come back today as late as twelve, like you did the other day. Eleven, yes, eleven o'clock, will you?'

But the priest did not turn back again, and Teuse withdrew indoors, grinding out through her teeth: 'I'll swear he never heard me . . . Not twenty-six, he ain't, and headstrong as a boy. True, for unworldliness, there's many a saint of sixty he could show points, but he's had no experience. He doesn't know anything of life yet. Dear boy! It's easy for him to be as good as an angel.'

CHAPTER IV

WHEN the Reverend Mouret no longer felt Teuse at his back, he halted, delighted to find himself alone at last. He looked back, His church stood on an insignificant hump of ground, from which there was a gentle slope down to the village. It was a longish building, like a disused farm building into the walls of which had been let large windows. The roof was of cheerful red tiles. The vicarage was a small grey cottage built up against the body of the church. As if sight of it awakened misgivings that that unquenchable flow of words which had buzzed in his ears since daybreak might catch him up, he immediately continued on his way, round to the right, and only felt safe when he reached the main church doorway, where he could not be seen from the vicarage. The bare, sun-baked, rain-swept west-end of the church was capped by a small stone turret, inside which one could see the outline of a small bell and the rope going down through a hole in the roof. Six broken steps, one end half covered with soil, led up to the tall main door. The timbers of this gaped badly. They were covered with cobwebs, and the iron-work was so rusty and so pitiable with the dust silting over it and the loose hinges that it looked as if at the first good puff the wind would break it in. He was rather fond of this decaying building, and mounted to the top of the steps, to lean against one wing of the door. From that point of vantage his eye could survey the whole countryside. Shielding his eyes with his hands, he scanned the horizon.

When May came round, this stony soil burst into stupendous vegetation. Immense thickets of wild lavender and juniper, and expanses of coarse herbage mounted the porch, to thrust armfuls of sombre greenery to the very edge of the guttering. With its very first upsurge, the sap threatened to bear away the church, engulfed in its dense tangle of growth. And in these morning hours, when growth was in full spate, the whole atmosphere throbbed with the sun's warmth, till at last the very stones of the church porch heaved in an immense shudder of life. But of these arduous labour pains the young priest had no knowledge. It was his impression merely that the stone steps were unsteady, and he changed his position, to lean against the other wing of the door.

He could see the country five miles ahead, where touched by black patches of conifers, a wall of yellow hills enclosed it; it was a frightful region of arid soil bursting asunder in ridges of outcropping rock. The rare patches of cultivable soil offered pools of blood, the red land of the fields with their ranks of scraggy almond trees, grey olives, and the straggling vines which ribbed the landscape with their stumpy ochreous trunks. One might have supposed some terrible conflagration to have swept over it all, scattering the cinders of burnt out forest trees far over the heights, scorching the pastures, leaving behind it only the flames and furnace heat of the deep ravines. It was only at rare points that the pale green of a field of wheat introduced a softer tone. It was an utterly savage horizon, dying of thirst, not a brook to be seen, and the least breath of wind in the air above it carried the soil away in fine dust clouds. Only in the ultimate distance was there a hill-enclosed corner of country with lush greenery, a side-arm of the next valley, which was rendered fertile by the Viorne, a river flowing down from the Seille Gorge.

Dazzled, the priest lowered his gaze to the village, the handful of houses of which straggled just below the church, wretched buildings, all of them, of grim stone and rough-hewn timbers, strung along a narrow road, with no precise side streets. There were about thirty of them, some poverty-black hunched against their own dunghills, others a little more spacious and cheerful, with pink tiles. Plots of garden won from the rock boasted their ranks of vegetables enclosed in hedges. At this hour, Artaud was deserted, not a woman at a window, not a child squatting in the dust, only the hens coming and going in flocks, scrabbling in the chaff, busy with their beaks up to the thresholds of the house-doors gaping passively at the sunshine. On the near side of the village, a large black squatting dog seemed to be on guard.

Gradually, lassitude overcame the Reverend Mouret. The rising sun bathed him in such warmth that he relaxed completely against the church door. Tranquil contentment took possession of him. He mused on this village of his, which had sprung up in this place, amid the stones, like the gnarled undergrowth of the valley. All Artaud's inhabitants were inter-related, all bearing the same surname to such an extent that they used double-barrelled names from the cradle up, to distinguish one from another. At some antecedent date an ancestral Artaud had come like an outcast, to establish himself in this waste land. His family had grown with the savage vitality of the vegetation, drawing nourishment from this stone till it had become a tribe, then the tribe turned to a community, till they could not sort out their cousinage, going back for generations. They inter-married with unblushing promiscuity. It was unknown for an Artaud to bring in a wife from any neighbouring village. There were merely occasional cases of girls going elsewhere to find husbands. These people came into the world and left it bound to their soil, proliferating on their own dung-hills with slow deliberation like the uncomplicated soul of trees which scatter their seed about their feet, with little conception of any larger world beyond the dun rocks among which they vegetated. Even so, there were still poor and rich among them. When hens vanished, hen-houses acquired heavy padlocks at night. An Artaud had once not long since killed another, one evening, behind the mill. Deep in this grim belt of hills they were a people apart, a breed sprung from the soil, a mankind of three hundred heads in whom time began all anew.

In Mouret there resided all the lifeless shadow of the seminary. For years he had not known the sun. Even now he was indifferent to it, his eyes sealed, inward-looking. He felt nothing but scorn for accursed Nature. For long, when in moments of contemplation his thoughts got him down, his dream had been of a hermit's deserted place, a nook in some mountain where no sign of life, no living being, no plant even, no living water, would come to distract him from the contemplation of God. There was in him the fire of unsullied love, coupled with frank horror of physical sensation. Turning his back to the light, in-dying on himself, he would have welcomed non-being, losing himself in the sovereign purity of all souls. The sky appeared to him uniformly white, with the whiteness of light, as if white lilies snowed from heaven, as if all modes of purity and all modes of innocence and all modes of chastity glowed there. But when he spoke out about his longing for seclusion and his need for divine frankness, his confessor used to reprove him, reminding him of the battles of the Church and the requirements of the priesthood.

Later, when ordained, the young priest came to Artaud at his own request, in the hope of there realising his dream of annihilation of the masculine nature within him. In the heart of this poverty, on this sterile soil, he would be able to stop his ears to the sounds of the world and would live in slumber, like the saints. And indeed, he had for some months now been quite radiant. There had been but rare, far-removed shudders of the village from time to time to perturb him. While he trod the paths, open to the sky, scarcely ever did he feel the sun's lips warmer at his neck, nor did he hear the uninterrupted act of generation through which he strode.

Suddenly, the big black dog which had mounted guard over Artaud decided to run up the hill to the priest. There, the animal squatted down again, at Mouret's feet. But the Vicar of Artaud noticed nothing. He was lost now in the gentleness of the morning. The evening before, he had begun the rosary of the Virgin Mary and now he attributed the great delight which had taken possession of him to her intercession with her divine Son. And how unworthy of attention the good things of the earth seemed to him! How grateful he was to feel poor! When after losing father and mother on the same day, fruit of a tragedy the horrible details of which were still unknown to him, he had begun to train for holy orders, he left all his share of the heritage to his elder brother. His

31

only link with the world was now his sister. Conceiving a sort of religious affection for her in her feeblemindedness, he had taken charge of her. She was so childlike, so innocent in her simple-mindedness that he saw in her one of the poor in spirit to whom the Gospel grants the Kingdom of Heaven.

Nevertheless, for some time now she had been worrying him. She was becoming too strong, too healthy, too much aware of life. He was, however, not seriously worried. His time was spent in that inward life he had made for himself, abandoning all to render his whole being to God. In his efforts to liberate himself from the exigencies of the flesh, he kept the doors of his senses closed, and had become but a spirit in the raptures of contemplation. Nature to him was all traps and filth, and it was his triumph to be harsh towards it, to scorn it, extricating himself utterly from human mire. The righteous man must of necessity be mad in the eyes of the world. Thus he considered himself as it were an exile on earth. All he thought of were the values of heaven. It was incomprehensible to him that a man should risk losing eternal joy for a few hours of perishable delight. His reasoning deceived him, his desires lied to him. And if he made progress in his achievement of chasity, it was above all by humility and subservience. He would be the last of all men, under all, so that the dew of divine grace should come to his heart as to an arid desert sand. He made himself out to be ever worthy of opprobium, a lost soul eternally unworthy of salvation from sin. To be lowly was to believe and to adore. He no longer even depended on himself; he was blind, deaf; he was a dead body. He was a thing of the Lord. This so, a hymn of praise swept him from the abjection into which he plunged up far above those who were merely happy or powerful and carried him into the dazzling light of unlimited happiness.

Thus Serge Mouret, Vicar, had at Artaud found the exquisite pleasure of the monastery which in days gone by, whenever he read the *Imitation*, he had so fiercely desired. Nothing in him had yet known battle. From the first time that he knelt, he was perfect, without struggle, without shock, as if striken by a thunderbolt of grace, in absolute oblivion of the flesh. It was an ecstasy of nearness to God such as some young priests do come to know, a period of bliss broken by no inner whisper and all the lusts known are but an immense demand for purity. When one believes that one thing is everything, one can never be shaken, and he did think that God, hence equally his own humility, subservience, and chastity, were everything. He could recall having heard temptation spoken of as an abominable torture experienced by the holiest of men. But at such talk, he smiled. He himself had never been thus abandoned by God. He walked in his faith as in perfect armour which preserved him from the least breath of evil. He remembered at eight having hidden in corners, weeping because of love. He did not know whom it was that he loved. He just wept because he loved, somebody unknown, very far away. He had then been in a constant state of intense emotion. Later, to assuage that desire for superhuman love which was his only torment, he wished to become a priest. He could not think where there could be greater love than in priesthood. In this he satisfied his being, the predisposition of his blood, his adolescent dreams, his first male desires. If temptation must come to him, he awaited it with all the calm of an ignorant seminarist. He felt that he had finally killed the man in himself, and he was happy to feel himself now one apart, a creature castrated, on a road all by himself, one whom the tonsure marked as one of the Lord's own flock.

CHAPTER V

ALL this time the sun was heating up the main door of the church. Gilded insects murmured in their flight as they circled about a large flower sprung up between the stones of the steps. Mouret felt a sudden faintness, and had decided to continue his way, when with fierce barks the black mastiff came racing across to the railings of the little graveyard to the left of the church. At the same time, a harsh voice cried: 'So there you are, you good-for-nothing little rascal, you play truant, and now I find you in the churchyard . . . Don't tell me *no*, I've been watching you for quarter of an hour.'

Mouret joined the dog against the railings, to see Vincent held roughly by the ear by the Friar who kept the church school. The boy was more or less dangling over the cliff which, the length of the churchyard, fell steeply away to the Mascle, a torrent whose white waters, five miles downstream, flowed into the Viorne.

'Friar Archangias!' the Vicar called, gently, to remind the big hulk of a man to have a care.

But the Friar would not let go the boy's ear.

'Oh, so it's you, Vicar, is it?' he grumbled. 'Did you know this young rapscallion is always lurking about in your churchyard? I don't know what mischief he gets up to . . . it would serve him right if I let him drop down and give his skull a crack on the rocks down there. Serve him right if I did!'

The boy did not utter a word, merely clung to the undergrowth, his eyes stubbornly closed.

'Take care, Friar,' the priest said, again, 'the boy might slip.' Then he leant over and gave Vincent a hand, to clamber up.

'Now, my dear boy,' he said, 'what were you after there? You really ought not to go playing in churchyards.'

The urchin had opened his eyes and timorously drawn away from the Friar, placing himself under the Vicar's wing.

'I'll tell you sir,' he half whispered, raising his tousled head to look at the priest. 'In the brambles under that rock there's a warbler's nest. I've been watching it ten days and more . . . As the babies had hatched out, I came to have a peep this morning after serving you at mass . . .'

'A warbler's nest?' cried Friar Archangias. 'You just wait a minute, you just wait!'

He moved away, to find a clod of earth on one of the graves, which he came back to throw down into the brambles. But he missed the nest. A second clod, however, better thrown, tipped up the fragile cradle and sent the little birds flying into the torrent below.

'Now,' he cried, rubbing his hands together, to brush the dirt off, 'perhaps you'll stop coming about in here like a little heathen . . . If you walk over the graves, you'll have the ghosts of the dead come back in the night to pull at your toes for you!'

Vincent, who had laughed when he saw the nest go flying, shot a swift glance all round him. Then he shrugged his shoulders, like a lad who was no coward.

'Pooh! I'm not afeared,' he said. 'Dead men never move any more.'

There was indeed nothing frightening about Artaud church-yard. It was a bare patch of ground with narrow paths which were beginning to be lost under the year's encroaching herbage. Here and there the soil bulged a little. One single stone, a fresh white piece of marble, that of the Reverend Caffin, reared its sharp outline in the centre. Otherwise, there was nothing but the torn-off arms of wooden crosses, sear box-trees, old flag-stones, broken and moss-grown. There were not two funerals a year in Artaud. Death seemed altogether to have deserted this ill-defined plot where every evening Teuse came to gather weeds for Désirée's rabbits. One single enormous cypress at the gate spread its shade over the bareness. It was visible three leagues round and known to everybody far and wide as *Le Solitaire*.

'It's full of lizards here,' said Vincent, eyeing the cracked wall. 'We could have such fun.'

But, seeing the lay brother thrust a foot forward, he leapt out of the way.

Friar Archangias made an observation to the Vicar about the bad state of the iron gate. It was badly rusted. There was a loose hinge. The lock was broken.

'It wants repairing,' he said.

The Reverend Mouret smiled, but made no reply. Then, turning to Vincent, who was now playing about with the dog. 'I say, littl'un,' he said, 'd'you know where M. Bambousse is working this morning?'

The boy's eyes flashed away to the skyline.

' He should be in his field out at Olivette,' he said, pointing away to the left. 'Anyway, Voriau'll take you there, sir. He's sure to know where his master is, that dog is.' And he clapped his hands and called: 'Eh? Voriau! Here, boy, here!'

After a moment's hesitation, tail a-wag, eyes on the boy's eyes, the mastiff barked with delight and started off down towards the village. Mouret and the Friar followed, chatting. After about a hundred paces, Vincent slipped slyly away and made his way back to the church, keeping his eyes on them, ready to fling himself behind a bush if they looked round. With the lissomeness of a snake, he slipped back into the churchyard, for to him it was a paradise, full of birds' nests and lizards and flowers.

Meanwhile, with Voriau racing ahead of them down the dusty road, the Friar was talking irritably to the Vicar.

'Come off it, Vicar, they're the seed of hell, this mob here. They all want a jolly good flogging to make them pleasing in the eyes of the Lord. They grow up irreligiously, like their fathers. I've been here fifteen years and I have not been able to make a single good christian yet. The moment they're out of my hands, it's all *u. p.* They all of them live on their land, with their vines and olive-trees. Not one sets foot in church. Wild beasts, they are, always squabbling over their stony fields. It's a stick about their backsides they want all the time, if you ask me, my dear sir.'

He paused to take breath, then, with a furious gesture, went on: 'I'm telling you, these Artaud folk are like these brambles which eat the rocks here. It only needed one root of them to poison the whole countryside. They creep and they multiply, whatever you do, and flourish. It would need the hell-fire of Gomorrha to cleanse that stuff.'

'We should never give up a sinner,' Mouret replied, walking slowly, in his inner peace.

'Wrong,' cried the lay brother, more fiercely, 'they're the devil's own, I tell you. I was once a peasant, like them, I swung a mattock till I was eighteen. And later, at the Institution, I swept and cleaned vegetables and did the roughest work. I'm not saying anything against their rough work. On the contrary, God likes best those who are lowly. But believe me, the Artaud folk behave like animals. They are just like their dogs. They don't go to church and they don't pay any heed to the commandments of God or Church. They love their patches of earth so much that they fornicate with them.'

Tail up, Voriau halted a moment, then, making sure that the two men were still following, he made off again.

'I admit, there are most regrettable shortcomings,' Mouret murmured. 'My predecessor, the Reverend Caffin . . .'

'Poor fellow,' the Friar interrupted. 'He came out to us from Normandy, after a dirty bit of business. Here, all he thought about was good living. He let everything go hang.'

'No, no, M. Caffin surely did all he could. Though I must admit that his efforts were rather fruitless. Indeed, my own are more often than not without result.'

Friar Archangias shrugged his shoulders. For a moment heaving his massive body jerkily along, he strode on without speaking. The sun beat full on the tanned skin of his neck. His hard, knife-edged peasant profile was in deep shadow.

'Listen to me, Vicar,' he resumed, at last, 'I am too lowly a man, of course, to venture to instruct you. All the same, I am twice your age, and I know this country here, and that authorises me to tell you that you'll get nowhere by gentleness . . . Do understand, you needn't go farther than the catechism. God has no pity for the impious. He burns them. You stick to that.'

And as the Reverend Mouret, head bowed, made no response, he ran on: 'Religion is going out of the countryside because it is being made too kindly. It was respected in the days when it assumed that it was a man's master, and a merciless one, too . . . I don't know what you are taught nowadays in the seminaries. The newer priests seem to cry like children side by side with their parishioners. God seems quite changed . . . Tell you what, Vicar, I'll bet you don't even know your Catechism properly by heart.'

The priest found this will, which tried so violently to impose itself on him, quite irksome. Raising his head, he said, rather drily: 'Very good indeed, my dear Friar, your zeal is most praiseworthy . . . But had you not something to tell me? You called at the vicarage this morning, did you not?'

Friar Archangias said uncouthly: 'I've just been letting you hear what I came to say . . . Those Artaud folk live like swine. Why, only yesterday, I learned that old Bambousse's eldest daughter, Rosalie, is in the family way. They all wait till that happens before they marry. In these last fifteen years I have not known one girl didn't go wallowing in the wheatfields before going to church . . . And then, all they do is laugh and make out it is their local custom.'

'Certainly,' Mouret said softly, 'it is all very shocking . . . I am as a matter of fact just looking for old Bambousse, to have a word with him about it. It would be best now for the marriage to take place without delay . . . Apparently the father of the child is that big lad Fortuné, the Brichets' boy. Unfortunately, the Brichets are poor.'

'That little bitch Rosalie,' went on the Friar, 'is only now turned eighteen. They go wrong, these girls do, while they're still on the school benches. Only four years ago, that little hussy was still in my hands. But she was already a lascivious little thing . . . Now I have her sister Catherine, a kid of eleven, and she promises to be more shameless even than the elder one. You'll find her at any time in a ditch with that little scoundrel Vincent . . . I tell you frankly, a lot of use it is pulling their ears till the blood comes, it's the female in them coming to maturity, that's what it is, all the time. They've perdition in their petticoats. All they're fit for is pitching on the muck-heap, with their filthy itch. It would be a jolly good riddance, if you ask me, to have all girls' necks wrung at birth.'

Disgust and hatred of womenkind now made the Friar swear like a drayman. Yet, listening to him, the Vicar of Artuad remained quite calm. He even smiled at the man's violence. All at once, however, he called the dog, which had suddenly raced off into a field.

'I say, hold!' cried the Friar, at the same time, pointing to a band of children playing at the bottom of a ravine, 'there are my beauties who should be at school. There, that's all there is in their excuse of going to help their parents in the vineyards . . . And you can be sure that hussy Catherine is the ringleader, too. She loves sliding down the slopes, that girl does. You'll see her skirts over her head any moment. There what did I tell you? Well, see you this evening, Vicar . . . Just you wait, just you wait, you young rascals!'

He made off down the slope at the run, his dirty cowl flapping on his shoulders, his voluminous, greasy cassock snatching at the thistles. Mouret watched him plunge into the midst of the children, who ran all ways like frightened sparrows. But he had contrived to get both Catherine and another one, a boy, by the ears and he led them off towards the village, holding them fast in his big, hairy fists, lashing them with his tongue all the time.

The Reverend Mouret continued on his way. Friar Archangias sometimes awakened unusual misgivings in him. For all his vulgarity and crudity he did seem to be a true man of God. He had no worldly ties. Though common and coarse, his mouth foul when opposing sin, he was a man entirely devoted to the will of Heaven. And Mouret felt despair because he could never divest himself any more of his own flesh, could not be ugly or foul-tongued or verminous like such a saint as this. Whenever Friar Archangias, as just now, outraged him by language which was too coarse or by his unreasoned brutality, the Reverend Mouret at once charged himself with his own fine sense of values and saw the features of his personal dignity as real shortcomings. Should he not by now be completely dead to all the weaknesses of this world?

Once again, a sad smile appeared on his face as he reflected that he had almost lost his temper at the Friar's arrogant lecture, and this, he told himself, this was personal pride, trying to ruin him, by making him scornful of unrefined folk. Yet, in spite of all those reflections, he did feel relieved at being alone again and able to continue slowly on his path, reading his breviary and free from that harsh voice which was so disturbing to his dreams of unsullied tenderness.

CHAPTER VI

THE road wound among the outcrops of rock amid which at widely scattered points the peasants had won a rod or two of chalky soil, where now grew veteran olive trees. As he trod the ruts, Serge Mouret's feet crunched into the thick dust as if it were snow. From time to time, when a warmer breath of air puffed in his face, he looked up from his book of prayers, as if to see whence came the caress, but his glance remained undefined, lost. On that horizon, aglow with fire, on the tortured contours of this passion-rent, dried-out landscape, sprawling in utter abandonment under the sun, hot and unassuageable as a childless woman, he saw nothing. To avoid that heated breath, he thrust his hat down on his forehead, then unperturbed resumed his reading, the cassock at his heels raising a cloud of dust which clung heavily to the road surface.

'Mornin', Vicar,' cried a peasant who met him.

Then the sound of spades in these little fields brought him back again into this world. He looked round, to see stalwart old men bidding him good day among their vines, as Brother Archangias put it, the men of Artaud in fornication with their very soil, in broad sunlight. Sweaty foreheads appeared from behind thickets, hard breathing torsos came slowly upright, fresh from their passionate labour of fecundity, through the midst of which he strode with even pace, unknowing and unmoved. No hint of the disturbing emotions of that great act of love with which this marvellous morning was full penetrated to his heart.

'N-n-no! Voriau! Don't eat me up!' laughed a vigorous voice, quietening the dog's fit of furious barking, and Mouret looked up.

'Oh, it's you, Fortuné,' he said, and crossed the road to the edge of the patch on which the young peasant was at work. 'The very person I wished to have a word with.'

'Big' Fortuné, as he was always called, was of the same age as the priest, a stalwart young man, insolent of bearing, his skin already leathery. He was busy now breaking up a small corner of this stony countryside.

'What about, Vicar?' he asked.

'About what has happened between Rosalie and yourself,' the priest replied.

Fortuné laughed cheerfully. He found it funny for a Vicar to concern himself with such a matter.

'Hang it,' he said, gently, 'Rosalie was willing enough. I never forced it on her . . . It's just bad luck if the old man won't let me marry her. Why, you saw their dog just now, didn't you? You see, old Bambousse is training Voriau to go for me.'

Mouret would have gone on, had not the elder Brichet, whom at first he had not noticed, at this point come out of the shade of a thicket, where, together with his wife, he had been busily lunching. He was a small-built man of humble bearing whom the years had dried up.

'What you've been hearing is all lies, Vicar,' he said, fiercely. 'The lad's as ready as anything to marry Rosalie . . . The young people have been keeping company some time, you see. Nobody's to blame for what's happened. There are others do the same and have a good life all the same . . . But it doesn't depend on us. You must talk to Bambousse. It's him, despising us, because of his money.'

'Yes, we are too poor for him,' complained the mother, a tall, peevish sort of woman, who now rose to her feet. 'This bit of field where the devil rained down flints, if he did anywhere, is all we have got. It doesn't even keep us in flour . . . Without you, Vicar, life would not be possible.'

Mother Brichet was the only devout woman in the village. After communion she always hung round the vicarage, sure that Teuse would have a couple of loaves left over from last week's batch of bread for her. Sometimes she even carried off a rabbit or a hen, given her by Désirée.

'It is one shocking thing after another,' Mouret went on to say, 'They ought to be joined in holy matrimony as soon as possible.'

'Right away if you like, provided the other parties will agree,' the woman assured him. She was always full of anxiety about keeping up the flow of little presents she acquired from the church. 'We're not likely to be such bad christian folk as to go against what Vicar wishes, are we, Brichet?'

Fortuné grinned. 'I'm ready enough,' he said, boldly, ' and so's Rosalie . . . I saw her yesterday down by the mill. We're not put out. On the contrary. It all makes us laugh . . . '

But the Reverend Mouret cut him short. 'Very well,' he said, 'I shall see Bambousse. I think he's out on his Olivette field.'

He was about to go on, when Mother Brichet asked what had happened to Vincent, her youngest. He had left the house at break of day, she said, to be server at morning mass. He was, she said, a young rascal, he needed the Vicar's good advice. And she accompanied Mouret a hundred yards along the road, bewailing their poverty,—they had run out of potatoes, the frost had cut back their olives, now the heat was threatening to scorch up their poor crops. Then, assuring him that Fortuné said his prayers every night and and morning, she left him.

Voriau ran some paces ahead of the Vicar, then all at once, at a curve in the road, shot off across country. Mouret had to take a narrow footpath which led to a hill side. This was Olivette—it was always spoken of in the plural, as 'the Olivettes'—the most fertile land in the whole district, where Artaud-Bambousse, the mayor of Artaud, owned several fields, variously under olives, grapes, and wheat.

Meanwhile, the dog had rushed straight into the skirts of a tall, dark girl, who grinned broadly with pleasure when she saw the priest.

'Is your father anywhere about, Rosalie?' he asked her.

'Right opposite,' she said, pointing. The smile did not leave her face.

Then, leaving the corner of the field, where she was busy with her hoe, she led the way. Her pregnancy, as yet in its early stages, showed only in a slight filling out of her hips. She had the powerful, rolling gait of a girl used to hard physical labour. She stood there, bareheaded in the sun, her neck bronzed, her swarthy hair upstanding like a mane. Her hands were stained green, and smelled of the weeds she had been pulling.

'Father,' she called out loudly, 'here's the Vicar wants to see you.'

She stayed close to him, insolently expectant, on her lips that artful, shameless, female, animal smile. Bambousse, a corpulent, square-jowled man, left his task and strode jauntily down, heavily perspiring, to meet his village's priest.

'I'll bet you've come to talk about repairs to the church,' he said, clapping his hands to get the soil off them. 'Well, Vicar, it's no, that's the answer, out of the question. There's not a penny in the kitty . . . if the Almighty likes to find the cement and lime and sand and tiles, then it's *all right*, the parish will throw in the builders.'

This canny, rustic humour prompted a burst of hearty laughter in the speaker himself. He slapped his sides till he coughed and nearly choked.

'It's not the church that I have come about,' replied Mouret, 'I want a word with you about your daughter Rosalie.'

'Rosalie? And what harm has she done you, eh?' demanded Bambousse, his eyes flashing.

Serge Mouret was conscious of the hearty peasant girl staring unabashed at him. Her eyes went from his white hands to his girlish-white neck, as if deliberately trying to make him blush. But his features retained their calm. Bluntly he said: 'You know what I mean, Bambousse. Your daughter is pregnant. You should marry her.'

'Oh, that's what you're after, is it?' the old fellow repeated, quite calmly, but in a narking sort of way. 'Thanks a lot for your attention, Vicar. It's those Brichets sent you along, I expect, isn't it? Of course, Mother Brichet is one of your faithful, so you would want to help to get her son fixed up. Not surprising. But it doesn't concern me. Oh, no, sir, that proposition does not suit me. That's all.'

In utter astonishment at this reception, the Vicar of Artaud explained that it was essential to cut the scandal of this pregnancy short. It was for him to forgive Fortuné Brichet, since Fortuné was willing to right the wrong he had done the girl. Besides, the honour of Bambousse's daughter required a prompt marriage.

'Ta-ta-ta!' cried Bambousse, cocking his head mockingly to one side and the other. 'What fine words! Well, let me tell you, I'm keeping my daughter. Fortuné's a mere vagabond. He hasn't a penny to his name. How easy it would be if all a man had to do, to get a girl for wife, was to put her on her back. Damn it, like that, we'd have all the young people marrying, morning to night . . . God in Heaven, man, I'm not worried about my Rosalie. We know all right what's happened to her. That won't make her bandy or hump-backed. She can still marry whomever she wants the length and breadth of this country.'

'But—the child?' the Reverend Mouret reminded him.

'The child? There isn't any child yet, is there? Perhaps there won't be one at all . . . And if she does have a kid, there's still time to think about it.'

Seeing what the end of the Vicar's intervention was going to be, Rosalie found it necessary at this point to put her fists to her eyes and begin to whimper. She even went so far as to fling herself on the ground, revealing blue stockings which reached well above her knees.

At that, her father lost his temper.

'You shut your trap, you little trollop!' he cried, and when she got up he continued to belabour her most shabbily, with the coarsest language, which however only made her giggle under her clenched fists. 'If I catch you with your fine buck, I'll rope the two of you together and show you off to the whole village . . Will you stop snivelling when I tell you! You just wait, you little hussy!'

Bambousse suddenly snatched up a big clod of earth and flung it savagely at the girl, from a distance of only four paces. It smashed against her knotted hair, the earth and dust covering her and pouring under her shift, right down her back. The blow staggered her, but all the same, she was on her feet in a second and made good her escape, covering her head with her hands against further missiles. And Bambousse was indeed quick enough to get two more clods home on his target. The first just glanced off Rosalie's left shoulder, but the second caught her full between the shoulder blades, such a savage blow that she fell to her knees.

'Bambousse!' cried the Vicar, and tore from his fist a handful of stones which he next took up.

'Now you let me be, Vicar!' cried the old farmer. 'That was only soft earth I hit her with. I would have done better to have made it stones . . . Anyone can see you don't know what girls are. I could douse that one in our well, or break a hawthorn stick over her backside, and it wouldn't stop her filthy goings-on. But I've got my eye on her and if only I do catch her . . . But they're all the same.'

He made the best of it. Taking a big, flat bast-covered bottle, warming on the burning soil at his feet, he took a good swig. Then, recovering his broad grin, he turned to the priest.

'Upon my word, Vicar, I'd offer your reverence a glass if only I had a glass wi' me.'

'Well,'—Mouret came back to the point,—'and our marriage?'

'No sir ! Out of the question. I'd be a laughing-stock. Rosalie's a fine lass. She is worth any man on the farm, believe me. The day she leaves me, I have to have hired labour . . . Look here, we'll talk it over again if you like after vintage. Besides I don't want to be robbed. If you don't look out, it's all give in this world, you know.'

The Reverend Mouret spent a good half hour more preaching to Bambousse and talking to him of God, with all the arguments which fitted the situation. But the old farmer merely resumed his work, shrugging his shoulders, shouting his wisecracks. Then, at last, he paused again, and shouted: 'Look-ee here, Vicar, it's like this—if you wanted a bag of corn off me, you'd pay me, wouldn't you? Why then do you expect me to let my girl go for nothing?'

Somewhat deflated by this, Mouret at last gave it up. On his way down the hill path he caught sight of Rosalie. She was rolling about with the mastiff under an olive-tree. The big animal was licking her face, making her roar with laughter. And as she writhed on the ground, petticoats flying, arms lashing the ground, he heard her shriek: 'But you're tickling, you great rascal! Do leave off!'

Then, seeing who was watching her, she pretended to blush, drew her skirts down over her legs, put her fists to her eyes. Mouret then made an effort to console her, promising he would try again to talk her father round. But, he added gravely, while she waited, she should be a good girl and have nothing at all to do with Fortuné. That was the only way not to make her sin still more serious.

'Oh, but now,' she murmured, with her saucy grin, 'there's no risk! I've had it.'

It was absolutely beyond Mouret's comprehension. He described hell fire to her and the fate of wicked women. Then, his duty done, he left her. And immediately, the serenity which made it possible to pass untroubled amid all the filth of the flesh, assumed its usual sway over him.

CHAPTER VII

THOUGH it was not yet midday, it had already become burning hot. As soon as summer really set in, the sun made the rocks of this vast amphitheatre glow like a furnace. By the elevation of the great orb, the Reverend Mouret realised that he now had just enough time to get back to the vicarage, if he was to be there by eleven and not get a scolding from Teuse. His prayers all read, his intercession with Bambousse made, he set off back at a quick pace. Afar off, he could see his church, a greyish patch and beside it the single tall black rod of the big cypress—*Le Solitaire*—against the blue horizon. Drowsy with heat, he was dreaming of how lavishly he could decorate the Chapel of the Virgin for the special prayers of May. Before him the road stretched out its soft carpet of dust of dazzling white purity.

At Green-Cross, just as he was about to cross the Plassans-La Palud road, a horse-and-trap coming downhill compelled him to take refuge behind a heap of stones. He was then crossing the crossroads when he heard a voice behind him crying: 'Hallo there, Serge, my boy!' The gig had stopped and a man was leaning out. Then he recognised who it was,—one of his uncles, Doctor Pascal Rougon, whom all Plassans folk, among whom he tended so many free of charge, knew as plain 'Dr. Pascal'. Though only just over fifty, Doctor Pascal was already snowy white, a bushy beard and luxurious head of hair framing a handsome face with regular features which breathed kindliness and sensitivity.

'So this is the time of day, is it, that you choose to trudge through the dust?' the doctor cried, cheerfully, leaning out still further, to press Serge's two hands in his. 'Aren't you afraid of sun-stroke?'

'No more than yourself, Uncle,' replied Serge, with a laugh.

'Ah, but this trap of mine has got a hood. Besides, if I go about in the middle of the day, that's because I cannot delay, I have to see my patients. Folk choose all hours of the day for dying in, my lad.'

And he went on to say that he was at this moment hurrying out to see old Jeanbernat, who looked after the Paradou estate. Jeanbernat had had a stroke during the night. A neighbour, a peasant, who was on his way to Plassans market, had dropped in to bring the news.

'It's probably too late by now,' Dr. Pascal continued. ' But there's no harm in hurrying out to see . . . These old rascals are often mighty tough.'

He raised his whip, when Serge stayed his hand.

'Wait' he said, 'what do you make the time?'

'Quarter to eleven.'

Serge hesitated. In his ears he heard Teuse's terrifying tones, shouting about his lunch already being cold. But he was not to be easily daunted, and quickly said: 'I'm coming with you, Uncle . . . Perhaps in his last moments the poor soul may wish to make his peace with God.'

The doctor could not help roaring with laughter.

'Him, you mean? Jeanbernat? Ah! I doubt if you will ever convert him . . . No matter, you can come along. The mere sight of you may shock him back to life.'

Serge climbed in. Doctor Pascal seemed rather to regret the wisecrack, and showed himself most attentive, as he clicked his horse to a nice trot. Meanwhile, out of the corner of his eye he quizzed his nephew with some curiosity, and that peculiar manner which your medical practitioner has when gathering information. In kindly fashion, he questioned him with curt phrases on his life, enquiring how he lived, what his habits were, and whether he was really happy at Artaud. And in reassured tones at every contented answer, as if talking to himself, he muttered 'Really? But that's very good, that's perfect.'

He was particularly insistent in his enquiries about the young priest's state of health. This surprised Serge, who assured his Uncle that he was marvellously well. No, he never had fits of dizziness, or sickness, no head-aches.

'But that's perfect,' said Doctor Pascal, again. 'I ask because, you know, in the spring any man's blood tends to get heated. But of course, you've got a very sound constitution. By the way, I saw your brother Octave last month at Marseilles. He is moving to Paris. He is to have a fine job there, in big business. The rascal, a fine life he leads.'

'What sort of life?' the priest asked, naively.

To avoid answering, the doctor clicked to the horse. Then he went on: 'In fact, they're all very well, your Aunt Félicité, your Uncle Rougon and the rest of them . . . That doesn't at all mean we don't stand in dire need of your prayers. You are the saint of our family, old man, I count on you to save the whole tribe of us.'

He was teasing again, but in such friendly fashion that even Serge himself felt he had to make a joke of it.

45

'The trouble is, there's some of the warren it won't be easy to get into Heaven. If they lined up for confession, you'd hear some rum things . . . As a matter of fact, I don't need to hear them spill the beans, I know all their doings, because I've got their medical records, you see, filed together with my herbals and all my other notes. Some day I shall be able to produce a really interesting picture . . . We'll see, we'll see.'

In his ever youthful enthusiasm for science, he was forgetting himself, when suddenly his nephew's cassock caught his eye again and stopped him short.

'But of course,' he said, 'you've done a wise thing, taking holy orders, you can be happy, now you're a parson. It's completely absorbed you, hasn't it, so you're well away now, aren't you? Fine! You'd never have been happy in anything else. Your parents were both like you when they were young. A lot of good it did them stooping to all their dirty tricks, and still they were not satisfied . . . There's hard logic in it all, my boy. A parson sort of rounds the family off. Besides, it had to be so . . . Our blood was bound to lead to it . . . And all the better for you . . . You have had the best luck of all.'

But this statement he corrected, a moment later, with a strange smile.

'No,' he said, 'it's your sister Désirée who has had the best luck of all.'

Then, with a sharp whistle and a crack of his whip, he changed the conversation. Having reached the top of a rather steep hill, the gig began to roll down through dismal-looking ravines, to come out at last on a patch of level ground, where a sunken road led beside an endless high stone wall. They had left Artaud far behind them and were in the midst of completely barren country.

'Nearly there, aren't we?' the young Vicar enquired.

'Yes, this is Paradou Park,' the doctor replied, with a nod at the wall. 'You've never been here before? But it's less than three miles from Artaud! . . . Ah, must have been a lovely place once upon a time, Paradou. On this side alone the park wall is more than a mile long. But for the past century the whole place has gone wild.'

'There certainly are some lovely trees,' Mouret remarked as he looked up in astonishment at the magnificent verdure thrusting lavishly above the wall.

'These are indeed,' said Doctor Pascal. 'This particular corner is the most fertile of all. The park, you see, includes a real forest set in the heart of all this dead rock country. This of course is where

46

the Mascle has its source. If I remember rightly, there are three, or even four, different springs.

In his jerky way of telling a story, constantly interrupting himself with asides foreign to his subject, the doctor now told Serge all about Paradou Park. It was a legend throughout this countryside. It went right back to Louis XV, when a nobleman built a magnificent palace there, surrounded by extensive gardens, with pools, running streams, and statuary, a miniature Versailles lost among these rocks, all under the rich southern sun. But the founder spent only one season there. He came down accompanied by a woman said to be of remarkable loveliness, and she must have died there, for she was never seen to leave the place. The following year, the castle proper was gutted by fire. Then the park gates were nailed up, and even the look-outs in the walls were filled in, so that all these many long years nobody had ever seen inside the vast enclosure, which covered the whole of one of the high plateaux of the Garigues.

'There must be enough nettles,' said the Vicar of Artaud, with a laugh. 'The place smells terribly dank all along this wall. Don't you agree, Uncle?' Then, after a moment of silence, he enquired who owned the place now.

'Upon my word, nobody knows,' the doctor replied. 'About twenty years ago, the owner did come down once, but this hotbed of reptiles so frightened him that he never came again ... The real owner is the caretaker, this eccentric old chap, Jeanbernat, who managed to make a home for himself in one of the lodges, which was still more or less intact when he came. Look, that's it—see that squat grey building over there, with big windows in ivy-covered walls?'

The gig bowled on, past the typical wrought iron gates of a nobleman's estate, which, however, were blood-stained now with rust, and boarded up from the inside with rough-hewn planking. The ha-has were black with brambles. The lodge occupied by Jeanbernat was set a good hundred yards deep in the park, which it faced. On the park side, however, the caretaker seemed to have walled his house off, at the same time, clearing a small garden facing towards the road. And here he lived, his back resolutely turned to Paradou, apparently entirely indifferent to the wealth of rioting vegetables behind him.

The young priest leapt to the ground, looked about himself in curiosity, then turned enquiringly to his doctor uncle, who with nimble fingers was tying his horse to a ring built into the wall.

47

'And you say this old fellow lives all by himself, in the heart of this lost world?'

'He does,' replied Uncle Pascal, ' absolutely alone.' Then he added: 'Oh no, he has a niece who lives with him, a queer girl, run rather wild. She fell to his responsibility some time back . . . Come, let's hurry. Everything seems frightfully dead inside.'

CHAPTER VIII

THE house was asleep.

The shutters closed, under the midday sun, amid the continuous hum of huge flies clustering all round the ivy which covered the walls from ground to eaves. Bathed in sunshine, the deserted place breathed a happy tranquillity. Dr. Pascal pushed open the gate leading into the narrow garden, which was enclosed by a tall hedge. And there, in the shadow cast by part of the wall, stood Jeanbernat himself, erect, calmly smoking a pipe in the tremendous silence and watching his vegetables grow.

'What's this, you old humbug,' cried the doctor, in surprise, 'you're on your feet?'

'So you'd come to bury me, had you,' the veteran growled, quite roughly. 'Ah! I don't need any help. I just bled myself . . .' Then, catching sight of the doctor's cassock-clad companion, he stopped short, with such a menacing gesture that the doctor was quick to intervene.

'My nephew,' he said, 'the new Vicar of Artaud, he's quite harmless . . . Damn it all, Grand-dad, we haven't come all this way at this hour of the day to gobble you up.' At this explanation, the old man seemed more at his ease.

'I don't want any of your sky-pilots here,' he muttered. 'They're enough to finish anyone off, they are. Get that clear, doc! When my time comes, no drugs and no parsons, or you and I are going to have a tiff . . . No matter, if he's a nephew of yours, let this one come in!'

Serge was so taken aback by this reception that he could not find his tongue at all, but just stood half way up the path, gaping at the unusual, deeply lined brick-burnt face of this hermit, his shrunken arms like knottled bundles of whipcord. Jeanbernat of Paradou Park wore his eighty odd years with an ironical scorn for life itself. When the doctor tried to get an idea of the old man's pulse, he was quite annoyed.

'Let me be,' he growled. 'Haven't I just told you, I took my knife and bled myself. It's all over, now. What clod was that came bothering you to see me, eh? Doctor and parson,—and where are the undertaker's men? Bah! I'm not blaming you, people are idiots, and it's no hindrance to our taking a glass together.'

He brought out a bottle and three glasses, and set them down on an old table which he drew out of the shadows. Filling the glasses to the brim, he held out his, for them to chink, his anger all dissolved in a new fit of roguish cheerfulness.

"'Twon't poison ee, Vicar,' he said, 'a bottle of good wine is never a sin . . . By God, it's the first time I've ever touched glasses with a dog-collar, no offence in the word, sir. Poor old Caffin, your predecessor, refused to talk to me at all . . . He was scared stiff of me.'

With a deep guffaw, he went on: 'Would you believe it, old Caffin really did make an attempt to prove to me that there is a God . . . After that, I never came across him without challenging him, and he'd always put his tail between his legs and skedaddle, every time, upon my word he would!'

'But however can you suggest that God does not exist?' Serge demanded, shaken out of his muteness.

'Oh!' returned Jeanbernat, mockingly, 'have it as you will. If it pleases you, we can start all over again, I'm game . . . Only let me warn you that I'm pretty tough. Upstairs, I've got several thousand volumes saved from the fire they had here at Paradou, all the eighteenth century philosophers, in fact, a heap of books on religion. I've got a lot of fine things out of them, I might tell you. I've been reading them for twenty years now . . . By Jove, Vicar, you've got somebody to sharpen your wits on, if you want,' he said.

Getting to his feet, he swept the whole horizon, earth and sky together, with a grand, sweeping gesture and repeated gravely: 'There's naught there, nothing at all . . . One good puff, and that sun would be out.'

Doctor Pascal nudged Serge pointedly. His studious eyes blinking at the old man, he kept nodding, just to encourage his tongue to run on. 'In short, Father Jeanbernat,' he said, now, 'you are a materialist?'

'Bah! I'm only a miserable human being,' the old man replied, lighting his pipe again. 'When the Count de Corbière was killed riding—my mother suckled him and me together, you know—his children, to get rid of me, sent me down here to look after this

49

'sleeping beauty' garden. I was sixty, and thought myself finished. But death missed me, so I had to fix myself up . . . It's like this, you know, when you live by yourself, in the end you get a funny outlook on it all. Trees cease to be mere trees, the very soil gets its moods like a living creature and every stone can tell you a story. In other words, a lot of nonsense! I know secrets which would take your breath away. But then, what would you have me do, in this hell of a desert? I have done a lot of reading. I found that more entertaining than shooting game . . . The Count, who swore like a heathen, had always said to me: 'Jeanbernat, my lad, I really count on meeting you again some day in Hell, so you can be in my service down there as well as you have been here'.'

With another expansive gesture taking in the whole horizon, he said: 'You must realise, though, it's all nothingness, all trickery.'

Dr. Pascal laughed heartily.

'Anyway, it's jolly good trickery, isn't it?' he cried. 'Jeanbernat, you're a sly dog, if ever there was one. You and your pretence of boredom! It's my suspicion you are in love. You were quite emotional just now, about sticks and stones talking.'

'Not a bit of it. I've got over all that, I assure you. There was a time, I'll admit, when you and I used to go botanizing together, time when I was fool enough to love all sorts of things about this tricking, cheating countryside. Luckily, book-reading put a stop to all that. I want my garden as small as possible now. I only go out of my gate twice a year. See this bench? That's where I spend my time, watching my salads growing.'

'But your strolls in the park?' Pascal interrupted him.

'My strolls in the park?' Jeanbernat repeated the words in utter astonishment. 'Why, it's more than twelve years since I last set foot in the place. What do you expect me to do in that great graveyard? It's far too big. It's idiotic, endless trees and moss everywhere, broken statuary, and holes all over the place you can break your neck in. The last time I went into it, it was so dark under the trees and all those flowers run wild poisoned the air so much, there were such funny gusts of breath down the rides, I was quite alarmed. Then it was I built this wall against it, at least to keep the place out of this little corner . . . A sunny corner with a rod of vegetables to look after and a big hedge to shut the horizon out is quite enough to make me happy. To have nothing, that's my desire, nothing at all, somewhere so small that the outer world cannot get in to disturb me. As little as six foot of ground, if you like, just enough to stretch out on my back and breathe my last.' He thumped the table with

50

his fist, raising his voice, suddenly shouted at Serge: 'Come on, Parson, another drop, the devil isn't in this bottle, come on!'

Serge felt quite uneasy. He felt powerless ever to get this strange old fellow back to God. Jeanbernat's mind seemed to him to be sadly disjointed. He had by now recalled something of his house-keeper's chatter about 'the Philosopher,' as the Artaud folk called the old man. He also had vague recollections of scandalous tales, and, with a sign to his uncle, he rose to his feet, anxious to get free from this house in which he felt he was breathing the odour of damnation. Yet, despite the dull fear he felt, a strange curiosity held him back. Lingering, he walked up the garden path to the house and peered into the hall, as he felt a need to see farther, beyond the walls. All he could distinguish, however, through the large open door, was the dark frame of the stairs. And he made his way back to the others, seeking a hole somewhere, a hiding-place in this sea of foliage which he felt closing him in, murmuring all the time with a sound which was like sea waves lapping against the house.

'And is your little niece all right?' the doctor asked, as he took up his hat.

'Not so bad,' replied Jeanbernat. 'She's never here, of course. She vanishes for whole mornings . . . For all I know, she may well be in one of the upstairs rooms.'

He threw back his head and shouted, 'Albine! Al-bine!' Then, shrugging his shoulders, he added: 'Ah, there's no getting away from it, she's a shocking baggage, she is . . . Well, so long, Vicar, at your service, sir.'

But the Vicar of Artaud had no time to take up this new challenge from 'the Philosopher,' for all at once a door at the back of the hall was flung open, and for a moment there was a dazzling hole in the blackness of the rear wall. It was like a vision of virgin forest, immense, fully-grown trees piled one upon another under torrents of sunlight. In that momentary vision he clearly distinguished precise details in the distance: he saw a huge yellow flower in the centre of a lawn, a stretch of water, pouring down over a tall rock, and an immense tree full of a flight of birds, all swallowed up, lost, ablaze in the midst of such a proliferation of verdure, such an orgy of vegetation, that the whole horizon was but one vast conflagration of blossom. Then the door had slammed, and it was all gone again.

'Ah, the little hussy!' cried Jeanbernat, 'she was still out in the park.'

She stood on the threshold, laughing at them. She was wearing

51

an orange skirt, a large red shawl tied behind her, giving her the appearance of a gypsy on Sunday. And still she laughed, her head thrown back, throwing out her bosom to the full with sheer delight, overjoyed by her flowers, wild blossoms braided into her golden hair, and made into garlands about her throat, draped her shoulders and her slender, bare arms with their soft flue of golden down, till she herself was entirely one huge, lavishly scented, bunch of flowers.

'You young limb, how lovely you are!' the old fellow chided. 'You fill the air with your smell of green sap.' He pointed at Albine. 'I ask you,' he cried, 'would anybody give this pet sixteen years?'

And when he said this, Albine daunted him with laughter more boisterous than ever. Doctor Pascal, who was clearly a great friend of this child, held his cheek for her to kiss him.

'So you're never afraid in Paradou Park, are you, lassie?' he asked.

'Afraid? Of whatever should I be afraid? Nobody can get in . . . I am all alone there. It is my garden, my very own. It is wonderfully big. I have still not found the real end of it.'

'And the wild animals?'

'The wild animals? But they are not dangerous, they know me well.'

'All the same,—under the trees it is dark.'

'Good gracious, it's shady, of course. Without some shade, the sun would burn my face . . . It's lovely in the shade, with the leaves all round you.'

She swung sharply about, filling the narrow garden with the flurry of her petticoats and scattering all round her that odour of greenery which she bore with her. She had given the young priest a smile devoid of any shame and seemed entirely undisturbed by the astonishment with which he followed her movements. He had moved away. This fair-haired young girl with the elongated face, so burning with life, seemed to him a mysterious, disturbing child of that forest lit by a swathe of sunlight of which he had caught that one glimpse.

'I say, I have a nest of blackbirds, would you like it?' she asked the doctor.

'No, thank you,' he replied, smiling. 'You should give it to your Vicar's sister, she is terribly fond of all creatures. Well, Jeanbernat, *au revoir.*'

But Albine had turned to Serge Mouret. 'You are the Vicar of Artaud, are you not? And you have a sister? Then I shall come to see her . . . Only—perhaps you would talk to me about God. My uncle does not like that.'

'Don't be tiresome, run along,' said Jeanbernat, shrugging his shoulders.

With one bound she vanished, like a chamois, leaving in her wake a veritable rain of flowers. There came the crash of a door closing, then laughter from behind the house, a ringing laughter which rapidly receded, as if a happy creature freshly turned out to pasture was galloping madly across the sweet meadows.

'You shall see, that girl of mine will end up by sleeping in Paradou Park,' muttered the old caretaker, unconcernedly.

He saw his visitors to the gate.

'Doctor,' he said, 'if one fine morning soon you find me dead, do me a service—just make a hole in the compost-heap there, behind my greenstuff, and pitch my body in . . . Good-night, gentlemen.'

He dropped into position the wooden barrier which served for gate, and the house regained its happy tranquillity, lost in the murmur of the huge insects clustering all round the ivy which covered the walls, to the roof, in the midday sun.

CHAPTER IX

THE doctor's trap was again following the sunken road which led round the never-ending wall of Paradou Park. Speechless, the Vicar of Artaud looked up at the enormous branches reaching out over the wall like the arms of giants in hiding. A medley of sounds came from beyond the wall—the rustle of wings, the shivering of leaves, then furtive leaps which snapped off branches and vast sighs which bent back the saplings, as if the very breath of life was stirring the summits of a race of tree-like people. And from time to time there came the definite voice of a bird, like human laughter. Beset by strange unrest, the young priest kept turning his head.

Uncle Pascal let the reins dangle loose. 'What a strange child that girl is!' he mused. 'She was nine when fate brought her into that old heathen's hands. A brother of his, ruined, I forget what it was all about. The kid was at a boarding school, when it happened, and the father committed suicide. When she came here, little Albine was already quite the young lady, a very worldly wise young lady, reading books, sewing fine seams, making elegant conversation, even playing the piano. And what a child for dress, too! I saw her when she arrived, open-work stockings, embroidered petticoats, lace here and starch there, all little fiddle-faddles . . . Ah, and long they lasted, too!'

He laughed uproariously. Then an outcrop of rock in their tracks nearly overset the gig. 'One of these days I shall be leaving one of my wheels behind on this damn road!' muttered Uncle Pascal. 'Hold tight, m' boy!'

The wall was endless, and Serge was all ears for the story.

'You can easily see,' the doctor resumed, 'Paradou Park, with its sunshine, its rocks, its thistles, would devour a frock a day. Her dainty garments were only a couple of mouthfuls for that wild place. She used to come in half naked . . . Now, she dresses like a wild thing. As a matter of fact, she was quite presentable today, but there are occasions when you find her in no more than shoes and an under-slip. . . . You heard what she said, didn't you? Paradou Park is *hers*. From the morning after her arrival, she took possession. She lives there. When Jeanbernat locked the door, to keep her in, she used to get out of the window. Whatever the old boy tried, she slipped out, and he never knew where she went, either, she had her secret hide-outs, which nobody ever knew of . . . A rare time she must have, in this deserted place.'

'I say, do listen, Uncle,' Serge insisted, interrupting his uncle's story. 'Surely that's some animal running along on the other side of the wall?'

Doctor Pascal listened.

'No,' he said, after a time, 'that's only our wheels on the stones. Well, well . . . the kid certainly doesn't do much piano-playing nowadays. I even imagine she has forgotten how to read. You have to picture a young lady brought back to the condition of a wild thing, absolutely untrammelled, on a desert isle, able to do whatever she likes. All she has kept of her fine upbringing is that perfect coquette's smile, and she can turn it on when she wants to . . . Upon my word, if ever you have a young girl to bring up, I don't advise you to hand her over to Jeanbernat. He has a thoroughly primordial gift for letting nature go its own way. When I once found the courage to talk to him about Albine, his reply was that trees should always be left to grow naturally. That in his view makes for a healthy expansion of a thing's true nature . . . All the same, those two are a most interesting couple. I never come this way without dropping in to see them.'

They had at last reached the end of the sunken road, where the wall of Paradou Park doubled off at an angle, and they could see it continue away out of sight over a hill-top. Just as the Vicar of Artaud was turning to take a last glance at that grey barricade, the stern impenetrability of which had in the end begun quite to upset him, the sharp sound of snapping twigs forced itself on the attention of them both and over the wall a cluster of young birch-trees seemed to bow to bid them farewell.

'I knew all the time there was some animal running along there,' said the priest.

But they saw nothing living, all they could perceive was those birch-trees swaying more and more furiously. Then suddenly, broken by laughter, there was a clear sounding voice, crying: '*Au revoir*, Doctor, *au revoir*, Vicar! I am kissing this tree and the tree is sending you my kisses.'

'Pah!' cried Doctor Pascal. 'That's Albine! She must have run all this way, keeping pace with us. The little sprite. Certainly mere bushes are not going to stop her!' And he shouted back: '*Au revoir*, darling . . . You are grown up, I must say, to bid us good-bye like that!'

The laughter grew gayer than ever, the birch tops swayed still lower, till leaves broke off and fluttered out as far as the doctor's gig.

'I am as big as the trees, and every leaf which falls is a kiss,' came the voice again, though changed now by distance. It was a voice so musical, so much part of the pulsation of the park's own deep breath, that the young priest was all a-quiver.

Gradually the road improved. As they went down hill, Artaud suddenly reappeared in sight, on the far side of the scorched plain. When the trap was crossing the village street, Serge insisted that his uncle should not drive him all the way to the vicarage. He leapt to the ground. 'No, thank you so much,' he insisted, 'I would rather walk, it will do me good.'

'As you please,' the doctor said, at last. He gave the younger man a handshake. 'Hm!' he said, 'if only all your parishioners were like that old animal, Jeanbernat, you wouldn't often have much trouble, would you . . . But coming here was your own wish . . . Look after yourself, boy. If ever you feel off colour, no matter what the hour, send for me. You know I always treat the whole family free . . . Good-bye, lad.'

CHAPTER X

WHEN the Vicar of Artaud found himself alone again, in the dust of the road, he felt relieved. The stony fields restored him to his dream of harshness and an inner life lived out in a desert place. Along that sunken road the trees had cast disturbingly fresh breathings on his bowed head, but now the savage sunshine dried them away. The scraggy almond-trees, the stunted wheats, the sickly vines, on either side of the road, soothed him and drew him out of the troubled state into which the too luscious breath of Paradou Park had cast him. Indeed, here in the midst of the blinding clarity of light which the heavens poured down on this naked soil, even old Jeanbernat's blasphemies cast no shadow. And when, looking up, he saw *Le Solitaire* on the horizon, and beyond the pink tiles of the church, he felt a swift stirring of delight.

At the same time, however, the farther he went, the more another worry overcame him. He was going to get a fine reception from Teuse, with her lunch all cold, for it must have been awaiting him these two hours now. He could just picture her glowering features, and the flood of words with which she would greet him, then the angry clattering of dishes which she would inflict on him for the rest of the afternoon. When he had gone through the village, his apprehension became so intense that he hesitated, overcome with cowardice, wondering whether it would not be better to go round about and come in through the church. But while he was deciding this, who should appear on the vicarage threshold but Teuse herself, her bonnet askew, her arms akimbo. He had no other course but to bend his back and climb the rise of ground under those eyes full of storm, the weight of which he could already feel on his shoulders.

'My dear Teuse,' he stammered, as he reached the last stretch of path, 'I am afraid I am a bit late.'

Teuse waited till she had him at close quarters, face to face. Then she gave him one furious look, straight in the eyes, swept round and preceded him into the dining-room, her massive heels banging the floor. She was so stiff with anger that she almost lost her limp.

'I have had such a lot to do,' he began, terrified by this silent reception. 'I've been on the go all the morning.'

But with a new flash of her eyes, so rigid, so angry, that he felt his legs collapse under him, she silenced him. He sat down and began to eat. She served him with the stiff movements of an automaton, risking breaking the plates, she banged them down so. The silence became so menacing that after the third mouthful he could not swallow at all, his feelings choked him.

'And has my sister lunched?' he asked. 'That was sensible of her. You must always have lunch, when I am detained by my duties.'

No reply. Teuse just stood there, waiting for him to empty his plate, before she took it away. Then, feeling quite unable to eat

56

under those two implacable eyes, which were really shattering, he pushed his plate back. That gesture of irritation was like the blow of a whip, it jolted Teuse out of her stubborn stiffness, and she leapt.

'Oh, that's how it is, is it?' she cried. 'It's you, thinks you, who is to be angry. Very well, I'm leaving. You can find me my fare back to my own country. I've had enough of Artaud and your church and all this!'

She pulled her apron together with quivering fingers.

'Surely you could see that I wanted to speak to you. Is this a life, I ask you? Only humbugs, Vicar, behave like this. Eleven o'clock, is it? Aren't you ashamed to be at lunch when it's nearly two o'clock? It's not christian, if you ask me, it's not decent behaviour.' Then, planting herself facing him. 'Now where have you been?' she demanded. 'What have you seen? What business was it kept you so long? If you were a child you would deserve a good whipping. It's no place for a clergyman, either, out on the roadside, in full sun, too, like a tramp without a roof over his head . . . And aren't you in a fine state! Your shoes are white, and your cassock is ruined with dust. Who's going to clean that cassock for you? Who will buy you another? Why don't you answer me? Tell me what you've been up to! I assure you, if I didn't know you I might think all sorts of things. What sort of things? Ah! you'd just like me to tell you, wouldn't you? Well, I'm not going to burn my fingers in it, but when a man starts eating his midday meal at this sort of hour, he may be up to anything.'

The Vicar, however, was relieved now, and let the storm pass over him. It even afforded him a sort of nervous relief to hear his old housekeeper nag like this.

'Now come, my dear Teuse,' he murmured, 'first of all, put on your apron again.'

'No, no,' she shrieked. 'I'm through, I'm leaving.'

But he got to his feet and laughingly tied the apron round her. Struggling, she stammered: 'But no, I tell you no! . . . You . . . Oh, you wheedler! . . . But I can see through your little game . . . You think you can soft soap old Teuse with your treacly talk, don't you . . . Where have you been? Tell me that, then we'll see.'

Cheerfully, he sat down again, a man who had won his victory. 'First,' he said, ' you must let me eat. I am dying of hunger.'

'And I'm not surprised,' she mumbled, suddenly all commiseration. 'Now, is there any sense in it? Shall I fry you a couple of eggs as well? It won't take a minute. Well, if that is enough for you . . .

But it's all cold. And all the trouble I took about those aubergine fritters. A fine sight they are now! Like old shoe soles . . . It's a good thing you're not so finicky as poor M. Caffin was. Yes, you've got your points, I'm not gainsaying it.'

She looked after him with maternal care, chattering all the time. Then, when he had finished, she hurried off to the kitchen to see if the coffee was still warm. She simply let herself go now, limping most outrageously, so delighted she was that it was all made up again. Usually, Serge avoided coffee, as it upset his nerves, but on this occasion, anxious to seal their peace, he accepted the cup she brought him. And when, sitting there before it, he suddenly became lost in thought again, she merely sat down opposite him and gently, like any woman agonised by curiosity, asked him again, wheedlingly, where he had been.

He smiled, 'Oh, I went to see the Brichets,' he said, 'and I had a heart to heart talk with old Bambousse too.'

He then had to tell her what the Brichets had said, and what Bambousse had told him, how they had taken it, and where they had been working. When she heard what Rosalie's father had said, 'Good Heavens,' she cried, 'of course, if the baby died, the pregnancy just wouldn't count.' Then, clasping her hands in an attitude of envious wonder, she cried: 'Dear Vicar, what a lot of talking you must have done! More than half a day, and all for this result! . . . And you came back very slowly, I am sure. It must have been terribly hot on the road.'

The Vicar of Artaud had risen to his feet, and he did not reply. He had been about to speak of Paradou Park, and ask more about it, but sudden fear of being questioned too closely, a sort of vague shame which he could not even admit to himself, made him hold his tongue about that visit to Jeanbernat and his niece. So he put an end to any further questioning, by asking a question himself. 'But wherever can my sister be?' he cried. 'I cannot hear her at all.'

'You just come with me, Vicar dear,' said Teuse, all smiles now, one finger on her lips.

They went into the neighbouring room, a country sitting-room papered with huge faded grey flowers and furnished with four armchairs and a settee upholstered in horsehair cloth, on which Désirée lay at full length, sound asleep, her head under her two clenched fists. Her petticoats dangled, uncovering her knees, while her arms, raised as they were, and naked to the elbows, revealed the powerful lines of her bosom. She was breathing rather hard, her red lips slightly open, showing her teeth.

'Isn't the darling sound, eh?' whispered Teuse. 'She didn't even hear you shouting so silly, just now . . . Goodness gracious, the child must be fairly worn out. Think, she was working, cleaning out her hutches and all, till nearly mid-day, and as soon as she had had a bite, she came in here and just flopped down and was off, and she hasn't budged since.'

With great affection, Serge watched his sister for some moments. 'You must let her sleep it off,' he said.

'But of course I shall . . . Isn't it a pity she's like she is? Just look at those bonny arms! Whenever I dress her, I always think what a wonderful woman she would have made, if she'd been in her right mind. I say, and wouldn't she have given you some fine nephews, Vicar? Don't you think she's rather like that stone statue in the Corn Exchange at Plassans?'

She meant a representation of Cybele, recumbent on sheaves of wheat, the work of one of Puget's pupils, a work piece of sculpture executed on the Corn Exchange façade.

Without a word, Mouret gently propelled Teuse from the room, enjoining her to make as little noise about the house as possible. And thus the vicarage sank into silence till evening fell. Teuse finished her washing out under the lean-to, while at the bottom of the small garden, his breviary fallen to his knees, the young priest sat on, deeply withdrawn into pious contemplation, while from the flowering peaches dripped a slow and gentle rain of pink petals.

CHAPTER IX

A LITTLE before six, the vicarage suddenly came to life again. There was a great banging of doors and cascades of laughter filling every room. Désirée appeared, her hair loose, her arms still bare to the elbow. 'Serge, Serge!' she cried, then, seeing her brother down the garden, rushed to him, and squatted on the ground at his feet. 'Do come,' she pleaded, 'do come and see all my creatures. You've never seen all my creatures. Do come! If only you knew how wonderful they are now.'

She had difficulty in persuading him. The farmyard rather frightened Serge Mouret. But when he saw large tears form in his little sister's eyes, he yielded. At once, she flung her arms round his neck, with the sudden furious delight of a young puppy, and her laughter rang louder than ever, though her cheeks were still wet with tears.

'Oh, what a kind boy you are!' she babbled, as she drew him away. 'You shall see the hens and the rabbits and the pigeons. And my ducks. I've given them fresh water. And my goat. Her room is as clean as my own now . . . Did you know I had three geese and two turkeys? Quick, you shall see them all.'

At this time Désirée was already twenty-two years old. Brought up deep in the country, with her wet nurse, a peasant girl of Saint-Eutrope, she had spent her whole life in the back yard of a small farm. Her mind vacant, with not a single serious thought, the rich soil and the fresh air of that village suited her well and all her development had gone to her body, turning her into a lovely animal, fresh, clear-skinned, rosy cheeked, her flesh firm. She was like a pure-bred little heifer with the gift of laughter. Though she was messing about the livelong day, she never lost a certain distinction of bearing, and her virginal body had all the lissomness of loin and delicacy of a girl of the moneyed classes, so that she was utterly one by herself, neither young lady nor peasant lass, a broad-shouldered child of mother earth, of limited intelligence but with the impressive forehead of a young goddess.

It certainly must have been her simplemindedness which made her so fond of animals. She was at ease only in their company, understanding their speech better than that of human beings, and she lavished all the tenderness of a mother on them. Though she lacked any power to put two thoughts logically together, she was on a level with her farmyard friends by force of instinct. At their first cry of distress, she always knew exactly what was wrong with them. She would invent delicacies on which they fed gluttonously. When they fought, one gesture from her, and there was peace. At a glance she seemed to be able to assess their character, and she would talk at great length and in tremendous detail too, with remarkable precision, on the mode of being of the smallest chick, a faculty by which she often staggered people to whom every pullet is exactly the same as the other. Thereby her farmyard was a whole realm to her, and in it she was the absolute ruler. It was, what was more, a country with its own very complex social history. It was shaken by revolutions and peopled by different species of being, and only she knew all its ins and outs. The certainty of her instinct went so far that she could even tell which eggs of a sitting were fertile and she always diagnosed rightly the number of rabbits to be in a litter.

At sixteen, when puberty caught up with her, Désirée never knew the dizziness or fits of sickness of other girls. She at once assumed the frame of a grown woman, bore herself better, and burst frock after frock, so magnificently did her body develop. From then she had an opulent, well-rounded figure, a fine swaying gait and the finely-balanced limbs of a goddess of antiquity. In short, she had all the allure of a powerful animal. It might be said that she had sprung from the very compost-heap of her farmyard, drawing its juices as if through roots into her powerful, white-skinned legs, round and firm as young tree trunks. Yet, with all that full ripening of her flesh, no bodily lust showed in her. She continued to find complete satisfaction in the creatures swarming about her. From the piles of dung and the beasts at their coupling flowed an unending stream of new life and in the midst of this she found all the delights of fecundity. Part of her even found satisfaction in the egg-laying of her hens. When she took her does across to the buck rabbit, it was with the laughter of an innocent girl whose nerves were utterly at peace. The delights of pregnancy she knew when she milked her full-uddered nanny. Nothing could have been healthier. In complete innocence she imbibed the very odour and warmth of life directly. No depraved curiosity prompted any concern about reproduction when she watched her cocks fluttering their wings and saw her female creatures giving birth, or her billy-goat spattering the close walls of his stable with his pestiferous ejaculations. She maintained her calm, a lovely creature, frank of glance, void of thought, happy merely to see her little world multiply, in this feeling as if her own body were fecundated and grew big, and to such degree in this wise identifying her own being with that of all her mothers that she became a sort of universal mother, a mother nature from whose finger-tips, yet without the turmoil of any orgasm, came a procreative dew.

Since she had come to Artaud, Désirée had passed her time in utter bliss. At last she could satisfy the dream of her life, the only desire which ever ravaged her in her infantile poverty of intellect: she had her own farmyard, a lost corner given over absolutely to her, where she could breed her creatures after her own fashion. From that moment, she buried herself there, herself making hutches for her rabbits, digging a pond for her ducks, hammering nails, bringing straw, intolerant of the assistance of others. All she would allow Teuse to do was clean the filth of it all from her when the day was done. This yard of hers lay beside the graveyard, and often enough Désirée had to clamber among the gravestones to catch an inquisitive hen which had mounted beyond the wall. At the far end of this yard was an outhouse, which contained her poultry houses and rabbit-hutches. To the right was her milk-goat, in own little stable. Otherwise all the animals pigged-in together, rabbits hopping about among the hens, the goat wallowing in the water among the ducks and the geese, and turkeys, guinea-fowls and pigeons fraternising with three cats. Whenever Désirée appeared at the wooden gate which alone prevented this population from getting into the church, there was a deafening din to greet her.

'Ah! Can you hear them?' she called back to her brother, as he emerged from the house. And when she had let him in and closed the gate behind them they rushed at her so fiercely that she almost vanished. Gaggling and quacking, the ducks and the greedy hens flew up on to her arms, pecking at her hands, while the rabbits clambered over her feet and tried to climb up as high as her knees. The three cats leapt on her shoulders, and the goat bleated in its stable because it could not get out.

'Creatures, creatures, do let me alone!' she cried, with her ringing laugh, as all those feathers and claws and beaks caressed her. But she did nothing to shake them off. As she used to say, she could have let them eat her up, it was all so lovely to her to feel all that life clustering round her, enclosing her warmly as in a feather bed. To the very end one of the cats would cling to its place on her shoulder.

'My Moumou,' she said, 'his paws are like velvet.'

Then, with pride, as she showed her brother all her yard, she cried: 'Isn't it spotless?'

It had indeed all been watered and swept and cleaned up. Nevertheless, from all that dirty water which had been stirred up and all that manure which had been forked over, there arose a stench so coarsely pungent that Serge Mouret felt it would choke him. Against the churchyard wall rose the enormous manure heap, a smoking mass.

'Isn't it a wonderful heap?' cried Désirée, leading her brother through its acrid clouds. 'I made all that myself, nobody helped me . . . Get away with you, that's not dirty, that cleans you. Look at my arms.'

She stretched them out. She had merely dipped them in a bucket of water. They were magnificent arms, wonderfully firm. Like lovely white and pink roses, they had grown lush from all this manure.

'Indeed, yes,' the young priest murmured, 'you have done a lot of work, darling. It's wonderful, now.'

And he made quickly for the gate. But she stopped him.

'No, no, wait! You must see everything. You have no idea . . .'

She drew him into the shed, along past the rabbit hutches.

'There are babies in every box,' she cried, clapping her hands with delight.

Then, at great length, she explained how long does carried their young. He had to bend down and put his nose to the wire while she gave him all the little details. The mother rabbits, their huge ears quivering anxiously, stared out of the corners of their eyes, breathing hard, frozen with fear. Then, in one box, he had to examine a nest of hair at the bottom of which was a little heap of swarming life, a confused darkish mass from which rose a heavy odour as if one single body were breathing it out. Next this, the little ones were venturing out of their nest and round it, their heads enormous. Farther along was a brood already strong, like young rats in appearance, nosing and hopping about, their hind-quarters with white buttons of tail high in the air. Yet others had the pretty movements of little children, as they scampered round and round their hutches, white ones with pale ruby eyes, black ones with eyes of gleaming jade. Then sudden panic would rush them all away, showing their tiny urine-raw paws at every leap. They would cluster in a heap again, so tight-packed that their heads could no longer be distinguished.

'It's you that frightens them,' said Désirée. 'They know me.'

She called them and drew crusts of bread from her pocket. The little rabbits regained courage, came up one by one, sideways, their noses puckered, then stood erect against the wire front of the cage, and Désirée kept them like that for a moment, so that her brother should see the pink soft belly fur. Then all the litter was against the wire, pressing close, struggling with each other. Sometimes three at a time gnawed the same crust. Others ran away and turned to face the wall, to eat in peace, while the does remained right at the back of the box breathing hoarsely all the time, mistrustful, refusing any offering.

'Oh, what greedy little things, cried Désirée, 'they would eat like that till morning ... Even in the night you can hear them chewing forgotten leaves.'

The priest had straightened his back, but she was never tired of smiling down on her dear little ones.

'See that big fellow, back there, yes, that one white all over, with black ears ... Well, he loves poppies, he always picks them out from a bunch of grass ... The other day, he had real stomach-ache. It caught him under his hind-legs. But I took him out and kept him warm in my pocket, and ever since he's been such a rascal.'

63

She stretched her fingers through the wire-netting and stroked their backs.

'Just like satin,' she ran on. 'They are dressed like princes. And so proud of it, too. Look, that one is always cleaning himself, using his little paws . . . And if you but knew what funny things they do! I don't talk about it, but I see all their little tricks. For instance, that grey one looking at us simply hated a little female, and I had to take her out of the cage. They had terrible quarrels. It would take too long to tell you everything. But the last time he beat her, just as I came along, wasn't I mad! And what do you think I saw next, it was that rascal huddled, right at the back of the box, pretending he was choking, just to make me think it was he who had to complain of her . . .' She broke off to talk to the rabbit: 'All very well, listening to me, you're a real rascal, that's what you are!'

She turned back to her brother. 'He understands everything I say to him,' she murmured, screwing her eyes up in a wheedling way.

Serge Mouret had by now really had more than enough of the heat coming up from all those litters of rabbits. The life swarming there amid all that hair torn from the does' bellies emanated a powerful odour which seemed to go to his head. Even Désirée seemed a little intoxicated, for she grew more hilarious than ever, her flesh more opulent, pinker.

'But there's nobody calling for you!' she cried. 'You always seem as if you want to run away . . . What about my little chicks? They hatched out last night.'

She took some rice from a pocket and scattered a handful where she stood. With chuckling call, a broodie hen came forward with great dignity, followed by a whole brood of chicks, rushing to and fro at high speed, twittering like lost birds. The moment they found themselves in the heart of that field of scattered rice, the mother started pecking furiously, cracking grains and throwing the pieces about, while under her eyes the little ones fed at top speed. They were adorable, so young, but half feathered, their heads round, their eyes like little steel beads, their beaks so comically set, their down so delightfully upstanding, just like toy chicks. Désirée laughed with sheer pleasure at the sight of them. 'Aren't they little pets?' she babbled. She took two, one in each hand, and smothered them with kisses, and the Vicar of Artaud was obliged to examine them from all angles, while with complete serenity she ran on: 'It isn't easy to recognize the cock-birds, but I never make a mistake . . . This one's a hen and that one, yes, that's a little cock.'

She put them down again, but now the other hens came hurrying up to get at the rice, with them a huge red cock, with fiery plumage. As he walked he lifted his huge claws with what seemed like conscious pomp.

'Alexander certainly is turning into a fine bird,' the Vicar remarked, to humour his sister.

Alexander was the cock's name, and he looked up at the young girl, his eyes like glowing coals, his head turned at an angle, his tail spreading. Then he came to stand up against her skirts.

'He's very fond of me,' she said. 'I am the only one who can touch him. He's a good cock, too. He has fourteen hens, but I never find an unfertile egg laid by his hens, do I, Alexander?'

She bent down, and when she stroked him, the cock made no attempt to escape. A fresh flood of blood seemed to set fire to his crest. Beating his wings and stretching out his neck, he uttered a long cry, which might have come from a brass trumpet. Four times he crowed, while all the other cocks in Artaud answered him from afar. Désirée found the agonised look on her brother's face very funny indeed.

'Ah, he deafens you, doesn't he?' she cried, 'He has a wonderful voice . . . But I assure you, he's not vicious. It's the hens which are savage brutes. Remember that big speckly who used to lay such golden eggs? The day before yesterday, she scratched her claw, and when the others saw the blood, they went quite mad. They followed her and pecked her and drank her blood, till by evening they had pecked her foot right off . . . I found her with her head behind a stone, like a loony, saying nothing, just letting herself be eaten.'

This voraciousness of the hens made her laugh, and she told her brother quite calmly about other cruel things, young pullets with their rumps torn open and the entrails picked out, so that all she found was neck and wings, and a litter of kittens in the stable which the hens ate up in a few hours.

'If you gave them a christian,' she ran on, 'they'd finish him off . . . And how tough they are. They can live quite well with a broken leg. Even when they are wounded, with gaping cuts you can stick your fist in, they want their dinners all right. That is why I love them so, their flesh mends up in a couple of days, their bodies are always so warm, as if they stored sunshine under their feathers . . . When I want to give them a real feast, I cut them up some raw meat. As for worms, you'll see how they love them.'

She ran across to the manure heap and found one, which without a sign of disgust she brought between her fingers. The hens simply stormed her hands, but she held the wriggling thing up high, taking pleasure in their gluttony. At last, she opened her fingers. The hens charged one another as they rushed at it, then with the worm in her beak off went one, pursued by all the others. Then the worm was snatched away and lost, and snatched again and again, till with a great jerk of her neck, one hen got it down whole. Immediately, they all halted, and their heads swung round to look behind them, expecting another worm from Désirée. She was so happy, she called them by pet names, lavished tender words on them, but her brother drew back in horror at the sight of such fierce voraciousness.

'No,' he said, 'you have not made me confident,' when his sister wanted him to feel the weight of a hen she was fattening. 'I hate the feel of live animals.'

He attempted a smile. But Désirée found him cowardly. 'And what about my ducks and my geese and my turkeys? Whatever would you do, if you had those to look after? Now ducks are dirty things. Hear their beaks clicking, in the water? When they dive, you only see their tails, straight up in the air . . . Nor are geese or turkeys easy to manage. But aren't they funny when they strut along, some quite white, the others all black, with their long necks? Just like fine gentlemen and ladies. Now they are things I wouldn't advise you to trust your fingers to. They'd gobble them up at one go. But they kiss me, my fingers, I mean, look!'

But she was interrupted by the delighted bleating of her goat, which at last had succeeded in forcing the badly closed stable door. In two bounds it was with her, kneeling down and stroking her with its horns. The priest thought its grin satanic, with that goatee beard and those slanting eyes, but Désirée put her arms round its neck and kissed its head. She pretended to run, she said she would suck its milk. Oh yes, she said, she often did that, whenever she felt thirsty out in the stable, she lay down on her back, under the goat, and sucked.

'But look, she's got plenty!' she cried, holding her hand under the goat's enormous dugs.

The young priest blinked, as if somebody had shown him something obscene. To his mind came a stone goat on a gargoyle in the monastery of Saint-Saturnin, near Plassans. That creature was fornicating with a monk. Goats, stinking of their billies, but with all the caprices and wilfulness of girls, would offer their milk to any who came along, and for that reason he always felt them to be creatures of hell, shiny with their own salaciousness. It was only after weeks of her begging that he had agreed to his sister's having one at all, and whenever he came into this yard, he took good care to avoid the touch of the creature's long, silky hair and always drew his cassock well away from her horns.

'All right then,' said Désirée, seeing how unhappy he was getting, 'I'll let you go again. But first, I must show you one thing ... Promise you won't scold? I have never said a word about it, because you would have been against. If only you knew how happy it makes me.'

She became all wheedling, her hands clasped in supplication, her head on her brother's shoulder.

'Some new craziness,' he grumbled, though he could not help smiling.

'You really won't?' she cried, delighted by how he was taking it. 'You won't be angry. He is such a lovely one.'

She raced across and opened a low door in the shed, and out bounded a young pig.

'Oh! the cherub!' she cried, absolutely ravished, as she watched her piglet escape.

He certainly was a delightful little pig, all pink, his loins oily with wetness and he had a ring of filth just under his eyes which his continual rooting in his trough left. Shouldering the hens aside, he trotted hastily up to get a little of the food thrown out for them, and was all over the yard in a second. His ears flapped down over his eyes, his belly rubbed the ground. On his tiny trotters, he looked like a toy on wheels, with a twist of string at the back in place of tail, for hanging him up.

'I will not have that animal here!' cried the Vicar, quite annoyed about it.

'Serge dearest, darling Serge,' Désirée pleaded, 'don't be unkind ... See how innocent the little darling is. I shall clean him up and keep him nice. Teuse got him for me. You can't send him away now ... Look, he's watching you. Don't be afraid, he won't eat you.'

But she broke into mad laughter as the little piglet suddenly charged between the legs of the goat, tripping her over, after which he rushed on, shrieking raucously, tumbling about, frightening the whole yard. To quieten him down, Désirée had to bring out the bowl of washing-up water. Into this he plunged his head, up to the ears, gargling and grunting, his pink skin shaken by little spasms of delight, while his tail slowly straightened out, then dropped and hung limp.

This was for Serge the last straw. He was disgusted. He could not bear the sound of the animal's suzzling in that filthy water.

67

Ever since he came into this yard, he had felt more and more stifled. Now his hands, his chest, and his face were simply burning. Gradually all this had gone to his head, mingling in one horrid stench, the poisonous fetid warmth of the rabbits and the poultry, the lascivious stink of the goat, and now this stale oily stench of the pig. The whole air seemed to be weighed down with fecundation, and the burden of it on his virginal shoulders was too much. It suddenly seemed to him in that moment that Désirée had grown larger. Her hips had spread. The arms she waved about were enormous. Her petticoats spread wide, sweeping the ground and stirring up all that pungency which suffocated him. Escaping, he had only just time to slip the wooden bolt of the gate, or he might have fainted. His feet stuck to the stones, still damp from manure, till it seemed to him that the very soil held him fast in a disturbing embrace. And then, all at once, amid this malaise, back to him came thought of Paradou Park, with its vast vegetation, its profound shadows, its powerful scents, and he could not escape from the memory.

'But how red you've gone all of a sudden!' cried Désirée, when she had reached him and closed the gate. 'Haven't you enjoyed seeing all my creatures? Listen,—hear them?'

Seeing her leave them the animals were all crowding around the wire-netting, and making a pitiable sound, especially that little pig, which now sounded just like somebody setting a saw. But Désirée waved back to them and blew them kisses. She laughed to see them all gathering round her like that, as if in love with her. Then, pressing close to her brother, she went back to the garden with him.

'Do you know what I want now?' she whispered in his ear, blushing to the tips of her ears, 'I want a cow.'

'No, not just now,' she said, quickly, 'later on. I'll talk to you again about it . . . There would be room in the stables. We'll get a lovely white heifer, with red patches. You'd see what lovely milk we should have in time. After all a goat doesn't give quite enough . . . And think, when she had her calves!'

She danced about, clapping her hands. But all that Serge Mouret could see in his sister was the traces of the farmyard which she had brought away in her skirts. He left her at the bottom of the garden, seated on the ground, in the blazing sun, just in front of a hive, the bees of which came buzzing up like little golden balls, some of them settling on her neck and climbing up and down her naked arms, even creeping into her hair, without stinging her.

CHAPTER XII

FRIAR ARCHANGIAS always dined at the Vicarage on Thursdays, to discuss parish affairs. It was he who for the past three months had kept the Vicar informed and told him about the whole valley's doings. This particular Thursday, while they waited for Teuse's summons to table, the two men paced slowly up and down outside the church. When the Vicar had related his interview with Bambousse, he was most astonished to find that the Friar found the peasant's response quite natural.

'Bambousse is quite right,' said the Ignorantine. 'A man does not lightly give away his goods ... Rosalie is not worth much, but it is hard all the same for the farmer to see his daughter throw herself at a beggar.'

'Nevertheless,' the Vicar insisted, ' only marriage can end the scandal of it.'

The Friar shrugged his shoulders most demonstratively, to express his disagreement. With a disturbing laugh, he said: 'Do you really think you are going to cure this part of the world with marriage? Before two years are out, Catherine will be pregnant. Then there will be others. All the girls go through that stage first. And the moment they're married, they cock a snook at everybody. Artaud folk flourish in illegitimacy, as if that were the sort of foul living that suits their natures. I've already told you, the only remedy would be to wring every female's neck. That is, if you want to keep the countryside clean ... It isn't a husband that girl wants, Vicar, it's a good stick across her backside, a good stick, I tell you!'

Calming down, he added: 'Besides, we should let any man do what he wants with his own goods.' And he turned pointedly to talk of the catechism time-table.

The Reverend Mouret, however, made only distracted answers. Below him he could see his village, in the setting sunshine. The peasants were making their way home, silent men, moving slowly, trudging like worried oxen back to their stables. Outside the squat houses were standing the women, shouting one to the other, from door to door, while hordes of children filled the streets with the clatter of their heavy shoes, pushing and tumbling and arching their backs one at another. From that pile of ramshackle houses rose a confused odour of humanity, till he found himself wondering if he were not back in Désirée's yard with that swarming of the incessantly multiplying lower creatures before him. There was the

69

same warmth of generation, there were the same incessant new births, the mere thought of which had always so upset him. Having lived the whole day through beset with the story of Rosalie's pregnancy, in the end that was all he could think of—the dirtinesses of life, the urges of the flesh, the fateful constant reproduction of one's kind, the sowing of men like grains of wheat. He saw the folk of Artaud as if a flock hurdled in by the surrounding hills, incessantly engendering and spreading over the face of the earth, each time the women produced a new litter.

'I say,' cried the Friar, interrupting his discourse to point at a big girl letting her sweetheart kiss her behind a bush, 'just look there, another hussy for you!' And he waved his long black arms, till he had put the couple to flight. Far off, on the red land and naked rock, shone the dying sun, in a last burst of conflagration. Little by little, night was gathering. The warm scent of the lavender freshened as the small gusts of wind which rose brought it their way. At moments there came a tremendous sigh, as if this terrible soil, scorched through all the day with its lust, had at last been cowered and subdued by the grey rain of dusk. Hat in hand, enjoying the chill air, the Vicar of Artaud felt himself pervaded by the peace of those shadows. Then came Teuse's sudden call : 'Vicar! Friar Archangias, quick, your soup is on the table!'

It was a cabbage soup, the strong reek of which filled the vicarage dining-room. The Friar took his place and at steady pace proceeded to deal with the huge plateful which Teuse had placed for him. He ate copiously, with noisy gulps as he swilled food down into his stomach, his eyes on his plate all the time, not breathing a word.

'Don't you like my soup, then, Vicar?' demanded the old housekeeper. 'Don't tell me you've come in only to sip at it like that.'

'I am hardly hungry at all, my dear Teuse,' he told her, with a smile.

'And I don't wonder either,' she replied, 'with the hours you keep ... You'd have an appetite all right, if you hadn't lunched after two.'

Pouring the last few drops of his soup from his plate into his spoon, Friar Archangias said sententiously: 'My dear Vicar, a man always ought to take his meals regularly.'

Meanwhile, Désirée, who had also swallowed every drop of her soup with great gravity and absolute silence, followed Teuse out into the kitchen. Left alone with the priest, the Friar now carved himself long fingers of bread, which one by one he popped into into his mouth, while awaiting the main dish.

'So you had a big round, I gather,' he said.

Serge had not had time to reply, when there was a sudden hubbub, quick cries and ringing laughter, from the far end of the corridor, which gave on to the yard. Then came a quick, flute-like voice, which sounded rather angry, a voice, however, which filled him with frightful uneasiness. Then followed a burst of general laughter.

'Whatever can that be?' he said, and would have hurried from the room, when in bounced Désirée, hiding something in her skirt. Excitedly, she cried: 'Isn't she a funny one? She wouldn't come in. I held her by her frock, but she's terribly strong, and she got away.'

'Whoever is it she's talking about?' demanded Teuse, hurrying in from the kitchen, with a dish of potatoes surmounted by a piece of bacon.

Désirée had sat down, then, with infinite precautions from under her skirt she drew a blackbird's nest, with three chicks in it, and put it on her plate. As soon as the chicks saw the light, they reached up their tiny necks, and opening wide their blood-red mouths, seeking food. Delighted, Désirée clapped her hands. She was overcome with astonishing emotion, at the sight of these birds, rare in the south. She had never seen any before.

Mouret suddenly recalling Albine's promise. 'It's that girl from Paradou Park!' he cried.

Teuse had gone to the window. 'You're right,' she said. 'I ought to have recognized her voice, she squeaks like a grasshopper . . . Oh! look! the gypsy! she's stopped, just over there, to spy on us!'

Serge went to the window, and certainly thought he could distinguish Albine's yellow skirt behind a juniper bush, but at this juncture, there was Friar Archangias reaching up from behind him, peering over his head, and shaking his fist at the window.

'The devil take you!' he shouted. 'You bandit's whelp! If I catch you at your witchcraft down here, I'll drag you through that churchyard by your hair!'

A burst of laughter, fresh as the night air, came up the path. Then they heard quick nimble footsteps and the rustle of a girl's frock through the undergrowth, just like the rustle of a snake. Mouret, at the window, followed a patch of lighter colour slipping away through the pine-wood. It was just like a reflection of the play of moonlight. The faint breath of wind coming from the country-side had bore that same powerful scent of greenery, that perfume of wild flowers which with her bare arms, her flowing robe, her unknotted hair, Albine had shaken free.

'Impudent hussy!' growled Friar Archangias, menacingly. 'Condemned to hell fire, a child of perdition, she is!'

Resuming his place at table, he devoured his bacon greedily, gobbling down whole potatoes, as if they were little pieces of bread. Teuse never could persuade Désirée to sit through the whole of dinner. Childlike, despite her size, Désirée was ecstatic about the blackbird's nest. She was all questions. What did blackbirds eat? Did they lay eggs? How could you tell which were the cock-birds among them?

Then the old housekeeper suddenly got suspicious. Resting all her weight on her good leg, she looked the young Vicar straight in the eyes and demanded if this meant that he knew those Paradou people? Without more ado, he told the truth, and related how he had called on old Jeanbernat, Teuse all the while exchanging scandalised glances with the Friar. For the moment, however, she was saying nothing, merely fidgetting round the table, limping terribly, her heel coming down heavy enough to go through the floor-boards.

'You really might have told me about these people three months since,' Mouret grumbled, as he concluded. 'At least I should have known what sort of home I was entering.'

Teuse halted sharply, as if something had broken in her legs.

'No lies, please, Vicar,' she stuttered. 'No lies, they can only make your sin the worse . . . How dare you say I never told you about 'the Philosopher,' as they call him, when that pagan rascal is the scandal of the whole countryside? The truth is that you never listen to what I say when I talk to you. It all goes in at one ear and out of the other . . . If only you would heed what I say, what a lot of trouble you would save yourself.'

'I, too, dropped you a hint about those abominable goings-on,' added the Friar.

The Vicar of Artaud shrugged his shoulders slightly.

'All I can say is that I certainly did not remember anything,' he replied, 'until, in fact, I went to Paradou Park, and then I admit I did have the impression that I had heard something about them. But that would have made no difference, I should in any case certainly have gone to call on the unhappy old man, the moment I heard he was in danger of dying.'

Friar Archangias's mouth was full, but he banged the table with his knife, then in a loud voice said: 'Jeanbernat is a vile hound. He deserves to die a dog's death.' Seeing the Vicar's head shaking in protest, he gave him no chance to speak. 'No,' he went on loudly, 'no God for Jeanbernat, no penitence, no mercy . . . Better cast the host before swine than offer it to that piece of rascality.' And he took another big helping of potatoes, got his arms solidly on the table, buried his nose in his plate and masticated furiously.

Teuse, white with rage, her lips a thin line, contented herself with saying drily: 'Don't say anything, the Vicar'll go his own headstrong way, the Vicar has begun to keep things from us, nowadays.'

There was a profound silence. For some time, all one could hear was the working of the Friar's jaws, accompanied by the peculiar, windy sound of his manner of swallowing. With her bare arms, Désirée encircled the blackbird's nest on her plate, bending over it, smiling at the chicks, endlessly whispering to them with little fluttering noises which they seemed to understand.

'When people have nothing to hide, they tell others about what they do!' cried Teuse, suddenly.

Silence set in again. What exasperated the old housekeeper was this fact that her Vicar seemed to have deliberately made a mystery of his visit to Paradou Park. She therefore assumed the attitude of a woman shamefully deceived. Her curiosity was raw. She prowled round and round the table, keeping her eyes off Mouret and saying nothing to anybody, merely talking to herself, to relieve her feelings.

'Heavens, and that's why we have lunch so late, is it? We go off without a word, and we're on the ran-tan till two in the afternoon. We go to houses so ill famed that we daren't say afterwards what we have done. Then we lie and try to deceive everybody . . .'

'But nobody ever asked me if I had been to Paradou,' the Vicar protested, gently. He had now been trying to eat, merely not to anger Teuse. 'I had nothing to lie about.'

But, as if she had not even heard him, Teuse just rambled on. 'Ruining his cassock in the dust, slinking back like a thief, and if any kind-hearted person, with your interests at heart, asks you something for your own good, you brush her aside and treat her like a worthless woman who does not deserve your confidence. Then hide crafty-like, rather die than let a word out, wouldn't even entertain the folks at home with a word about where you've been.'

She swung round suddenly, and faced him. 'Yes, it's you I mean, you I'm talking about . . . You're sly by nature, that's what you are, you are a wicked man!'

She burst into tears, and Mouret had to try to console her.

73

'M. Caffin used to tell me everything,' she cried, through still more tears.

However, she did at last get control of herself. Meanwhile, Friar Archangias had finished off an enormous portion of cheese. The scene did not seem to disturb him at all. In his view, the Reverend Serge Mouret needed a dressing-down and Teuse was quite right to tighten the snaffle a bit. He drained a last glass of rough wine, then, pushing it back, slumped into his chair, to digest his meal.

'Well, now, and what was it you saw at Paradou?' the old house-keeper demanded. 'At least you might tell us that.'

With smiles, Mouret briefly told the singular way in which Jeanbernat had received him. Teuse showered questions on him and punctuated his story with outraged cries. From time to time, Friar Archangias clenched his fists and shook them. 'May Heaven strike them down!' he cried. 'May they burn in Hell, he and his witch.'

Then Mouret went on to try to find out more about the Paradou people, and listened with deepest attention while the Friar told him monstrous things.

'Yes, that she-devil came to school one morning and sat herself down. That was a long time ago. She must have been ten. I just let her. I thought her uncle had sent her to prepare for communion. In two months she turned the whole class upside-down. The little wretch had them worshipping her. She knew games, she concocted the girls furbelows out of tree-leaves and scraps of coloured rag. A clever girl, too, like all Hell's trollops. She was top in catechism. Then, one morning, right in the middle of school, in came the old man, threatened to smash the place up, shouting about priests getting hold of his child. I had to send for the bobby, to get him out. The girl had run away while this was happening. I could see her through the window in the field opposite, laughing at her uncle's rage . . . She had been coming to school by herself for those two months and he didn't know a thing. Did you ever hear of such a thing?'

'She never was christened properly,' Teuse said, in awed tones, and shuddered as she spoke.

'Quite true, she never was. She must be sixteen now. She has grown up like an animal. I have seen her running in a ditch, La Palud way, on all fours.'

'On all fours!' murmured the housekeeper, and turned anxiously to the window.

74

Mouret tried to express his doubts, but the Friar got quite worked up.

'Upon my word, on all fours. And she could jump like a wild cat, with her skirts up, showing her thighs. If I'd had a gun I could have shot her. People kill animals more pleasing in God's sight. Besides, everybody knows that at night she comes miaowing round Artaud. She miaows like a female cat on heat. If any man falls into her grip, she won't leave a scrap of flesh on his bones.'

All his hatred of womenkind rose up in him. With a blow of his fist he shook the table, while he shouted out his usual insulting words: 'They have Satan in their bodies. They stink of Satan, they do, they stink in the legs and the arms and the belly, everywhere . . . That is what gets fools into their clutches.'

Mouret nodded his assent to all this. Friar Archangias's violent words and Teuse's babbling tyranny were like blows of the plaited ropes the scourge of which he often felt about his shoulders. He felt a pious delight in sinking into utter abasement, in the hands of this elder man whose mouth was so full of the most vulgar foul language. He felt that this scorn for the world, this vilification of his whole being, must ultimately lead to the peace of heaven. These were wounds he was delighted to inflict on his flesh, a sewer in which it was his delight to drag his delicate temperament.

'The world is all filth,' he whispered, folding his serviette.

Teuse began to clear away. She tried to take the plate in which Désirée had her blackbird's nest.

'You're not going to sleep here, Miss,' she said. 'Let go those wretched birds.'

But Désirée defended her plate. She put her bare arms over the nest, and the laughter left her lips. She was very angry at being interfered with.

'I hope you are not going to keep those birds,' cried the Friar. 'That would bring misfortune . . . You should want to wring their necks.'

He even reached his massive hands forward, but the girl leapt to her feet and drew back, shivering all over, clutching her nest to her bosom. Her eyes fastened wildly on the Friar. Her lips suddenly seemed swollen. One would have said she was a she-wolf, about to bite. 'Don't you dare touch these little ones,' she stuttered. 'How—how ugly you are!'

She put such extraordinary scorn into the words that Mouret shuddered, as if the Friar's undoubted ugliness had now struck

75

him for the very first time. But all that body did was mutter. He had anyway always felt an obscure hatred for Désirée. The marvellous physique of the girl outraged him. When she had left the room, withdrawing backwards, keeping her eyes on him, he shrugged his shoulders, and muttered an obscenity that no one quite heard.

'It is better for her to go to bed,' said Teuse, 'she would only disturb us during the service.'

'Has anybody come?' asked Mouret.

'Oh, the girls have been there a long time, outside the church, with armfuls of foliage . . . I'll go and light the holy lamps. We can begin when you like.' And a few seconds later, they heard her swearing in the sacristy because her matches were damp.

Alone with the Vicar, the Friar asked if it was the service for the month of the Virgin that evening.

'Yes,' Mouret said. 'For the past few days the girls have not been able to come, in the usual way, to decorate the Chapel of the Virgin, they have all been busy in the fields, so we put the ceremony off till this evening.'

'A fine custom that!' muttered the Friar. 'When I see them putting down their branches, I feel I want to get each one down on the ground and make her confess all the wickedness she has been up to, before letting her touch the altar . . . It is shameful for us to let such wenches even brush their garments so near holy things.'

With a gesture, Mouret indicated that, alas, he felt that as a recent arrival at Artaud, he was bound to observe the customs.

'When you're ready, Vicar!' cried Teuse.

But Friar Archangias kept him a moment longer. 'I am going home,' he said. 'Religion for me is not a girl to be decked up in flowers and lace.'

With slow steps he made his way to the door. There, he halted again, raised one of his hairy fingers, and added: 'And you beware, Vicar, of your devotion to the Virgin!'

CHAPTER XIII

IN the church, the Vicar found a dozen big girls holding branches of olive, rosemary, and bay. As garden flowers hardly grew at all on the rocks of Artaud, it was customary to decorate the altar of the Virgin with greenery hardy enough to last the whole of May.

76

To this Teuse would add wallflowers from the churchyard wall, and the stalks of these were already soaking in old wine decanters.

'Will you let me manage it, Vicar,' she asked. 'You haven't got the hang of it . . Here, you stand over there, in front of the altar and tell me if it looks all right.'

He agreed, and it was Teuse who really managed the whole ceremony, clambering up on to a stool and nagging the grown-up girls who came up, one at a time, with their foliage.

'Now then, steady, gi' me time to set these up firmly. We don't want faggots like these falling on the Vicar's head . . . Come on now, Babet, your turn next. If only you could turn your big eyes this way. Hm! A fine piece of rosemary, yours is, yellow as a thistle, anyone'd think every moke in the place has been pissing on it . . . You now, Rousse. Now, that at least is a nice bit of bay, isn't it? I expect you picked this in your Green Cross field, eh?'

The girls all put down their branches on the altar, and kissed it, then stayed for a moment leaning against the cloth, handing branches one by one to Teuse. By now they were becoming quite forgetful of the sly air of piety with which they had mounted the altar steps, till they all of them ended up by laughing. They freely hitched their knees up on the altar table and they spread their broad hips all over it, till their bosoms were quite inside the tabernacle, with the big gilded plaster Virgin with her painted face, and her pink lips smiling at the stark naked little Jesus she held in the crook of her left arm, just above them.

'That's right, Liza,' cried Teuse. 'Squat yourself down on the altar, now you're about it! Will you pull your skirts down now! Is that the way to behave, showing your legs like that? If any of you dares lean right over again, she'll get a good swipe with her own branches . . . Can't you hand it up to me quietly?' Then, swinging round. 'How's that for you, Vicar? Does it go like that?'

She had built up a niche of greenery behind the Virgin so that the ends of the branches hung well over her, forming a sort of cradle and drooping down like palms. Curtly, the Vicar approved, then ventured a suggestion.

'I wonder whether a bunch of more delicate flowers wouldn't look nice on top.'

'Perhaps they would,' grumbled Teuse. 'But all these girls bring me is rosemary and bay . . . Has anyone of you got olive branches? Not one? For shame! The little heathens, they're afraid of losing half a dozen olives.'

But Catherine was mounting the steps, holding out an enormous olive branch, which quite hid her.

'Oh, so you've got some, have you, you little hussy," cried Teuse.

'Good gracious,' came a voice, 'she's pinched that. I saw Vincent breaking it off, while she kept watch.'

Furious, Catherine swore this was a lie. She turned round, without letting go of her branch, wriggled her swarthy head free of the leaves, and lied with astonishing adroitness, inventing quite a long story about it all, as proof that the olive-branch was really hers.

'Besides,' she wound up, 'all trees belong to the Holy Virgin, don't they?'

The Vicar was about to intervene, when Teuse demanded loudly if they were making a fool of her, leaving her up in the air empty-handed, and she fixed the olive-branch firmly, while Catherine clambered on to the stool at her back and imitated the painful way she twisted her enormously stout body on her one good leg, and at this even the Vicar had to smile.

'There,' cried Teuse, coming down, to stand beside him and have a look at her own work, 'that's the top done . . . Now for some tufty stuff between the candlesticks provided you wouldn't rather have it looped all along the gradines.' Mouret decided on the tufty stuff.

'Come along with ye, forward here,' cried Teuse, mounting her stool again. 'We don't want to sleep here . . . Now will you please kiss the altar, Miette? Do you think you're in your stable at home? Vicar, can you have a peep what they're all at, down there, I can hear them laughing like mad things.'

One of the two lamps was hooked up at the dark end of the church, to light it, and under the gallery three hefty lasses were playing at pushing one another. One fell, with her head in a holy-water stoup, which made the others laugh so uproariously that they lay down, to be able to laugh at their ease. Then they got to their feet again, their arms waving up and down as they slapped their haunches. When the Vicar appeared, they gazed brazenly at him, and seemed to enjoy his scolding. But what particularly angered Teuse was suddenly to see Rosalie with her contribution of greenery on the altar steps like the others.

'Will you come down this instant!' she commanded. 'Have you no shame, my girl? Hurry up with you, and take that stuff outside at once!'

'Good gracious, and why ever should I?' asked Rosalie boldly. 'You aren't going to accuse me, too, of stealing, are you?'

The other girls gathered round, with an air of complete innocence, but with many a sidelong bright-eyed glance at each other.

'Get outside!' ordered Teuse. 'You must know this is no place for you in your condition!'

Then, losing patience, she spat out a coarse word which made the peasant lasses all giggle with delight.

'And then?' Rosalie asked. 'Do you know everything the others do? You haven't been to watch them, have you?'

After that outburst she thought it proper to burst out sobbing. She tossed her branches away, then allowed the Vicar to take her a few steps aside and speak to her very severely. He had tried to silence Teuse. As a matter of fact, he was beginning to be quite embarrassed amid all these shameless young hussies filling the church with their greenery. They crowded right up to the footpace of the altar, surrounding it with a corner of living forest, and bringing to his nostrils the harsh scent of odiferous woods, as if it were the very breath rising from their limbs, the limbs of bodies accustomed to hard toil.

'Come along,' he cried, clapping his hands lightly, 'we really must hurry.'

'Gracious me, wouldn't I rather I was in bed myself?' grumbled Teuse. 'Do you imagine it's easy work, setting up all this greenery?'

However, in due course she succeeded in arranging lofty plumes of foliage across from one candlestick to the other. She folded the stool, and Catherine took it back to its place behind the main altar. All that remained to be done was to set up two big displays of greenery one on each side of the altar. The last armfuls of branches were ample for this, there were even some branches left over, and these the girls arranged along the wall, all the way to the wooden balustrade. The altar of the Virgin was now a grove, an enclave of forest growth, with a greensward before it.

At last Teuse consented to give place to the Vicar. He mounted the steps to the altar, and again clapped his hands lightly.

'Girls,' he said. 'Tomorrow we shall begin the special prayers for the month of May. Any of you who are unable to come should make a point of saying your rosaries at home.'

He knelt down, and with a tremendous rustle of skirts, all the girls at once squatted down on their heels, and accompanied his prayer with a confused mumble of voices, broken every now and then by bursts of laughter. One girl, when another behind her gave her bottom a pinch, actually squeaked out, then tried to hide her squeak in a fit of pretended coughing, just as they said an

79

Amen which the others all found so funny that for a moment they could not raise their heads, but huddled up writhing on the stone flags.

Teuse at once sent the guilty ones outside, while the Vicar, making the sign of the cross, remained at the altar, completely absorbed, no longer able to hear anything which took place behind him.

'Come on, skedaddle, quick, you good for nothing little things, you can't even respect Almighty God,' cried Teuse. 'Shame, whoever saw such things as girls wallowing on the ground in church like cattle in a meadow ... What are you at there, Rousse? If I catch you pinching anybody, I'll show you what for! Yes, all right, put your tongues out, I shall tell the Vicar all about you. Come on, outside, outside with you, you hussies!'

Inch by inch, she drove them to the door, hobbling to and fro round and round them, barking furiously. She had just succeeded in getting all of them, as she thought, outside, when her sharp eye saw that Catherine had quietly tucked herself into the confessional with Vincent. Inside the box, the young couple were busy munching something, a blissful expression on their faces. Them, too, she hustled out. Then, poking her head outside, for one look round before closing the door, when what should she see but Rosalie, with her arms round the neck of Fortuné, who had been waiting for her. With a distinct sound of kisses, the young couple vanished into the darkness, towards the churchyard.

'To think that hussy could dare approach the altar of the Virgin,' stammered Teuse to herself, as she shot the bolts. 'And the others are about as bad, I know. Hussies, flocking in with their bundles of greenery, all laughing, then kissing the boys the instant they get outside. And there isn't one will put herself out to come, to-morrow. The poor Vicar will have to say all his *Aves* by himself. Not one of these trollops with sweethearts to see will turn up.'

She handled the chairs and benches roughly as she put them in place and peered about her to make sure there was nothing suspicious, before going up to bed. In the confessional she found apple-cores. She tossed them out of the way behind the main altar. She also found a piece of ribbon torn from somebody's bonnet and a lock of black hair. These she screwed up together in a scrap of paper, to pursue enquiries later. But apart from this, the church seemed in good order. There was enough oil in the holy-lamp for the night, and the chancel flagstones could well go till Saturday before getting a wash.

'It's nearly ten, Vicar,' she said, going up to the Reverend Mouret, who was still on his knees. 'Far better go to bed now.'

He made no reply, except to bow his head slightly.

'Very well, I know what that means,' Teuse ran on. 'In an hour's time, the man will still be here, on this stone floor, giving himself the collywobbles. I'm off, it makes me too riled, it does . . . When all's said and done there's no sense in it all, lunching when other people dine and going to bed when the hens get up . . . I annoy you, no doubt, dear Vicar. Good-night, then. But I must say, you are not very sensible, are you?'

She had made up her mind that she would leave him there, but nevertheless, she did come back again, to put out the two lamps, muttering that praying so late at night was 'mortal hard on the paraffin.' Then at last after sweeping her sleeve across the main altar-cloth, which suddenly seemed to her very dusty, she did withdraw. Eyes raised, arms crossed on breast, the Reverend Serge Mouret was alone.

CHAPTER XIV

LIT solely by the lamp burning in the midst of the verdure on the altar of the Virgin, both east and west end of the little church had now filled with vast, fluctuating shadows. The pulpit projected a big column of shadow up to the rafters of the ceiling. Under the gallery the confessional suggested the outlines of a decrepit sentry-box. What light there was, softened and turned to a soft green by the verdure, enfolded in slumber the gilded Virgin who seemed to be descending from above in royal splendour, borne by a cloud from which the heads of winged angels protruded. At first glimpse of the round lamp glowing amid the foliage, one would have said it was a pale moon rising on the edge of a wood, lighting some sovereign apparition, a princess of heaven with a golden crown on her head, come to carry her divine child in glorious nudity down the mysterious rides of the forest. All round the tall tufts of green, cradled in the broad arch, starry rays of drowsy light poured through the leaves like the milky rain of moonshine which pervades forest thickets on clear nights. From the two ends of the darkness of the church came cracklings of wood and other indefinite sounds. On the left side of the chancel, the big clock ticked slowly, with the heavy breathing of a machine which had gone to sleep, while the radiant vision, the Mother, with tightly braided chestnut hair, came down lower, as if this nocturnal peace of the nave gave her confidence, and the airy flight of her cloud sent faint waves pulsating through the grass of the rides.

The Vicar of Artaud's glance rested on her, examining her. This was the hour in which he loved his church. The deplorable crucified Christ in death throes at his back, in the Chapel of the Dead, the tortured limbs plastered with ochre and lacquer, was forgotten. The harsh, bright light of the windows, all that morning gaiety which had poured in with the sun, all that outer life, those sparrows and that mountain ash foliage thrusting through the missing panes, were no longer there to distract him. In this night hour Nature was dead, the whitened walls drawn with black crêpe, and the night chill drew a salutary hair-shirt round his shoulders. He was then able to lose himself utterly in absolute love, without the play of a light-ray or the soft touch of wind or any odour or the beat of an insect's wing drawing him away from his delight in loving. Never did morning mass afford him that superhuman delight which his evening prayers afforded.

His lips fluttering in prayer, he gazed at the large Virgin. He saw her come forward towards him in mounting splendour from the depths of her green niche. It was no longer the mere light of the full moon on its course above the summits of the trees. She seemed clad in sunlight. Her progress was majestic, glorious, magnificent, so all-powerful that at moments he was tempted to fling himself face down on the ground to avoid the blaze of light pouring from that door opening into heaven. Then, amid that worship coming from every fibre of his being, by which the very words died on his lips, he suddenly recalled the Friar's parting words, and was aware of the blasphemy of them. This lay brother of the Ignorantine order had frequently complained about this special devotion of his to the Virgin. He claimed it was nothing less than allegiance stolen from God himself. According to him, it had a softening effect on the soul, it put religion into petticoats, engendering hyper-sensitivities of devotion unworthy of men, who should be strong. Friar Archangias had his knife in the Virgin simply as a woman, as a beautiful woman too, and as a woman who was a mother. He was always on his guard against her, obsessed with a blind fear of being tempted himself by her charm and falling to her seductive gentleness.

'She will lead you badly astray!' he had one day cried to the young priest. In love for the Virgin he saw the first seeds of all man's concupiscence, a downward slope leading straight to the physical charms of lovely auburn hair, large limpid eyes and all the mystery of female garments draping from shoulder down to toes. It was the revolt of an ascete who made a sharp division between Mother and Son, and put such questions as that of his cry : 'O Woman, what can there be in common between you and me?' But Mouret resisted the Friar's coarse words and now made deepest obeisance in his effort to blot them from his mind. This brought him back to his condition of rapture at the immaculate purity of the Virgin, and this elevated him out of the self-vilification in which he now strove to make himself as nought. When alone, face to face with the big gilded Virgin, he induced self-hallucination to such point that he actually saw her bend forward to let him kiss the plaits of hair bound tight about her head, he was once again very young, very good, very strong, very righteous, his whole being pervaded by a life which was all gentleness.

This devotion to the Virgin dated from Serge Mouret's early youth. Even when quite a small boy, and a rather wild uncouth one at that, always hiding away in corners, he used to find pleasure in imagining himself under the protection of a lovely lady, whose blue eyes of rare gentleness and kindly smile followed him everywhere. Often, at night, feeling a faint breath of air stir his hair, he would maintain that the Virgin had come to put her arm round him. He had grown up under that womanly caressing, the very air musical with the rustle of the divine skirts. After the age of seven, he satisfied all his demands for affection by spending every penny of his pocket-money on religious figurines, which he hid jealously from everybody else, to be able to play with them all by himself. He had on the other hand never been tempted to buy a statuette of Jesus carrying a lamb or a crucifix, let alone those of God the Father with a long beard, leaning down over the edge of a cloud. It was always to sentimental representations of Mary that he came back, Mary with rosebud lips and a smile, Mary with the delicate hands outstretched. Little by little he had made quite a collection of all that were to be had: Mary between a lily and a distaff, Mary like a big sister, carrying the Child, Mary with a crown of roses, Mary with a crown of stars. They were his family of lovely girls, all imbued alike with grace, all with like air of kindness, all with the same gentle features, all of them under their veils, so young, that though they were all called The Mother of God, he never felt a trace of fear of them, as he did of grown ups, nor did he feel them as adults.

They seemed to share his age with him. They were little girls he would have loved to meet, the little girls of Heaven with whom surely little boys who died when they were seven played eternally in a corner of Paradise. But, already serious, as he grew up he kept the secret of his religious love, even when the exacting sense of shame of adolescence had taken possession of him. For Mary grew up as he himself grew up, always a year or two his senior, as was but fitting, if she was to be both his friend and his governess. When he was eighteen, she was twenty. No longer did she kiss his forehead at night, but now stood withdrawn a few paces away from him, her arms crossed, on her lips that adorably gentle, ever chaste smile. Now he no longer mentioned her name but in a soft whisper, and every time that in his prayers the precious syllables passed his lips, he felt his heart overcome by faintness. He no longer dreamed children's games in the celestial garden, but endless contemplation, with that unblemished face before his eyes, so pure that he could not admit that his mere breath should touch it. Even from his mother he concealed what he loved so dearly.

Some years later, however, when he was at the seminary, that lovely affection for the Virgin, which had hitherto always been so straight and so spontaneous, began to be perturbed by profound unrest. Was the worship of Mary essential to salvation? Was he not robbing God by giving Mary part of his love, the greatest part indeed, thoughts, heart, and all he had? These were disturbing questions, an agonising inner conflict, which drew him but closer to her. He began now to probe deep into the finer shades of his attachment. He found unbelievable sweetness in debating the very legitimacy of his feelings. The books which dealt with devotion to the Virgin delighted him, justifying him and filling him with arguments in favour which with meditative prayer he constantly repeated. The path by which he approached Jesus now led through Mary, and he adduced a variety of proofs of the rightness of this, drawing distinctions and consequences from them: since Jesus had obeyed Mary on earth, all men without exception should obey her; in Heaven, Mary retained her maternal powers, she was there the great dispenser of God's treasury, the only person who could intercede with him, and the only one who could grant thrones. Thus, originally a humble creature in comparison with God, Mary became exalted to God's level and thus the bond between Heaven and earth, the agent of all grace and all mercy. The conclusion to be drawn was that Mary was to be loved above all others, loved even in God.

Beyond this came even hotter theological curiosities, such as the marriage of the Heavenly Bridegroom, the Holy Ghost putting his seal on the Chosen Vessel, placing the Virgin Mother in a state of eternal miracle, giving her inviolable purity to men for their devotions. There was the Virgin victorious over all heresies, the Virgin who was Satan's irreconcilable enemy, the new Eve declared to be She who would Crush the Head of the Serpent, the Virgin as the august Portal of Grace through which the Saviour had entered the world once already and would enter again, on the day of judgment, undefined prophecy adumbrating a still vaster role for Mary and bringing Serge to a dream state in which by love alone he lost all consciousness. This entry of woman into the jealous, cruel Heaven of the Old Testament, this figure of perfect whiteness taking her place at the feet of the awesome Trinity, meant the introduction of grace itself into religion, a consolation for all that was so awesome in faith, the refuge of a man lost amid all the mysteries of dogma. And when point by point with logic he had demonstrated to himself which was the way to Jesus, the easy way, the short and perfect reliable way, with no trace of misgiving, he once again abandoned his whole being to Mary, and all his study was bent on making him her true devotee, his own individuality withering away, annihilated in its total submission.

What divine moments of loving thrill! The books of devotion to the Virgin burned his fingers. They spoke a language of love redolent as incense. The Virgin was no longer the white veiled adolescent, standing with folded arms a few paces only from his couch. She came to him amid splendours such as St. John saw her in, clad in sunlight, crowned with twelve stars, under her feet the moon. She anointed him with her fragrance, she ignited in him the longing for Heaven, bearing him up into the ardent glow of the stars which burned on her forehead. He cast himself down before her, cried aloud that he was abjectly hers, nothing sweeter to him than this word *slave* which he kept repeating the more he abased himself at her feet, the sweeter ever on his quivering lips, so that he became her thing, her nothing, mere dust brushed in passing by the sway of her blue gown. Together with David, he said : 'Mary is made for me.' With the evangelist, he added: 'I have taken her for all my goods.' From poverty of words he called her *my beloved mistress*, descending to the baby-talk of child and of lover, till he could but gasp incoherent words of love. She was the Blessed One, the Queen of Heaven lauded by nine choirs of angels, the Mother of glorious Love, the Treasure of the Lord. Vivid images multiplied, comparing her to an earthly paradise made of a virgin land, with flower borders of virtue, green meads of hope, invincible towers of strength, delectable houses of confidence. Or again, she was a fountain on which the Holy Ghost had set its seal, a sanctuary in which the most Holy Trinity found rest, the Throne of God, the City of God, the Altar of God, the Temple of God, the World of God. And Serge Mouret himself trod the paths of that garden, through shadow and sunshine, amid verdure enchanting. He sighed for the water of that fountain. He dwelt in the lovely house of Mary, resting against her, hiding himself in her, losing himself in her without reserve, drinking the milk of infinite love as it oozed drop by drop from her virginal bosom.

In the seminary his first act on rising was to greet Mary with a hundred inclinations, his face turned towards the segment of sky which he could perceive through his window. Every evening, he took his leave of her by the same number of inclinations, his eyes on the stars. Often, when the night was intense peace, and Venus burned fair and reflective in the warm night air, he would lose himself, in contemplation and like a faint song murmur the *Ave maris stella*, the hymn of tenderness which far from blue beaches conjured for him a tranquil sea which rippled but faintly in the tremendous spasm of a caress, lighted by that one smiling star as large as any sun. Thereafter he would proceed to recite the *Salve Regina*, the *Regina caeli*, the *O gloriosa Domina*, all the prayers and all the canticles. He read the *Office of the Virgin*, the sacred books in her honour, the little Psalter of Saint Bonaventure, all with such devout emotion that the tears would hinder him turning the pages. He fasted, he mortified himself, to make her the offering of his murdered flesh. From the age of ten he wore her symbol, the holy scapulary, the double image of Mary, sewn on to cloth, the warmth of which with shivers of contentment he felt on back and bosom, against his naked skin. Later, to declare the enslavement of his adoration, he assumed the chain. But his supreme act of devotion was certainly always the angelic greeting, the *Ave Maria*, perfect prayer of his heart. 'I greet you, Mary,' he would murmur, then see her come towards him, all grace, blessed among all women. At her feet he cast down his heart for her to trample in all her gentleness. This salutation he multiplied, repeating it in a hundred ways, and was full of inventiveness, to make it more efficacious. He said a dozen *Aves*, to recall the crown of twelve stars which bound her forehead, he said fourteen, to recall her fourteen delights, he said seven times ten, in honour of the years which she spent on earth. For hours he passed the beads of her rosary through his fingers. Then, in all their inordinate length, on certain days of mystic meeting he undertook the infinite whisper of the prayers of the Rosary of the Virgin.

When, alone in his cell, with time for loving, he knelt on the stone flags, the garden of Mary flourished entire about him, with immense flowers of chastity. Like a garland of white roses mingled with Annunciation lilies, the blood-stained flowers of the Crucifix and the stars of her Coronation, through his fingers slipped the rosary's garland of *Aves* alternating with *Paters*. With measured pace he trod the sweet-scented avenues, halting at each of the fifteen tens of *Aves*, finding repose in the mystery to which it corresponded. As the mysteries took their places in three series, the happy, the sorrowful and the glorious, he was alternately overcome with delight, with sorrow and with pride. It was a legend without compare, the story of Mary, the perfect human life, with its smiles, its tears, its triumphs, which would flash through his soul in an instant, from beginning to end. First came her delight, in the five smiling mysteries, bathed in the serenity of dawn. Here was the message of the archangel, a ray of fecundation shooting from Heaven to Earth, bringing the lovely relaxation of faultless union; next, the visit to Elizabeth, in the clear morning of hope, in that hour when the fruit of her bowels for the first time brought Mary that shock at which a mother's cheeks turn pale; then the confinement in the Bethlehem stable, with the long queue of shepherds come to greet divine motherhood; next, the new-born carried to the temple in the arms of its mother, who though still exhausted by her labour smiles, already happy to offer her child for God's justice to be accomplished, for Simeon to kiss, for the lusts of this world to assail; finally, Jesus grown up, declaring himself to the learned men, amid whom is his mother again, proud of him and consoled. Then, after that morning, with its light of supreme delicacy, it seemed to Serge that the Heaven was suddenly curtained off from him. He trod then on nothing but thorns, and the beads of the Rosary lacerated his fingers. With their terrible weight the five mysteries of sorrow broke his back: Mary living through her son's agony in the Garden of Olives, receiving the blows of the flagellation with him, feeling on her own brow the tearing spikes of the Crown of Thorns, bearing the frightful weight of the cross, dying at his feet on Mt. Calvary. These essentials of suffering, this frightful martyrdom of the venerated Queen, for whom he would have given his blood as Jesus did, caused in him a revulsion of horror that even ten years of the same prayers and the same special

87

services had been powerless to assuage. But beyond this he still tore his fingers on the rosary beads, and there came a sudden gap in the darkness of the Crucifixion, the splendid glories of the five final mysteries blazing out over him with all the delight of the free stars. Mary, transfigured, sang the alleluiah of resurrection, of victory over death, of eternity of life. Her hands reached out, her head was thrown back in wonder, she was present at the triumph of her son as in clouds of gold fringed with purple he ascended to Heaven. She gathered the Apostles about her, enjoying as she had done on the day of annunciation the great conflagration of the spirit of love come down in fierce flames. In turn, she was borne up on a flight of angels, borne up on white wings like an ark immaculate, to be deposited gently amid the glory of heavenly thrones. And there, as supreme glory, in such dazzling light that she put out the sun, God crowned her with the stars of the firmament. Burning love knows but the one word. Reciting his hundred and fifty *Aves*, one after the other, Serge never repeated one, yet in them that insistent murmur, that never-changing word which like the 'I love you' of lovers recurred again and again, every single time assumed significance more profound. He lingered over it, and by the aid of that single phrase of Latin, contrived to hold converse with the Virgin, knowing her absolutely, to such point that as the last bead of all of the Rosary slipped from his hands and separation drew near, he felt himself grow perilously weak at the mere thought.

Many a time did the young man thus pass his nights, beginning the dozens of *Aves* many times over, putting off and putting off the moment when he would have to take leave of his dear beloved mistress. When day broke, he would still be whispering away. Even then, to deceive himself, it was the moon, he would say, that made the stars grow pale. His superiors were obliged to scold him for those night vigils, from which he would emerge worn out, so pale that he seemed to have lost every drop of blood. For a long time, he kept on the wall of his cell a coloured engraving of the Sacred Heart of Mary. Smiling serenely, the Virgin bared her corsage, to reveal the red gash in her bosom where, transfixed with a sword and surrounded by white roses, her heart was burning. That sword caused him agonies. It induced in him unbearable horror of suffering in woman, the mere thought of it making pious resignation impossible for him. He removed the sword, leaving only the crowned, flaming heart, half torn from that exquisite body in offering to him.

It was then that he felt himself loved. Mary offered him her heart, her living heart, her heart exactly as it beat within her own bosom, from it dripping the scarlet drops of her own blood. It was no longer a mere symbol of passionate devotion, but something material, a prodigy of tender affection which whenever he faced the engraving and prayed made him extend his wide-open hands religiously to receive that heart torn from a bosom of absolute purity. It was as if his whole being lost all control, in its desire to kiss that heart and submerge itself in it, nestling with it in the seclusion of that bosom thus laid open. She loved him actively to such point that she wanted him to be close to her for eternity and always hers. She loved him effectively, ever concerned about him, following him everywhere, ensuring the non-committal of the slightest act of infidelity. She loved him tenderly, more than all other women, with love that was like the heavens themselves, profound, infinitely azure blue. Where could he ever have found so desirable a mistress? What earthly caress could be compared with this breath of Mary in which he moved? What wretched union, what dirt-fouled physical satisfaction could ever outweigh that eternal flower of desire for ever swelling yet never breaking into bloom? In such moments the *Magnificat* broke from his lips like a delicate puff of incense and he sang the song of Mary's delight and tremor of happiness at the approach of the divine Spouse. He glorified the Lord casting down the mighty who sat high on thrones and sent Mary to him, yes, to him, poor naked boy, dying of love on the ice-cold flagstone of his cell.

And when he had rendered all to Mary, body, soul, earthly goods, spiritual goods, when he lay thus naked before her, his prayers exhausted, from his heat-cracked lips burst forth the litanies of the Virgin, with all their repetition of supplication, so persistent, so frenzied, in supreme need of heavenly aid. It seemed to him that he was mounting a ladder of desire. At every leap of his heart, he accomplished another rung. First, he pronounced her Holy. Then he called her Mother, Most Pure, Most Chaste, Lovable and Admirable, and again his fire rose, as sextupled he declared her virginity, his lips as it were made fresh again each time he pronounced the mere sounds of the word virgin, associated by him with the concepts of power and kindness and loyalty. As his heart bore him higher and higher on the rungs of light, a strange voice welling from his own bloodstream spoke within him and spread out in dazzling blossom. He would have liked to melt away in the perfume thereof and grow great in clarity, dying in a sigh that was music. While he called her Mirror of Justice, Temple of Wisdom, Source of Delight, he saw himself in that mirror, pale from ecstasy, he knelt on the warm stones of that temple, he drank long draughts of intoxication from that spring. Still further did he transform her, giving free rein to his mad affection to seek ever closer union with her. She became the Vessel of Honour elected by God, the Chosen Bosom into which he aspired to pour his whole being, for ever there to sleep. She was the Mystic Rose, a huge flower which had unfolded its petals in paradise, a flower made of the angels who enfolded their Queen, so pure, so sweet-smelling that in his abysmal unworthiness he breathed her fiercely in, swelling so with delight that his very bones cracked. She turned into a House of Gold, a Tower of David, a Tower of Ivory, of unappraised richness, of the envied purity of swans, tall of stature, imbued with strength, rounded of limb, till he longed to make of his outstretched arms a girdle of subjection. She stood erect on his horizon, she was the Gate of Heaven which he glimpsed beyond her shoulders when a breath of wind spread the folds of her veiling. She grew mighty behind the mountain in the hour when night grew pallid. Star of the Morning, Succour of the Lost Traveller, Dawn of Love. Then, at that height, lacking breath, before his strength was recovered, though the words bewrayed the strength of his heart, he could not do more than glorify her with the title of Queen which he cast before her nine times to mark the nine strokes of the thurible. In these cries of ultimate triumph, his song of songs died away in sheer delight: Queen of the Virgins, Queen of All the Saints, Queen Conceived without Sin! Ever higher, she glowed with her glory. He was on the final rung, the rung which only those who were Mary's intimates could attain, and there he poised for some moments, breathless in that rarefied atmosphere which bereft him of his senses, yet still too far removed from her even to kiss the hem of her blue robe. Then, oh, how soon despite his eternal longing to climb yet higher and attain superhuman satisfaction, he felt his footing too insecure by far.

What countless times those litanies of the Virgin, recited together, in the Chapel, left this young man with faltering knees, void of thought, as if fallen from a great height! And since he left the seminary the Vicar of Artaud had learned to love the Virgin still more, devoting to her that passionate cult in which the Ignorantine Friar detected the ill odour of heresy. According to Mouret, it was the Virgin who would save the Church, and this in virtue of a tremendous miracle, the forthcoming manifestation of which would delight the world. She was the sole miracle of our impious age, the lady in blue revealed to little shepherds, that nocturnal whiteness to be seen between two clouds, the edge of her veil trailing above the thatched roofs of peasant homes. When Friar Archangias roughly put the question to him of whether he had ever really seen her, all he did was smile and knit his lips tight, as if to preserve a secret.

The truth was that he saw her every night. She no longer came to him as joyous sister or fervent maid of beauty. Now, she wore the garments of a bride. In her hair were white flowers. Her eyelids were lowered yet not quite closed, for under them came humid glances of a hope which shed soft light upon her cheeks. And he vividly felt her approaching him, promising him she would tarry no longer, saying to him: '*Here I am, now take me.*' Thrice daily, when the *Angelus* bell rang—at dawn, in the maturity of midday, and when gentle dusk enveloped the earth—he bared his head and said an *Ave*, looking about him the while to be sure that this was not the day when the bell had finally announced her arrival. He was twenty-five years old, and he was expectant of her advent.

In May, the young priest's expectation became rich of contented hope. He no longer gave heed to Teuse's grumbling. If he stayed so late in the church at his prayers, it was with the mad idea that the large gilded Virgin would at last some down to him. And yet he still feared her, feared that Virgin who was so like a Princess. He did not like all Virgins in the same way. This Virgin instilled sovereign respect. She was the Mother of God. She had the breadth of body of fecundity, the august features, the powerful arms of the Divine Spouse who carried Jesus in her womb. Thus he imagined her in the centre of the court of heaven, the train of her regal cloak trailing behind her among the stars. She was too lofty for him, so powerful that were she but to deign to lower her eyes to look into his, he would collapse in dust. She was the Virgin of his days of weakness, the stern Virgin who by the terrible vision of paradise gave him inner peace.

This particular evening, Serge Mouret remained more than an hour, kneeling in the empty church. His hands clasped, his eyes on the Golden Virgin rising like a star amid the greenery, he sought the nerve-deadening effect of ecstasy, the pacification of the strange unease which he had felt all that day. But now he was unable to slip down into the half-sleep of prayer with the happy ease which he usually achieved. The motherhood of Mary, however glorious and pure she seemed, those rotundities of the fully mature woman, that naked child which she carried on one arm, all troubled him, all suddenly seemed like a continuation in Heaven of that over-

91

abundance of new generation and birth which here on earth had somehow surrounded him everywhere he moved all that day. Just like the vines on the stony slopes, like the trees of Paradou Park, like the human warren of Artaud itself, Mary, too, offered the burgeoning and the engendering of new life. He therefore lingered over his prayers, seeking oblivion in distractions, perceiving things he had never seen hitherto—the gentle waves of the auburn hair, the dainty fullness of the chin with its pink colour-wash. She should now show herself sterner, she should crush him with the brilliance of her all-powerfulness, and thereby bring him back to the broken phrase of his prayer. It was in the end by reason of her crown of gold, her golden cloak, by all that gold, which made an awe-inspiring princess of her, that she was able to crush him back into slavish submission, with prayer flowing steadily from his lips and his mind lost in the profundities of single-minded adoration. Raised thus to that ecstatic stupefaction, he slept till the hour of eleven, conscious no longer of his knees, feeling as it were in a state of defiance of gravity, rocked like a child in its mother's arms, yielding to that rest, though all the time aware of a weight burdening him at heart. Around him, the tall greenery darkening the varnished features of the big Virgin, and the lamp-wick choking, the church filled with shadows.

When, just before it sounded the next hour, the church clock began to grind harshly, he suddenly shook all through. He had not felt the chill of the night wrap about his shoulders. Yet now he was shivering with cold. As he made the sign of the cross his awakening mind was crossed by a sudden memory. His teeth thus chattering recalled to him the nights once passed on the flags of his cell, with agued limbs, facing the Sacred Heart of Mary.

He rose painfully to his feet, full of discontent with himself. As a rule he left the altar with peace in his body and the sweet breath of Mary on his brow. But tonight, when he took the lamp to go to bed, he felt as if his temples would burst. His prayers had been bootless. After brief assuagement, here, back again, was that terrible fever which had grown in him, from heart to head. Reaching the door of the sacristy, and about to go on into the house, he swung round and mechanically raised the lamp, once again to take a look at the big Virgin behind him. She was drowned now in the enfolding shadows of the rafters, deep in the verdure, through which only the cross of gold of her crown could be seen.

CHAPTER XV

The Vicar of Artaud's bedroom, one of the corner rooms of the vicarage, was enormous. Each of the two outside walls had a huge rectangular window, one opening on to his sister's farmyard, the other on to the village, with the valley and hills, all the horizon, in fact, behind it. The four-poster had yellow curtains, while the walnut tallboy and the three rush-bottom chairs were lost under the lofty ceiling with its limewashed rafters. From the tiles, which were redded and shone like glass, there arose a faint acridity, that slightly sour odour of old country houses. On the tallboy a large statuette of the Immaculate Conception introduced a note of grey gentleness, set between two pots which Teuse had filled with white lilac.

He put his lamp down on the edge of the tallboy, in front of the Virgin. He felt so shivery that he decided to put a match to the dried vine cuttings already laid in the fireplace. And there he stood, his pince-nez between his fingers, watching the wood burn up, the flickering flames lighting his face. The silence hummed in his ears till it assumed the sound of whispering voices, and little by little these forced their way into him, increasing the anxiety which during the day he had felt more than once clutch at his throat. Whatever could be the origin of this mental discomfort? What on earth was this unfamiliar trouble, which had grown so insidiously, till now it was unbearable? Throughout the day he had committed no sin. He felt as if he left his seminary but yesterday, with all the ardour of the fervour of his faith, so strong in opposition to the world that he walked among men but saw only God.

Next, he thought he was in his seminary cubicle, one morning, at five, on the point of rising. The deacon on duty had passed, tapping on all doors, with the regulation cry: '*Benidicamus Domino!*' and though but half awake, eyes still heavy with sleep, he replied with '*Deo gratias!*', leapt to the narrow rug, washed, made his bed, swept his room, changed the water in his jug. This slight domestic chore was a delight in the morning freshness which played on his skin. He heard the sparrows of the plane trees in the courtyard rise simultaneously with himself, with much flapping of wings and deafening cries. He reflected that they too were saying their prayers.

He went down into the Meditation Room, where after prayers, he spent half an hour on his knees reflecting on the following

93

thought of Ignatius': '*What serves it to a man to conquer the whole world, if he lose his soul.*' It was a subject pregnant with good resolutions, one which made him renounce all worldly goods, with the dream so often cherished of a life in a desert place, where the only wealth would be the blue sky above.

After ten minutes his knees, numbed by the flags, began to hurt him so much that he gradually felt he was losing consciousness entirely, an ecstatic state in which he saw himself as a great conqueror, master of a vast empire, casting away his crown, breaking his sceptre, trampling underfoot unheard-of luxury, caskets of gold, showers of jewels, cloth sewn with precious stones, to don a horsehair shirt which excoriated his back, and bury himself in a Theban retreat.

Mass, however, drew him from these fantasies, from which he emerged as if from true happenings through which he had lived in a former age. He took communion, he sang the psalm for the day, ardently, hearing no other voice than his own, a voice of crystal purity, so clear that he felt it reverberate to the ears of the Lord God. And when he came up to his room again, he climbed only one stair at a time, as Saint Bonaventure and Saint Thomas Aquinas recommended, walking slowly, seemingly in deep meditation, head slightly dipped, finding inexpressible satisfaction in following the most petty prescriptions.

Next came the midday meal. In the refectory the crusts of bread laid out by the glasses of white wine delighted him, for he had an excellent appetite and was of cheerful temperament, saying, for instance, that the wine was most christian wine, a very daring allusion to the water which the steward was accused of adding to the bottles. That did not prevent his resuming his serious bearing when he came into class again. He took his notes on his knees, while, fists on the edge of his lectern, the professor spoke the customary Latin, eked out now and then when the Latin failed him, by a word of French. A debate arose, and the pupils argued solemnly, in a strange jargon.

Then, at ten, came a reading of Holy Writ for twenty minutes. He went for the holy book, richly bound, the cut edges gilded, and, kissing it with special veneration, read it bareheaded, bowing every time he came to the names of Jesus, Mary or Joseph. The second meditation then found him fully prepared to bear a second bout of kneeling, longer than the first, for the love of God. He avoided relaxing back even for a second on to his heels, and this examination of conscience he underwent with passion for three-quarters of an hour, till he came to the conviction that he was damned for having forgotten the evening before to kiss the two images of his scapulary or for having fallen asleep on his left side, abominable sins he would gladly have expiated by torturing his knees till evening, yet happy sins for so engaging him and without which he would not have known how to occupy his frank heart in the soporific state induced by the eventless life he led.

He entered the refectory quite relieved, as if he had shaken a major crime from his bosom. The seminarists on duty, the sleeves of their cassocks drawn up, an apron of blue twill tied about their waists, brought the vermicelli pottage, the boiled beef cut up into little dice, and the portions of leg of mutton with haricot beans. There came a monstrous din of jaws, not a man in his gluttony speaking a word, a ferocious assault of massed forks, broken solely by envious glances cast at the horseshoe table, where the principals ate tenderer meats and drank redder wines. And all the time the thick voice of the son of some peasant household who was endowed with powerful lungs droned away with fine disregard for commas or full-stops, reading out above the din some pious matter— missionaries' letters, episcopal exhortations, articles from the religious press. And in between mouthfuls he gave ear to it all, for these snatches of polemic and tales of distant voyages astonished him, even frightened him, for beyond the walls of his seminary they revealed the existence of a turmoil, indeed, of immense horizons on which he had never before reflected.

They would still be eating, when a rattle announced recreation. The yard was sanded and planted with eight tall plane-trees which yielded fresh shade in summer. On the south side was a fifteen-foot high wall surmounted with broken bottle glass, above which only the tip of the spire of St. Mark of Plassans could be seen, a short needle of stone thrusting into the azure sky. From one end of the yard to the other he paraded slowly, with a group of fellow students. They all trod the same track. Each time they turned to come back, facing the high wall, he gazed at the tip of the spire, among the free-flying clouds, and that point of stone became the whole town, indeed, the whole earth, for him.

Under the plane-trees, excited groups were busy in debate. Other men, friends, separated off in couples, in corners, while one of the principals, peeping from behind some window curtain, kept his eye on them. There were others playing tennis or skittles with great excitement, disturbing quiet lotto players crouching on the ground over their cards, which wildly flying balls would cover with sand.

When the bell rang, there was sudden silence, and with a cloud of sparrows flying up from the trees, and the pupils, still out of breath from their games, made their way, arms folded, heads bowed, to a lesson on plain-song. Thus he finished this day of May, lost again in that tranquillity, a pupil on the seminary benches again, under the spire of St. Mark. Again he supped amid the din of hard-plied jaws, with a rough voice completing the morning's reading. Again he made his way up to the chapel to recite the evening graces. Again he retired to bed at a quarter past eight, after having sprinkled his bed with holy water to obviate ill dreams.

What countless such lovely days he had passed there, in that old monastery of the ancient city of Plassans, a building saturated with the odour of centuries of devotion. For five years the days of his life flowed on there, one after the other, unchanging like the murmur of a limpid stream. Now he found himself recalling a thousand little details which moved him. He remembered his first outfit, and how he had gone to buy it with his mother: two cassocks, two belts, six bands, eight pairs of black stockings, surplice, three-cornered hat. And how his heart had beaten that gentle October evening when the seminary gates first closed behind him. There he had come, after his years of high school, at the age of twenty, full of a need to believe and to love. From the first morning he had forgotten everything and as it were sunk to a sleep in the depths of that great house of tranquillity. Again he saw the constricted cell in which he had passed his two years of philosophy, a cubicle with bed, table and one chair, separated from other cubicles by badly joined planking, in an immense dormitory which contained about fifty such boxes. Again he saw the cell which he occupied for three years as theologian, larger, this one, with an armchair, a wash-hand-stand, book-shelves; a happy room this, full of dreams of his faith. Down those endless corridors and long stone stair-cases he had known sudden revelations, gifts of unexpected succour. From the lofty ceilings came the voices of guardian angels. Not a flagstone of the halls, not a stone of the walls, not a branch of the plane-trees which did not speak to him of the satisfactions of his contemplative life, of those stammerings of affection, of his slow initiation, of the caresses he received in return for the gift of his being, all the happiness of his first loves of divine things. There was, for instance, that day on which, awakening, he had seen a bright light which bathed him with delight. There was the evening when, closing the door of his cell, he had felt warm hands about his neck, so gentle that when he recovered consciousness he found himself prostrate on the floor, sobbing his heart out. Then, on many occasions, particularly under the low vaulting which led to the chapel, he felt soft arms encircle his waist, and abandoned himself to them and was levitated from the ground. At that time Heaven in its entirety was concerned with him, walked at his side and inspired his least act, the accomplishment of the commonest of his needs being a special sense, a surprising perfume which seemed for long thereafter to hover faintly about him, in his clothing, even in his skin. He also remembered the Thursday walks. They would set out at two o'clock for some verdant nook, two or three miles from Plassans, most frequently on the banks of the Viorne, at the far edge of a meadow, where gnarled willows dipped their leaves in the waters. He saw nothing, neither the big yellow flowers of the meads or the swallows dipping in flight, their wings skimming the still surface of the little river. Till six, lolling under the willows in little groups, his fellow-students recited together the Office of the Virgin or paired off and read to each other the small seminarists prayer-book.

Poking the fire, Serge Mouret smiled. In this past of his he found nothing but enormous purity, perfect obedience. He was a lily the sweet scent of which delighted his masters. He could not recall a single bad act. He never once profited by the complete liberty of those country walks, while the two principals in charge went to chat with a neighbouring rector, to smoke behind a hedge or run for a glass of ale with a friend. He never concealed novels under his mattress or bottles of anisette in his bedside table. Indeed, for long enough he did not even know about the sins which surrounded him, wings of chicken or cakes smuggled in during Lent, guilty letters brought by acolytes, shocking whispered conversations in certain corners of the courtyard. He wept scalding tears the day he first realised that few among his fellow seminarists loved God for himself. There were among them peasant sons who were taking holy orders to avoid the army, lazy characters whose dream was an idle sort of job, and ambitious men already much concerned with the cross and mitre. But when he thus discovered the dirt of the outer world so close to the foot of the altar itself, he merely withdrew still more into himself, abandoning himself more than ever to God, to console God for the way in which others neglected him.

Nevertheless, there was one memory: how one day, in the lecture-room, he crossed his legs, and the lecturer reproached him for this, whereupon he turned scarlet, as if he had committed an indecent act. He was one of the best pupils, never arguing back, learning all texts by heart. He would prove the existence and the eternity of God by proofs drawn from Holy Writ, by the opinions of the Fathers of the Church and by the universal consent of all peoples. Such reasoning filled him with unshakeable certainty. During his first year of general humilities, he worked so hard at logic that his professor hauled him up and reminded him that the cleverest were not necessarily the most holy. Thus, from his second year on, in metaphysics he did no more than was in the schedule, and did very little indeed about the daily exercises. He was beginning to mistrust knowledge as such. He wanted to remain ignorant, in order not to lose the humility of his faith.

Later, in theology, it was only because he was told that it was a fixed item of the syllabus that he followed the course of Rorbacher's *Ecclesiastical History*. He went as far as Gousset's *Disputations* and Bouvier's *Theological Guide*, without daring touch on Bellarmin, Liguori, Suarez, or St. Thomas Aquinas. It was only Holy Writ itself that really excited him. In it he found the knowledge so much desired, a story of infinite love which is doomed to suffering as example to men of good will. He accepted only what his masters laid down for him, leaving all concern for choice of study to them, for such fuss was no aid to loving and he held that books robbed him of time for prayer. He even succeeded in obliterating in memory his high school years. Knowledge ceased in him, leaving him but the simplicity of a child reduced to stammering the answers to its catechism.

This is the manner in which, step by step, Serge Mouret rose to priesthood. And here memories crowded in, charged with emotion, still warm from celestial delights. With every year he drew closer to God. He passed his holidays in sanctity, staying with an uncle, confessing daily, taking mass twice a week. He set himself fasts and in his trunk kept boxes of coarse salt on which he knelt with naked knees for hours together. During recreation, he stayed in the chapel, or went up to the room of one of the principals, who told him astonishing stories of piety. Then, the day of the Holy Trinity coming round, he was rewarded beyond measure, permeated by that emotion which runs through any school for priests on the eve of ordination. It was the grand feast, the day when Heaven opened its portals to allow the elect to mount yet a step higher. A fortnight before the great occasion he put himself on bread and water. He drew the curtains of his window, so he might no longer even see the daylight, prostrating himself in darkness, imploring Jesus to accept his sacrifice. The four last days, terrible anxiety overcame him, frightful scruples bringing him from his bed in the middle of every night, to go to knock on the door of the visiting priest in charge of the retreat that night, a discalced carmelite, once and more than once, a converted protestant regarding whom the remarkable story was told, and to him would make a lengthy general life-confession, his voice broken by sobs.

Only absolution then set him at rest again, refreshed him as if he had bathed in grace. On the morning of the great day, he was of perfect whiteness, so vividly conscious of his spiritual cleanliness that he seemed to see the glow of his body all about him. Then the seminary bell rang out, of incredible clarity, while June scents— Lenten lilies, stocks, mignonette and heliotrope, were wafted over the high courtyard wall. In the chapel, relations were waiting, all in their best, so moved that the women would be sobbing under their veils. Then came the procession: deacons, about to be ordained, in gold chasubles, under-deacons, in dalmatics, minorites, tonsured, surplices flowing behind them, their black collar-pins in their hands. The organ breathed music, spreading far and wide its joyous flute-like sounds. At the altar, assisted by two canons, the bishop officiated, crosier in hand. The chapter was there and the priests of all the parishes were crowded round. There was unheard-of luxury of vestments, a glow of gold lighted by the heavy rays of the sun pouring down through the west-end window. After the epistle commenced the ordination.

In this moment, young Mouret vividly recalled the chill of the scissors, when the tonsure was marked on his head, and he began his first year of theology. A faint shudder had passed through him, though then the tonsure was very small, scarcely as large as a two-shilling piece. Later, as one by one he received new ordinations, it had grown steadily, till it crowned him with a white patch as large as a full-sized communion wafer. Now the organ breathed more softly, the thuribles fell to rest with the silvery sound of their slender chains, dispersing a trail of smoke which unfolded like lace. He could see himself in his surplice, young man tonsured, led to the altar by the master of ceremonies. He knelt down, and bowed his head very low, while with golden scissors the bishop cut from his head three locks of hair, one from the forehead, the others above his ears. A year later, he could see himself again in the incense-filled chapel, receiving the four minor orders: he was being led by an archdeacon to close the large door noisily, then open it again, to signify that he was commissioned to care for churches. He jingled a little bell in his right hand, to declare that he had the right to summon the faithful to their devotions. He came back to the altar, where the bishop conferred new privileges on him ; those of intoning the lessons, of blessing the sacrament, of catechising children, of exorcising devils, of serving deacons, or lighting and extinguishing candles. Then there came back to him memory of the ordination which followed, more solemn, more alarming, amid the loud music of the organ, the diapason of which seemed to be the wrath of the Lord. On this occasion he wore the dalmatic of an under-deacon on his shoulders and engaged himself for ever by the vow of chastity, and at the terrible *Accedite* of the bishop he shook all over, despite his faith. The bishop's cry put to flight two of his comrades, who turned pale at his side. His new duties were to serve the priest at the altar, to prepare the altar-cruets, to intone the epistle, to wipe the chalice and to bear the cross in processions. And then, at last, he was in procession in the chapel for the last time, with the June sun pouring down on him, but this time he headed the long file of men, at his waist he had the alba knotted, over his breast was crossed the stole, from his neck dangled the chasuble. Weak with supreme emotion, he could see the features of the bishop conferring priesthood on him in all its sacerdotal fullness by triple imposition of hand. After giving the oath of obedience to the church, he felt as if raised above the stones of the floor when the reverberating voice of the prelate pronounced the Latin words: *Accipe Spiritum sanctum: quorum remiseris peccata, remittantur eis, et quorum retimeris, retenta sunt.*

CHAPTER XVI

THIS evocation of the great happiness he enjoyed in his youth warmed the Reverend Mouret's blood slightly, and he ceased to feel the cold. He lay his pince-nez down and went across to his bed, as if intending to get into it, then crossed the room again, to lean his forehead against the window-pane and stare out with unseeing eyes into the night. Was he ill, he wondered, feeling this strange lassitude in his limbs, while his blood seemed to boil in his veins? At the seminary he had twice had fits like this, a sort of physical unease which made him most unhappy. Indeed, on one occasion he had gone to bed and been quite delirious. Then into his mind came a young girl who, the Friar said, had been possessed, but exorcised merely by the Friar's making the sign of the cross over her one day when she fell at his feet in a fit. This memory turned the Reverend Mouret's mind to certain spiritual exercises which one of his tutors had once advocated: prayer, general confession, frequent communion, choice of a sensible tutor possessed of great authority over the spirit of his penitent. And with a sudden switch which astonished him, deep in his memory he perceived the rotund features of an old friend, a peasant, choir-boy at eight, whose board at the seminary had been paid by a lady who had taken charge of him. That friend had always been laughing and with great disingenuousness managed to enjoy the slight benefits of his office in advance: twelve hundred francs salary, a vicarage set in a garden, presents, invitations to dinner, wedding, baptismal and burial fees. He must have been happy when he obtained his living.

The melancholy regret which this memory brought him surprised the Vicar of Artaud extremely greatly. Was he then not happy himself? Until today he had regretted nothing, desired nothing, been envious of nothing. Even in this moment, while he was questioning himself, he found no cause for rancour. He was, he believed, just the same as he had been when his deaconate began and the obligation to read his breviary at appointed hours had filled his days with endless prayer. Since then the weeks, the months and the years had flown by, without the leisure of any evil thought. No doubts disturbed him. Before mysteries which he could not understand, he abased himself, and he found it easy to sacrifice his powers of reason, since he disdained them. When he left the seminary, he had been delighted to find himself a stranger among other men. He no longer walked as they did, he carried his head differently, and he had the gestures, the vocabulary and the feelings of a being apart. He felt himself feminised, brought nearer to the angels, washed clean of sex, purified of all odour of maleness. This thought that he no longer belonged to the human species, that he had been brought up for God, painstakingly purged of human filth by an exacting education, made him almost proud. He felt as if for years he had been kept in a holy oil, prepared according to special rites, and that this oil had permeated into his very flesh, the beginning of a process of beatification. Certain organs had disappeared, gradually dissolved away; his members and his brain had been drained, in return to be filled with spirit, so ethereal that at times he was overcome with sheer dizziness, as if the ground suddenly fell away beneath his feet. He exhibited the timidities, the ignorances and the franknesses of a young girl brought up in a nunnery. He would sometimes say with a smile that he was continuing his childhood, and would imagine that he had remained quite small, with the same sensations, the same ideas and the same judgments. Thus he had known God at six just as well as he knew him at twenty-five, for prayers to God he had the same inflections of his voice, coupled with the same childish delight in putting his hands together exactly right. The world seemed to him like the world he had known long ago, when his mother led him by the hand. He had been born a priest and had grown up a priest. When he revealed to Teuse some monstrous ignorance of life, she would look slyly at him in utter astonishment and with a strange smile say that 'he was certainly Miss Désirée's brother.' In all his life he could recall only one shameful shock. This had been during his final six months at the seminary, after becoming deacon, before holy orders. He had been required to read a work of the Reverend Craisson, Superior of the large seminary of Valence. It was entitled *De rebus venereis ad usum confessariorum*. Out of that reading he came staggered, sobbing. That clever tissue of casuistry about vice which revealed all man's abominable nature, and sank to the most monstrous instances of perversions, was a brutal violation of the virginity of his body and his spirit. He remained for ever vilified, like a young bride, totally innocent before the bridal bed, suddenly initiated to all the carnal violences of love. And every time he confessed he was afterwards led fatally back to that questionnaire of shame. Though the obscurities of dogma, the duties of the divine service and the death of all free will left him serene, content to be but the child of God, despite himself he continuously felt the bodily disturbance of those filthy things he was by that study obliged to stir up, and on his conscience he thereafter had an ineffacable blot. It was somewhere deep down in him, but any day it might grow big and cover him with filth.

Beyond the Garigue hills the moon was rising. Feeling still more feverish, he opened his window and leant on the sill, to feel the freshness of the night on his cheeks. He did not know at exactly what hour he had first felt this uneasiness. He could only recall that that morning, when he said mass, he had been very quiet, very sober. The fever must have begun later. Perhaps it was during that long tramp in the sun? Or was it shivering in the shade of the trees at Paradou Park? Or was it perhaps the stifling air of his sister's farmyard? And thus he ran back through the events of the day.

Below him the level ground stretched far out, more tragic under the pallid, slanting rays of the moon. The olives and almonds, scraggy trees all, were greyish patches in a chaos of large rocks, all the way to the gloomy line of the hills on the horizon. There were large patches of shadow, wooded ridges, pools of blood-red earth where the red stars seemed to seek their image, and there were chalky whitenesses like the garments of rejected women, revealing bodies drowned in obscurities, engulfed in the hollows of the countryside.

By night this land assumed the strange arching spasm of lust. It slept, but with coverlets torn aside, hips naked, limbs contorted, legs straddled, while from its bosom rose heavy, tepid sighs and the pungent odour of women's bodies moist with sweat as they slept. One might have said it was some tremendous Cybele fallen on her back, bosom upthrust, belly bare to the moonlight, intoxicated still from the sunshine of the past day and crazed in expectation of new impregnation. In the far distance, following that vast body, Mouret's eyes followed the Olivette road, thin pale ribbon outstretched like the disengaged cord of a corset. He heard Friar Archangias lifting back the skirts of his little hussies and whipping them till the blood came, he saw him spitting scornfully in the faces of the bigger girls, he felt the man himself stinking goat-like in his person and never to be satisfied in his lust. He saw Rosalie laughing at mother earth, like an animal on heat, while her father flung clods of soil at her loins.

But so far, so it seemed to him, he was quite well, conscious merely of the warmth of a lovely morning on his nape. He merely felt a shiver behind his back, a hazy whisper of life which he had caught, though never distinctly, ever since he rose that morning, even in the heart of mass, when the sun peeped in through the broken window panes. But never had this countryside so disturbed him as in this night hour, with its giant bosom, its flaccid shadows, its glimpses of gleaming amber-like skin, all that nudity of a goddess scarce hidden by the silvery muslin of the moon.

Lowering his eyes, the young priest looked down and peered at Artaud. The village lay prostrated in the heavy slumber of exhaustion, in that utter extinction in which country workers sleep. Not a light. The hovels were black blots breaking up the white lines of the transverse streets down which the moon shone. Even the dogs must be snoring, on the threshold of the closed doors. Was it possible that these Artaud folk had instilled some abominable plague into the vicarage? Behind him he could hear an incessant breathing, which as it approached filled him with anxiety. Now he seemed to catch the sound of the feet of a flock of sheep, with a cloud of dust about them, all greasy with their animal exhalations.

His thoughts of the morning brought back to him that idea of a handful of men starting the world all anew and growing among these naked rocks like a handful of thistles brought by the wind, and he had the impression of looking on at the slow expansion of a whole race. When he was a boy, nothing surprised him or frightened him more than the myriads of insects to be heard rising up from a crack when one raised a damp rock. Even in slumber, fagged out in the depths of shadow, the Artaud folk troubled him with their mere sleeping, which he found in the air he was breathing himself. The village was not dead enough. The thatched roofs swelled like human bosoms. The gaps of the doors let out sighs and faint cracklings, living silences, to reveal in the hole the presence of a swarming breed rocked in the darkness of the night. It must be that path and that alone which gave him that feeling of nausea. Yet he had often enough before breathed hard of it without feeling any other need than to recuperate himself by prayer.

His temples wet with sweat, he went to the other window to open it and get a keener breath of air. Below him, to the left, stretched the graveyard, and he could see *le Solitaire* erect against the skyline, and not a breath of wind stirring the shadows that way. From the vacancy before him rose the scent of freshly cut grass. The big churchyard wall, full of lizards, topped by wallflowers, was cool now in the moonlight, and one of the big church windows gleamed, the panes like sheets of steel. The sleeping church at this hour should be living but by the non-terrestrial life of God and the host, shut away in the tabernacle. He thought of the yellow patch of light of the holy-lamp, engulfed in shadows, and was tempted to go down again, to ease his sick head amid that darkness which was pure of any befoulment. But a strange terror held him back. All at once, his eyes fixed on the lighted windows of the church lighted by the moon, he thought he saw the church glow from within as if it were a furnace, glow with the splendour of an infernal fête, where now in May-time plants and animals and Artaud girls with whole trees clasped in their bare arms all whirled in mad dance. Then, leaning out, beneath him he perceived Désirée's farmyard, a patch of fumy blackness. It was impossible to see the rabbit hutches, the hen roosts, or the ducks' little shanty clearly. Everything there was transformed to a single mass piled close in all its reek, sleeping with a single pestiferous breathing. The acrid stench of the goat came from under its stable door. On its back, the little pig was snorting its greasy breath beside its empty trough. Suddenly from his copper gullet that monstrous, savage cock-bird Alexander produced a cry which, far away, one after another, awoke the lustful cries of all the cock-birds of the village.

Then all at once, it came back to him : this fever which he felt trying to master him and had first attacked him in Désirée's farmyard, when he was close up to all those hens still warm from their laying and those does tearing the soft nest-hairs from their bellies. And at that moment the sense of something breathing on to his neck was so precise that he turned sharply, thinking at last to see who it was it thus touching him. And then to his mind came the girl Albine as she burst into his sight, banging the door of Paradou Park behind her, but not before he glimpsed that enchanted garden. And he remembered how she had raced all along that endless wall, following Doctor Pascal's trap as it bounded along, then scattering birch leaves into the wind like so many kisses. He also recalled her as she had been again in the twilight, laughing at Friar Archangias's oaths, her petticoats flashing over the ground as she escaped, just like a miniature whirlwind of dust in the evening air.

She was sixteen, a strange girl, her features rather elongated. She was redolent of the open air, of the grasses of the meadows and of the very soil. And his memory of her was so precise that he could see even a scratch, a red line across the pale skin of one of her expressive hands. Why had she laughed so when she stared at him with those blue eyes of hers? He was prisoner of that laugh, it was like a penetrating sound wave which resonated through his flesh. He breathed that laugh, he felt it vibrate all through him. Yes, all this trouble of his came from that laugh which he had absorbed.

He stood in the middle of his room, both windows open, and shivered. He was the victim of a fear, and the fear made him hide his head in his hands. Was this long day then to end in this evocation of a fair-haired girl with rather long face and blue eyes? For through his open windows the whole past day surged in. Far away was the heat of the red soil, far away the physical desire of the huge rocks and the olives thrusting out from among them, the vines with twisted trunks bordering the roads. Closer to him were the exudations of humanity wafted down the wind up from the village, the fetid odours of the churchyard, the residue of incense from the church, corrupted as it was by the smell of all those girls and their greasy hair. In addition, came the odours of the manure-heap, all the reek of the farmyard, all the suffocating stifling ferment of germination on germination. And all these exudations filled his nostrils together in one great choking cloud, so harsh, and filling his lungs so swiftly that he gasped. He closed his senses, strove to

105

make all this not be. But whatever he did, before him Albine rose again, like a large flower thrusting up in all its beauty out of this universal compost heap. She was the nature-born blossom of all this foulness, delicate herself in the sunshine, as she unfolded the young buds of her shoulders, so joyous of life that she leapt from her stem and, flying on to his lips, scented his body with her long laugh.

He uttered a cry. He felt fire on his lips. He felt a burning injected through his veins. And, seeking protection, he knelt down before the statuette of the Immaculate Conception, pressed his hands together in prayer and cried:

'Holy Virgin of all Virgins, pray for me!'

CHAPTER XVII

THE Immaculate Conception on the walnut tallboy smiled affectionately, the corners of the thin lips indicated by a stroke of carmine. She was a small Virgin, and quite white, the voluminous white veil which flowed from head to foot merely edged with a scarce perceptible thread of gold. Her garment draped in long straight folds down her body, which was sexless. It was also drawn high up in the yoke, only her neck showed. Not a single lock of her auburn hair escaped from the veil. Her cheeks were pink, her bright eyes directed to Heaven. The hands, those of a child, were pressed together, revealing her finger tips from under the veiling. Beneath them was a blue shawl by which two floating ends of the universe seemed to be bound into her torso. Not one of the seductive points of the female body was bare, save her feet. But these, treading the mystic wild rose, were lovably naked, and from their nudity grew roses of gold, as if by the natural flowering of flesh that was doubly pure.

'O faithful Virgin, pray for me!' the young priest murmured, again and again.

This particular Virgin had never troubled him. She had not yet become a mother. Her arms held out no Jesus to him, her body never assumed the rotundities of fruitfulness. She was not the Queen of Heaven, descending with golden crown, clad in gold, like an earthly princess borne triumphant by a flight of cherubs. This Virgin had never been awesome, had never addressed him with the sternness of an implacable mistress, the mere sight of whom bent men's eyes to the dust. He dared look her in the face, dared love her, with no fear of being moved by the soft waves of auburn hair. Her naked feet merely filled his heart with tenderness, lovable feet, blooming like a garden of chastity in too miraculous a wise for him to feel any desire to touch them with fondling hands. She perfumed his room with an odour of lilies. She was the silver lily, set in a golden vase, priceless purity, eternal, impeccable purity. In her white veiling, so tightly drawn about her, there remained no trace of human flesh. She was essentially and only virginal flame burning for ever and never faltering. By night when he lay down and in the morning when he awakened she was always there with unchanged, ecstatic smile. He stripped his body in her presence with no trace of embarrassment, as if only his own modesty were with him in the room.

'Mother most pure, Mother most chaste, Mother ever Virgin, pray for me!' he murmured in his fear, pressing close to the Virgin's feet as if at his back he had caught the ring of Albine's racing feet. 'You are my refuge, the source of my delight, take me, I implore you, and draw a corner of your veil over me and hide me in your innocence, behind the sacred ramparts of your robe, so that no carnal breath shall attain me. I need you, without you I die, if you do not bear me in your succouring arms far from here into the burning whiteness which is our habitation, I feel I shall be parted from you for ever. O Mary, conceived without sin, make me as nothingness, deep in the immaculate snow which falls from your every limb. You are the prodigy of eternal chastity. You and your Son are blood grown from a ray of light, as from a miraculous tree knowing no seed. Your Son Jesus was conceived by the breath of God, and you yourself were born without the flesh of your mother knowing any abasement, and I crave the belief that such virginity shall pass on for ever from generation to generation in never-ending ignorance of the flesh. Oh, to live and grow outside the shame of our earthly senses! Oh, to multiply and bear offspring without the loathsome necessity of sex, merely at the touch of a Heavenly kiss!'

This desperate appeal, a cry purified of lust, brought the young Vicar some calm. The Virgin in all her whiteness, her glance Heavenward, seemed with her thin pink lips to smile more gently. In a voice full of emotion, he resumed:

'I should like once again to be a child. I should like never to be more than a child walking in the shadow of your gown. I was once quite small, laying my hands together to whisper the name of Mary. My cradle was white, my body was white, all my thoughts were white. I saw you clearly, I heard you call me, I went to you in smiles, I trod the petals of the rose. There was nothing more than this. I felt not, I thought not, I lived but to be a flower under your feet. People should never grow up. Then you would be for ever surrounded by fair haired little ones, by a race of children, who would love you pure-handed, healthy-lipped, gentle-limbed, without blemish, as if fresh arisen from a bath of milk. On the cheek of a child one kisses its soul. Only a child can pronounce your name without befouling it. Later, the lips become unclean and the love spilled out by them is poisoned. Even I who love you so and have given you myself dare not always call upon you, for I would not have you brought into contact with the impurity of a grown man. I have prayed, I have afflicted my flesh, I have slept under your protection, I have lived in chastity, yet I weep today when I see that still I am not sufficiently dead to this world to be your groom. O Mary, most lovable Virgin, why am I not five years old, why did I not remain the child pressing his lips to images of you? I would take you to my heart, I would lay you down at my side, I would kiss you as a well-beloved friend, as a girl of my own age. I would have your narrow gown, your child's veil, your blue shawl, all the signs of childhood by which you are but a big sister. I would not seek to kiss your hair, for that is a nudity which should not be seen, but I would kiss your bare feet, one after the other, the whole night through, night after night, till my lips detached the last petal of your golden roses, mystic blossoms of your veins.'

He broke off, and waited for the Virgin to lower her blue eyes and bring her veil down over his forehead. But she remained enveloped in muslin to the neck, to the finger-nails, to the ankles, completely given over to Heaven, her body weightless, no longer resting on this ground, in its urge to rise.

'Come, come,' he cried, more frantically now, 'kind Virgin, powerful Virgin, make me a child again! Make me five years old! Remove my five senses from me and take my virility away. Let a miracle strip from me all the man who has grown up within me. You reign supreme in Heaven, nothing is easier to you than to strike me with a thunderbolt, dry away my parts, leave me sexless, incapable of evil, so drained of vigour that I could not raise up were it but my little finger without your consent. I want to be without any guile, with that guilelessness which is yours, and no human shudder can disturb. I do not want any longer to feel nerves, muscles, beating of heart, or labour of desires. I want to be a thing, a white stone at your feet, in which all you will leave will

108

be a perfume. I want to be a stone which will not stir from the place where you will cast it, a thing sans ears, sans eyes, content to rest beneath your heel, unable to dream of unclean commerce with any other stone of the road.

Ah, what beatitude that will be! Without effort I shall immediately achieve that perfection which I dream. I shall at last declare myself your true priest. I shall be that which neither my studies, nor my prayers, nor my long five years of priestly initiation could make of me. Yes, I renounce my life, I declare that the death of my kind is better far than that unending vility which propagates it. Original sin befouls everything. It is a universal stench which ruins love, poisons the spouses' bedchamber, sullies the cradle of the newborn child, spoils even the flowers breathless in the sun, even the trees which freely send forth their buds. The whole earth wallows in this foulness, the least drops of which burst forth into shameful vegetation. But for me to be perfect, oh Queen of the Angels, Queen of all Virgins, hear my cry, and answer it! Make me one of the angels who have but two large wings behind their countenances, who have no trunk, no parts, so I may fly to you if you call me, and be no more than lips whispering your praise and a pair of wings to waft you on your journeys through space. Death, death, O Venerated Virgin, render me the death of everything. I shall love you in the death of my body, in the death of all that lives and multiplies. With you I shall consummate the only marriage which my heart desires. I shall rise higher and ever higher, till I attain those clear burning fires from which you shine forth. There shall there be a great star, an immense white rose, each petal of which burning like a moon, a throne of silver whence you shine forth with such rich glow of innocence that all paradise is ablaze merely by the light of your veil. All that is white, the daily dawn, the snows of inaccessible peaks, the opening lily, the waters of unknown springs, the milk of plants which the sun respects, the smiles of virgins, the souls of the babes who lie in the cradle, rain down on your white feet. Then shall I rise to your lips like a tongue of delicate flame and enter into you through your half-opened lips and our marriage shall be consummated while the archangels tremble from the great shudder of our delight. To be virgin, to love virginally, and mid the softest of kisses to maintain virginal whiteness! With all love, couched on the wings of a swan in a cloud of purity, in the arms of a mistress of light whose caresses are the orgasms of the spirit! Perfection, superhuman dream, longing by which my very bones creak, delights which elevate me to Heaven!

Oh Mary, Vessel Elect, castrate what is man away from me, make of me a eunuch among men, so I may be without fear be awarded the treasure of your virginity!'

Here, his teeth chattering wildly, overcome at last by his fever, the Vicar of Artaud lost consciousness on the tiled floor of his room.

BOOK TWO

BOOK TWO

CHAPTER I

CALICO curtains painstakingly drawn over the two enormous windows flooded the room with the muted whiteness of dawn. Lofty and very spacious, it contained white-painted furniture with red flowers on a background of foliage, dating from Louis XV. In recesses above the doors on either side of the alcoves, were paintings in which could still be distinguished the pink tummies and rounded bottoms of little cupids. They were flying about in flocks, playing at some game or other. The oval panels built into the wainscoting and the double doors, and the arched ceiling, which had once provided a sky-blue background and frames for other insets, medallions and knots of pink ribbon, were now fading to a very soft grey, a tone indeed which tended to suit the rather sentimental charm of this decayed paradise. The large alcove opposite the windows offered the sight of billowing clouds held aside by plaster cupids which bent down over them, some quite standing on their heads, as if to peep naughtily in at the bed. Like the windows, the entrance to it was shut off by roughly tacked calico curtaining of a rustic simplicity remarkable in an apartment still warmly redolent of the emanations of a voluptuousness which was now very remote.

Seated beside a bracket table on which a kettle was heating over a spirit-lamp, Albine was attentively watching the alcove curtains. She was dressed in white, her hair tied back with a scarf of old lace. Her hands hung relaxed at her sides. She was keeping watch with all the solemnity of adolescence. The utter stillness was broken solely by a faint sound of breathing, the respiration of a sleeping child. But after some minutes she took sudden alarm, and could not refrain from tiptoeing across, to peep behind the curtain. Serge Mouret lay on the edge of the enormous bed, to all appearances asleep, his head resting on an arm folded under on the pillow. During his illness, his hair had grown long; his cheeks were now bearded. He was very pale, his eyes sunken in blue sockets, his lips bloodless. He had the charm of a convalescent girl.

With great tenderness, Albine was about to let the curtain fall back into position, when he spoke, in a very low voice. 'I am not asleep,' he murmured. But he did not stir. He remained exactly as he was, his head resting on his arm, as if overcome with a pleas-

113

ant tiredness. Slowly, his eyes opened. The soft breath from his parted lips stirred the fair down on his uncovered hand.

'I could hear you,' he whispered again. 'You walked so softly.'

He addressed her tenderly, with 'thou,' as intimate friends—and lovers—do, and the fact that he had slipped into this mode of speech filled her with great pleasure. She went across to him and squatted down beside the bed, to bring her face on a level with his.

'How do you feel?' she asked him, and found new pleasure in the lovely sound of the 'thou' which she herself pronounced for the first time. 'Why, you are cured now,' she ran on. 'Do you know that when I heard the terrible news that you were ill and delirious and had a frightful fever and even if you recovered it might rob you of your reason, I cried all the way home . . . How I kissed your Uncle Pascal when he brought you here to get better!'

She tucked him in, all motherly.

'You know, those sun-scorched rocks down in Artaud, they are no good for you. You need fresh vegetation, fresh air and peace . . . Doctor Pascal has not told a soul that you are hidden here. That is a secret between him and those who love you. He thought it was the end of you . . . Don't fear, nobody will disturb us. Other people get reports of your condition without knowing where you are. Even the doctor is not coming back again. From now on, I am your doctor . . . Apparently, it's no more medicine for you. What you need is affection, see?'

One might have said that he did not hear her, his mind was still vacant. As without moving his head he probed every corner of the room with his eyes, she concluded that he was getting worried about where he was.

'This is my room,' she said. 'I have given it to you. It's a lovely room, isn't it? I furnished it with the nicest things I could find in the barn. Then I made these calico curtains so the daylight would not blind me . . . And there's absolutely no need for you to worry your head about it. I sleep upstairs now. There are still three or four other empty rooms.'

Yet he was still uneasy. 'Are you alone?' he asked.

'I am. Why do you ask?'

He made no reply, merely said, rather anxiously: 'I dreamt . . . I am always dreaming . . . I hear bells. That is what tires me.' Then, after a short silence, added: 'Go and shut the door. Bolt it. I want you to be alone, quite alone.'

When she came back, bringing a chair, and sat down beside him, he was as pleased as a child, and kept saying: 'Now, no one will

114

come in, will they? I shan't hear those bells any more . . . Now, when you talk to me, that rests me.'

'Are you thirsty?' she asked him.

He nodded. He stared at her hands with an air of surprise, obviously so delighted to see them that she held one out to him with a smile, and lay it beside his pillow. He slipped his head sideways till his cheek rested on the fresh dainty fingers. Then, with a fragile laugh, he said: 'Oh, how soft, just like silk! It seems to breathe fresh air through my hair . . . Don't take it away. Please!'

There was a lengthy silence.

They looked into each other's eyes with great friendliness. She could clearly see herself reflected in her patient's vacant glance. He seemed to be listening to something undefined which the fresh little hand whispered to him.

'It's so good, your hand is,' he said. 'You cannot imagine what good it does me . . . It seems to enter my very heart, get right inside me and take out of me the pains in my limbs. It caresses the whole of me, it eases me, it heals.'

He rubbed his cheek softly, roused from his torpor as if new life had been put into him.

'Promise,' he said, 'promise you won't give me nasty things to drink or torment me with all manner of medicine? I only need your hand, you see. That is what I came here for—so you could lay it there, under my head.'

'Dear Serge,' Albine murmured. 'You have had a terrible time, haven't you?'

'A terrible time? Yes, yes . . . but long ago . . . I slept badly, I had frightful dreams. If I could I would tell you it all.' For a moment he closed his eyes. Then he made a great effort of memory. 'I can see only blackness,' he stammered. 'That's funny. I know it was at the end of a long journey . . . I haven't the slightest idea where I was travelling from. I had a temperature, my blood was pounding through my veins like a wild animal . . . I have it! I remember I kept having the same nightmare, of having to climb and climb an endless underground passage. At certain stabs of pain the passage would suddenly be walled up. Heaps of stones fell from the vaulting and the walls closed in. I panted, I burned with a terrible desire to go on farther, and I flung myself at the obstacle and struggled with feet and hands and head, despairing whether I should ever get through the pile of collapsed debris, which got bigger and bigger . . . Then, often, all I needed to do was touch it with my finger, whereupon it all vanished, I could walk freely forward again, the tunnel widened out, and I was merely rather exhausted by the tension I had been through.'

Albine would have laid her hand over his lips.

'No,' he said. 'No, it does not tire me to talk. See, I will whisper into your ear. I have the feeling that you understand me merely if I think my thoughts to you . . . The queerest thing is that in this underground passage of mine I never for a moment thought of going back. I was determined to go on, though it was in my mind that I should need thousands of years to clear away any one of those obstacles, but it was a desperate task which I had to fulfil under pain of greater misfortunes. My knees went numb, my forehead banged against the rock, I deliberately made the most agonising efforts to get through as quickly as I could . . . it is all so strange, all so strange . . .'

He closed his eyes, thinking about it, puzzling, then, with a scornful little twist of his lips, nestled against her hand again and laughingly said: 'Come, how stupid! I am only a little child.'

But then it was Albine's turn to be anxious. She had to discover whether he was really hers, absolutely. She asked him questions, bringing him back to the confused memories he had just tried to recover. But, he now recalled nothing, he was truly back in a state of radiant childhood. He felt he had been born but yesterday.

'You see, I am not strong yet. My earliest memory is of being in a bed which burned every inch of my body. My head tossed about on the pillow as if it were a brazier. My feet grew sore, I chafed them together so . . . I tell you, I really must have been very ill. I had the impression my body was being changed, everything removed and repaired, just as when a piece of machinery breaks down . . .'

The image made him laugh again. Then he resumed: 'I shall be quite reconditioned. Being ill has jolly well overhauled me . . . But what was that you were asking me? No, there was nobody with me. Nor was there anything beyond. At least, I saw nothing . . . I suffered all by myself, deep in a black hole. Nobody, nobody there. I am your boy? But will you have me? You can teach me to walk! You are the only person I see, now. I don't want anything that is not you. I tell you, I simply can't remember. I came, you took charge of me, that is all.' And then, reassured, wheedling, he added: 'Now your hand is quite warm, it is as good to feel as the sunlight . . . Now we won't talk any more. I am getting hot again.'

A tremulous silence filtered down from the blue ceiling and filled that enormous room. The spirit-lamp had gone out, the vapour

116

from the spout of the kettle had ceased. Together on the same pillow, Albine and Serge gazed into the long calico curtains which hid the windows. Serge's eyes were drawn to them, white source of light. He bathed in it, contented, for it was daylight thinned down to suit his convalescent weakness. Beyond a yellower corner of the calico he could guess at the sunshine, and that was enough to do him good. From afar he could hear the rustle of masses of foliage and on the window to his right fell the greenish shadow of a high-up branch. The clear outline filled him with disturbing dreams of the forest which he felt so near.

'Would you like me to open the curtains,' asked Albine, suddenly, prompted by his fixed stare at them.

'No, no,' he replied, hastily.

'It is a lovely day. You would have some sunshine. And see the trees.'

'No, no, please not . . . I want nothing beyond this room. Even that one branch I can see makes me feel tired, with its constant moving and growing, as if it were alive . . . Leave your hand under my head, I am going to sleep. Everything white . . . How wonderful . . .'

And he did indeed fall to sleep, like an infant, with Albine watching over him, breathing over him, bringing freshness to his slumbers.

CHAPTER II

THE following morning the good weather ended, and it rained. Feverish again, Serge had a bad day. He stared in distress at the curtains, from which there now came only a cavernous light, ashen-grey, forbidding. No longer could he sense the sunlight. Instead, he sought out every source of the shade which had frightened him, that tall branch of the tree which, as it was now, lost in the hazy soupiness of the downpour, began to seem to sweep the whole forest away with it. As evening approached, he became delirious and through sobs assured Albine that the sun had died, he could hear the sky and the whole countryside weeping over the mortal remains, and she had to console him like a child, promise him the sun, persuade him that it would return, that she would give it back to him. But he was also smitten with grief for the plants. All the seed, he muttered, all the seed under the soil, awaiting the light, suffering so, all the seed had nightmares, all the seed dreamt that it was fighting its way up a long underground slope, frustrated by collapses of the ceiling of the tunnel, struggling madly to reach the sunlight again. And he began to whimper in a very low voice, telling her that winter was a disease of the earth, and he would die together with it, if spring did not cure them both together.

For three days on end the weather was frightful. Torrents fell on the trees, it sounded as if somewhere in the offing a river had burst its banks. Gusts of wind beat periodically against the windows, like enormous waves of a flood. Serge had insisted on Albine closing all the shutters. With the lamp lighted, he was freed from that funereal atmosphere cast by the dimming curtains, no longer felt the grey of the skies thrusting in every tiny crevice and flowing towards him, like gravediggers' soil which would cover him. He relaxed now, lying with shrunken arms, pale countenance, feebler than before, in tune with the growing debility of the outer world. At times, when inky-black clouds swept over the house, the contorted trees groaning and the herbage laid flat like the hair of a drowned girl trailing in the water, he collapsed. He fell so low that he scarcely breathed at all, vanishing from this life, stricken down by the tempest. Then, the moment there was a break in the clouds, at the first patch of blue amid the greyness, he could breathe again and enjoy the peace of the rain-washed foliage, the white-gleaming paths, the fields gulping the water to the last drop. Now it was Albine who longed for the sunshine. Twenty times in the day she went to the landing window to con the skies, overjoyed by the tiniest hint of the sky lifting, depressed again by any darker cloud which would threaten to kill her cherished convalescent. She spoke of sending for Doctor Pascal. But Serge was against anybody coming.

'Tomorrow,' he said, 'tomorrow the sun will shine on the curtains and I shall be well.'

One evening, when he was worse than usual, Albine gave him her hand, for him to rest his cheek against. But when that no longer eased him, she shed anxious tears, seeing herself so impotent. Since he had sunk back into this winter depression she no longer felt herself strong enough by herself to draw him out of the nightmare through which he was struggling. She needed the spring as ally. She herself drooped, her arms chilled, her breathing short, unable any longer to infuse life into her. For hours she wandered about the big room in misery. When she passed the mirror, she saw a sombre figure, and found herself ugly.

Then came the morning when, re-making his pillows and afraid again to try the broken charm of her hands, she thought she caught on Serge's lips that smile of the first day as her fingers accidentally happened to touch his neck behind.

'Open the shutters,' he whispered.

She thought he was still delirious. An hour previously, all she had seen from the landing was a sky in mourning.

'Try to sleep,' she said sadly. 'I do promise, I will waken you at the first ray of sunshine . . . Sleep on, the sun has not come yet.'

'But yes, it has, I feel it,' he replied, 'the sun is here, open the shutters.'

CHAPTER III

IT was quite true, the sun was there. When Albine opened the shutters, beyond her big curtains, the good yellow glow again warmed a corner of the pale hangings. But what made Serge sit up in bed was once again seeing the shadow of that branch, for that limb of a tree declared his return to life. To him, this greenish patch, which quivered sensitively at the slightest breath of air, summed up the whole countryside restored, with its greenery, its waters, its vast circle of hills. It no longer upset him. He followed its every motion greedily, for he needed the vigour of the sap of which it was so eloquent. And there was Albine, supporting him in her arms and so happy, crying: 'Darling Serge, darling, the winter is over . . . We are saved.'

He lay down again, but already there was a light in his eyes and his voice was firmer.

'Tomorrow,' he said, 'I shall be very strong . . . Now draw the curtains back. I want to see it all.'

The next day, however, he was overcome with childish fear, and absolutely refused to have the windows wide open. He murmured: 'In a little while, later.' He was still anxious, full of the uneasiness which that first burst of light had brought his eyes. Evening was there before he had made up his mind to face the sunshine again. He stayed all day with his face turned to the curtains, on the transparency of the curtain following the pallor of morning, the fire of mid-day, the violet shades of evening, all the colours and all the emotions of heaven. It was all painted there, even the shudder which a bird's beating wings lent the warm air, yes, even the delights of the scents were there, quivering on a ray of light. Beyond that veil, beyond that moving dream of the powerful outdoor life, he could hear springtide rising. There were moments when it even choked him as despite the obstacle of the curtains earth's flow of new blood reached him too brusquely.

The following morning, he was still asleep when, thinking to speed up his cure, Albine cried: 'Serge! Serge! Here is the sun!' and, drawing back the curtains, swiftly flung the windows wide. Gasping and weak, he brought himself to his knees on his bed, his hands pressed to his chest to prevent his heart from bursting.

Opposite him was the vast sky, blue from horizon to horizon, nothing but infinite blueness, and in this he cleansed himself of pain, yielding himself up to it, as if gently cradled by it and from it now he thirstily drank in gentleness, purity and youth. But now the branch of which he had seen the shadow, growing past the window, stained the ocean of blue with its vigorous foliage, and this proved too violent an influx of vitality for so sensitive and weak a patient, for whom even the distant swallows in their flight seemed to mar the beauty of heaven. He was in the throes of rebirth, and uttered involuntary little cries when the brilliant light lapped him about and floods of warm air pressed against him and he felt it all pour over him and into him, as if life had swallowed up his whole being. He thrust out his hands, then fell back to the pillows in a faint.

But what a happy day that had been, what a moving day. The sun had entered the room from the right of the window, far from the alcove, and all day long Serge had watched it creep slowly forward. He saw it draw close to him, golden yellow, smoothing the lines of the ancient chairs, playing in corners, sometimes slipping across the floor, like a roll of cloth unfolding, a slow, confident progression, as a beloved mistress comes. It stretched its fair limbs till it had gradually pulsated as far as the alcove itself, came up to him with a voluptuous lingering which raised to frenzy the desire to possess it, till at last, towards two o'clock, the field of sunlight left the last armchair behind, crept over the counterpane, to spread across the bed, like long hair unknotted. Serge let the ardent caress of those rays caress his shrunken arms. He half-closed his eyes, as he felt kisses of fire run from finger to finger. He lay in a bath of light as if the glowing orb held him alone in its embrace. And then, Albine being then at his side, bending over him, smiling, he stammered: 'No, no! Leave me alone now!' His eyes were closed. 'Do not hold me so fiercely,' he babbled on, 'however can you hold the whole of me so easily, so completely, in your arms?'

The sun then slithered away off the bed again and with the same languorous pace moved towards the other side, when Serge saw it turn yet again, to creep first on to one chair, then another, and he

120

was all regret that he had not held it back, clutched close to his own bosom. Albine was still fast at the bedside. She had slipped an arm under his neck. Together they saw the sky slowly grow paler and paler. At moments the tremendous shudder of a sudden surge of emotion seemed to drain it of blood, and in this changing scene, Serge's own languorousness found more and more satisfaction discovering fine shades which he had never before imagined could be there. It was not blue at all, it was a pinkish blue, a violet blue, a yellow blue, it was living flesh, it was a vast immaculate nudity which at a mere breath palpitated like a woman's breast. At every new glance the distant vision offered new surprises, unknown angles of the firmament, subtle smiles, delightful rotundities, fine muslins which in the depths of the paradise there before him concealed the magnificent and massive bodies of goddesses. He too had now taken flight, his limbs incorporeal from pain, and was wafted into the midst of that fugitive silk, lost in that innocent down of blueness, his feelings borne weightless above his faint flesh. The sun was sinking, the blue melted away into pure gold, the living flesh of the heavens turned to paler gold, slowly to fade away into all the shades of shadow. Not a cloud marred that unobtrusiveness of a virgin at her bedside in an undressing which showed but a single ray of modesty on the far off skyline. And the great heavens were asleep.

'Darling boy!' whispered Albine, as she gazed down at Serge, who had fallen asleep on her bosom, together with the sky.

She tucked him in, she closed the windows. But, the next day, as soon as day broke, they were open again. He could not live without the sun. He gathered new strength, he grew hardened to the gusts of wind which snatched at the alcove curtains. Even that blueness, that eternal blueness began to seem dim to him. He was tired of being a swan, a whiteness, tired of floating endlessly on the clear waters of the lake of heaven. He found himself actually longing for a flight of black clouds, a rock-fall of cloud which would break the monotony of that immense purity.

As his health returned to him, he began to feel the need for stronger sensations. Now, he passed whole hours watching the green branch. He would have liked to see it grow larger, to see it actually expanding, to thrust its twigs right into his own bed. It fell short of what he desired, it merely exacerbated his desires, speaking to him of trees whose voices he could hear, but whose summit he had never glimpsed. There was an intimate whisper of foliage, a babble of running waters, the murmur of wings beating, then high-pitched, long-drawn-out, vibrant voices, all together.

'If I could but get you out of bed,' said Albine, 'you could sit by the window . . . You would see the lovely garden.'

He closed his eyes, murmuring: 'But I do see it, I hear it . . . I know where the trees are, where the waters, and where the violets grow.' Then, again: 'Only I do not see it very well, I see it without any light . . . I shall have to be very strong to go to the window.'

Other times, when she thought he had gone to sleep, she would vanish for hours, and when she returned, always found his eyes a-gleam with curiosity, burning with impatience.

'Where have you been?' he would ask. And he would grip her arms, smell at her skirts, her bodice, her cheeks.

'You smell of so many good things . . . Tell me, do, have you been walking over grass lawns?'

She laughed and held up for him to see her boots, wet with the dew.

'You've come straight from the garden, straight from it,' he repeated, rapturously. 'I knew as much. When you came in, you looked just like a big flower . . . You bring me the whole garden in your frock.'

He kept her beside him, smelling her as if she were herself a bunch of flowers. There were times when she came in with scraps of bramble, or leaves, or twigs sticking to her garments. He would then take these fragments of the life burgeoning without and hide them under his pillow, as if they were talismans. One day she brought him a bunch of roses, and he was so moved that tears streamed from his eyes. He kissed the flowers, lay them in bed beside him, hugged them to him. But when they faded, that hurt him so that he forbade Albine ever to gather him roses again. He would rather, he said, have her. She was just as fresh, just as redolent of sweet odours, and she would not fade, the sweet fragrance of her hands and her hair and her cheeks never left her. In the end he himself sent her out into the garden, with an injunction not to return for a whole hour.

'Do see, understand!' he pleaded. 'Like that, I have sunshine, I have fresh air, and I have roses too, to last till tomorrow.'

Often when he saw her re-enter the room, out of breath, he plied her with questions. Which walk did she follow? Did she go in deep under the trees, or did she merely skirt the edge of the meads? Had she seen any nests? Where had she sat? Behind a wild rose? Under an oak? In the shade of a group of aspens? But whenever in response she tried to explain the garden to him, he lay his hand on her lips. 'No, no, silence!' he would whisper. 'My mistake. I do not want to know . . . I would rather see for myself.'

122

In such moments he just sank back into the dream he always fondled, the thought of all that green growth that he felt in close proximity, only two paces from him. For days on end he lived merely by that dream. In the early part of his life there, he said, he had visualised the garden more clearly. But as he recovered strength, his dream was clouded by the spate of warm blood which now flooded his being. He had ever greater vacillations. He could no longer say whether the trees were to the right, the waters flowed at the far end, or even whether or not the great rocks were piled just under the windows of the house. He would mutter to himself, in debate about it all. On the slightest clues he would build up marvellous lay-outs, which the song of a bird, the snap of a branch the scent of a flower would then make him re-shape, here to plant an enormous lilac, there instead of lawns to lay flower-beds. He was constantly plotting new gardens, to Albine's intense delight. And whenever she caught him at it she would laugh uproariously and cry: 'But no, it's not a bit like that, I do assure you. You just cannot imagine it. It is lovelier than the loveliest thing you ever saw . . . But don't put yourself out, trying to picture it. It is my garden, and I shall give it to you. Don't worry, it won't run away.'

Having once known fear of the light, Serge was in a state of considerable agitation when he was at last strong enough to lean his elbows on the window-sill. Evening after evening he spoke of doing this 'tomorrow,' but when Albine entered the room and in cheerful tones told him it was break of day, and she had scratched her hands making a gap in the hedge to bring him all the scent of dawn, he turned over to face the wall. She was at last one morning obliged to take him in her arms and half carry him to the window, holding him there, compelling him to look out.

'Aren't you a big coward!' she cried, with that lovely, ringing laugh of hers, and waved her hand to the whole sweep of the horizon, repeating with triumph which held so many tender promises: 'It's Paradou, Paradou, my dear!' And then, speechless, Serge at last looked out.

CHAPTER IV

FACING him, a sea of greenery, to right, to left, everywhere. An ocean, the deep-sea swell of the leaves of which reaching the skyline, broken by no building, no hint of wall, no dusty road. An ocean without a single sail, ocean virginal, sacred, in the innocence of solitude, displaying all its untamed charm. Here only the sun had the entry, a golden sheet of light unrolling over the meads, shooting its vagabond rays down the rides, loosing its burning, silken hair to drape the trees, and at the springs of fresh water sipping with golden lips which imbued every pool with shivers of delight. Under this dissemination of conflagration the vast garden lived exuberantly, like a wild creature entirely happy, at journey's end the great freedom, from all habitation far, from all duty free, such a debauch of foliage, such an overflowing lake of herbage, that from one end to the other it constituted a new world, lost, drowned in its own overbordering life. Nought but green slopes, shrubs burgeoning into flower-like fountains, piled masses of green, tightly drawn curtains of forest, climbing plants so thickly swarming that they cloaked the earth, flights of enormous trees, their summits arching over it all.

Indeed, so far here had the tremendous invasion of nature's superabundant seeding gone that it was with the greatest difficulty that one could surmise the original lay-out of Paradou Park. Immediately opposite, in a sort of vast amphitheatre, must have been a sunken garden, though now the walls of the fountain pools had collapsed, marble steps had fallen away, statuary had largely fallen, prostrate now with whitish gleam glimpsed here and there on the overgrown lawns. Beyond this, on the far side of a stretch of water, was a confusion of orchard growth, and beyond this a lofty wood, dense with purplish undergrowth shot with rays of sunshine, a forest turned virginal, its summits shot with yellowish greens, pale greens, and all the pungent greens that ever were, billowing on without end. To the right, this forest climbed high ground, broke up into copses of conifers, died out in meagre scrub, till beyond that the rocks themselves piled in a tremendous slope, as if a collapsed mountain barred the horizon. Here, out of the soil thrust fierce, monstrous growth of twisted trunks frozen in the fierce heat like crouching reptiles. Here a thread of silver, with broken light in the distance like pearl dust blowing, indicated a waterfall, source of the limpid waters which lay lazy about the garden. Finally, on the left there was a river, flowing in through a vast mead, where four separate streams converged to make it, with play of light under reeds, among willows and round larger trees. As far as the eye could reach, patches of vegetation added to the freshness of the low-lying ground, a landscape washed in bluish haze, a break of daylight gradually merging into the greenish blue of the setting sun. Paradou Park, with its sunken garden, its forest, its rocks, its waters, its meadows, offered the vastness of heaven itself.

'Paradou,' Serge stammered, spreading wide his arms, as if to press the whole garden close to his own bosom.

He nearly fell. Albine had to get him to an armchair. Once there, he was speechless for two hours. Chin on his cupped hands, he gazed out. At moments his eyes blinked and the colour flooded to his cheeks. He examined it all slowly, in absolute amazement. It was too big, too complex, too strong.

Then, with a gesture of utter exhaustion, he held out his hands to her and muttered: 'I see nothing, I understand nothing.'

She leant on the back of the chair and took his hand, compelling him to look again. Half-whispering, she said: 'It is all ours. Nobody will come in. When you are well, we can go for walks in our garden. We could walk there all our lives. We shall go where you like . . . Where do you choose?'

Smiling, he whispered:

'Oh, not far. The first day, two steps from the door. You can see for yourself . . . I should fall . . . When I go, I only want to be just under this tree, here, by the window.'

Softly, she repeated:

'Wouldn't you like to walk out into the garden itself? You shall see the rose bushes and the enormous flowers which have spread everywhere. They have even filled the old walks with their growth . . . Or would you like the orchard, I wonder, where I have to crawl to get in, so laden are the branches with fruit? We shall go farther still, if you feel strong enough. We shall go all the way to the forest, into its caverns of shade, a long way, so far that when night overtakes us we shall sleep out there . . . Or, one morning, we shall go high up there, on those rocky cliffs. You will see the plants which frighten me. You will see the water-springs, where the spray is like rain, and it will be such fun for us to let it play over our faces . . . . And if you would rather go along the hedgerows, beside a stream, we shall have to cross to the meadow side. It is so lovely there, in the evening, under the willows when the sun goes down. You can lie in the deep grass and watch the little green frogs jumping on to the reeds.'

'No, no,' said Serge, 'you tire me, I do not want to go so far . . . I shall only go a couple of paces. That will be a lot for me.'

'But even I,' she continued, 'even I have not yet been able to go everywhere. There are many spots I do not know. For all the years I have gone for walks here, I still feel unknown nooks all round me, places where the shade must be fresher and the grasses softer . . . Do you know, I have always told myself that in it must be the nook in which I should like to spend the rest of my life. It must be somewhere. I have probably passed close by it, or it may be hidden so far away that in all my wanderings here I have never been within reach of it . . . Serge, shall we seek it out, you and I, shall we live there?'

'No, no, please stop,' the young man stammered. 'I do not know what you mean. You will kill me.'

For a few moments she let him weep his alarm off in her arms and was heart-broken not to be able to find words to soothe him.

'Then is not Paradou so lovely as you dreamed it would be?' she asked him, again.

He freed his face and replied:

'I really cannot say . . . It was once quite small to me, but look, now it is getting bigger and bigger . . . Take me away, hide me!'

She took him to his bed, soothing him like a child, nursing him with falsehood.

'No, no, of course not,' she whispered, 'there's no such great garden, it's all a silly story I told you. Sleep quietly, my dear.'

CHAPTER V

EVERY day, while the air was still fresh, she had him sit at the window. Then he began to attempt a few steps, clinging to the furniture. A tinge of pink entered his cheeks and his hands lost their waxen appearance. In this stage of recovery, however, he was overcome with a dimming of his senses which reduced him to the vegetative state of a newborn creature come into the world but overnight. He was suddenly no more than a plant, his impressions reduced to mere awareness of the air which bathed his body. He remained in-turned, still too anaemic to make any outward effort, seeking only, letting his flesh absorb all its life-giving sap. It was a second gestation, a slow development in the warm egg of springtime. But when she recalled certain things that Doctor Pascal had said, Albine was terrified to see him remain like that, a dazed little infant, who knew nothing. She had heard the doctor remark that there were illnesses from which one could recover, but bereft of one's intelligence. For hours she would be lost in bewilderment, watching over Serge like a mother, contriving to get him to see her smile at him, so he should smile back at her. And still he did not smile. When she held her hand in front of his eyes, he saw nothing, did not notice the shadow of it. He would scarcely turn his head even a trifle in the direction of the sound, when she spoke to him. She had only one consolation. He was growing magnifi-cently. He was a bonny boy.

There followed a whole week of tenderest care for him. She was patience itself, waiting for him to grow up. When at last she observed an occasional hint of response, her mind was more at rest and she told herself that time would bring manhood back to him. She saw the faint tremors which passed over him now, in response to her touch. Then came the evening when there was a frail little laugh.

The following day, having sat him at the window, she went down into the garden and there began running, calling to him, vanishing under trees, re-appearing again, flashing through patches of sun-light, all out of breath, clapping her hands. At first his eyes just vacillated, he did not even see her. But when she began to play hide-and-seek with him, making every shrub an ambush from behind which to emerge with excited cry, at last his glance did follow the white patch of her skirt. And when she came right up to him, under the window, her countenance raised to him, he suddenly held out his arms and made a gesture as if he would try to go to her. She ran indoors to him, and kissed him, gloriously proud.

'Why, you saw me, you saw me!' she cried. 'You would have liked to come into the garden to me, wouldn't you? If only you knew how sad you have made me, these last few days, pretending like that, never seeing me or hearing me.'

She had the impression that he listened, with a hint of pain, straining his neck, the very movement timid.

'But now you really are better,' she continued. 'Why, you are strong enough now to come out, when you feel ready . . . Why do you never say a word to me now? Have you really lost your tongue? Oh, what a monkey! I shall have to teach him to speak, you'll see!'

She did indeed start calling out the names of anything which he touched. He could only mumble, repeating single syllables. He could not say a single word clearly. Nevertheless, she began to walk him about the room, supporting him, leading him from bed to window, a tremendous journey. Two or three times, on the way, he nearly fell, making her laugh. One day he just sat down on the floor, and she had enormous difficulty getting him up again. Next, she made him undertake a round of the whole room, sitting him down, first on the settee, then on one armchair after another, on all the chairs, all round this little world of his, and that took a good hour. At last, he could risk a few paces by himself. She would stand in front of him, arms wide spread, then draw back, calling to him, to get him to cross the room to reach her supporting arms. When he sulked, and refused to walk, she would take the comb from her hair and hold it out to him like a toy. He would then go forward, to take it from her, then for hours be quiet in a corner, playing with it, using it to scratch gently at his hands.

One morning, however, she found him already out of bed. He had even contrived to open one of the shutters. He was trying to walk, without leaning on any furniture.

'Just look at him, the rogue,' she cried. 'Tomorrow, he'll be jumping out of the window, if we let him . . . So we are really strong now, are we?'

Serge's response was a childlike laugh, for his limbs had regained the health of early boyhood, without his mind awakening in concert with them. He spent whole afternoons looking out at the park, with the blank expression of an infant which only sees whiteness and to which sounds are but so many modulations of the air. He still had all the unknowingness of a child, was still so innocent that he could not even distinguish between Albine's frock and the upholstery of the old armchairs. He still stared in open-eyed wonder, uncomprehending, his gestures devoid of purpose. It was the early stage of a purely instinctive existence, quite without any sense of what his surroundings really meant. The man in him was not yet re-born.

'Very well, then,' murmured Albine, 'be an animal. We shall see.' And, removing her comb, she offered it to him. 'Want my comb?' she asked him. 'Then come and get it.'

But when, treading backwards, she had got him out of the room, she slipped her arm round his waist and held him up at every step. She put her comb back into place now, and engaged his attention by tickling his neck with the tip of a lock of her own hair. In this way also she hid from him realisation that he was going downstairs. But when she had got him down, before she could open the door, he was suddenly stricken with fear in the darkness of the hall.

'But look!' she cried, flinging the door wide open, to bring him sudden dawn, a curtain of shadow ripped aside, revealing the light of day in all its early delight, the park far flung, open before them in its green clarity, fresh and transparent as the waters of a spring. Delighted by it all, he remained on the threshold, full of a hesitant longing to essay one foot before the other in that lake of light.

'Anyone would think you were afraid of getting your feet wet,' said Albine. 'Get away with you, the ground's dry enough.'

He then hazarded a step and seemed astonished by the soft resistance of the sand. This first contact with the earth was like a shock to his body, an upsurge of life into him which made him rear erect, growing taller, breathing deep.

'Come, come,' cried Albine, 'courage! You know you promised me you would take five steps. We are going just up to that mulberry, which is under your window . . . There, you may rest.'

It took them quarter of an hour to cover those five steps. At every effort he paused, as if the movement had torn from the ground the roots which kept him there. The young girl, egging him on, with a laugh, said: 'Why, you're just like a tree trying to walk.'

She got his back up against the mulberry. He stood under the shower of sunlight, dripping freely from the branches above him. Then, leaving him, she raced away from him, quickly telling him not to move. His arms hanging limp, he turned his face slowly, till he was gazing into the park. This was childhood. The pale verdure was drowned in a milk of adolescence, bathed in a golden glow. The trees were still childlike, the flowers had the bodies of babies, their eyes innocently blue, lovely and wide to the world. Under every single leaf one saw exquisite new life.

Serge halted at the yellow tunnel made by a large broad walk cutting into the dense mass of foliage. At the far end, to the east, meadows drowned in gold seemed like the field of light on which the sun made its first descent to earth, waiting new morning to open this alley too, when it would come all the way to him. He felt the approach as a warm breath, at first very faint, scarcely stirring his skin, then little by little gathering strength till it was so fierce that it made him tremble all through. He revelled in that coming, ever more precise to the senses, bringing the healthy acidity of the open air, laying on his lips its feast of sugared aromatics, acidulous fruits, milky woods. His nostrils breathed in that approach, with the scents it gathered on its course, the smell of the soil, the smell of shady woods, the smell of hot herbs, the smells of living animals, all together a bouquet of scents of such violence that it made him quite dizzy. He could hear its approach, with the light flying of birds swooping close to the greensward, drawing the whole garden from its silence, lending whatever it touched a voice, till the music of inanimate things and living creatures resonated together in his ears. He saw its approach, at the far end of the ride, out of those gold-drenched meads, the air pink, so joyous that it lighted the road with a smile in a distance vast as a corner of day itself, in a few onward leaps becoming the very glory of the sun. Thus the morning came surging in waves all round the mulberry against which Serge was leaning, and in this childhood of the morning he was born anew.

'Serge! Se-erge!' he heard Albine calling from somewhere unknown beyond the tall flower thickets of the sunken garden. 'Do not be afraid! I am here!'

But Serge was not afraid. In this sunshine, this pure bath of light which poured over him, he was coming to life. He was being born at twenty-five, his senses suddenly awakened, enraptured by the open sky, the happy soil, the marvel of the landscape spread out all round him. This garden, unknown to him the day before, was of astonishing satisfaction. Everything went to fill it with ecstasy, even the blades of grass and pebbles of the walks, even the breathing of the life which he could not see, yet felt on his cheeks. His whole being entered into possession of this corner of nature, his limbs enfolded about it, his lips drank it in, his nostrils imbibed it, he bore it away in his ears and it was hidden in the depths of his eyes. It was his. The roses of the garden, the tall tree summits of the woods, the ringing rocks at the spring and the waterfall, the meadows where the sun planted its ears of light, were all his. And he closed his eyes, yielding himself up to the voluptuous enjoyment of slowly opening them again, to be dazzled by a repetition of his own re-awakening.

'Oh, those birds,' cried Albine, running up to him, pouting, 'they've eaten all the strawberries. Look, I could only find these two.' But then, still some paces away from him, she stopped short, staring at him in rapturous astonishment, and smitten at heart. 'But how handsome you are!' she cried, and then, drawing closer, again paused, submerging herself in him, and whispered: ' I never saw you before.'

There was no doubt, he had grown up. His clothes loose-fitting, he stood very erect, still very thin, of slender build too, yet full-shouldered and deep of chest. His white-skinned neck was now deeply tanned at the nape. He looked freely about him, his head held a little back, and on his features were written health, strength, power. He was unsmiling, his face in a state of repose, the lips solemn, yet gentle, his cheeks firm. His nose was prominent and he had very bright grey, dominating eyes. His hair, grown long, a thick head of it, fell to his shoulders in raven curls. His beard was thin and rightly curled away from lips and chin, revealed the whiteness of the skin beneath.

'You are lovely, lovely,' Albine repeated, slowly, crouching in front of him and looking up most tenderly. 'But why are you cross with me even now? Why do you say nothing?'

He did not reply, but just stood, his eyes gazing afar off, so that he did not even see the child at his feet. And when he did speak, he was alone. He addressed the sunlight. 'How good this light is!' he breathed.

One could have thought the words a mere vibration of the sun. They left his lips scarcely more than a whisper, like a musical breath, a tremor of warmth and life. For some days now, Albine had not once heard his voice. She found it as changed as he himself was. It seemed to her to spread throughout Paradou more softly than the song of the birds, more imperious than the winds that bent the branches of the trees. It was a regal, commanding voice. The whole garden heard it, though it was but breathed, and the whole garden shivered with the delight that it brought.

'But speak to me,' Albine begged him. 'You never spoke to me like that. Up there in your room, before you lost your voice, you used to chatter just like a child . . . How can it be that your voice is no longer recognizable? Just now it seemed to me that your voice came from the trees, from the whole garden, one of those deep sighs which so upset me in the nights before you came here . . . Sh! See how silent everything has become—waiting to hear you speak again.'

But he continued to remain utterly indifferent to her presence. And then she became more loving.

'But no, don't speak, if you find it tiring. Sit here, beside me. We can talk, stay here on this grassy bank, till the sun goes down . . . And do look, I have two strawberries here for you. It was such a trouble, finding them, naughty! The birds eat them all. Look, one for you, both, if you like. Or shall we share them both, you and I? You will say thank-you to me, I shall hear you.'

He would not sit down, he rejected the strawberries, and scornfully, Albine threw them away. She herself would not utter a word, now. She would rather he were ill, as during the first few days, when she lent her hand for pillow and felt him come back to life under her very breath. She cursed the health which now made him stand so erect there in the glow, like a supercilious young god. Was he then going to be so for ever now, and never vouchsafe her a glance? Was he never to gain still greater health, till he might see her and love her? To think that she had dreamt she would again be his real doctor, by the mere power instinct in her two small hands achieve the recovery of this second youth of his! She could see

131

only too clearly that deep in his grey eyes a fire was lacking. There was a deathly pallor in his handsome face, he was like that statuary in the sunken garden, collapsed and overgrown with nettles. So, rising to her feet, she went to him and again lay her arm about his waist and breathed on his neck, to bring new life to him. But on this occasion Serge was not even physically aware of that breath which stirred his silky beard. And then the sun had passed, and it was time to go in. Once indoors, Albine dissolved into tears.

From that morning, however, the convalescent took a short walk in the garden every day. He came to venturing beyond the mulberry, to going as far as the edge of the terrace, reaching the broad broken steps which once had led to the sunken garden. He grew hardened to the open air. Every sun bath brought him out more. A young sweet chestnut, sprouted from a nut fallen between two pillars of the balustrade, spread the fans of its foliage and burst in resinous buds with less vigour than Serge now displayed. The day even came when he tried to go down the steps. That, however, proved beyond his strength, and she found him sitting on one of the stones, among the feverdew which had sprung up in the crevices between the flags. Below them, to the left, his eye had been caught by a veritable coppice of roses run wild. It was his dream to reach that point.

'Wait a while yet,' said Albine. 'The scent of all those roses is too strong for you. I can never sit under them myself without feeling all my strength go. They go to my head. I feel I have to cry . . . All right then, I will take you there, under the roses, and cry there. You make me very unhappy.'

CHAPTER VI

ONE morning she was at last able to help him to the very bottom of the steps. With her foot she cut a path in the herbage for him to follow, treading down the dog-rose briars which barred the lower steps with their lissom arms. Then, at slow pace, they went to the rose garden. It was now a complete wood of them, dense groups of bush and tree-roses, bosky with foliage as voluminous as that of tall trees, roses blooming on shrubs, thickets of them as impenetrable as scrub oak. Once there had here been the most lovely collection of species roses that one could see, but ever since the garden was abandoned it had run wild, turning to virgin forest, a dense scrub of roses invading the paths, with a thick tangle of suckers so mingling the varieties together that roses of all scents and colours seemed to blossom on the same roots. Climbing roses formed a thick carpet, ramblers, thrusting up clouds of their green, clung to other species like voracious ivy, and as the wind stirred them their petals showered down like coloured rain. Throughout this wood, natural paths had formed, some narrow, some broad, lovely covered-in rides, where one could walk in fragrant shade. There were cross-roads in this rose world, broad clearings. One moved cradled among tiny red roses and one walked between walls covered with tiny yellow roses. There were patches of sunlight gleaming like green silk shot with light, and shady corners like discreet alcoves. It was one long lovers' path, it was a bouquet of flowers warm from a woman's bosom. The blossoms had their own whispering voices. The bushes were full of nests of song.

'We must take care not to lose our way,' said Albine, as they entered the wood. 'Once, I did get lost here. The sun had set by the time I had got free from these roses. They clung to my skirt and hampered every step.'

They had, however, not been walking more than a very few minutes, when, broken with fatigue, Serge wished to sit down. He immediately stretched out and fell into a deep sleep. Sitting at his side, Albine was pensive. They were at the point where the path came out on to a clearing. The path ran on a long way, barred with rays of sunlight, and at the far end a narrow circle of blueness showed where it finally came out on the open sky. Other small paths plunged some distance into the impassable verdure. The clearing was formed by large roses, one above another, a wall of them rising in a profusion of branches, a tangle of spiny creepers fastened high up by their serried thorns, forming a tenting above them, from bush to bush. Through this tissue of roses, it was only through narrow channels, slashed like fine lace, that touches of daylight passed, an open-work of azure through which day came in the form of intangible sun-dust. And from the vaulting hung branches like chandeliers, huge tufts of foliage dangling by slender green stems, armfuls of flowers reaching the ground from a rent in the ceiling and dragging there like torn curtains.

Albine all this time watched Serge sleep. She had hitherto never seen him so exhausted, his fingers outstretched on the grass, his features lifeless. He seemed so dead that she thought she would be able to implant a kiss on his cheek without him feeling it. Sad and despairing, she idly plucked petals from blooms within reach. One enormous bunch was dangling just above her head, actually touching her hair, mingling its blossoms with her own knotted locks, laying them on her neck, draping her shoulders with a wrap of roses. Higher, at the touch of her fingers, the flowers rained large, soft petals of miraculous roundness, and the faintly blushing purity of virginal breasts. Like a sudden fall of living snow, the petals already concealed her feet, crossed in the long grass. They rose to her knees, covering her skirt, immersing her to the waist, while three petals, slipping away and falling past her bodice into the valley of her bosom seemed to reveal three points of her exquisite nakedness.

'Ah!' she cried, 'the lazy boy!'

It was too much, she felt, and she scooped up a couple of handfuls of petals and flung them at Serge's face, to waken him.

Still heavy with sleep, he sat up, blinking, with rose petals in his eyes and on his lips. She had to laugh. Bending down, she gave him hearty, heartfelt kisses, first one between the eyes, then one on his lips. At the same time, she blew, to drive the petals away, but they clung to his lips, and she then laughed more loudly still, finding this loving contact amid flowers ever so funny.

Slowly, he drew himself up, and stared at her, all astonishment, apparently quite startled to see her there.

'Who are you?' he demanded, 'where have you come from? What are you doing, here with me?'

Still smiling, overjoyed to see him thus awakened at long last, she still smiled. Then only did he seem to remember things, and, with a gesture of contentment and confidence, resumed: 'I know, you are my love, you come of my flesh, you are waiting for me to take you into my arms, so we may be one again... I was dreaming of you. You were in my bosom and I gave you of my blood, my muscles, my bones. I suffered nothing. You took half my heart, so softly that I found that sharing it with you the greatest pleasure. I sought of my best and finest to give to you. Even had you taken it all, I would but have said *thank-you* ... And when you emerged from me, I awakened. You came out of my eyes and my lips, I felt it quite clearly. You were so warm, so fragrant, so caressing that it was the very tremor of your flesh that made me sit up.'

Ecstatically, Albine listened to what he said. So at last he saw her, at last his birth was complete, at last he had began to get well again. Reaching out her hands to him, she begged him to go on.

'However was I able to live without you?' he murmured. 'I did not really live at all, that is how, I was like a sleeping animal... But now you are mine. You are but myself. Listen, you must never leave me, for you are my breath, you would carry my life from me. We shall remain within ourselves. You shall be in my flesh as I shall be in yours. If ever I leave you, may I be cursed, may my body shrivel up like a noxious weed.'

He took her hands, and in tones of quivering admiration, he cried:

'How lovely you are!'

The dust of the sunshine illuminated her, and her skin was of milk, faintly gilded by the reflected light, while the downpour of roses all around her and upon her, drowned her in rose hues. Her fair hair, loosely contained by her comb, was like a glorious sunset to crown her, showering over her shoulders the unbridled glow of its final fanned-out flames. She wore a white gown, so true to her form, so neatly baring arms, bosom, knees, that it really left her naked. She displayed a skin that was all innocence, full-blooming with the sinlessness of a flower, musked with its own odour. She lay at full length, her person dainty, lissom of line, a symphony of soft curves which in places rose richly into voluptuous hills in all the grace of charm of a young girl, body, flesh still drenched with childhood, yet already swollen with puberty. Her long countenance, with its narrow forehead and her rather full lips possessed that smiling light of delicate young life which shone in her blue eyes. Moreover, she was so grave, her cheeks so unassuming, her chin firm. She was as natural in her beauty as the trees in their own loveliness.

'And how I love you!' murmured Serge, drawing her to himself.

They remained, close held, in each other's arms. They exchanged no kiss, but held each other by the waist and lay cheek against cheek, at one, speechless, enchanted to be thus united. All round them the rose-bushes flowered, with crazy profusion, lover's profusion, all scarlet laughter, pink laughter, white laughter. The living blooms revealed their petals as when corsages reveal the naked riches of the bosom. There were yellow roses brushing the golden skins of barbarian maidens, straw roses, lemon roses, sunshine roses, every shade possible of blossoms bronzed by blazing skies. Then the flesh grew more tender still, the tea roses assumed lovely moistness, exposing beauties which modesty had hid, crevices of the body not usually shown, of silken softness, with faint blue transparency of minute capillaries. The laughing rose life expanded to the full, pink whiteness with subtle tinge of the fine red brush, the snow of a virgin foot trying the waters of the spring, pale rose, more discreet than the fiery whiteness of the knee half seen, or the flash of upper arm glimpsed up loose sleeve, frank rose, blood under

135

satin, naked shoulders, naked hips, all a woman's nakedness, caressed by light, vivid rose, the budding blossoms of the bosom, the parting blooms of the lips as they draw in the scent of warm breath. And the climbing roses, vast growth with their downpour of white blossoms, enwrapped all these roses, all this flesh, in the lace of their sprays, in the innocence of their gossamer muslin, while here and there red wine lees roses, roses almost black, roses of blood, thrust the wound of fierce love deep into that purity of the bride. Wedding of sweet-scented coppices, bringing the virginities of May to the impregnation of July and August, first innocent kisses, culled like a posy of flowers on the marriage morn. Even in the grass underfoot, a froth of roses, roses in long high-necked gown of green cloth, awaited love. All down the ride, barred by rays of sunshine, flowers wandered, faces turned towards them, as the summoning zephyrs wafted them.

Under the widespread tenting of that glade, every smile was radiant, yet not any two blooms the same. The roses had their own ways of living. Some would but bring bud to bud, half opened, facing each other, all timidity, blushing at the heart, while others had corsage ready loosened and were breathing hard, roses fully open, as if of loose muslin, flesh crazed to the point of death. Some were small, alert, laughing roses, following one after the other, with cockades in their caps. Others were enormous, bursting with their charms, and all the full fire of plump harem wives. There were shameless creatures there, with the allure of courtesans, temptingly revealing themselves, their white petals all powerful. There were the circumspect bourgeoises, their bosoms revealed just the prescribed amount, the lissom, chic aristocratic wenches, assuming their right to shock, in frocks cut with startling ingenuity to reveal. Roses opened cup-like offered as it were crystal goblets of perfume, others, drooping, urn shaped, spilled their precious nectar drop by drop. There were roses round like cabbages breathing out from their petals of sleep with regular rise and fall of breast, and rose-buds which clutched their petals close into their bodies and yielded no more than the faintest sighs of their virginity.

'I love you, I love you,' Serge cried, again and again in a whisper. And Albine was one of those large pale roses which had opened only that same morning, rose with white feet, pink knees and arms, fair neck, pale bosom, adorably veined, with exquisite bloom. She was most fragrant, she held out lips, in coral goblet offering a perfume which was still of great fragility. And Serge drank her in, took her into his bosom.

136

'Oh!' she cried, laughing, 'you do not hurt me, you can take me all.'

Her laughter made him rapturous, like the cadences of the birds which sang.

'This is your song,' he said, 'I never heard so sweet a melody... You are my joy.'

And she laughed, louder now, with pearly scales of little sharp, flute-like sounds which merged into slow, soft sonorities. It was an endless laughter, a bosom murmur, sonorous music, music of triumph which marked the supreme satisfaction of the awakening. Everything was laughing in this laughter of a woman now born to beauty and to love, the roses laughed, the sweet-scented copses all laughed, the whole of Paradou Park laughed. Till then, that enormous garden had lacked enchantment, lacked grace in its voice, to be the living merriment of trees, waters, sunshine, but now it was suddenly endowed with that enchantment of laughter.

'How old are you, dear Serge?' Albine asked, as her song faded out in a descrescendo of trills.

'I shall soon be twenty-six,' he replied.

She was amazed. What? Twenty-six? But even he was surprised —surprised at having answered with this figure so easily. For he felt not a day, not even an hour old.

'But you,' he in turn asked, 'how old are you?'

'Me? Sixteen!'

And she was off at once, vibrant with delight, repeating her age in song, laughing to be sixteen, her laughter a subtle thread flowing like clear water, vibrant as her speaking voice. Serge examined her now from close to. The vitality of that laugh, which shed its lovely light over all her young face, made him marvel. He hardly recognized her thus, her cheeks dimpling, her lips arched, revealing the moist scarlet of her mouth, her eyes like points of blue sky lit by the rising sun. When she flung her head back to laugh freely, he felt the warmth of her laughter-filled throat pressed against his shoulder. With automatic movement he reached out his hand and felt at her nape.

'What do you want?' she asked him. Then, guessing, cried:

'Of course, my comb, you want my comb!'

So unfastened, the heavy plaits of her hair cascaded over her shoulders, she gave him the comb. It was like golden cloth unknotted. The torrents of it covered shoulders and bosom in a royal garment. At this swift flourish of flame, he uttered a faint cry. Then he kissed every strand of it, scorching his lips against that flood of sunset glow.

Meanwhile, Albine was revelling in this end to his long-drawn-out silence. She chattered away, no stopping her now, all questions.

'Oh, how you have been worrying me! I was suddenly nothing to you, I spent day after day useless, unable to do anything, and so worried by my uselessness . . . Yet during your first few days I did help you. Then you saw me and spoke to me . . . Don't you remember lying there and falling asleep against my shoulder, with the whisper that I did you good?'

'No,' he said. 'No, I do not remember it . . . I had never seen you till just now. I have just seen you for the first time, and you are so lovely, so radiant, unforgettable.'

But she clapped her hands with impatience and protested.

'And what about my comb? Surely you remember how I used to give you my comb, to soothe you, when you turned back into a baby? Why, just now you wanted it again.'

'No, I do not remember,' he said. 'Your hair is finest silk. I have never kissed your hair before.'

She became nettled, reminded him of various details, then told him about the whole of his convalescence in the blue-ceilinged room. After this, his only reply was to lay his fingers on her lips and say, with rather troubled weariness:

'Please don't talk about it now. I no longer know, nor do I even want to know . . . I have just wakened up and have found you here, all roses, and that is enough.'

And he took her into his arms again and held her a long time, dreaming out loud, whispering:

'Perhaps I have had a previous existence. It must be a very long time ago. I loved you in a sorrowful dream. You had blue eyes, the same rather long face, and this same air of early girlhood. But in that dream, you used to hide your hair so painstakingly under a linen kerchief, and I never dared pull it aside, for then your hair was a terrifying thing, and if I had touched it, I might have died. Today, it is the essence of your sweet personality. It is your hair which preserves your fragrance and delivers all your lissom beauty straight into my hands. When I kiss your hair, when I bury my face in it,—like this—I imbibe your very life.'

He ran the long locks through his fingers, pressed them to his lips, as if he thought to draw every drop of Albine's life-blood from it. Then, after some silence, he went on:

'Strange, before being born, one dreams one's birth . . . I was

138

buried somewhere and I felt very cold. I heard the life of the outer world above my head, but I sealed my ears. In my mental agony I had become accustomed to my tunnel of darkness and found monstrous delights in it, but I never made any effort to get free from the mass of earth which weighed me down. Wherever then was I? And who can it have been that at last brought me out into the light?'

He made efforts of memory, while Albine waited anxiously, terrified now lest he should recall that past life. Smiling, she took a handful of her hair and knotted it about his neck, binding him to her. This play brought him out of his reverie.

'You are quite right,' he said. 'I belong to you, and what does all else matter? It was you, of course, drew me up out of the underground world in which I lingered. I must have been under this garden, and what I heard was your feet, stirring the little stones of these paths. You were looking for me, you brought the song of birds above my head, the scent of carnations, the sun's warmth . . . And I suspected that in the end you would discover me. I had been waiting, you see, a long time. But I never hoped you would give yourself to me without your veil, with your hair undone, or that that awesome hair would prove to be so soft.'

He drew her to him as he lay there, lay her back over his knees, bent over her till his cheeks touched hers.

'But let us stop talking,' he murmured. 'We are alone for ever. We love each other.'

They remained innocently in one another's arms, for a considerable time oblivious of all else. The sun was mounting higher in the sky, the dust of the hotter part of the day was already filtering down from the tree tops. The yellow, the white, the red roses, were now lost in the total radiance of their own delight, and by this effusion knew each other's smiles. There was no doubt, they had brought their every bud into laughing bloom. And these roses were their crown, casting down garlands to bind their union, and the perfume of the roses became so penetrating, so rich in loving tenderness, that it seemed as if it were the very scent of their own breath.

Then Serge did up Albine's hair for her again, taking the tresses by the handful with delightful clumsiness and jabbing the comb into the enormous knot which he contrived at the top of her head. Thus she was clothed with a wonderful head-dress, and he stood up and offered her his hands to assist her to her feet, and both were speechless, yet wreathed in happy smiles as they slowly made their way back down the path.

139

CHAPTER VII

ALBINE and Serge went into the sunken garden. She eyed him
anxiously, afraid he would be over-fatigued. But he laughed
lightly and put her mind at rest: he felt strong enough to carry her
wherever she wished to go. When he found himself back again
in the full sunlight, he gasped with delight. At last he was really
alive, no longer a mere vegetable thing at the mercy of winter's
trials. And what affectionate gratitude he felt for this care of hers!
He would have liked to save Albine's dainty feet from the roughness
of the paths, thought of her clinging to his neck while he carried
her, like a mother a sleeping babe. He was already the eagle-eyed
protective guardian, kicking aside stones and brambles, seeing that
the wind on her beloved hair did not steal caresses which belonged
exclusively to him. She had nestled close in to his shoulder, yielding
herself to him, at perfect peace.

Thus Albine and Serge for the first time walked together through
the sunlight. Behind them the air was sweet, the path all a-quiver,
the sun unfolding a golden carpet under their feet. They went
slowly forward, rapturous, on either side flowering shrubberies and
these were so desirable that the distant walks which led all ways
called to them, greeting them with murmurous admiration like that
with which crowds greet long awaited royalty. They were one
being only, of sovereign beauty, Albine's white skin but the white
counterpart of his sunburn. They trod slowly, clad in sunshine.
They were the sunshine itself and the flowers bent towards them
and worshipped them.

The sunken garden was one long thrill in itself. It was their
escort. A huge area laid out in flowers and shrubs, but run wild
for a century now, a corner of paradise where the wind had sowed
the rarest flowers. The fortunate peace of Paradou, slumbering in
the fierce sunlight, had prevented degeneration. The temperature
was equable and the soil had been long enriched by the plants
growing there in their silent strength. The vegetation was stupendous, vigorously wild, and the rich play of chance brought out
giant blooms such as the gardener's spade and watering-can could
never have produced. Left to herself and free to grow without shame
deep in this solitude, under the protection of natural wind-breaks,
Nature with every spring grew more expansive, lavish with striking
fancies, taking delight in every season in lavishing on herself

unusual bouquets which no hand was ever to pick. She even seemed to find particular delight in upsetting whatever man's hand had laboriously done. She rebelled, sending flowers helter-skelter down the walks, she assailed the rockeries with a mounting horde of mosses, she overturned marble statues and laced them to the ground with the supple ropes of her creeping bonds. Thrusting the roots of shrubs into them, she broke the flagstones which floored the water pools, and formed the steps and terraces. She climbed till the least cultivated corner was in her possession, then made havoc of them all as she chose, planting the flag of revolt in the form of seeds gathered by the wayside, humble weeds which here she turned into giant verdure. There had once been a time when the sunken garden was the pet of a master gardener, a man with a passion for flowers, who displayed a marvellous selection in trim beds and borders. Today, the same plants were still there, but on a permanent footing, multiplied into such countless families and so running wild everywhere that the garden was now but vagabondage, a free riot, forbidden territory where Nature in her intoxication hiccoughed verbenas and carnations.

And though she might seem to give herself into his care, as if so weak that only his shoulder could support her, it was in fact Albine who led Serge. First she took him to the grotto. At the end of a small wood of poplars and willows, an outcrop of rock was hollowed out, eroded. Blocks of stone had fallen into a shallow basin and rivulets of water now streamed over them. There was also a grotto which had disappeared under the oncoming wall of vegetation. From below, ranks of hollyhocks seemed to bar the entrance with a portcullis of red, yellow, mauve and white flowers, the stems lost amid enormous bronze-green nettles ready effortlessly to exude the fire of their poison. Beyond this the vegetation leapt several paces at once: jasmines starred with their gentle blossoms, wistarias with the delicate lace of their leaves, dense, clean-cut ivy, like varnished canvas, lissom honeysuckle, loaded with tufts of coral-pink flowers, amorous clematis, reaching out its arms, with all its white spikes of flowerets. There were other plants too, frailer things, entangled with these, binding them more tightly together, weaving of the whole a sweet-scented backcloth. Nasturtiums, with their bare, greenish flesh, opened ruddy gold lips. Scarlet runners, with rough, ropy stems, bore aloft the fiercely red little coals of their burning blossom. Convolvulus extending its foliage, each leaf a truncated heart, little bell blossoms in their thousands ringing out inaudible carillons of exquisite shades. Sweet peas, like flights of dignified

141

butterflies, folded their wings of buff and pink, ready to be carried farther by the first puff of wind. It was a mane of greenery, through which came a torrential rain of flowers, so immense, its wild tresses so out of control on all sides, that one could think it a giant maiden in the throes of love somewhere beyond, haunches doubled back, in the momentary throes of oblivion from satisfaction, her head still forced back by the sheer culmination of her orgasm, her glorious locks streaming loose like those of a superb animal, and spreading wide in a cloud of sweet odours.

'I have never dared go into that black hole,' Albine whispered, into Serge's ear.

He reassured her, carried her through the thick growth of nettles, then, finding a block of stone closing the threshold of the cave, held her up for a moment so that she could lean over the hole which gaped a few feet beyond.

'Here, in the running water,' she whispered, 'lies a woman of marble, full length. And the water is wearing away her features.'

Next, he too had to see. He heaved himself up. A breath of chill air struck at his cheeks. Amid the reeds and water lilies, in the arm of daylight flowing from the hole, she lay on her back. She was naked to the waist. Her thighs were concealed by drapery, century-old victim of death by drowning, the slow suicide of a marble statue by tribulation fallen to the bottom of the waters by this spring. The incessant translucent flow had turned her countenance to featureless stone, smooth whiteness, but her breasts, which the neck muscles by immense effort seemed to thrust above the water, had remained intact, still tense with the orgasm of long ago.

'No, no,' said Serge, when he lowered himself back to the ground again, 'she is not really dead. One day we must come and get her out.'

But Albine shuddered, and led him away from the spot. They came back to the sunshine, amid the wild confusion of overgrown beds and borders. They walked through a flowering meadow, where the whim took them, for there was no marked path to follow. For carpet their feet had delightful dwarf plants which once edged the garden walks but had now spread far beyond, in great patches. At moments they were ankle deep in the speckled silk of pink fly-catchers, the gaudy satin of pinks, the blue velvet of forget-me-not, with all its myriad tiny, mournful eyes. Farther, they strode through enormous mignonette beds, reaching to their knees, making a bath of scents. They trod a field of lily-of-the-valley to spare a nearby field of violets, so gentle that they seemed to shiver if the smallest tuft of them was touched. Then, hemmed in on all sides by them, they had no choice, in the heart of this atmosphere of spring breath, but to tread on that embalmed freshness. They kept coming on more and more violets, a sea of violets everywhere, smothering their feet with their precious scent, following them with the breath of their leaf-hidden flowers.

Albine and Serge lost their way. A myriad taller plants formed hedges and disposed of the narrow paths which they wished to follow. The paths made sudden twists and vanished, they ran one into another, they led to impenetrable thickets: ageratums with their sky-blue puffs of blossom, woodruffs with a delicate musk-like scent, mimulus with their coppery throats and cinnabar spots, scarlet phlox, and superb violet phlox, rearing distaffs of blossom swayed by the wind, red flax with blades as fine as hair, chrysanthemums like golden full moons thrusting out their subdued, short, whitish lilac and pink tinted rays. The young couple came upon one obstacle after another as they persisted in their promenade of joy between the two hedges of greenery.

On their right reared airy fraxinellas, their central anthers drooping back in perfect snow and there were greyish hound's tongues with a drop of dew in each of the minute cups of their blooms. To the left was a long road of columbines of every variety, white, pale pink, dark violet, almost black, with the sadness of mourning, the petals drooping from their lofty stems pleated and goffered like crêpe. And farther on, as they went forward, the hedges changed yet again, with lines of larkspur in immense bloom, all lost in the haze of its foliage, between them thrusting the open jaws of beige snap-dragons, the slender leaves of schizanthus, with masses of butterfly blossom, the sulphur wings spotted with delicate red. Campanulas raced beside them, throwing their blue bells out like discus-throwers, to top the tall asphodels whose golden stems served as bell-towers. In a corner, a giant fennel was like a lady in fine lace putting up her water-green satin umbrella. Then, all at once, they found themselves faced with an impenetrable obstacle and could go no farther, a massif of flowers completely sealing off the path, such a profusion of plants that it was like an orchid-house of blooms, more splendiferous than believable. At the bottom, acanthus provided a foundation, above which shot scarlet bennet and rhodantias, the white petals of which were crackled as if of painted paper, and clarkias with immense white worked crosses, like the symbols of some pagan order. Above these were lavish pink viscarias, yellow leptosiphons, white colinsias, while among all these colours the lagurus thrust their bobbles of greenish ash. Higher still, red digitalis and blue lupins raised their slender columns and reared aloft a byzantine cupola, with violent daubs of purple and azure, while at the very peak was a colossal castor-oil plant with blood-red leaves, spreading what looked like an oxidised copper dome.

And as Serge reached forward, in his intention of getting through, Albine begged him not to hurt the flowers.

'You might break them down, you might crush their leaves,' she said. 'All the years I have lived here, I have always taken care never to kill anybody ... Come, let me show you the pansies.'

She made him withdraw from this place, taking him out of the narrow paths to the centre of the sunken garden, where once had been the larger water-pools. Now that they had broken up, these were no better than huge flower-pots edged with shattered, fragmented marble. In one of the largest of them, the wind had sown the seeds of a marvellous basket of pansies. The velvety flowers seemed almost sentient things, with their violet head-dressing, their yellow eyes, their paler lips, their delicate flesh-coloured chins.

'When I was younger, they used to frighten me,' she whispered. 'But just look at them. Would you not think they were thousands of little faces looking up at you from the ground? And they turn their faces round, all together. One might think they were dolls buried here, with their heads sticking out.'

Again she led him on, and they went to all the other pools. In the next one, amaranthus had grown, rearing tall crests which Albine was afraid to touch, for they made her think of enormous bleeding caterpillars. There were balsams too, pale yellow, peach colour, line grey, white stained with pink, filling another sunken bed, the springs of their seed-pods popping with minute dry crackle. Next, amid the debris of a fountain, there was a collection of marvellous carnations, white blooms pouring over the edge of the basin, dazzling carnations which had set the multicolour of their slashed muslin ruffs in crevices between the stones, an enormous red one breaking from the cavernous mawl of a lion, the colour thrusting out so harsh, so vivid, that the mutilated animal seemed to be spitting clots of his blood into the sunlight. And here beside it was the principal stretch of water, once a lake where swans had

swum, and bordering this a thicket of lilac, in the shade of which
all moist with their fragrance, forty-day stocks, verbenas and day-
lilies found shelter for their delicate shades.

'But we have not seen half the garden yet!' cried Albine, proudly.
'Over there are the really big flowers. There are whole fields
of them in which I am as lost as a partridge among the
wheats.'

They made their way across the garden, and down a long flight of
steps past overturned stone urns, still glowing with the tall violet flames
of irises. Down the steps liquid gold, poured a flood of wall-flowers.
On both sides the slender-stemmed thistles raised their candelabra
of greenish bronze, their spikes erect, bent in on themselves like the
beaks of fantastic birds with all the curious footing and elegance of
Chinese perfume braziers. Between the broken banisters clustered
sedums with pale dangling tresses, greenish mildew stained river
hair. Beyond this stretched yet another sunken garden, intersected
by shrubs as stout-trunked as oaks, all ancient growth, straight-
trained, once clipped into spheres, pyramids, octagonal towers, now
one untidy mass of verdure with here and there gaps revealing
patches of blue sky.

Albine took Serge to a patch of ground to the right which was like
a sort of graveyard of the garden which once had been. Here
scabious flaunted its mourning. Long columns of poppies marched
in procession, dispersing an effluvium of death, their heavy blooms
outspreading with febrile brilliance. Tragic anemones clustered
in little groups, dull-complexioned, sickly with the breath of epi-
demic. Squat daturas spread their violet-tinted cornets, and in
them insects tired of life came to drink the poison of suicide.
Marigolds, blocks of death-throe stars already breathing out the
pest of their decomposition, buried their blooms under congested
foliage. There was also many another grim blossoming: fleshy
ranunculus, the dull colour of rusting metal, hyacinths breathing
suffocation, tuberoses expiring in their own scent. But it was the
cinerarias which here dominated the scene, a close-packed army of
them in slow progression in the half-mourning of their violet and
white velvet robes, some striped, some all of one colour, but all alike
of lavish, costly severity. In the very centre of this melancholy field
one marble cupid still stood erect, though even he was damaged.
The arm which had held the bow now lay deep in nettles, yet under
the lichens which made the childlike body shiver, the lips still
smiled.

Albine and Serge forced their way through, into a clump of

145

paeonies which reached to their shoulders. The lavish white blooms were already breaking up, the large petals fresh to the hands of the young couple as the rich-splashing rain-drops of a thunder-shower, but the red blooms were still like apoplectic faces, leering with a laughter which made the young man and woman uneasy. Moving to the left, Albine and Serge came to a patch of fuchsias, a coppice of gracefully drooping, loose-growing bushes, the countless little red bells of which delighted the eye like Japanese toys. Next, their path led through fields of veronicas, with their lilac-coloured racemes of flower, and fields of geraniums and pelargoniums, over which seemed to play the greedy little flames, the reds and the pinks and the fierce white glow of a brazier, ceaselessly fanned anew by the breath of the wind. They had to draw aside curtains of gladioli bull-rush tall, holding aloft poles of blossom burning against the glowing light with all the richness of flaring torches. They turned aside through a wood of sunflowers, a veritable forest of stems as tall as Albine, a forest sombre with rough leaves, each large enough to cradle a baby, peopled with giant faces, sun-like faces, splendid as the great orb itself. And at last they reached yet another wood, that of the rhododendrons, so compact now with blossom that the branches and leaves were completely hidden, basket upon basket of soft calyxes billowing to the very horizon.

'Get away with you!' cried Albine. 'We have not reached the end. Come on, my dear, farther yet.'

But Serge made her pause. They were now in the heart of an ancient, but ruined colonnade. The pediments of broken columns formed seats, with thick growth of primroses and periwinkle all round them. Farther on, among columns still standing, were other stretches of flowers: tulips with all the gay show of the painted china of their petals, fields of calceolarias, the airy blisters of flesh speckled with gold and blood, fields of zinnias, like large, angry daisies, fields of petunias with petals soft as the batiste which reveals the pink of flesh, and beyond, other fields, endlessly, flowers of which they did not know the name, the carpets of which lay outstretched in the sunshine, a vivid patchwork of startling blocks of colour, all half-submerged in delicate greenery.

'We shall never be able to see it all,' said Serge, holding out his hand, and smiling. 'This should be a good place for us to sit, with all this perfume filling the air.'

Beside them was an expanse of heliotropes, their breath so vanilla sweet that it was like a touch of velvet in the air. They had been walking for more than an hour. They found a seat on one of the

146

overturned pillars. From roses, by way of so many other flowers, they had come to the superb lilies which now enclosed them, affording a retreat into a sweet simplicity after their lovers' walk amid the hot suggestiveness of the luscious honeysuckle, the musk-odoured violets, the verbenas with their fresh exhalation of kisses, and the tuberoses, breathing that love swoon of the satisfaction which leads at last to death. With their uplifting stems, these lilies made a white summerhouse for them, their calyxes a roof pure as snow, the only touch of colour the delicate gold dust of the pistils. And here they lingered, like children affianced, triumphantly chaste, as if around them was a bastion of purity, an ivory tower none could assail, where their love still knew but the sorcery of their own innocence.

Albine and Serge stayed among the lilies till the sun began to go down. It was exquisite there. The process of birth found its continuation. Cradled in those blooms, Serge lost the last traces of his indisposition, and Albine was a white without blemish, a milk white which no hint of blush stained with redder hue. They were no longer aware even of the nudity of their arms, their bosoms, their shoulders. Their uncovered hair no longer seemed a display of nakedness. Pressed close one to another, they laughed with limpid laughter and in each other's constraining arms found true freshness. Their eyes retained the translucent tranquillity of spring water and from their bodies rose no impurity to tarnish that crystallinity. Their cheeks were fruit of velvet, and when they at last left the lilies, they were but ten years old, and it seemed to them that in these very moments they met for the first time ever, alone in this huge garden, to live on there for ever in endless friendship and play. And as they made their way again, returning to the house at dusk, through the main treasury of garden, in their delight to see them so young the very flowers seemed to feign not to see them, determined not to shatter their innocence with any carnal thought. Those thickets of paeonies, those basketfuls of carnations, those carpets of forget-me-not, those draperies of clematis, no longer opened to them any alcove for love. Instead, their bowers were withdrawn deep into the evening air, with frank little faces, sleeping an infant sleep as pure as their own. The pansies peeped up at them as playmates. Even the resedas, languid now as day came to its end, seemed overcome with compassion as Albine's white skirt brushed them by and were at no pains now to hasten their fever by even the faintest breath.

CHAPTER VIII

THE next day it was Serge who called Albine, and at break of day, too. She had turned an upstairs room into her bedroom, but he never thought of such a thing as going up to her. He leant out of his window, to shout. And then he saw her. She had just got up too, and was opening her shutters. With one accord, thus meeting, they broke into happy laughter.

'Now, you're not going out at all today,' said Albine, when she came down. 'We must both rest . . . Tomorrow, I mean to take you for a long, long walk, so that we can really be free.'

'But it will be so dull today,' he murmured.

'I should think it will not!' she cried. 'I shall tell you stories.'

They passed a delightful day, the windows wide open, so that Paradou came inside with them, and laughed with them. At last Serge had taken full possession of this happy room, where he imagined he had been born. He wanted to examine everything and have it all explained to him—the plaster cupids somersaulting round the edge of the alcove delighted him so much that he climbed on to a chair to turn Albine's belt into a necklace for the smallest of them, a little chap, bottom uppermost, at very roguish tricks. Clapping her hands, she insisted that the cupid was just like a hornet on a string. Then, as if in an access of pity. 'No, no, untie him,' she cried, 'with that on, he won't be able to fly.'

But it was more than anything else the cupids painted above the doors that engaged Serge's attention. The colours had faded considerably and he was annoyed not to be able to make out what games they were at. With Albine's help, he moved a table underneath them and they both climbed on to it. It was Albine who explained: 'See, those over there are throwing flowers. But all you can see under the flowers are three legs. They are bare. But I seem to remember that when I first came it was still possible to see a lovely lady lying on her back. Since then she seems to have faded right away.'

They examined each panel in turn, but in all the petty little lewdnesses of the boudoir they saw nothing unclean. The paintings, now flaking like any cheeks made up over a century before them, were now dead enough to reveal no more than a medley of knees and elbows, whose owners lolling in all the satiety which endless adorable pleasures could give. These details, which were too blunt but in which apparently that old-time love of which the alcove retained the lingering aroma had found its pleasure, had vanished, eaten away by the fresh air, so that now, like the park, in the calm glory of the sunlight, the room had by natural courses returned to its pristine virginity.

'Pooh!' said Serge, as he got down from the table, 'it's only some children at their games ... I say, do you know how to play hot cockles?'

Albine knew all the games. But for hot cockles one needed at least three. That made them laugh. What did it matter? Serge said they were too well off as two to want to be three. They swore never to be more than two.

'We are absolutely our own masters here,' he said, stretching out on the settee. 'And this furniture smells so old-world and so good ... It's as cosy as any bird's nest. It really is a nook of happiness.'

Solemnly, she nodded acquiescence.

'If I had been at all timid,' she murmured, 'I should have been terribly afraid here, at first ... As a matter of fact, I was going to tell you the story about it some day. I heard it talked about round here. Perhaps it is only make-up. Even so, it will pass the time.'

She sat down by Serge's side.

'It was years and years ago ... Paradou Park then belonged to a rich nobleman who came here to live in seclusion with a very beautiful lady. The gates were so firmly locked and the park walls were so high that nobody even saw the hem of her skirts.'

'I know,' Serge said. 'She disappeared.' And, seeing Albine look at him in astonishment, even annoyance at seeing her tale was already familiar to him, he ran on, surprised by himself. 'You've already told me all about it,' he said, 'the story, I mean.'

She assured him she had not. Then, apparently thinking better of it, she nodded agreement, then went on herself to end her story.

'When the nobleman left, his hair was white. He had all the entrances built up, so nobody should disturb the lady ... But—she died in this room.'

'In this room!' cried Serge. 'You never told me that ... Are you sure she died here?'

Irritably, Albine repeated that everybody knew it. The nobleman had had this very lodge built for this unknown lady, who was like a princess. Later the folk of the chateau swore that he had spent day and night there. What was more, they often saw him down one of the walks, guiding the dainty feet of the strange lady into the darkest coppices. But they would not for anything in the world

149

have made so bold as to spy on the couple, who wandered about in the park for many weeks.

'And this is where she died?' cried Serge, seemingly agitated. 'You took over her room, you use her furniture, you sleep in her bed.'

Albine smiled.

'You know very well that I am not timid,' she said. 'Besides, if a long time has passed . . . Why, you yourself found the room full of happiness.'

Neither spoke. For some moments, they stared into the alcove, at the lofty ceiling and the grey shadowiness of the corners. There seemed to be an amorous sensitivity about the faded colours of the furniture, a sigh of the past, so subtle, so yielding a breath that one could have thought it the warm gratitude of a woman replete with love.

'True,' murmured Serge, 'it would be impossible to be afraid. It is too peaceful.'

Then, drawing closer to him, Albine resumed: 'What very few people know is that in Paradou gardens those two discovered a realm of absolute bliss, where in the end they spent the live-long day. And—I have it from a reliable source—they spent it at a spot hidden deep in impenetrable thickets where the shade is fresh and so wondrously beautiful that in it one forgets the whole world. And here apparently this lady was laid to earth.'

'In the sunken garden?' Serge enquired, with curiosity.

'Oh, how do I know, how do I know exactly where?' the girl cried, with a gesture of hopelessness. 'I have searched everywhere, but never have been able to discover the fortunate clearing where she lies . . . She is not among the roses or the lilies, or even where the violets carpet the ground.'

'Perhaps it was that corner with the dismal flowers, where you showed me that boy standing, with broken-off arm.'

'Oh, no!'

'Perhaps it was the far end of that grotto, near that clear water in which the big marble woman without any face is drowned.'

For some moments Albine was pensive. Then, as if whispering to herself, she continued:

'Almost as soon as I came here, I began the search. If I passed countless days in Paradou Park, if I probed into the smallest corner of the greenery, I had only one aim, and that was to be able to sit for an hour in that particular glade. What lost mornings, creeping under brambles, penetrating to the farthest parts of the park! . . .

150

But I should at once have recognized that enchanted retreat. An enormous tree that must stand there, to roof her over with its lofty leafage, and there must be fine grass like silken plush, walled in all round by green: shrubs that even the birds cannot penetrate!'

Suddenly lacing an arm about his neck, in firmer tones she implored:

'Now we are two, we will look till we find it, won't we ... You who are strong can hold the bigger branches out of my way so that I can get into the remotest thickets. When I am tired you will carry me, you will help me leap over brooks, you will climb the trees, and at last we shall sit together, side by side, under the leafy roof, in the heart of that glade. I have been told that in but one minute there one lives a whole lifetime out ... Serge darling, shall we? Tomorrow, shall we set out? To beat our way through the park, bush by bush, till we satisfy desire?'

Smiling, he shrugged his shoulders.

'But why?' he asked her. 'Are we not all right in our garden? Why, far better stay with the flowers than go seek greater happiness in so remote a place.'

'But it is there that the lady who died here was buried,' whispered Albine, and lapsed again into meditation. 'The great happiness of being seated there destroyed her. It is a tree the very shade of which enchants to death. I would love to die like that. We would lie down, in each other's arms and thus pass over into death and nobody would ever find us again.'

'Sh! enough of that,' he interrupted, uneasily. 'You fill me with horror. I want us to live in the sunshine, far from such mortal shade. Your talk worries me, I feel it prompts us on to some irretrievable misfortune. Sitting under trees the shade of which so strangely excites should be condemned.'

'But of course,' Albine declared most gravely, 'it is condemned. Everybody about here tells me it is.'

There was silence between them. Serge rose from the settle on which he had been outstretched, and laughed. He made out that such stories did not entertain him, but the sun was already sinking when at last Albine consented to go into the garden for a few moments. She led him now over to the left, along the enclosing wall, as far as a patch of ruins overgrown with brambles. Here were the ancient foundations of the chateau, still black from the conflagration which had brought the edifice down in ruins. Under the brambles were stones baked and cracked. Collapsed timbers here lay rotting. It was like an outcrop of sterile, fissured, rough piled rock, overgrown with coarse grass and rampant creeping plants, fastening into every crevice like snakes. But they found great delight in wandering over the whole of these ruins, climbing down into holes, poking over the debris, trying to decipher something of the past in the ashes. But they did not give response to any curiosity. They merely ran after one another over the shattered flooring and overturned partitions. Yet their only thought now was of the stories told of these remains, of the lady more beautiful than daylight whose skirts had brushed these steps where today only the lizards idly played.

Finally, Serge mounted the highest pile of ruins and thence surveyed the immense green expanses of the park, trying to spot the grey blotch of the lodge among the trees. Erect at his side, solemn again, Albine was silent, then: 'There's the lodge,' she cried, 'to the right.' She had not needed to ask him his thoughts. 'That is the only building that is left. Can't you see it? It's quite clear, just beyond those lime-trees.'

Again they were silent. As if continuing to translate into sounds the reflections passing through both his mind and hers, she resumed:

'Whenever he went to see her, he must have gone along that path. Then he would turn by the big chestnuts and go deep in, under the limes . . . He did not need quarter of an hour to get to her.' Serge said nothing.

When they set out back, they took that very same path, turning by the big chestnuts, then on under the limes. It was the path of love. One might have thought they were looking for footprints in the grass, or a knot of fallen ribbon, seeking a whiff of ancient scent, at least some sign to show them clearly that they really were on the path which led to the delight of being together. Night was stealing in on them, and the park now spoke with vast, dying voice, calling them back into the depths of its foliage.

'Wait out here,' said Albine, when they had reached the lodge again. 'You stay out three minutes more.'

She scurried away, all laughter, and shut herself in the blue-ceilinged room. Then, when at last Serge had knocked three times on the door, she opened it a discreet inch, then with an old-world curtsey ushered him in.

'*Bonjour*, my dearest lord,' she cried, kissing him.

This game afforded them enormous pleasure, and with all the childishness of the very young, babbling the terrible love which had once known its death throes here, they proceeded thus to play being lovers. They learned it all like a lesson which they mimed through adorably, though ignorant even of how to kiss properly on the lips, seeking each other's cheeks. Finally, they danced as they stood, facing one another, roaring with laughter, utterly ignorant of any other way to give proof of the delight they found in loving one another.

CHAPTER IX

THE following day, Albine wanted to set out as soon as the sun was up, for the great expedition she had been planning since the day before. She danced up and down with delight, assuring him that it would take them the whole day, till darkness.

'But wherever do you mean to take me?' he wanted to know.

'You shall see, you shall see.'

But he seized her by the wrists and peered into her eyes.

'We've got to be sensible, you know. I'm not going to have you looking for that glade or that tree or that grass where people die. You know it is forbidden.'

With a slight blush, she protested that these were things she had never thought of. Then added:

'All the same, if we did happen to stumble on them without looking for them, you don't mean you would not sit down there, do you? Do you then love me so little?'

They set out. Crossing straight through the sunken garden, without halting for the awakening of the flowers, naked in their dew bath. The morning was rose-tinted and had the smile of a lovely infant opening its eyes to the whiteness of its pillow.

'Where are you taking me?' Serge kept asking, and Albine replied with a laugh, but never a word. Then, when they reached the stretch of water which flowed through the far end of the sunken garden, she stared in consternation, for the recent rains had deepened the stream considerably.

'We shall not be able to get across,' she murmured. 'I usually take off my shoes and tuck up my petticoats, but it would come up to our waists today.'

For some moments they followed the bank, looking for a shallow place. But Albine assured him it was pointless. She knew every detail of that water. Once there had been a bridge across. When it broke up it filled the river bed with the stones over which the waters now eddied and foamed.

'Get on my back,' said Serge.

'No, on no account,' she said. 'If you were to slip, what a ducking we should both get ... You don't know how treacherous those stones are.'

'Get on my back, I say.'

That was sufficient to get to try. She took a run and leapt like a boy, so well that she was at once a-straddle on his shoulders. Then, feeling him stagger, she shouted that he was not strong enough, and would get down. But now, twice more, she leapt up again. The game delighted them.

'Well, when you've had enough of that,' the young man cried, at last, laughing himself, 'we'll go. Now hold tight! We'll risk it together!'

With springy steps, he crossed the stream, the water hardly coming over his ankles. Halfway across Albine certainly thought he was going to stumble and she shrieked and snatched at his chin with both hands. But he already had her over, galloping like a horse over the fine sand of the farther bank.

'Gee-up, gee-up!' she cried, now quite at ease, and full of fun about their new game, and he raced about as long as she wished him to, stamping about and imitating the sound of a horse's hoofs. She clicked at him with her tongue, and seized two strands of hair as reins to steer him right or left.

'Now then, now then, we're across,' she cried, giving him little slaps on the cheeks, and leaping to the ground, while he leant against a tree, perspiring heavily, to get back his breath. Then she scolded him, threatened she would not look after him again, if he made himself ill.

'Don't be silly,' he cried, 'that did me good, I tell you. When I really do get my strength back, I'll carry you about the whole morning ... Where are you taking me?'

'Here,' she said, sitting down with him under an enormous pear-tree.

They were now in the former orchard of the park. A hawthorn hedge, a dense wall of greenery with gaps in it, marked the end of the garden on this side. The orchard was a forest of fruit-trees, which had not been pruned at all for a century. Some had grown frightfully lopsided and now flourished horizontal, where storms had laid them, while others, marked with calloused stumps, their trunks hollow, seemed to be borne up solely by the remnants of

154

their bark. High up branches, which every season were weighed down with fruit, held their enormous sprays of fruit far and wide. There were even some which had been so heavily laden that they had snapped, and now half-rested on the ground, but still they bore, so powerful was the spring upsurge of sap. Indeed, the trees served as mutual props, one to another, till they were merely twisted columns supporting a common vaulting of foliage which was shaped into long galleries, here and there suddenly expanding into airy halls, or bending earthwards like the sagging roofing of an ancient house. Round each giant, wild offshoots formed a dense thicket, adding the confusion of their own branches, the fruit of which was of delightful acidity. The greenish light beneath this vaulting was like clear running water and the only sound to break the vast silence of the moss was the soft thud of falling fruit.

There were also patriarchal apricots, bearing their age magnificently, paralysed, some of them, on one side. Whole forests of dead wood reared thus like scaffolding on a cathedral but so vigorously alive in the other half, so young there, that the thick back was bursting all over with tender new shoots. Cloaked in moss, veteran plum-trees still towered in their effort to get at the sunlight, every leaf rich in colour. Cherries formed entire cities of many-floored houses, complete with stairways and lofty flooring of branches big enough to quarter half a score of families. Next there were apple-trees, their backs broken, their limbs rheumaticky, veritable invalids, their scaly hide blotched with a rust of green mould, and fastigiate pears, rearing their masts of fine twigs high, towering trees which seemed to have slipped out of harbour, to rear up their dun lines on the sky-line. There were rubicund peaches, which like pretty girls lost in a crowd, with cheerful laughter and persistent shoving made the mellay round them give way. And there were some trees, formerly espaliers, which had riven in the low walls which supported them and now, free of the trellis-work, the torn off slats of which still dangled from their arms as they grew at their own pleasure, were running amok, the only vestige of their special shape being a suggestion of being wild, rag-costumed carnival creatures which were really still well-brought-up maidens underneath. And from every trunk, every branch, from one tree to another, ran runners of vine. Like crazy laughter they climbed, hooking here, hooking there, on and on to high-up knotting joints, then branching forth again in a fresh scatter of still more sonorous laughter, spattering all the other foliage with the happy intoxication of their succulent shoots, all a gilded tender green shedding the glow of a touch of inebriation over the time-torn polls of the grand old men of the orchard.

To the left came more widely-spaced trees, almonds with slender leaves letting the sun pass on the ground to ripen gourds like fallen moons. Farther, beside a stream which cut through this orchard, there were warty-skinned melons lost among sheets of rampant foliage and varnished ellipsoids of water-melons, as perfect in their form as ostrich eggs. At every step, gooseberry bushes barred former paths, exposing the timid chains of their fruit, each single berry a ruby glowing with a touch of daylight. Hedges of raspberries stretched away like wild brambles. The ground they trod was nought but a carpet of strawberries, and the plants were thick sown with ripe fruit, in the scent of which there was a definite suspicion of vanilla.

The really enchanting corner of this orchard, however, was farther over to the left, against the rising rocks where the hills beyond Paradou began. Here one found oneself on burning soil, in a natural greenhouse, the sun striking the earth at ninety degrees. First, one had to get through past giant gawky fig-trees, their branches extended like greyish arms heavy with slumber and so encumbered by the hairy leather of their leaves that to get through one had to thrust back trunks dessicated with age, till one broke in through the young growth. Then came thickets of arbutus, their foliage like that of giant box-trees, their red fruit like maize ornate with tassels of scarlet silk. Then came a thicket of medlars and jujubes, bordered by the tufty evergreen foliage of grenadines. The fruit of these were hardly set, yet already as large as a baby's fist. The flowers, at the tips of the branches, were purple, and suggested the frail wings of humming-birds, which do not even bend the leaves of grass on which they alight. And at last, in open country, one reached a wood of oranges and lemons growing vigorously. The trunks of these were straight, and together they formed brown colonnades. The leaves set the sharp cheerfulness of their varnished green against the blue of the sky and shot shadows so precisely outlined on the ground that their innumerable out-spread lanceolate blades suggested palms on some fine Indian cotton. This was tree shade of totally different charm, against which that of European trees was dull. It was all warm enjoyment of its veiled light full of flying gold dust. There was in it a certainty of perpetual greenery, a vigour of continual fragrance, the pene-trating odour of its bloom and the more solemn redolence of the fruit, lending the limbs the relaxed suppleness of hot climes.

'And now we shall lunch!' cried Albine, clapping her hands. 'It is at least nine o'clock. I have an enormous appetite!'

She had risen to her feet as she spoke. Serge too admitted that he would certainly have nothing against a bite.

'You big gook,' she said, 'didn't you realise I was taking you out to lunch? And we aren't likely to die of hunger here, are we? Look! It is all ours!'

Thrusting the branches aside, they went under the trees, slipping in to get at the best fruit. Albine, who went first, her skirts tucked between her legs, suddenly turned back and in her flute-like voice asked her companion what he really preferred.

'Pears? Apricots? Cherries? Gooseberries? I warn you, the pears are still greenish. All the same, they are jolly good.'

But Serge chose cherries, and Albine agreed. Yes, they might as well start with cherries. But, just as he was rather foolishly preparing to climb the first cherry-tree he came to, she made him carry on another good ten minutes through a frightful tangle of growth. The first cherry had rotten fruit, no good at all she said. Those of this other were too sharp, those of that would not be ripe for another week. She knew every tree.

'Here!' she said, at last, halting at a tree so laden with fruit that some clusters hung to the ground with what might have been coral necklaces dangling from them. 'Get up into this one.'

Serge settled himself comfortably in the fork of two branches and began his repast. He could no longer hear Albine, and had concluded that she was up some other tree, a few paces away when, glancing down, he saw beneath him, her lying at her ease on her back under the low-drooping branches. She had slithered in under the fruit and was busily eating without even using her hands, just grabbing the fruit with her lips.

When she saw that he had discovered what she was at, she laughed endlessly, rolling about on the grass like a fish dancing on a river bank. Then, lying on her belly and supporting herself on her elbows, she crawled all round the tree, nibbling off the biggest fruit.

'What do you think they're doing to me?' she cried, suddenly. 'They're tickling me! Ouf! There's another, fallen straight down my back. Aren't they wonderfully juicy? I'm full of them, ears and eyes and nose, everywhere. I might even crush one and make myself whiskers . . . These bottom ones are so much sweeter than those high on top.'

'Get away with you,' said Serge, with a laugh. 'It's only because you funk climbing it.'

For a moment, she could not speak, she was so indignant.

'Me? Me?' she stammered, and, drawing up her skirts and fastening them in front to her belt without the least concern about the amount of lovely thighs she was showing, she angrily grabbed hold of the trunk, and with one easy motion swung herself into the tree. She ran nimbly out onto the first branch, without even bothering to take hold anywhere. She darted forward, lissom as a squirrel, swinging round side branches, her feet free. She held on exclusively by balancing from the waist, and when at last she was quite at the top, and out on a very thin branch, which her weight made sway dangerously, she shouted down to him:

'Now what about it? Dare I not climb?'

'Will you come down, at once,' Serge implored. He was quite alarmed. 'Please. You will be hurting yourself.'

But in her triumph she insisted on climbing still higher. Then she clung to the very end of a branch, which she had straddled, and hitched herself out, farther into space, little by little, clutching handfuls of leaves with her hands.

'That branch is going to break,' cried Serge. He was most alarmed.

'And what if it does? A lot that worries me!' she replied, with a huge laugh. 'I shan't have to bother to come down.'

And then the branch did indeed break, though slowly, so long about it that it drooped little by little, as if especially in order to put Albine down gently. She was not in the least alarmed, but rolled over, brandishing her half-naked thighs, and crying: 'It's so lovely, you know, just like riding in a cab.'

Serge had leapt down from his branch to take her as she fell. Seeing him pale from the anxiety he had gone through, she mocked him.

'But, silly, people fall off trees every day. It never hurts . . . Why, laugh, you big ninny! But, I say, do put a little spittle on my neck, will you, I've got a scratch.'

With his lips he moistened his finger and did as she asked.

'There, that's better now, isn't it?' she cried, and gambled off like a young child. 'Shall we play hide-and-seek?'

She hid. She vanished completely. Her cry of 'Cuckoo, cuckoo!' came from the depths of dense greenery which she alone knew, and he could not find her. The game, however, did not pass without a terrible slaughter of the fruit. Wherever these two grown-up children chased after each other, they continued their midday meal. As she slipped between the trees Albine reached out a hand and snatched a green pear or gathered a skirt-full of apricots. There were hiding-places where she had wonderful finds for which she would sit down, forgetting the game altogether, and eat seriously. Then, suddenly, she could no longer hear him, and had to seek him out in turn. It was a surprise, indeed, she was almost annoyed, to find him under a plum-tree, what is more, a plum she did not even know the existence of, but the fruit of which had a wonderful musky scent. She gave him a fine dressing-down. Had he meant to gobble them all, without a word to her? All very well to pretend to be such a ninny! He had a sharp nose! Indeed, he could scent out so good things from a distance, it seemed! She was particularly angry with the plum-tree. It was a sly tree, which she did not even know by sight. It must have sprung up overnight, just to be annoying. She scolded so that Serge refused to touch a single plum, but suddenly gave the tree a sharp shaking. Then the plums just rained, or rather, hailed down. In the thick of the shower, Albine had plums on the arms, plums down the back, even plums on her nose. Then she could not restrain her laughter, but, standing there in the deluge, cried for more and more, full of delight as the fruity bullets bounced off her. She huddled into a ball on the ground to make herself small, and held her open mouth and hands treewards.

It was childhood's morning, with all the tricks of two children set at liberty in Paradou Park. They spent together, lovely childlike truant hours, running, shouting, clapping hands, without their bodies in their innocence ever once feeling the swift quiver of love. It was still only the comradeship of two romping children, to whom later it might perhaps occur to give each other a peck on the cheek, though only when the fruit trees could no longer tempt them with their dessert. But what a happy natural nook for such a first venture, a retreat deep in dense foliage, with many a perfect hiding-place. There were paths on which nobody could ever have been solemn, on either side the very hedges, greedy for gaiety, lavished so many eager laughs. Here in this happy orchard the park possessed a wild frolic of carefree trees and bushes growing as they listed and fresh shade which stirred the appetite, all overlooked by veteran ranks of fine old grandfather trees, all ready to spoil the young ones. Even in the depths of green, mossy retreats, making their way under and over fallen trunks which forced them to clamber one behind the other down such narrow corridors of leaves that Serge would cling laughing to Albine's bare legs, they never found the dangerous reveries of silence. There was nothing whatsoever in that holiday wood to make their minds restive.

And when they were tired of the apricots, the plums and the cherries, they raced away under the gaunt almond trees, munching the green nuts, hardly as big as peas, looking for strawberries in the thick grass carpet, and regretting that the melons were not yet ripe. Finally, Albine set off running as fast as she could, Serge at her heels, unable to catch her. She plunged in among the fig-trees, leaping over big branches, snatching handfuls of leaves, to fling in her companion's face. In a few bounds she was through the strawberry-tree thicket, tasting some of the scarlet fruit as she ran, and then, in the thick coppice of sorbus, azaras and jujubes, Serge lost her. First, he thought she was hiding behind a pomegranate, but found that what he thought were the two pink knots of her fists were two still unfolded buds. Then he beat his way through the orange grove, rapturous at its beauty, picturing it as the entry to the realm of the sun fairies. In the heart of this wood he sighted Albine and she, who had thought him much farther away, darted wildly off, her eyes quickly seeking where to plunge again into the green depths.

'What are you looking for there?' he cried, sharply, 'you know very well you must not look for that!'

She started guiltily, and faintly blushed, the first time that day, then, sitting down beside him, began to talk of the glad days when the oranges ripened. This wood was then all gold, lighted through and through by those bright round stars, yellow eyes piercing the green vault with a myriad holes of light.

And when at last they left to return, she halted at every wild seedling, filling her pockets with tart little pears, tiny acid plums, saying these would do to eat on the way, they were a hundred times better than what they had so far tried, and, notwithstanding the way they twisted his face at every bite, Serge himself had to try them. And thus at last they returned, worn out but happy, having laughed so much that their sides ached. Albine was even so worn out that she could not bring herself to go upstairs to her room. She fell asleep at Serge's feet, lying cross-wise on his bed, dreaming that she was still climbing trees, still munching in her sleep the fruit of the seedlings, which she had hidden at her side under the counterpane.

CHAPTER X

A week later there was another great excursion into the park. The idea this time was to go over to the left, beyond the orchard, on the side where there were large meadows crossed by the four brooks. They would have miles to walk across those meads, and if they got lost, they would catch fish for food.

'I'll take my knife,' said Albine, and showed him a real peasant knife, a heavy-bladed weapon.

She also stuffed a little of everything into her pockets: string, bread, matches, even a small bottle of wine, scraps of clothing, a comb, and needles. Serge was to take a blanket. But when they got past the lime-trees and reached the chateau ruins, this was already such an encumbrance that he left it behind, under the shelter of a fallen wall.

The sun was now fiercer. Albine's preparations had delayed her. For this reason, they were almost sedate today as, side by side, they strode through the hot morning air. They would go as much as a score of paces without once pushing each other for fun. Instead of such play, they talked.

'I never waken in the night,' said Albine. 'I slept wonderfully last night. And you?'

'I too,' said Serge.

'Tell me, what does it mean when you dream of a bird talking to you?'

'I don't know. But what did your bird say to you?'

'I really seem to forget . . . But it certainly talked and said a lot of funny things . . . I say, look at that enormous red poppy over there. You shan't have it, you shan't have it!'

And off she rushed. But, thanks to his long legs, Serge outpaced her and picked the poppy, which he flourished triumphantly. She halted in her tracks, pursing her lips, speechless, on the point tears. All he could think of doing was to throw the flower down. Then, to make peace, he said:

'Are you going to climb on my back? I will carry you, like I did the other day.'

'No, no.'

She sulked. But she had not taken thirty steps farther when she swung round, all laughter again. A bramble had caught her skirt.

'Why!' she cried. 'I thought it was you, treading on my frock, on purpose . . . But look, it won't let me go. Do get it off, please dear Serge!'

And when she was off the thorn, once again they walked side by side, sweetly now. Albine made out that it was more interesting to go for a walk like that, like grown-ups. They had just reached the meadows. As far as the eye could see vast stretches of herbage unfolded before them, broken but rarely here and there, by the rare delicate leafage of a curtain of willows. The reaches of mead were all fluffy, like velvet, and of a vivid green, gradually paling into the far distance. On the very sky-line, under the sun's flaming rays, it melted into strident yellow.

The clusters of willows, all of them at some distance, looked like pure gold in that vast quivering glow. Dancing dust grains stippled the greensward with a fluidity of lighting, while at certain breaths of the zephyrs which played unhindered across this bare loneliness, the herbage took on the shot silk play of light of the shimmering of all the young growth the wind caressed, and all along the nearest meadowland, crowds of tiny white daisies growing in profuse clusters, close-pressed like the crowds on a great public holiday, peopled the dun pastures with their widespread delight. Little golden birds had all the gaiety of tiny polished copper bells which the mere touch of a fly's wing would set a-tinkling. Enormous, lone-standing poppies broke their scarlet dynamite against the green. Farther off they collected in bands to spread out in rejoicing meres, of a colour like the bottom of the viner's vat still purple with his lees, while large cornflowers swayed their light, blue-goffered mob caps and at the merest breath threatened to fly right away over beyond the windmills. Then came carpets of velvet-grass, fragrant antho-xanthum, hirsute bird's trefoil, sheets of fescue, dog's tail, bents and spear-grass. The sainfoin reared its long and slender locks of hair, the clovers outlined their featly leaves, plantains brandished their broad blades, lucerne offered soft bedding, eiderdowns of river-green satin buttonholed with lilac-tinted flowers. Thus ahead, to their left, to their right, everywhere, unfolded over the level land-scape, softening the lines of the mossy surface of a stagnant lake, slumbering under a sky which seemed vaster still. In places, in this immensity of growth, the weeds of limpid blue, as if they had reflected the sky itself.

All this time, Albine and Serge trod on and on, the grasses reaching to their knees. They had the impression of moving forward through fresh waters which lapped round their calves. There were moments when they found themselves countered by real crosscurrents,—the tall stems leaning so intently as they streamed by that Albine and Serge heard the very murmur of the motion past their feet. Then would come somnolent lakes, shallow pools with short-cropped grass, coming no higher than their ankles. As they thus walked on, they played, not, as in the orchard, at crushing the lush growth underfoot, but, on the contrary, at dawdling, their feet as it were entramelled by the supple fingers of the herbage, for in it all they revelled in a purity, a fresh brook-like caress which soothed the childlike brutality within them. Albine suddenly slipped to one side and ran to stand in the midst of a patch of growth so lush that it reached to her chin, only her head rising above it. For some moments she was still there, calling to him.

'But come here, Serge darling, it is like being in a bath, there is green water all round you here.'

Then, with a single bound, without even waiting for him to reach her, she escaped and they went along the first river which barred their road. The water was tranquil and shallow, flowing between wild cress which clung to both banks. Away it flowed, so softly, with slow meanders, so clean, so precise, that like any mirror it reflected every single reed along its banks. Albine and Serge were obliged to walk downstream, for some considerable time, outstripping the slow-moving waters, before they found a tree whose shadows bathed in that stream of idleness. As far as the eye could see on either side there was now only this clear water, flowing over its grassy bed, stretching its pure limbs, falling to sleep in the full sunlight with supple, semi-relaxed sleep, like a blue-hued serpent.

At last they reached a group of three willows, two of which had their feet in the water, the other set a little back from the brook. The trunks were split and backless with age, but the crowns of the trees were graced with all the fair growth of youth. The shade was so clear that its faint outlines scarcely marked the sunlit bank. But here these waters, so unitary in their rise and fall, shuddered an instant, a mere ripple disturbing the translucent skin, witnessing the river's astonishment as it felt that frail gauge drawn so lightly across it. Between the three willows a tongue of the meadow sloped gradually towards the water, here and there planting poppies in the very fissures of the split trunks. It was like a tent of green foliage erected on three poles beside the water in this far-rolling landscape of herbage.

'Here, here, this is the spot!' cried Albine, as she ran in under the willows. Serge sat down beside her, his feet dangling just above

163

the water. Looking about him, he murmured: 'You know it all, you know all the best spots . . . Here, one might be on an island ten feet square in the heart of the ocean.'

'Yes, this is our very own spot,' she agreed, banging the grass with her palms in sheer delight. 'Our own house . . . We can do whatever we like here.' Then, as if a sudden triumphant idea had occurred to her, she lay against him and in a burst of happiness, whispered in his face: 'Would you like to be my husband? And I shall be your wife?'

He found the novel idea enchanting, and laughing more uproariously even than she did, said he would very gladly be the husband. But she was then at once very grave, pretending all the fussy anxiety of the mistress of the house who is a good housekeeper.

'I'm the boss, you know,' she said. 'We can lunch when you lay the table.'

She continued to shower imperious orders on him. He had to lock all that she drew from her pockets away in the hollow trunk of one willow, which she christened the cupboard. The rags were their linen, the comb stood for all toilet articles, the needles and string were to repair their explorers' clothes, while the inner man was to be looked after by the little bottle of wine and a few of yesterday's crusts, though of course one should also not forget the matches which were to cook the fish they were to catch.

When he had completed table preparations, the bottle in the centre and the three crusts round it, he ventured the observation that the feast was going to be a little on the lean side. But with all a woman's superiority she shrugged her shoulders. Her feet already in the water, she said sternly.

'I am just getting the fish. You may watch me.'

For the next half hour, with infinite trouble, she contrived to catch some little fish with her hands. She had tied her skirts high about her waist with a piece of string, and entered the water with every precaution not to cause eddies. Whenever she got quite near a small fish caught between two stones she stretched out her hand and, making a frightful splash, would plunge it in, to bring it out again with a handful of shingle. Serge roared with laughter, which eventually brought her to the bank most put out, to shout at him that he had no right to laugh.

'Besides,' he said at last, 'what were you going to cook your fish on? We've not got any wood!'

That was the last straw, especially as the fish themselves were not so plentiful. She came ashore and, without thinking of pulling on

her stockings again, raced about the meadow to get dry, which
brought back her laughter, because some kinds of grass would
tickle her feet so.

'But look!' she cried, suddenly, dropping to her knees, 'burnet!
Burnet's wonderful! Now we really shall feast.'

Serge now had to grace the table with a dish of burnet, and this
they ate with their bread, Albine insisting that it was better than
hazel-nuts. She acted the mistress of the house, cutting Serge's
bread for him, even refusing to let him have the knife. However
much he protested, she insisted that she was the wife. Then he had
to put the the few drops of wine which were left back into the
cupboard and even sweep the grass, before they could leave the
dining-room and go to the bedroom. Albine got into bed first,
stretching out full length, then saying:

'Now I hope you understand that we really are going to sleep . . .
You have to lie down beside me, and quite close, too.'

He stretched out, exactly as she ordered, and they lay as still as
stones, touching from shoulders to feet, their empty hands behind
them, over their heads. It was their hands principally that embarrassed them now, but their maintained all the gravity of pretend
and stared straight up into the sky, their eyes wide open, telling
each other that they were asleep and very, very comfortable.

'You see,' she said, meditatively, 'you're warm when you are
married . . . Can't you feel how warm I am?'

'Of course, you are like an eiderdown . . . But we ought not to
be talking, because we are asleep. Better not talk.'

They were then silent a long time, all very solemn, turning their
heads away from each other surreptitiously, as if the warmth of
their breath disturbed them. Then Serge suddenly broke the long
silence.

'I do like you very much,' he said.

It was the love which comes before sex, the love instinct which
makes little men of ten keep vigil for little girls in white frocks.
Around them, the widespread meadows tended to alleviate the
slight fear they had of one another. They were conscious of all
those grasses and weeds looking at them and the sky too peering
down through the willow foliage, and they were not worried by it.
The willow tent over their heads was merely a sheet of transparent
cloth, as if Albine had strung up a corner of her frock. The shade
remained so bright that it did not instil them with the same languor
as the dense thickets had done or the demands of those obscure
corners and green alcoves. From the far skyline came the open air,

healthy breezes bringing them all the freshness of this ocean of greenery with its sweet swell of blossom, while the river at their feet was merely another childhood, a frankness the descant of whose fresh voice seemed the distant cry of a friend laughing there. Happy solitude, so saturated with serenity, exposing its nakedness with all the adorable outrageousness of ignorance. The vast field with all the green pastures which were their first bed together assumed all the naivety of the cradle.

'That's enough, now,' said Albine suddenly, and got up. 'We've had our sleep.'

He was a trifle taken aback to find it over so soon. Reaching out, he plucked at her skirt, as if to draw her back to his side. But she merely knelt down, laughing.

'And now what is it? Now what is it?' she demanded.

He could not say. He just stared up at her, and took her elbows in his hands. Then he took her by the hair, but that made her cry out. Then, when she stood up again, he buried his face in the grass, which still bore the warmth of her body.

'There, that's all,' he said, suddenly, and also got up.

Till evening they raced about over the meadows. They ran far ahead, to peer into the distance. They went to their garden. Albine led, with the nose of a young dog, never mentioning it, but always seeking that happy glade, even though here there were none of the big trees of which she dreamed. Serge was all clumsy gallantry, rushing so roughly ahead to brush tall growth aside that he would nearly fall over and when he wanted to help her over brooks, picking her up with his arms so tightly round her waist that he hurt her.

Their great delight was coming upon each of the other three rivers. The first flowed over a pebbly bed, running between two long lines of willows, so that they had to ford it amid all the willow branches, with the risk of stumbling into a deep pocket of water. But Serge went first, and the water only came up to his knees. Then he took Albine in his arms and carried her across so that she should not get wet at all. The next river was dark withthe shade of a file of tall trees, under which languorously and with faint murmur it drew the white folds of the satin skirts of a meditative lady of noble birth deep in the heart of woods. It was a deep belt of water, icy and disturbing, which luckily they were able to cross by a tree which had fallen across it. They rode astride this trunk and delighted to disturb the burnished steel mirror of the waters with their feet. Then they hurried on, terrified by the eyes that stared at them suddenly from even the smallest drop of water breaking away from the drowsy deeps.

But it was principally the last of the three rivers that held them. This was a stream as playful as they were, sedately slow at some bends, then rushing in pearly laughter forward among large rocks, then out of breath and still all a-quiver, becoming tranquil again in the lee of a clump of arbutus. It exhibited all the moods in the whole world, its bed now fine sand, now flat eroded rocks, now clear gravels, now rich loam, from which leaping frogs kicked little slow puffs of yellow smoke. Here Albine and Serge had a wonderful game. Barefoot, they went some distance upstream for the pleasure of paddling down again, preferring that watery way to the meadow-land and lingering at every islet they came upon, going ashore on them and conquering savage lands, and resting amid the tall reeds and sedge which seemed to rear its shipwrecked sailors' huts specially for them.

It was a wonderful journey back, with all the fun that the banks and that dancing smiling water laid out for them to enliven them. But when they had left the river, Serge suddenly realised that all along those river banks and in the islands, even among the plants which drowsed in the flow of the water, Albine had persistently been looking for something. Once he had to go and take her by force from the heart of a patch of water-lilies whose large leaves ringed her legs with the scalloped lace of a noblewoman. He said nothing, merly scolded her with upraised finger. That at last, aglow with the day's delights, they went back, arm in arm, a young married couple, as they pretended, on their way back from a really adventurous outing. They gazed at each other and found each other more handsome and stronger than ever and in their laughter there was undoubtedly a note which that morning had not been there at all.

CHAPTER XI

'AREN'T we ever going on any more excursions?' Serge asked her, some days later. And when he saw her give a rather wearied shrug of her shoulders, he added, as if to tease her: 'Does this mean you have given up looking for that tree of yours?'

This they turned into a joke which lasted all day. There was no tree. It was a nursery tale. Yet it rather gave them the shivers to talk about it. The next day, however, they resolved to make a trip to the far side of the park, where the wood was dense and tall.

That was a region which Serge did not yet know at all. When they set out, in the morning, Albine refused to take anything with her. She was meditative, even a little sad, with her very gentle smile. So they lunched, and did not go down till late. The sun, already hot, made them slack, so they walked very slowly, close together, seeking out patches of shade. Neither the sunken garden nor the orchard, which they had to cross, prompted them to linger. When they reached the coolness of the heavy shade, they walked even more slowly, plunged into the emotion-charged forest retreat with not a word spoken, merely uttering a huge sigh, as if this escaping from the broad daylight afforded them relief. Then, when they could see nothing on all sides but leaves, with not a single gap to reveal the sunlit vistas of the park, they turned to each other, smiling, yet vaguely uneasy.

'Isn't it wonderful here?' murmured Serge.

Albine nodded. Her heart was so full that she could not speak. They had not got their arms round each other's waists, as they usually had, but walked without any physical contact, their arms swinging free, their eyes intent on the ground. Then, seeing tears suddenly trickle down Albine's cheeks and mingle in her smile, Serge halted.

'Whatever is it?' he cried. 'Does something hurt you? Have you knocked yourself?'

'But of course not! I am smiling, I really am,' she assured him. 'I cannot tell why, the mere scent of these trees brings tears to my eyes.' Then, with a glance at him, she added: 'But you are crying too. Then you do know how good it is.'

'Yes,' he murmured, 'the immensity of this shade—it takes one's breath away. One would think one was entering something so astonishingly sweet that it hurt, wouldn't one? But if there is anything worrying you, you should tell me. Have I perhaps upset you somehow, are you angry with me?'

She swore she was not. No, she was very happy.

'Then why are you so sad? Shall we race each other?'

'Oh, no, not that,' she replied, with a grown-up girl's pout of disapproval.

And when he went on to suggest other games—climbing trees after birds' nests, looking for strawberries or violets, at last she lost patience.

'We are too grown-up for all that,' she said, sharply. 'It's silly always to be playing. Don't you like it better just walking side by side quietly with me, like this?'

She was certainly walking beside him so delightfully that the mere click of her little footsteps on the hard-beaten path had been giving him the greatest pleasure in the world. Never before had he actually noticed the graceful sway of her body or the exciting sweep of her skirts, which rustled in her wake like lissom snakes. He felt it was an unexhaustible delight to see the fine dignity with which she walked at his side, with all the new enchantments he kept finding in each soft, easy movement of her limbs.

'You are right,' he cried. 'That is far better than anything else. If you wanted, I would go beside you to the end of the earth.'

And yet, only a few steps farther on, there he was interrogating her, wondering if she were not tired. Next, he suggested he would have nothing against a little rest himself.

'Here's a nice place to sit,' he faltered.

'No,' she said, 'I don't want to sit down.'

'You know,' he said, 'what we might do is lie down together as we did in the meadows the other day. We should be so snug and comfortable.'

'I don't want to,' she said, 'I don't want to.'

And she leapt a pace away from him, suddenly terrified of those male arms reaching out to take hold of her. He said she was a great ninny, and tried to catch her. But when his fingers just caught up with her she cried out so agonisingly, that he halted, and found that he was shaking from head to foot.

'Did I then hurt you?'

She did not answer at once. She was already re-emerging into a smile, and really quite surprised at her own cry.

'No,' she said, 'let me be, don't keep worrying me . . . What is there for us to do if we did sit down? I would rather walk.'

Then, gravely, yet pretending to joke, she said: 'You know very well that I am looking for my tree.'

At this, he too laughed and offered to look with her. He became specially gentle, not to frighten her any more, for he could see that although she had resumed her slow pace at his side, she was still very timorous. What they were going to do there was forbidden, it would bring them bad luck, and he felt himself shaken by the same exquisite fear which was making her tremble at every far-off sigh of the forest. The scent of the trees, the greenish daylight seeping down from their lofty summits, the soft whisper of the undergrowth, all instilled them with anxiety as if round the very next bend of the path they were going to enter an awesome happiness which was to be feared.

For hours, it seemed, they strode on among the trees, maintaining the same tempo and scarcely speaking a word to each other; yet were never a moment apart, following one another through the depths of gaps in the darkest greenery. At first, they made their way through growth where the young trunks were no thicker than an infant's arm. These they had to thrust aside to get through, where the fluttering lace of the foliage brushed against their eyes. At their backs, the path they had made closed in behind them and their tracks were lost.

They went forward blindly, lost, swept this way and that, only the tall tree-tops swaying behind them. Tired of not being able to see three steps ahead, Albine was very glad when she was able to jump free of an enormous thicket, the far edge of which they had been striving for some time to reach. They found themselves in the very centre of a glade from which led a number of narrow paths. All round them were narrow channels between high hedges, twisting, criss-crossing, turning back, strung out most capriciously. They raised themselves up to peer over the hedge-growth. But they were really in no great hurry. They would even gladly have stayed where they were, losing themselves in their continual detours and enjoying the mere pleasure of walking on through this, but never arriving anywhere, had they not sighted ahead of them the proud outline of the really tall timber. These woods they now entered, with religious feeling, touched with holy awe, as when one mounts the steps under the portal of a church. The trunks, straight and white with lichens which stained them with the frail greyness of old stone, rose immensely high in ranks like pillars towering into the empyrean. In the distance, those pillars opened out into naves, with side-aisles which were more encumbered, naves of a wonderful boldness of design, rearing on the slenderest of pillars, the vaulting so lace-like, so richly worked, so sensitively channelled that the blue sky showed all over it. From the giant arches a religious silence came down and there was an austere bareness in the soil below, making it like well-worn stone flags, hardening its surface, without a blade of grass, only dusted with the rusted leaves of yesteryear. And so absorbed were they into the immense remoteness of this temple that their footsteps rang loud in their ears.

Here, surely, was that tree which they had searched so long, the shade of which rendered perfect bliss. They felt its proximity by the enchantment which flowed through them, in the half-light of the immense vaulting. The trees appeared to them as creatures of loving-kindness, powerful and full of silence and happy stillness too. They looked at them one after the other, they loved each one, and from their sovereign calm they expected some vow which should make them grow up as these trees had grown, delighting in vigorous vitality. Maple, ash, hornbeam and dogwood were together a nation of giants, a throng proud in their gentleness, fine stalwarts of peace alone, for the fall of one alone of them would suffice to slay and mutilate a whole corner of the wood. The elms were enormous, their limbs swollen, bursting with sap and scarce hidden at all behind their tiny leaves. Beech and alder, with their maiden-like whiteness, their slender forms bent in lissom abandon to the wind which swept their grand, goddess-like hair and combed out their long locks, as if they were giant goddesses in process of trans-formation into trees.

The planes reared their straight torsos, their satiny red-tattooed skin releasing its large flakes of enamel painting. The larch came streaming down the slope like a troop of young savages, draped in their long waistcoats of woven greenery, all fragrant with their balsam of resin and incense. And the oaks were the kings, huge oaks, square set on paunchy bodies, dominating arms widespread, assuming all the sunlight for themselves, titanic trees, some struck by lightning and recoiling in postures of invincible wrestlers whose wide-apart legs were a forest to themselves.

Was that sound not the muscles of one of those gigantic oaks straining? Or one of the lovely plants, or a white birch woman, or was it an elm? Deeper and deeper went Albine and Serge, losing all sense of space, lost amid this throng. There was a moment when they thought to have found what they sought: they were in the centre of a block of walnuts, where the shade was so chill that they shivered. Then, farther, there came a further thrill, when they entered a small wood of chestnuts, the ground below these green with moss, the bizarre branches widespread, of vast enough expanse to have built hanging villages there. Still farther, Albine discovered a glade, where both of them ran, breathing hard. In the centre of a stretch of very fine grass reared a carob tree, with dense, pell-mell, Tower of Babel branches drooping all ways higgledy-piggledy, over them all, astonishing vegetation. There were even stones caught up in the wood, torn from the ground by the rising flood of the sap. The uppermost branches bent earthwards again, to take root in a farther ring, surrounding the main trunk with enormous arches and a population of new trunks which were also multiplying farther. And on the bark, split with many a bleeding cut, the carob beans

171

were ripening. The very fruit of this monster was a concentration of force, for it ravaged the skin. Slowly they went round this tree, penetrating under the widespread arms, where the streets of a town intersected, and stared at the gaping gaps where the roots came bare of the soil. Then, failing to find the superhuman happiness they sought, they went on farther.

'But wherever are we now?' Serge suddenly asked.

Albine could not tell him. She had never been on this side of the park. They were at the moment in a thicket of laburnum and acacia, the racemes of which exuded a scent which was very sweet, almost sugary.

'I think we're lost,' she murmured, and laughed. 'I certainly don't recognize these trees.'

'But surely,' he argued, 'the park has an end somewhere? I thought you knew every corner of Paradou?'

She spread her arms wide, in sweet assurance that she had never claimed that. 'Oh, no,' she said.

Silent wonder took possession of them, for hitherto they had never known so glorious a sense of the vastness of the park. It was ravishing to be thus alone in the heart of so large a realm of their own that even they were obliged to give up trying to know it all.

'Well, then, we're lost,' Serge laughed. 'It's better still, now we don't know where we are going.' He went up close to her. As if timidly, he murmured: 'Not afraid, are you?'

'Of course not,' she replied. 'There's only you and me in the garden ... Of whom should I be afraid? The outside walls are too high. We can't see them, but they protect us, you know.'

Close pressed to her, he whispered: 'But a little while back, you were afraid of me.'

Nevertheless, with absolute serenity she faced him, and not an eyelid flickered.

'You were hurting me, that's all,' she said. 'Now you seem very nice again. Why should I be afraid of you?'

'Then let me take you in my arms. Like this. We shall go back under the trees.'

'Very well. Hug me tight, I like it. And we will walk ever so slowly, won't we? We don't want to find our way back too quickly.'

He had enlaced her waist with his arm, and thus they made their way back under the tallest trees, where the majesty of their vaulted roof made this walk of grown-up children awakening in unison to love, slower still. She told him suddenly that she was a little tired and rested her head on his arm. But neither one nor the other now mentioned even the idea of sitting down. It did not even occur to them. It would have interrupted their dream. What enjoyment could resting on the greensward give them in comparison with that vivid pleasure of thus walking side by side? The legendary tree was forgotten, and their only thought was to bring their faces closer, to smile more closely into each other's eyes. And it was the trees, the maples and the hornbeams, which by their transparent shadows whispered to them their first words of sentimental love.

'I love you!' cried Serge, his voice zephyr-like, faintly stirring the stray golden hairs about Albine's temples. He would have liked to discover other words, but he could only repeat:

'I love you, I love you.'

Albine heard his murmur with radiant smile and learned the melody of it.

'I love you, I love you,' she herself sighed, even more deliciously, in her pearl-like girlhood's voice. Then, raising her blue eyes, in which a dawn of light was growing more intense, she asked: 'In what way do you love me?'

Serge was at once pensive. There was a grave gentleness in that impenetrable wood. The immense nave of that cathedral shuddered with the young couple's muted steps.

'More than all else,' he replied, at last. 'You are lovelier than anything I see mornings when I open my window, and when I see you, I want nothing else. With only you in life, I should be happy.'

She lowered her lashes. Her head swayed from side to side as if she were being cradled.

'I just love you,' he went on. 'I do not know you, I do not know who you are, or where you come from. You are not my mother or my sister, and I love you, till you can have all my heart, and I keep nothing for anybody else. Listen! I love your cheeks, silky as satin! I love your lips, with the perfume of roses! I love your eyes, in which I see all myself and my love. I love even your eyelashes, even these little threads of blue vein at your temples . . . And that, Albine, means that I love you, I love you!'

'Yes, and I love you,' she said again. 'You have soft hair on your lips and cheeks which never hurts me when I rest my forehead on your throat. You are strong, you are big, you are handsome. I love you, Serge.'

For a time they were silent in their rapture. It seemed to them that before them went the song of a flute and their own words came from a mellifluous orchestra which they never could see. They took the tiniest steps possible now, in and out among the huge trees,

173

leaning one against the other. In the far distance, away down the colonnade, rays of the setting sun slanted through, like a procession of young maidens in white gowns entering a church for affiancement, while the organ murmured softly.

'And why do you love me?' Albine asked again.

He smiled and did not reply at first, then said:

'I love you because you came to me. That tells everything . . . Now we are together and love each other. I think I should cease to live if I did not love you. You are my breath.'

He lowered his voice, speaking now out of a dream.

'Of such things one does not know all at once. They grow with one's heart. One needs to grow up, one needs to have strength. Remember how we used to love each other, yet never spoke of it. When one is a child, one is silly. Then, one glorious day, it becomes too plain, and it slips out from one . . . But no matter, we have nought else to do, we love each other because it is our life to love each other.'

Her head thrown back, her eyes firmly closed, Albine held her breath, as she revelled in the silence which ensued, still warm from those words' caress.

'Do you love me? Do you love me?' her lips fluttered quickly, her eyes still closed.

But he was now silent, terribly unhappy to have nothing more he could say to show her that he loved her. His glance moved slowly over her rose-tinted countenance. It was all yielding, as if she slept. Her eyelids had the delicacy of living silk, her lips curled into the lovely, moist curves of a smile. Her forehead was purity itself, circled with a zone of gold at the edge of her hair. And he longed to give her his whole being in one single word which was on the tip of his tongue, yet would elude him. At last, he bent his head lower, as if seeking on which precious corner of this countenance he should lay that word of all words. Yet in the end he still said nothing, did not even breathe, merely lay his lips on hers, and kissed her.

'Albine, I love you, dearest one!'

'I love you, Serge darling.'

And here, they halted, all a-quiver from this first kiss. She had opened her eyes wide. He was still poised, his lips slightly thrust forward. Thus, without any blush, they both watched each other. Something most powerful, a sovereign force, had entered their being. It was like a long-awaited meeting, in which they saw themselves grown up, made one for another, for ever bound together. For a while they were astonished, raising their eyes towards the religious vaulting of the tree-tops, as if to enquire of this tree people and recover the echo of their kiss. But, confronted with the serene acquiescence of the dense wood, they experienced the joyousness of lovers unpunished, a joyousness which was lasting, sonorous, full of the eloquent blossoming of their affection.

'Oh,' she cried, 'do tell me about all the days you have loved me! Tell me everything . . . Did you love me when you slept on my hand? Did you love me, when I fell out of the cherry-tree, and you were down below, so pale, holding out your arms? Did you love me, out in the meads, when you took me by the waist to get me over the brooks?'

'Sh! Let me speak! I have always loved you . . . But you, did you then love me, did you?'

Till night, they lived on that word love which came back to their lips without end, ever with new sweetness. They sought it, they brought it into every sentence, they spoke it when it had nothing to do with what they were talking about, but for the mere pleasure of saying it. Serge had no intention of laying a second kiss on Albine's lips. Their ignorance had enough merely with the perfume of the first kiss. They had now found their road home, without for a moment having worried about it. As they emerged from the forest, dusk had fallen, the moon was rising yellow amid the dark hues of green. And what a wonderful walk back that was, through the heart of the park, accompanied by that orb of discretion which peeped at them through gaps in the trees! Albine maintained that the moon was following them. From afar, the deep forest whispered softly, and Serge, hearing it, said to himself: 'They are talking about us.'

When they crossed the sunken garden, they walked through a fragrance of astounding sweetness, that fragrance which flowers possess at night, a more caressing fragrance than that of day, such fragrance that it might be the very breath of their slumber.

'Good night, Serge dearest.'

'Good night, Albine.'

Without going into the room, they had taken each other's hands on the landing, where they were accustomed to saying good-night to each other. They did not kiss.

When he was alone, seated on the edge of his bed, Serge Mouret listened long to Albine going to bed in the room above his head. He was worn out by the bliss which then brought sleep to his own limbs.

175

CHAPTER XII

DURING the next few days, however, Albine and Serge felt a constant sense of mutual embarrassment. They avoided any mention of that excursion in the wood. They did not exchange a single kiss, nor did they once tell each other again of their love. Yet it was not shame that prevented them speaking. It was apprehension. They were afraid of spoiling their happiness. When they were apart, it was by that lovely memory that they lived. They immersed themselves in it, reliving those lovely instants with their arms about each other's waists, brushing their cheeks against each other's breath. In the end the fever of it quite took possession of them. They would stare at each other, hollow-eyed and melancholic, and talk of things which did not interest them at all. It was only after long bouts of silence that at last Serge anxiously asked Albine if she was not well. But she shook her head.

'Of course I am all right,' she said, 'it's you who's poorly. Your hands are quite hot.'

Paradou now instilled in them a dull unrest which they could not fathom. At every bend of a path lurked some menace, ready to leap at their throats, bring them to the ground, hurt them. But though every now and then timorous glances admitted that mutual anxiety which made them both so strange, as if they were enemies, they never mentioned such things. Till at last, one morning, after much hesitation, Albine decided to speak.

'You ought not to be so much indoors,' she said, 'you'll be getting ill again.'

Serge gave a troubled laugh.

'Nonsense,' he murmured. 'Besides, we've been everywhere, we know the whole garden now.'

She shook her head. 'Oh no,' she said in a low voice. 'We don't know the rocks, and we've never been to the springs. That is where in winter I go to get warm. There are spots where the stones seem alive.'

The following day, without another word said on the matter, they set out. They climbed up to the left, beyond that cave where the marble woman slept. As they set foot on the lower rocks, Serge said: 'Yes. I think this did rather leave us with a worry, for we ought to see everything. Perhaps we shall feel better after we have been to the springs.'

It was a close, sultry, stormy day. They did not venture to walk with arms enlaced about each other, but walked in Indian file under scorching sun, Albine taking advantage of a spot where the path widened to let him go on in front. The touch of his breath when he walked beside her made her uneasy, and it disturbed her equally profoundly to feel him just behind her back, so near her skirts.

On either side here the rocks were piled high in broad layers. Easy slopes led from one broad ledge to another, the ledges covered with coarse herbage. First they came on golden broom, patches of thyme, patches of sage, patches of lavender, all manner of aromatic plants, together with pungent juniper and bitter rosemary, so powerfully scented that it all went to their heads. On either side of the path here and there the luxuriant hops made hedges like fine metal work, oxidised copper fences, wrought iron, polished copper, complicated ornamentation, florid with spiny arching. Next, to reach the springs, they had to pass through a pine wood. The thin shade weighed like lead on their backs. Underfoot, the sere pine needles crackled, with faint resinous dust which dried their lips.

'There's no gainsaying it, this part of your garden is not easy going,' said Serge, turning to Albine.

At last, they smiled at each other. They had reached the rock springs and the limpid waters of the pools were a relief to them. These were not hidden under green vegetation, like springs in the plains, which gather thick, bosky growth about them, to slumber idly in their shade. These gushed from the rock face in full blaze of sunlight, without a blade of grass to veil their blue waters. Drenched with dazzling light, the waters were silver jets. The sunlight played on the sand at the bottom of their pool, a wafted dust of vivid light. From the first pool the water drained by channels of absolute purity, lightly playing with all the happy nakedness of a child, then leapt out into the waterfall, the gentle curve of which was a woman's fair body bending back.

'Dip in your hands,' cried Albine. 'The water in this pool is like ice.'

It was a good idea to re-freshen themselves. They splashed water on their faces and stayed some time, bathed in the constant fine spray breathing out from the streaming waters. Even the sunlight was moistened by it.

'Oh! do look back!' was Albine's next cry. 'There is our garden, there are the meads, there is the forest!'

For some time they gazed down at Paradou Park, which now lay at their feet.

'See,' she said, 'there's not a bit of the outer wall in sight, the whole world is ours, to the very edge of the sky.'

They had at last, without noticing it, enlaced their arms about each other. They were suddenly at their ease, mutually trusting again. The water of this spring had cooled their fever. Yet, as they moved away, Albine seemed to yield to a memory, and she brought him back, saying suddenly: 'And yet, right over there,—look under the rocks,—I did once get a glimpse of the wall. Long ago.'

'There's certainly nothing to be seen now,' murmured Serge, turning rather pale.

'But I assure you . . . it ought to be immediately behind the chestnut avenue, beyond this undergrowth.'

Then, suddenly aware that Serge's arm was holding her tighter, she hastily said: 'Perhaps I am mistaken . . . All the same, I do recall suddenly finding it right in front of me, when I came out of the ride. It barred my road. It was so high that it frightened me . . . A few paces away from that spot, I had a real surprise. The wall was broken down. There was a great gap in it, through which you could see the country beyond.'

Serge shot her an uneasy, begging glance, but to reassure him, she shrugged her shoulders.

'Ah, but I sealed up the hole, you see,' she said. 'Don't fear, I tell you, we are quite alone . . . I sealed it up at once. I had my knife. I cut brambles and I rolled big stones up. I defy a sparrow to get through. If you like, one of these days, we will go and see. That will set your mind at rest.'

He shook his head. They went their way again, arms round each other's waists, but they were now troubled once more. Serge glanced down sideways at Albine's face. She blinked nervously, sensitive at being thus watched. Both of them would have liked to retrace their steps and avoid the ill ease of any further excursion. Then, against their wills, as if they yielded to some force which drove them on, they rounded a rock and reached level ground, where the renewed intoxication of full sunlight awaited them. But here it was no longer merely the joyous drouth of sweet-scented plants, with musky breath of thyme and incense of lavender. They trod growth which stank: wormwood with bitter headiness, rue, with foetid smell of human flesh, acrid valerian, saturated in aphrodisiacal exudations. Mandrake, hemlock, setter-wort and belladonna sent up clouds of dizziness to their temples, made them feel faint, so that as they bore each other up, they staggered, and their hearts were on their lips.

'Shall I carry you?' he asked her, as he felt her yield herself to him, and before she could answer, he crushed her to him in full embrace. Breathless, she freed herself.

'No, don't, you suffocate me,' she said. 'Let me be . . . I do know why I feel so strange. The ground is swaying under my feet . . . Serge, this is where I feel funny.'

She took one of his hands and lay it on her bosom. He turned white as a sheet and was suddenly weaker than she was. Seeing each other in this state, they both had tears in their eyes, yet could not guess what remedy there might be for their great disorder. Were they going to die suddenly here, of an unknown ill?

'Come into the shade, here, and sit down,' said Serge. 'It is these plants killing us, with their powerful scent.'

He led her by the finger-tips, for she shook all over merely at the touch of his hand on hers. The green-leaved nook in which she sat down was formed by a lovely cedar, and the flat roofing of its branches spread more than thirty feet. Behind them also grew strange pungent conifers, cypresses with leaves soft and flat as thick lace, silver firs, erect and solemn, like ancient dolmens, still stained with the blood of sacrifice, yews, their sombre garments fringed with silver, and many another plant of tenacious foliage, standing all the winter through, trees squat of growth, their leaves dark as of varnished leather, bespattered yellow and red, so tough that the sun slithered off them and was powerless to make them flaccid. A monkey-puzzle was the strangest thing of all, with its huge angular limbs. It was like a building constructed of rigid reptiles morticed one into the other, the imbricated leaves erect like the scales of the angry creatures. Here, in this heavy shade, the heat was voluptuous with drowsiness. The very air slept, breathless and mouldy as a closed room. There arose an oriental odour, the redolence of the lovely lips of the Shunammite perfumed that timber.

'Are you not going to sit down?' she murmured, and made a little more room for him. But he recoiled and remained standing. But, invited again, he slipped to his knees, but still some paces from her.

'No,' he said, 'I am more feverish than you, I should scorch you . . . Albine, were I not afraid of hurting you, I would take you in my arms, so powerfully, that we should cease for ever to feel our discomfort.'

Dragging himself on his knees, he drew nearer to her.

'Oh, to have you in my arms, in my flesh . . . That is my only thought. At night, I waken, clutching emptiness to myself, clutching

179

a dream of you. I would like first to take you but by the tip of your little finger. Then I would gradually have all of you till there was nothing left of you and you had all become mine, from your feet to the last hair of your lashes, and I should keep you for ever. It must be a wonderful gift, thus possessing the one whom one loves. My heart would melt away into yours.'

He drew still closer, till had he reached out his hand, he would have touched the hem of her skirt.

'But, why I cannot tell, I feel far away from you . . . There is a sort of wall between us that my fists could never break down. Yet I am strong today, I could bind you fast in my arms and fling you over my shoulder and carry you away as if you were a mere thing belonging to me. And yet be frustrated, for I should still not possess you sufficiently. When my hands take you, they hold a mere nothing of your being . . . Tell me where the whole being of you is concealed, so I may go and seek it out.'

He had bent forward till he rested on his elbows, in a posture of abysmal adoration. He imposed a kiss on the hem of her skirt. Then, as if she had taken this kiss on her naked skin, she sat bolt upright and clapped her hands to her temples, aghast and stammering:

'No, I beg you, let us go on with our walk.'

Yet she made no attempt to escape. She let Serge follow her, slowly, desperately, feet stumbling against roots, her head still between her hands, to stifle the clamour rising within her. And when they emerged from the little wood, they took a few steps up the ledges of rock, where an ardent race of luscious herbage grew, a riot, nameless creatures glimpsed in nightmare, a stampede of monsters holding spiders, caterpillars, wood lice, all amazingly enlarged, some with glaucous, bare skin, others set with obscene down. Behind them they dragged infirm limbs, abortions of legs, stumps of arms. Some were swollen like immodest pregnancies, the spine of others was lumpy with multiple humpinesses, yet others were loose-knit, ramshackle, loose-jointed skeletons. Like a profusion of greenish turtles, monstrously bearded with long spines harder than steel points, the nipple-cacti were a mass of live pustules. There were echinocacti, revealing more skin, but just like nests of young vipers knotted together. The globe-thistles were but a single brush, an excrescence with red bristles, giant insects rolled into balls. Like trees, the opuntias raised their fleshy leaves, spattered with reddened needles. They were like swarms of microscopic bees, threadbare pouches of vermin. The gasterias held out their feet, looking like large grasshoppers on their backs, their limbs blackish, spotted, striped, damascened. There were cereus with their shameful vegetation, huge polyparies, sickly from this over-heated soil, mere debauch of poisoned sap. But it was above all the aloes, crowds of which displayed their lavish, love-swooning hearts, and all the shades of green, soft, violent, yellowish, greyish, brownish, rust-spattered and edged with pale gold. They were of all possible shapes, the large leaves heart-shaped, the narrow ones like sword-blades, some lace-worked with prickles, others finely hem-stitched. There were huge specimens bearing their flowers separately on tall stems and with pale coral collars hanging from them, others whose flowers grew in little bunches on stalks, fleshy growth darting the swift snakes' tongues to all sides.

'Let us go back to the shade,' Serge implored her, 'and you sit down as you sat just now and I will kneel and talk to you.'

At this point there was a downpour of sunlight, huge drops of it. In triumph the great orb took the naked earth and pressed it to its scorching bosom. Faint with the heat, Albine stumbled. She turned to Serge.

'Take me,' she whispered, in a dying voice.

The moment their flesh touched, they fell to the ground, lips to lips, without a cry. There seemed no end to their fall, as if the rock gave way infinitely beneath them. Madly now their hands sought knowledge of each other, of features, of throat and beyond, of all their clothing. It was, however, a sudden nearness so tense with anxiety that almost at once they got to their feet again, their nerves on edge, yet unable to go further in the satisfaction of their desires. And then, each by a different path, they fled. Serge did not stop till he reached the lodge, where he flung himself face down on his bed, his head afire, his heart despairing. Albine did not come back till night. She had shed all her tears in a corner of the garden. This was the first time that they had not come back together, wearied by the delight of their long walks. For three days now they sulked and were terribly unhappy.

CHAPTER XIII

Now, nevertheless, the park was entirely theirs. They had taken possession of it, sovereign possession. Not a corner of that realm but belonged to them. For them the sunken garden maintained that mingled languorous fragrance which came in by their open windows at night and lulled them to sleep. The orchard fed them, filling Albine's skirts with fruits, it afforded them refreshment by the musky shade of its foliage, under which it was so good to break their fast after the sun was up, and in the meads there were all the grasses, and the waters. The grasses enlarged their kingdom, ceaselessly unrolling before them their carpets of shot silk, while with their immense purity, their immense innocence, the rippling of that coolness in which they delighted in bathing their youth, the waters were the greatest of their joys. They also possessed the forest, from the vast oaks which ten men together hand to hand could not have encompassed, to the slender birch sapling which a child could have snapped off without effort, they possessed the forest with all its trees and shade and avenues and glades, its green nooks which even the birds did not know, the forest which they disposed of as they thought fit, as of a giant tent in which at midday they could always find shelter for the tenderness born in the morning. They reigned everywhere, even over the rocks, the springs, and the terrible soil, with its monstrous plant growth, this soil which had quivered with emotion under the weight of their bodies and was dearer to them than the other soft beds of the garden, loved for the strange emotion they had tasted there. Thus, now, they were masters of all that lay before them and all that lay on either side, they had mastered their domain, they walked amid a nature which knew them, nature their friend, which as they passed gave them with a smile, offered itself to their pleasures, was their submissive servant. They also found delight in the sky, in that vast expanse of blue stretched above their heads. This the park walls could not enclose, yet the sky too belonged to their vision and became part of the happiness of their life, day with its triumphant sun, night with its warm rain of stars, making them rapturous at any minute of the day, offering all the shades of light of living flesh, at break of day whiter far than any maiden rising from her bed, gilded at midday, yearning for fruitfulness, and at evening sinking back to rest in the contented weariness born of the pleasures of love. Never did it twice reveal the same countenance. Every evening it made them marvel above all at its farewell hour. As the sun slipped close to the horizon it always found a new smile. Occasionally it even left them, amid serene peace, without a cloud, gradually engulfed in a bath of gold. At other times, it broke into rays of purple, and tore its robe of mists aside, to escape in waves of flame which barred the heavens with the tails of giant comets whose streaming locks set fire to the summits of the high-grown woods. Then, on banks of red sand and red coral came the final eclipse of the great orb, glorious,

182

when one by one it blew out its rays, discreet, behind a vast cloud, draped as by an alcove curtain in grey silk, only the red glow of its night-lamp to be seen in the depths of the increasing shadow, or perhaps a sunset of passionate love, flaming disc of biting fire which finally rolled below the horizon, a chaos of twisted limbs sinking from sight in glowing ruin.

Only the vegetation had not admitted their allegiance, but among all the creatures which owed them allegiance and obedience Albine and Serge walked like monarchs. When they walked through the garden, flights of butterflies rose to delight their eyes, fanned them with beating wings, followed them like a vital orgasm of the sun, as if the very flowers took flight, and shed their fragrance in their wake. In the orchard they found the greedy birds in the tree-tops, sparrows and finches, orioles and bullfinches, showing which fruits were ripest, scarring them with their beaks, with the din of school-children at playtime, a turbulent frolic of robbery, brazen flocks of them coming to filch the cherries at their feet, while straddled in the trees they dined. Albine found pleasure too in the meadows, picking up the little golden-eyed green freshers which climbed into the bull-rushes, with all the gentleness of contemplative creatures. And Serge would take a straw and get the crickets out of their holes, tickling the abdomens of the cigales to make them sing, gathering other insects, blue and pink and yellow, to set them walking up his sleeves like buttons of sapphire, ruby and topaz. There was also the mysterious life of the rivers, fish with dun backs slipping through the rippling water, eels to be guessed at by faint agitation of water grasses, small fry scattering at the slightest sound like puffs of blackish smoke, flies mounted on large pattens sweeping in vast silvery curves over the motionless surface, all that soundless swarming of life which made them cling to the banks, often giving them the longing to stand bare-legged in very midstream, just to feel those millions of minute lives slipping past them.

Other days, days of soft languorousness, it would be under the forest trees, in the sonorous shade, that they would repair, to hear their musicians serenade them, the nightingales with crystal flutes, blue tits with their tiny silver horns, and the cuckoos making their distant accompaniment. The swift flight of the pheasants, tails like rays of sunshine among the branches of the trees, made them marvel and they would pause smiling to let a happy troop of young goats, or a couple of solemn deer, slow down as they trotted by, to stare at them.

Yet other days, when the sky was burning, they climbed the rocks and took pleasure in the clouds of grasshoppers which, crackling like a brazier caught by a sudden gust of wind, their feet sent flying from the stretches of thyme. The snakes stretched out on the edge of red-burnt bushes, the lizards lying full length on the hot white rocks, followed them with friendly eye, and, dipping their webbed feet in the spring water, the pink flamingoes stood still as they approached and by their trusting calm reassured the water-hens which drowsed in the centre of the pool.

It was only since that day when they first felt their own vital pulse in a kiss, that Serge and Albine had thus felt the life of the park in its growth all round them. Now at moments it left them dazed, for it would speak a tongue they did not comprehend, addressing suggestions to them to which they did not know how to yield. It was this life, all these voices and this living animal warmth, all these scents and colours of the multitudinous forms of the park *flora* which disturbed them, to the point of making them impotent one with another. But, despite this, the park was to them only a numerous and loving family. Every blade of grass, every little creature, became their intimate. Paradou Park was one great caress. Before their advent, for more than a century, only the sun had reigned here, unrestricted master, adding its splendour to every branch. In those days this was all the garden knew. It saw the sun in the morning leap the enclosing wall with its slanting rays, neatly seat itself at midday on the fainting earth, and when evening came leave at the other side with a farewell kiss that gently lay on all the foliage. Thus the garden had lost its shame and accepted Albine and Serge, just as long since it had accepted the sun, seeing in them good children of whom it need never be shy. Animals, trees, waters and stones remained gloriously free, their voices unmuted, their bodies unclothed, having no secrets, exposing all the innocent boldness and lovely tenderness of the very creation of the world. This corner of nature laughed discreetly at the fears which Albine and Serge felt and this made it kinder still, unfolding under their feet the softest of greensward, drawing the bushes close together to make narrow paths for them. If it still did not throw them fully into each other's arms, that was because it took pleasure revealing their desires, delighting in their clumsy kisses, which in the bosky shadows would ring out like the cry of angry birds. But they suffering as they did from the immense voluptuousness which enveloped them, they would curse the garden. That afternoon when Albine cried so much, after their walk over the rocks, suddenly feeling Paradou so vital and so ardent about her, her words were: 'If you are our friend, why do you make us so unhappy?'

CHAPTER XIV

THE next day, Serge began to shut himself away in his room. The fragrance of the garden had overcome him. He drew the calico curtains so as not even to be able to see the park and to prevent it entering the room. Perhaps far from all that verdure, the mere shade of which made his skin quiver with life, he would be able to recover childhood's peace of mind. Now, in long hours shut away together, Albine and he never mentioned rocks or waters, trees or sky. Paradou was non-existent. They strove to forget it. Yet all the time they felt it there, beyond those flimsy curtains, vast, immensely powerful. The redolence of the grasses crept in through every crack in the woodwork. The window-panes were vibrant with drawn-out voices. All that outdoor life lurking under the windows kept up its laughter and its whisper. The colour would leave their cheeks, they would raise their voices, seeking some distraction which might permit them not to hear.

'You had never noticed it?' said Serge, one morning, in one such moment of disturbance. 'Over the door, a painting of a woman? Why, it's just like you.' He laughed, rather noisily.

They went to look at it close-to. Once again they pulled the table up to the wall and climbed up.

'Oh, no!' murmured Albine. 'She is much fatter than I am! Besides, it's hard to make her out, but with her head thrown back like that she's lying in such a funny position!'

With that, they were silent. From the faded, time-worn painting emerged a scene they had neither of them hitherto noticed. Delicate forms of flesh floated up again from the grey of the wall, life returning to a representation of the details till it seemed that it would show even its intimate details, one after the other, in the summer heat. The prostrate woman lay back in the embrace of a faun which had the legs of a he-goat. The arms flung back over the head and the lavish rotundities of this grown-up naked maiden's sprawling body could clearly be made out. She had been taken, by surprise, on sheaves of flowers cut by little cupids which, sickle in hand, were still adding fresh armfuls of roses to her simple couch. It was also possible to make out something of the efforts of the faun tumbling down on the girl. He was quite out-of-breath. But beyond this one could distinguish no more than the woman's two feet. They were flying up into the air like a couple of pink pigeons.

'Oh no!' said Albine, again. 'She's not like me at all . . . She is ugly,' she added, with sudden vehemence.

Serge said nothing, but looked, first at the woman, then at Albine, as if insisting on comparing them. Albine drew one of her sleeves back to the shoulder, to show how much whiter her skin was. Then silence again fell between them. They turned back to the painting, and to their lips came questions that they preferred not to admit to themselves. For a moment, however, Albine's large blue eyes did rest on Serge's, and he saw a fierce flame flare up in them.

'Have you re-painted the whole room?' she cried suddenly, leaping down from the table. 'One would have said that all this old world was coming back to life.'

They laughed at this thought, but their laughter was uneasy, and they kept glancing at the cupids and their rogueries and the extensive nudity which exhibited nearly ever part of some of them. They wanted to look at all this scene again and again, to dare it. Every panel astonished them. They called on one another, pointing out human limbs which had certainly not been there a month earlier, supple loins supported on eager arms, legs naked to the hips, women come back to life in the embrace of men whose outstretched hands before had clutched only at space. Even the plaster cupids in the alcove seemed to somersault more brazenly than they had previously done. And Albine now stopped talking as if these were merely children at their play, nor did Serge try any more to suggest what was there depicted. They both became very solemn, yet they still lingered at those pictures, secretly wishing the paintings could recover all their pristine brilliance at once. The imprecision which still partly masked the coarse events of these paintings made them both quite languid with uneasiness. It was these ghosts of dalliance completing their education in the science of love.

Albine, however, at last took fright. Suddenly feeling Serge's breath on her neck grow fiercer, she slipped lithely from him, and sat down by herself, at the far end of the settee, murmuring: 'In the end I think they frighten me. The men are like gangsters, and the women have the dying eyes of somebody being killed.'

Serge went to an armchair which stood several paces away from her, and spoke of something else. They were both of them suddenly very wearied, as if they had been for a very long walk. What was more, the thought that those pictures were looking at them made them uneasy.

Bands of cupids were tumbling out of the panelling, where was depicted a confusion of amorous bodies, with a crowd of impudent

186

little boys tossing flowers over them, and threatening to tie the couples together with the blue ribbons with which in one corner of the ceiling they had already roped one pair of lovers. The couples were all vivacity in their depiction of the same story as that of the big wench without a stitch of clothing on her being loved by a faun. At this they could guess from the faun's lair behind a rose thicket and other clues, including the abandon of the girl herself on her rose-petal bed. Were they all going suddenly to leap down out of the ceiling? Was that perhaps they already heaving meaningful sighs, they whose breath now charged the room with the effluvium of the ancient rites of love?

'It's frightfully stuffy in here,' murmured Albine. 'For all the airing I've given it, this room always reeks of age.'

'The other night,' said Serge, 'I was awakened by so powerful a fragrance that I called your name, thinking you had come into the room. I could have sworn it was the warm breath of your hair when you stick heliotrope flowers in it ... When I was first here, it seemed to come from afar off, like the memory of a perfume, but now it keeps me awake, so strong it nearly stifles me. Especially at night, the alcove is so hot that in the end I shall sleep on that settee.'

Albine lay her finger on her lips and whispered: 'It is the beautiful lady who died, you know, she lived here.'

They started sniffing about the alcove, as a joke, but at bottom in all seriousness. It was true, the alcove had never exhaled so disturbing a smell as now. The walls seemed still vibrant from the touch of musk-scented petticoats. The parquet had still the balm-like sweetness of a pair of satin mules slipped off at the bedside. And on the bed itself, against the head-board, Serge made out he found the imprint of a dainty hand which had left behind it a persistent scent of violets. Now from every object in the room rose the scented ghost of the woman who died.

'But look, that must be her favourite armchair!' cried Albine. 'You can smell her shoulders on the back of it.'

And, sitting there herself, she commanded Serge to drop to his knees and kiss her hand.

'Don't you remember the day when I received you here with the words: *Bonjour, my dear Lord?* But that was not enough, surely, for when the door had closed again, he surely kissed her hands ... Here are mine. They are yours to kiss.'

They tried now to return to their former light-hearted games, to forget Paradou, for they could hear its broad laughter wax louder, also no longer to see the pictures and yield to the languorous alcove air. With many a grimace, Albine rocked with laughter at the ridiculous sight Serge made at her feet.

'You big ninny, put your arms round my waist, and say pretty things to me, since now you are reputed my lover . . . Do you mean to say you don't know how to love me?'

But the moment he had taken her in his arms and raised her impulsively from the floor, she was all struggle, and slipped out of his grasp, quite angry, indeed.

'No, let me be, I won't . . . This is a room people die in!'

From that day, they became afraid of the room, just as they feared the garden. Their final refuge became an awesome spot where they could foregather together without keeping a furtive eye on one another. Albine hardly ever went in. She would remain on the threshold, the large door open at her back, as if to keep open a rapid line of flight. Serge lived alone there, miserably anxious, finding it even more stuffy than before. He slept now on the settee, trying to escape the sighs of the park and the emanations of the old furniture. At night, the nakedness of the paintings gave him mad dreams, and when he wakened his nerves were all on edge. He thought himself ill again. If it was to be completely restored, his health had still some final need. There was need for a supreme fullness, for an all-absorbing satisfaction which he had no notion where to find. The result was that he passed whole days in silence, his eyes heavy, only waking with a slight trembling of his body when Albine came to see him. They would remain facing one another, eyeing each other gravely, exchanging rare words of tenderness, which merely exacerbated their nerves still more. Albine's eyes had darker rings even than Serge's. Now, they constantly begged something of him.

Then, after a week, Albine would not stay with him more than a few minutes. She seemed to avoid him. She would come in, looking worried, stand and talk a bit, then hurry away again. When he asked her what this meant and reproached her with no longer being his dear friend, she turned her head away, not to have to answer him. Nor would she ever tell him what she did with the mornings she spent far from him. She would shake her head as if he embarrassed her and make some remark about her own laziness. If he insisted, with one bound she would dart away, merely calling back to him a formal good-night from the doorway. But often he could clearly see that she had been crying. On her countenance he could trace the sequence of hope eternally deceived, the endless rebellion of desire fiercely bent on satisfaction, but ever cheated of it. There were days when she was deadly miserable, discouragement written all over her. She dragged herself slowly about as if she would never even try again to be light-hearted. On other days, she would give restrained laughs, her features lighting up with some triumphant thought of which she was still loth to speak, and fidget about, unable to keep still, anxious as soon as ever possible to run to meet some final certainty. But the following day, she would be sunk back again into her misery, and only on the morning after would her hopes show again. But what it soon became impossible to hide was her tremendous weariness, a fatigue which broke her limbs. Even when she was hopeful she would wilt, and with eyes wide open she seemed to slip into a trance.

Serge finally stopped questioning her, for he grasped that she did not want to answer him. Now whenever she came in, he looked at her anxiously. He was beginning to fear that soon the evening would come when she had not even the strength to come to see him. Wherever could she tire herself so? What constant struggle made her so miserable, yet so happy? One morning, the sound of light footsteps immediately under his window made him tremble. It could never be a squirrel so bold. Too well he knew that rhythmic step which never harmed a blade of grass. It was Albine he could hear scampering about in the park, without him. That meant that it was from Paradou that she brought her falling spirits and anxious hopes, all that stress and exhaustion which were wearing her down. And he had a very shrewd idea, too, what she was seeking all alone there, deep in the greenery, without a word to him, and with all the mute stubbornness of a woman who has sworn she will find the thing she wants.

From that night he specially listened for her steps. He dared not raise the curtain, to follow her in the distance among the trees and shrubs, but he did experience a strange emotion, almost sorrowful, at the knowledge that she had gone over precisely either this way, or that, or merely into the garden, and how much of the park she had covered in her search. Amid the noisy life of the park, with the murmur of the trees, the rippling of the waters, the never-ending song of the wild creatures, he could now distinguish the tiny tap of her footsteps so clearly that he could have told whether she was treading the gravel of river bottoms, the crumbling forest soil, or the naked rocks. He even learned to tell from the nervous tapping of her heels when she came back whether she was happy or sad. The moment she began to mount the steps of the porch, he left the window. He never once let her know that he had followed her like that everywhere she went. But she must have guessed, for ever since his first discovery of this she had reported her search with a mere glance.

'Stay in now, don't go out any more,' he pleaded, clasping his hands, one morning when he saw her still exhausted from the previous evening's search. 'You worry me so.'

She hurried away in great indignation, and for him there now began suffering when that garden rang with her footsteps. The tip-tap of her shoes was one more voice calling to him, a dominant voice the echo of which grew ever more clamorous within him. He sealed his ears, tried not to hear, but the distant steps still echoed in his heart. Then, one evening, when she returned, the whole park flooded in at her heels, calling to mind their walks together and the gradual awakening of their caresses in the heart of conniving Nature. She seemed bigger, more solemn, as if matured by those lonely chasings of hers. There was now no trace left in her of the joyous child, the change so complete that at moments, looking at her, his teeth chattered, to see her so desirable.

It was one day, towards noon, that Serge suddenly heard Albine come racing back. He had forbidden himself by now to notice when she went out. As a rule, she did not return till late. And he was astounded now at the way she seemed to be bounding along, seeming to run so straight towards the house, crashing down what branches barred her path. Then there she was under the windows, all laughter. She raced up the steps, panting so fiercely that he seemed to feel her hot breath on his cheeks. Flinging the door wide open, she cried:

'I have found it!' And she sat down, repeating softly, in choking voice: 'I have found it, I have found it!'

But he lay his hand on her lips. Aghast, he stammered:

'Please, please, don't tell me anything about it. I don't want to know. If you tell me, it would kill me.'

At that, she was silent, but her eyes burned and she had to pinch her lips bloodless for the words not to gush out despite her. And she remained there with him till evening, trying to catch his eyes, and as soon as she succeeded, entrusting to him a little of what she knew. Her features seemed illuminated. She smelt so good, she rang so clearly with life, that he breathed her into his lungs and she entered his being as much by hearing as seeing. Though he fought desperately against that slow mastery of his being, all his senses drank her in.

The following day, as soon as she was up, she installed herself in the same way in his room.

190

'You are not going out?' he asked, feeling that if she stayed there, he was conquered.

No, she said, she was not, she would go out no more. The more she relaxed, the stronger and more triumphant he felt her. Soon she could have taken him by her little finger and led him to that grassy bed, on the sweetness of which her silence was so eloquent. That day, she said not another word, contenting herself with drawing him to her feet, where he sat on a cushion. It was only the day after this, that she went on to say:

'Why do you shut yourself up in here? It is so lovely under the trees!'

He stood up and held out his arms, imploring her. But she laughed.

'But of course we won't go, if you don't want to ... But this room has such a funny smell. We should be better in the garden, more comfortable, more sheltered. You are wrong to be against the garden.'

He had stood up again. He was silent, his eyes closed, and little shivers ran over his face.

'We won't go,' she said again. 'Do not be angry. But don't you really prefer the herbage of the park to these paintings? Remember all that we have seen together ... It is these paintings that make us sad. They are irksome, always staring down on us.'

And as he relaxed gradually against her, she slipped an arm round his neck and lay her head back on his knees, murmuring again, ever so softly: 'That's where we should really be comfortable, in a corner I know. There, nothing would worry us. The open air would cure your feverishness.'

She stopped, for she felt his shudder, and was afraid lest too brusque a word should bring his terror back. Bit by bit she won him over, merely by caressing his face with the blue light of her eyes. He was looking at her now and was at peace, his nervous reaction over, all hers.

'Oh, if only you knew!' she breathed softly, in his ear.

Seeing that now the smile did not leave his lips, she gained courage.

'It is a lie, it is not prohibited,' she murmured. 'You are a man, you should not fear ... If we went there, and any danger threatened, you would defend me, would you not? You would be able to pick me up and carry me away? I assure you, I am never afraid when I am with you ... See what strong arms you have. Does one fear anything, when one has arms as strong as yours?'

With one hand she stroked his hair, his neck, his shoulders, for a long time.

'No, there is no prohibition,' she resumed. 'All that yarn is for silly people. Those who set it going long ago just did not want anyone to come and disturb them in the most delicious corner of the garden . . . Tell yourself that the moment you were seated on that grassy carpet you would be perfectly happy. Only then shall we know everything and be the real masters . . . Listen to me, come with me.'

With a shake of the head, he refused, but without anger, rather as if the game entertained him. Then, after a silence, very put out to see her sulking, and wanting her to caress him again, at last he opened his lips to ask:

'Where is it?'

She did not reply at once. Her eyes seemed fixed on the far distance.

'Over there,' she murmured, at last. 'I cannot tell you. We have to follow the long walk, then turn left, and left again. We must have passed it by a score of times . . . No, no it would be vain for you to look for it, you would not find it, unless I led you there. I can go straight there, though I could not really tell you exactly how.'

'And who showed you?'

'I do not know . . That particular morning, the plants seemed to urge me that way. The long branches whipped me from behind, the grasses contrived paths, the rides opened of themselves. I rather think the animals too had a part in it, for I saw a stag galloping in front of me as if to invite me to follow him, while a flight of bullfinches flitted from tree to tree and warned me with chirping when I was tempted to take the wrong road.'

'And is it very lovely?'

Again, she did not reply. Her eyes swam with supreme ecstasy. And when she could speak, she said:

'So lovely that I could never tell you . . . I was permeated with such enchantment that I was merely aware of nameless delight falling from the foliage, slumbering in the grass. And I came running back, to take you with me, not to enjoy that happiness of sitting in that shade without you.'

Again she lay her arms about his neck, quite close, begging him ardently, her lips almost on his.

'Yes, you will come,' she stammered. 'Think that if you did not, my life would be blighted . . . I have within me a longing, a far-off need, which has grown with every day, and now causes me real suffering. You surely cannot want me to suffer? And even if you had to die of it, even were this shade to destroy us both, would you then hesitate, would you have the least regret? We should stay there, reposing together, at the foot of the tree, we should sleep for ever, pressed to each other, and that would be so good, would it not?'

'Yes, yes,' he stammered, won over by the fervour of that quivering heat of desire.

'But we shall not die,' she continued, raising her voice, and laughing the victorious laugh of a woman. 'We shall live to love each other ... That tree is the tree of life, a tree under which we shall be stronger, healthier, more perfect. You will see, everything will become more natural. You will be able to take me as you dreamt of doing, so closely that not one inch of my body but will be absorbed into yours. After that, I think something heavenly will come down and enter us ... Will you come?'

The colour left him, his eyes shrank back, as if some dazzling light worried him.

'Yes? Yes?' she repeated, more ardently than ever. She had already half risen to her feet.

He stood up, he followed her, uncertain on his feet at first, then linked to her waist, unable to be separate from her, and he went where she went, drawn into the warm air flowing from her hair. And since he was just a little behind her, she half turned back, her countenance gleaming with love, her lips and her eyes full of temptation, calling him on, with such dominance that he would have gone anywhere with her, her mere faithful dog.

CHAPTER XV

THEY went out and straight to the centre of the garden. A smile now played unbrokenly on Serge's lips. He saw the greenery only as mirrored in Albine's limpid eyes. From the garden, as they emerged from the house, there arose a drawn-out laugh, a contented murmur flitting from leaf to leaf all the way down the deep avenues. For all this time, the garden must have been awaiting them to come thus, arms enlaced about each other, at reconciliation with the trees, on greensward bed again to find their lost love. A grave hush spread under the branches. At two in the afternoon the hot skies were heavy with slumber. Flowers reared their heads to watch the couple pass.

'Can you hear them?' asked Albine, in low tones. 'They become silent when we draw near, but while they await us afar off they whisper one to another which path they should show us . . . Did I not tell you we should not have to worry about the way? It is the trees, with their outstretched arms, which show me where to go.'

It was true, the whole park urged them gently on. Behind them it seemed as if a barricade of thick growth reared its thorns to prevent them from drawing back, while before them was unrolled a carpet of soft grass so smoothly that they did not even glance down at their feet, merely followed the easy, down-sloping lay of the ground.

'The birds too are accompanying us,' Albine continued. 'Today it is the tits. See them? Flitting along the hedges, stopping at every bend, to make sure we do not get lost? Oh, if only we understood their song, we should know that they were calling on us to hurry.'

Then she said:

'All the creatures of the park are with us. Can't you feel them? That great rustle which follows us, that is the birds in the trees, the insects in the grasses, the squirrels and the deer in the under-growth, even the fishes' rhythmic fins stirring the voiceless waters . . . Don't turn round, that would alarm them, but I am sure we have a wonderful procession behind us.'

All this time, with tireless step, they pressed forward. Albine spoke merely to enchant Serge by the music of her voice. He was obedient to the slightest pressure of her hand. In their certitude of going straight to the place they desired, they paid no heed, either of them, to where they were going. And as they advanced the garden became more discreet, restraining the sighing of its fields of shadow, the chatter of its waters, the burning life of its creatures, and there was everywhere nothing but profound, quivering silence, religious expectation.

Then, instinctively, Albine and Serge raised their heads. Facing them was a collossal mass of verdure. And as they hesitated, a squirrel who had been watching them with his lovely, gentle eyes, with one leap plunged into the thick undergrowth.

'It is here,' said Albine.

It was a tree in the centre drowned in such dense shade that one could not make out the nature of it. It was a tree of immense height, with a trunk breathing like a thorax, and branches wide-stretched like protecting arms. In appearance it was sound, robust, powerful, fertile. It was the doyen of the garden, the father of the forest, the pride of all the herbage, the friend of the sun which every day rose and set in a flood of light cast over its summit. From its green vaulting, all the delight of creation descended, the scents of flowers, the song of birds, the raindrops of light, dawn's fresh awakenings, the drowsy warmth of twilights. Its sap was of such energy that it oozed and trickled down the bark, bathing it in a drenching of fecundity, making it the very virility of the soil. From it derived all the magic of this glade. The other trees, round it, formed an impenetrable wall which isolated it deep in a tabernacle of silent half-light. There was but one continuous mass of verdure, without a chink of heaven, or glimpse of horizon, solely this rotunda, every inch of which was draped with the loving silk of the leaves, the floor below covered with the satin velvet of the mosses. Entering it was like plunging into the crystal water of a spring, a world of greenish clarity, sheet of silver lulled beneath the reflections of the reeds. Colours, scents, all vibrant sound and quivers of delight preserved a vagueness, a transparency, an anonymity, rapturous with a delight in which all consciousness faded away. The languor of an alcove, the dream of summer nights dying on the naked shoulder of a loving mistress, a scarce distinct murmur of love suddenly sinking to the tremor when all words disappear, all clung to the immobility of those branches, which not a breath stirred. A nuptial retreat, where all were laced in loving coupling, an empty room in which behind the drawn curtains of a bed, one sensed Nature, in the arms of the sun, satiate in fiery union. At moments the loins of the tree creaked and its limbs stiffened like those of a woman in childbed, and the sweat of life which drained from its bark then poured down more copiously on the greensward all round, breathing out the languor of love's desire, soaking the air with its yielding, till the glade turned pale at sight of such enjoyment. And then the tree with its shade, its grassy carpet, its belt of dense undergrowth, was nothing but the weakness and the sweetness of sex.

Albine and Serge were enraptured. The moment that tree gathered them in to the gentleness of its branches, they felt themselves healed of the unbearable tension which had agonised them. No longer did they feel that fear which had put them to flight, those heated, desperate struggles by which they tortured each other, without knowing what enemy it was they resisted so wildly. On the contrary, they knew absolute trust, a supreme serenity poured into them, and they yielded themselves one to another, slowly sliding down into the joy of being together, far off, deep in a miraculously hidden retreat. No longer puzzled about what the garden wanted of them, they gave it full liberty to do what it would with their love,

195

and then, their minds at ease, they left it to the tree to whisper to them what they should do. And the tree brought them to such blindness of passion that, regally immense though it was, the glade vanished completely and they were borne up on nothing but the sweet fragrance of life itself. And then, with faint sigh, caught by that musky freshness, they paused.

'The air itself tastes like a fruit,' Albine murmured.

And Serge spoke, very softly: 'The grass is so living that I feel as if I were walking on the hem of your gown.'

In a feeling which was religious, they lowered their voices. They were not even curious to look up and see the tree. They were too conscious of its majesty upon their shoulders. With a glance, Albine asked if she had exaggerated the enchantment of her glade. Serge replied with two limpid tears, which trickled down his cheeks. Their delight in being there at last remained inexpressible.

'Come,' she whispered in his ear, her voice lighter than mere breath.

She walked ahead across the grass and lay down at the foot of the tree. A smile on her lips, she offered him her hands, while, standing there, and taking them, he smiled back at her. Feeling the grip of his hands, she drew him slowly down to her, and he lay beside her, taking her at once closely to him, and the embrace filled them with immense relief.

Serge Mouret heaved a sigh of relief.

'Remember,' he said, 'that wall which seemed to separate us . . . Now I feel you and there is no longer anything stands between us . . . You are really contented now?'

'I am all right,' she replied. 'It is all so very good.'

They preserved silence, still holding one another. A delicious sensation, gentle and shockless as a lake of milk, invaded them. He passed his hands over her whole body.

'Your face is mine, your eyes, your lips, your cheeks . . . Your arms are mine, your knees are mine, every part of you is mine.'

He kissed her cheeks, her eyes, her lips, then, with little fluttering kisses, her arms, from fingers to shoulders. He kissed her feet and her knees, bathing them with a rain of kisses, which fell in large warm drops like a summer shower, then watered every part of her, her throat, her breasts, her thighs, her loins. With utter calm, little by little, he took possession of her, conquering the most minute filigree of veins under the rose-tinted skin.

'I take you, in order to give you myself,' he said again. 'I want to render my whole self up to you, for ever. For in this moment I know so well that you are my sovereign mistress, the mistress to be worshipped kneeling. I am here but to obey you, to lie at your feet, observant of your wishes, my arms held out to protect you, to ward off the breath of any flying leaf which might disturb your peace . . . Oh, grant me permission to disappear, to absorb myself into your being, so I become the water you drink and the bread you eat. You are my be-all and end-all. Ever since I awakened in this garden I have progressed towards you, have grown up for you. Always, as aim and reward, I saw your grace. You and your hair of gold passed through the sunlight and were a promise telling me that the day would come when you would make me know the necessity of this creation of ours, this earth, these trees, these waters, this sky, you will tell me the supreme word for which still eludes me . . . I belong to you, I am your slave, I shall listen to you, my lips on your feet.'

All this he said bent to the ground, adoring the woman, and Albine was proud and let him adore her, offering her fingers, her breasts, her lips, for his devoted kisses. When she saw this man, so strong, so humbly low before her, she felt herself queen. She had conquered him, she held him at her mercy, by a mere word she could do what she would with him. And what made her all-powerful was that all about them she could hear the garden rejoicing in her triumph, aiding her with a chorus of voices now subtly raised in delight.

Now, Serge could only stammer, and his kisses fell but at random, yet still he murmured:

'Oh, how I want to know . . . I would like to take you and keep you, dying perhaps, or flying away with you, I cannot say where . . .'

They both lay prostrate, silent, breathless now, their heads spinning. Albine had strength enough to raise one finger, to invite Serge to listen.

It was the garden that willed this sin of theirs. For weeks it had lent itself to the gradual training of their ability to love each other. Then, on this last day, it had brought them to the green alcove. Now it was the tempter, its every voice instructive of love. From the sunken garden came the scent of swooning flowers and a long whisper which told of the marriage of the roses and the satisfaction of the violets, and never before had the invitation of the heliotropes been of more sensuous ardour. From the orchard came puffs of the odour of ripe fruit, brought by the wind, a rich scent of fertility, the vanilla of apricots, the musk of oranges. The meads raised a deeper voice made of the sighing of millions of grasses kissed by the sun, the vast cry of countless creatures on heat, assuaged by the fresh caress of the rivers, the nakedness of running waters, beside which the willows dreamed at the summit of desire. The forest breathed the giant lust of the oaks, the diapasons of the tall massed trees, a solemn music, bringing the marriage of the ash trees, the birch, the hornbeam, the plane, deep in leafy sanctuaries, while the undergrowth and young copses were all lovely roguery, a glorious confusion of lovers pursuing each other, flinging themselves down on the edge of ditches, stealing their pleasures amid the tremendous shudder of the tree-tops. And in this coitus of the whole park the most rustic of embraces could be heard afar-off, on the rocks, where the heat made the love-swollen stone fend and spiny plants knew their tragic love, without the nearby springs being able to alleviate them, themselves being set on fire by the great orb, pouring down into their bed.

'What are they saying?' Serge murmured, in utter astonishment. 'What do they want of us, to supplicate us so?'

Without a word, Albine drew him tighter to herself.

The voices had become more distinct. The animals of the garden in their turn cried out to them to love each other. The cigales sang of the tenderness of which one dies. The butterflies distributed kisses by the beating of their wings. The sparrows exhibited the swiftest of play, caresses of Sultans hastening through their seraglios. In the clear waters was the swooning of the fishes as they deposited their fry in the sun, the ardent melancholy of the cry of the frogs, in their occult lust shockingly accomplished in the glaucous dimness of the reeds. Deep in the woods, the nightingales scattered pearly laughter of bodily love, the stags bellowed, intoxicated with such lust that they lay dying, exhausted by does which they had almost eviscerated. And on the steps of the rocky cliff, beside the sparse bushes, were the snakes, knotted, two by two, hissing sweetly, while large lizards, their spines a-quiver, and their throats croaking faintly with the delight of it, laid their eggs. From the remotest corners of the patches of sunlight and from the shady nooks rose an animal odour, warm with universal heat. All that swarming life shuddered with the shudder of childbirth. Under every blade of grass, some insect conceived, in every tuft of grass a new family grew, flies flew by on heavy wings glued one to another, unable to wait for solid ground for their fecundation. Even the particles of invisible life peopling all matter, even the very atoms themselves, loved and coupled, lending the sun its voluptuous quiver, turning the park into one immense fornication.

Then, Albine and Serge understood. Without a word, he enlaced

198

her with his arms, ever more closely. The fatality of generation surrounded them. They yielded to the demands of the garden. It was the tree that whispered in Albine's ear what mothers whisper to daughters on the marriage night.

Albine now yielded to him, and Serge possessed her.

And the whole garden was engulfed together with the couple in one last cry of love's passion. The tree-trunks bent as under a powerful wind. The blades of grass emitted sobs of intoxication. The flowers, fainting, lips half-open, breathed out their souls. The sky itself, aflame with the setting of the great star, held its clouds motionless, faint with love, whence superhuman rapture fell. And it was the victory of all wild creatures, all plants and all things natural, which willed the entry of these two children into the eternity of life. And the park applauded with formidable sound.

CHAPTER XVI

WHEN Albine and Serge awakened from the stupor of their bliss, they looked at each other and smiled. They were returning from a land of light. They were coming to earth again from immense heights. Then they pressed each other's hands, in gratitude. They were aware of each other and they said:

'I love you, Albine.'

'Serge, I love you.'

And never had the word love had so sovereign a meaning for them. It stood for everything, it explained everything. For a time which they could not measure, they stayed there in delicious rest, still clasping each other close. They were experiencing an absolute perfection of their being. The delight of creation bathed them, making them equal to the mother forces of the world, and making them the very strength of the earth. In their happiness in addition there was the certainty of a law accomplished, the calm of the goal logically reached, step by step.

Taking her again in his strong arms, Serge said: 'See, I am cured, you have given me all your health.'

And, yielding herself up to him, Albine replied: 'Take me entirely, take my life.'

They were filled with life till their lips over-ran. In the possession of Albine, Serge had at last discovered his masculine sex, the courage of his heart, the final health which his long-drawn-out adolescence had lacked. Now he felt complete. His senses were sharper, his understanding broader. It was as if he had suddenly awakened as a lion, lord of the plains, the open sky his realm. When he stood up, his feet were set firmly on the ground and his body drew to its uttermost height, proud of all its parts. He took Albine's hands and lifted her too to her feet. She swayed a little, and he had to support her.

'Do not fear,' he said, 'it is you whom I love.'

Now, she was his servant. She lay her head back on his shoulder and looked at him with an air of uneasy gratefulness. Would he never be angry with her for having brought him there? Would he not some day reproach her for this moment of adoration in which he called himself her slave?

'You are not angry?' she asked, humbly.

He smiled, plaiting her hair again, soothing her with his finger-tips as if she were a child.

She continued: 'Ah, you will see, I shall be so retiring. You will not even know I am there. But you will let me lie in your arms like this, won't you, for I need you to teach me how to walk . . . it seems to me now that I no longer know how to walk.'

Then she was suddenly very grave.

'You must love me always, and I shall be obedient, I shall work for your delight, I shall give up everything to you, even my most secret will.'

At sight of her so abject and caressing, Serge felt as if his strength grew to double. He asked her: 'Why are you shaking so? Whatever should I reproach you with?'

She did not reply. Almost sadly, she looked at the tree, the walls of green, the grass they had crushed.

'You child,' he went on, with a laugh. "You don't say you are afraid I should resent the gift you have made me? Nonsense, that cannot be a sin. We just loved as we should do. I would like to kiss the imprint your feet made when you brought me here, as I kiss your lips which tempted me and as I kiss the breasts which have just completed the cure begun, have you forgotten, by your tiny, fresh hands.'

She nodded. Then, turning her eyes aside, avoiding further sight of the tree, in a low voice she said: 'Take me away.'

Serge slowly led her away. He gave one last, all-embracing look at the tree, thanking it. In the glade, the shade grew denser. The shudder of a woman surprised on her bed fell from the green leaves. When, emerging from the greenery, they saw the sun and its splendours still filling a sector of the skyline, they felt relieved, particularly Serge, who in every creature and every plant now found new sense. Everything about him bowed down, everything rendered homage to their love. The garden was now no more than an appendage of Albine's loveliness, and it seemed to have grown larger and more beautiful in the kiss of its master and mistress. Yet Albine's happiness remained restless. She broke off her laugh again to listen, and sudden shivers shook her body.

'But whatever is the matter?' Serge asked.

'Nothing,' she replied, casting furtive glances behind her.

They had no idea in what lost corner of the park they now were. Generally they were delighted when they did not know where their whim had led them, but this time they experienced a peculiar uneasiness and embarrassment. Gradually, they hastened their steps, plunging deeper and deeper into a maze of shrubbery.

'Did you not hear that?' said Albine, timorously, and halted, out of breath suddenly.

And while he listened, caught up in turn by the anxiety which she could no longer conceal, she continued: 'The thickets are all voices. As if there were people, mocking us. There, was not that a laugh, came from that tree? And back there, when my skirts brushed them by, did not those grasses mutter something?'

'Of course not,' he said, anxious to reassure her, 'the garden loves us. If it did speak, that would not be to frighten us. Have you forgotten all those lovely words which the leaves whispered to us ... Your nerves are on edge, you are imagining things.'

But, with a nod, she murmured: 'I know the garden is our friend ... That means that somebody else has got into the garden. I assure you, I did hear somebody. I am shaking so. Oh, please take me away and hide me.'

They went on walking, peering at the bushes all round them, thinking to see faces behind every tree-trunk. Albine swore that there were far-off footsteps tracking them down.

'Let us hide, let us hide,' she kept begging him.

She had flushed pink. Shame was being born in her, shame taking possession of her like an illness, soiling the frank purity of her skin, hitherto never soiled by blushes. He would have taken her in his arms again and soothed her with a caress, but she drew away from him and with desperate gesture indicated to him that they were no longer alone. Blushing still more, she glanced down at her frock. It was unhooked, revealing her nakedness, arms, throat, bosom. The free-flowing locks of her hair were a shudder on her shoulders. She tried to re-knot her hair over her head, then was afraid to reveal her bosom so. Now the mere touch of a tree-branch, the fragile collision of an insect's wing, the slightest breath of wind, made her tremble as if at the improper touch of an unseen hand.

'Do stop worrying so,' said Serge. 'There is nobody . . . Why, you are as scarlet as if you had a fever. Let us rest a moment. Do!'

She had no fever, but she wanted to go back to the house at once, so nobody should laugh, if they saw her. And she hurried, faster and faster, she gathered leaves from the shrubs to hide her nakedness. Over her hair she bound a branch of mulberry, round her arms she bound convulvulus, fastening it to her wrists, and about her throat she strung a necklace of wild clematis stems plucked long enough to conceal her breasts by the leafy veil.

'Are you going to a fancy-dress ball?' he asked her, thinking to make her laugh.

But she threw foliage she had just picked at him and in frightened tones, in a low voice, said: 'Can't you see that we are naked?'

Then he too felt shame and bound foliage over his unfastened clothes. But still they saw no way out of the thickets. And suddenly, at the end of a path, they found themselves up against an obstacle. It was a tall, grim grey mass. It was the outer wall.

'Come, come,' cried Albine.

She would have drawn him away, but they had not gone twenty paces, when there was the wall again. After that they ran along the length of it, for panic took possession of them. It was a wall of unbroken gloom, not a cranny to reveal what lay beyond. Then, at the edge of a meadow, it suddenly seemed to break away, and there was a breach, a window of light giving on to the neighbouring valley. This must be the gap of which Albine had spoken one day, the gap she said she had blocked up with brambles and loose stones. But now the brambles trailed wide to either side like severed ropes and the stones had flung far back, as if the gap had been enlarged by infuriated hands.

CHAPTER XVII

ALBINE uttered a terrible cry.

'Ah! I knew it, I begged you to take me away . . . Serge, for Heaven's sake, don't look!'

But despite his will something held him to the gap. Down below, at the far edge of the plain, the setting sun was lighting the village of Artaud with a sheet of gold. It was like a vision rising from the dusk in which the surrounding fields were already drowned. The hovels loosely built along the road could clearly be seen and their little yards with the masses of manure, the narrow, vegetable-planted gardens. Higher up, the big cypress of the churchyard reared its sombre outline. And the red tiles of the church were like a furnace. Above them the black outline of the clock-tower reared what might have been a loosely sketched head, while beside it stood the old vicarage, doors and windows open to the evening air.

'For pity's sake,' Albine repeated, with sobs, 'do not look! . . . Have you forgotten that you promised to love me always? Oh, can you ever love me enough, now? Look, let me seal your eyes with my hands. You know so well that these are the hands that cured you . . . You cannot now reject me.'

Slowly, he thrust her away. Then, while she laced her arms about his knees, he wiped his face with his open hands, as if to take from forehead and eyes the last vestiges of a sleep. So this then was that unknown world, that strange world on which he had never pondered lately without a dull fear. But where had he seen this countryside before? From what dream was he wakening now, with pain so biting rising from his bowels and swelling in his breast till he was choking?

The village was coming to life, as the men and women returned from the fields. The men carried their coats thrown over their shoulders and their gait was that of worried men. The women, on the threshold of the houses, seemed to be calling to them, while the bands of children were chasing the poultry with stones. Two young rascals, a boy and a girl, had just slipped into the churchyard and, not to be seen, were creeping on all fours along under the wall. Flights of sparrows gathered under tiles of the church. On the threshold of the vicarage appeared a blue print petticoat so vast that it filled the whole door embrasure.

'Oh, misery!' gasped Albine, 'he is looking, he is looking! Will you listen! Just now, you promised to obey me. I implore you, turn back and look at the garden . . . Were you not happy in the garden? It is the garden gave you to me. And what happy days it reserves for us, what long-lasting felicity, now that we know all the happiness of the shade! Instead of death coming in by that gap, if you escape, if you do not carry me back. Look, it is the others, it is all the world which will come between us. We were so alone, so lost, so well guarded by the trees . . . The garden is our love. Look at the garden, I on my knees beg you.'

But Serge was shaken by a great tremor, for his memory was returning. The past was coming back to him. Far-off, he clearly

203

heard the life of the village. Those peasants, those women, those children—why, that was Mayor Bambousse, on his way back from his Olivette field, where he had been counting the coming grape harvest. Those were the Brichets, the man dragging his feet, the woman groaning in her poverty. And there behind the wall was Rosalie, letting grown-up Fortuné embrace her. He also recognized the two scamps in the churchyard, that good-for-nothing Vincent and that brazen hussy Catherine, catching the big flying grasshoppers among the tombs. They even had Voriau with them, Voriau the black dog, who was helping, sniffling in the sear herbage and at every crack in the old flags. Under the church eaves the sparrows were fighting before sleep, the bolder among them flying down again and fluttering through broken squares of window into the church. And as he followed all this with his eyes he recalled the lovely din those sparrows made under the pulpit and on the altar steps, where there were always crumbs for them. And on the vicarage threshold, Teuse in her blue cotton gown seemed to have grown fatter than ever. She was turning round, smiling at Désirée, who had just come all laughter from her farmyard with a whole flock of animals. Then both women disappeared. At that point, aghast, Serge held out his hands.

'No use, it is too late,' murmured Albine, and she slumped down on the torn brambles. 'You will never love me enough.'

She sobbed, while he listened, ardently, striving to catch the slightest distant sounds, waiting for a sound which might complete his awakening. There came the faint tinkle of the church bell, and slowly, through the drowsy evening air, the strokes of the *Angelus* floated all the way to Paradou Park, a silvery breath, very soft, very regular call. Now the bell seemed a living thing.

'Dear God!' cried Serge Mouret, falling to his knees, when the zephyr breath of the bell overbowled him.

He lay prostrate, and felt the three strokes of the bell, passing over his shoulders, re-echo in his inner heart. The bell sounded louder now and came back, implacable, for minutes which seemed years to him, calling up all his past life, his godfearing childhood, his happy seminary years, his first masses in the scorched valley of the Artaud folk where he had dreamt of the seclusion of the saints. It had always spoken to him thus and he recognized the slightest inflexion of that voice of the church rising ceaselessly to his ears, like the grave, sweet voice of a mother. Why had he not paid more attention to it? It had once promised him the coming of Mary. Was it Mary who had led him deep into happy groves, where that

204

voice of the bell had never reached? He would never have forgotten it all, had the bell not ceased to sound. And now, as he crouched lower, his own beard, brushing across his clasped hands, suddenly instilled fear into him. He did not recognize himself with this long hair, this silky hair which lent him the magnificence of a wild creature. He twisted the hair of his beard, then he clutched at his head, to feel for the nakedness of his tonsure. But his hair had grown richly all over his head and the tonsure was lost in a virile flood of thick curly locks from forehead to nape. All the flesh of his face and chin, formerly shaven, now sprouted this savage growth.

'Oh, how right you are,' he said, casting a desperate glance at Albine. 'We have sinned, we have merited terrible punishment . . . But, I assure you, I never heard the threats which came to you through the leafage.'

Albine tried to take him into her arms again, murmuring: 'Get up, darling, let us run away together . . . There may still be time for us to love each other.'

'No,' he replied, 'I have no longer any strength, the smallest pebble would bring me stumbling to the ground . . . Hear me. I am aghast at myself. I know not the man who is within me. I have killed myself, and my hands are all stained with blood. If you take me away, my eyes from now on can give you nought but tears.'

She kissed his weeping eyes. With all her vigour she cried: 'No matter, if you only love me!' But he was terrified, and could not reply.

A heavy step beyond the wall dislodged a stone. Albine had not been mistaken, there was somebody there, disturbing the peace of these thickets with jealous breath. Then, overcome with a new surge of shame, they would both have liked to hide behind a bush, but already, erect in the gap in the wall, there stood Friar Archangias, glaring at them.

The Friar remained motionless without a word for some moments, his fists clenched. He examined the couple, Albine seeking protection with her arms round Serge's neck, and on his countenance was the disgust of a man who on the edge of a ditch comes upon filth.

'I thought as much,' he ground out, between his teeth. 'Just where they would hide you.'

He took several steps forward, then cried:

'I see you, I know your nakedness . . . Abomination! Are you a wild animal, to run the woods with that female thing? She has certainly gone a long way with you. She has dragged you into filth and you are covered in hair like a billy-goat . . . Why don't you break off a stout stick and break it over her backside?'

Albine, in her burning voice, whispered: 'Do you love me? Do you love me?'

Serge, his head lowered, kept silence, but still did not reject her.

'A lucky thing I found you,' continued the Friar. 'I found this gap . . . You have disobeyed Lord God Almighty, you have destroyed your own peace. Now, temptation will always bite at you with its flaming teeth and from now on you will no longer have your ignorance to fight it with . . . It is this trollop who tempted you, isn't it? Can't you see the serpent's tail twisted into the locks of her hair? She has a bosom the mere sight of which make a man want to puke . . . Let go of her, stop touching her, for she is the gateway to hell! . . . In the name of Lord God, get you out of this garden!'

'Do you love me? Do you love me?' Albine repeated.

But Serge had drawn away from her, as if in truth scorched by her naked arms, her naked shoulders.

'In the name of Lord God, in the name of Lord God!' cried the Friar, in a voice of thunder.

Invincible now, Serge strode towards the gap. When, with a brutal gesture, Friar Archangias finally dragged him outside Paradou Park, Albine, who had slipped to the ground, her arms madly outstretched towards her love as he went away from her, stood up, choking with sobs, then fled, disappearing into the heart of this world of trees, against which her unknotted hair lashed desperately.

BOOK THREE

BOOK THIRD

CHAPTER I

AFTER the *Our Father*, with a bow to the altar the Reverend Mouret crossed to the Epistle side. Here, descending, he came forward to make the sign of the cross over big Fortuné and Rosalie, kneeling side by side on the edge of the altar platform.

'*Ego conjugo vos in matrimonium in nomine Patris, et Filii, et Spiritus sancti.*'

'*Amen*,' came the prompt response from Vincent, who was serving this mass, out of the corner of his eye following with some curiosity how his brother took it all.

Even though they had nudged one another as they knelt down, to prompt a laugh, both Fortuné and Rosalie were as a matter of fact rather moved, and at this point they ducked their heads. Meanwhile, Vincent had gone for the stoup of holy water and the sprinkler. Fortuné dipped the ring in the basin, it was a heavy one, solid silver. When the priest had blessed it, by sprinkling it in the form of a cross, he passed it back to Fortuné, who then took Rosalie's hand, which vigorous use of soap had not robbed of its green sap stains, and slipped the band on to the ring finger.

'*In nomine Patris, et Filii, et Spiritus sancti*,' murmured the Vicar of Artaud, yet again, giving them a second blessing.

'*Amen*,' came the response, from Vincent.

It was early morning, and the sun had not yet reached the main windows of the church. Outside in the branches of the mountain-ash, the foliage of which seemed to have broken in several panes of the windows, the sparrows were wakening noisily. Teuse, who had not yet had time to do dear God out, was dusting the altars, hitching herself up on her good left leg to give the ochre-daubed feet of the crucifix Christ a good wipe. With as little noise as possible, she re-arranged things, all the time bowing repeatedly, crossing herself and striking her bosom, as she followed the service, though without missing a single stroke of her feather brush. Alone, at the foot of the pulpit, was the sole witness of the marriage, Mother Brichet, who prayed most extravagantly, continually on her knees, mumbling away so loudly that the church might have been full of bluebottles. And at the far end was Catherine, down by the confessional, in her arms a swaddled babe, and since the little thing had begun to cry, she had been obliged to turn her back to the altar to dandle it and amuse it, for which the bell rope, dangling just above its nose, came in handy.

'*Dominus vobiscum,*' intoned the priest, turning round, hands outspread.

'*Et cum spiritu tuo,*' piped the response, from Vincent.

At this point in came three lasses, jostling one another, to get a better view. Not one of them dared to come too far forward. These were Rosalie's three best friends. They had slipped across, on their way to work. They were inquisitive to know what the Vicar of Artaud would say to the newly-weds. They had their secateurs, for work in the vineyards, dangling at their waists. Finally, they took up a sheltered position behind the font, pinching each other and wriggling, loose-forked, big hussies as they were, smothering their constant giggles with their fists.

'There's one thing,' whispered Rousse—'Ginger'—hoarsely—she was a magnificent young creature with hair and skin of copper— 'They'll have room at the door to get out when it's all over, won't they!'

'Pooh! Old man Bambousse is quite right,' murmured Lisa, a swarthy, dainty little thing, with eyes like hot coals. 'People with vines look after them. If the dear Vicar absolutely insists on getting Rosalie and Fortuné to the altar, well, let him get on with it by himself.'

The third, Babet, a lame girl, with over-large bones, just cackled with malicious laughter.

'There's always Mother Brichet,' she said. 'She's dopey enough about church for the whole family . . . I say, doesn't she half mumble! She'll get what she wants, though. Mother Brichet knows what she's about, I can tell you.'

'She's the organist,' suggested Rousse. And all three went into hysterics again, Teuse threatening them from a distance with her brush.

At the altar, the Vicar had now reached the act of communion. When he went to the Epistle side, for Vincent to pour on his thumb and first finger the wine and water of ablution, Lisa said more softly: 'It'll soon be over now. Then we'll have his little talk.'

'Like that,' observed Rousse, 'big Fortuné'll still have time to get out to his field, and Rosalie won't miss her day in the vineyard, either. It's handy, having your wedding in the morning. Doesn't Fortuné look silly.'

'Not half!' whispered Babet. ' It's hard for that boy to stay so long on his knees anyway. I'll bet he hasn't knelt like that since his first communion.'

But their attention was suddenly drawn away by the brat that

210

Catherine was amusing. He wanted that bell pull, and was reaching out his hands, purple with rage, choking till he yelled.

'I say,' cried Rousse. 'They've got the babe here.'

The child's voice rose and he struggled like a little devil.

'Lie him on his belly, let him suck,' whispered Babet to Catherine. With all the brazenness of a hussy of ten, Catherine looked up and giggled.

'Not my sort of fun,' she said, shaking the child. 'Will you shut up, you little wretch! . . . Rosalie just dumped him on me.'

'Of course she did,' said Babet, maliciously. 'Did you think she'd give him to the Vicar to mind?'

This time, Rousse nearly fell over backwards, she laughed so uproariously. She just let herself stumble back till her shoulders were up against the wall, fists on her hips, laughing fit to burst her sides. Lisa flung herself against her and found relief by taking handfuls of her shoulders and buttocks and pinching them. Babet had a typical hunchback's laugh, the sounds ground out between her clenched lips like a saw screeching.

'If it hadn't been the brat,' she continued, 'the good Vicar's holy water would have gone to waste . . . Old Bambousse was set on marrying Rosalie to the Laurents' boy, over Figuières way.'

'Aye,' cried la Rousse, in a sober moment. 'Do you know what old Bambousse did? Hit Rosalie in the back with clods to stop the babe coming.'

'All the same, the babe's a jolly big 'un,' murmured Lisa. 'Clods did him good.'

And in an instant they were all three biting one another in a fit of crazy hilarity, which brought Teuse limping furiously down the aisle. She had gone behind the altar to get her broom. Now the three girls were scared. They fell back, sober.

'You little bitches!' stammered Teuse. 'Fancy daring come in here with your dirty little tongues . . . Rousse, you've no shame in you. You ought to be on your knees at the altar like Rosalie. Another sound, and I'll turn you out, do you hear?'

At this, Rousse's coppery cheeks took a slightly darker hue. With a leering laugh, Babet squinted at her friend's belly.

'As for you,' continued Teuse, turning to Catherine, 'will you leave that babe alone, and this instant! You keep pinching it, just to make it cry, don't you dare deny it . . . Give the child here to me!'

She took the baby, rocked it for a moment, then put it down on a chair, where it at once fell into a cherubic sleep. The church

211

relapsed into a melancholy calm, broken solely by the sparrows in the mountain-ash outside. At the altar, Vincent had taken the missal to the right-hand side and the Vicar had just folded the corporal again and slipped it into the burse. He was now saying the final prayers, with stern concentration, which neither the crying of the baby nor the laughter of the girls had been able to disturb. He seemed to hear nothing, to be entirely absorbed in the supplications he was addressing to Heaven regarding the happiness of the couple the union of whom he had blessed.

This particular morning, the sky, overcast with heat haze, was drenched all through with sunlight, and through the broken panes came a lurid luminosity foreboding a day of storms. All along the walls, the harshly coloured engravings of the Road of the Cross exposed the scowling crudity of their blotches of yellow, blue and red. At the far end of the nave the dry timbers of the gallery creaked, while the weeds outside, in the main porch, growing enormous, thrust long ripened straws, to which clung little brown grasshoppers, in under the portal. All at once, the mechanical lungs of the wood-cased clock harked loudly, as if to clear the time-piece's voice, then, dully, the hammer struck half past six.

'*Ite, missa est*,' declared the priest, turning to face the church.

'*Deo gratias*,' responded Vincent.

Then, after kissing the altar, the Vicar of Artaud turned again, and murmured the final prayer over the bowed heads of the newly-married couple:

'*Deus Abraham, Deus Isaac, et Deus Jacob vobiscum sit . . .*'

The words faded away into a single gentle monotone.

'That's it,' whispered Babet to her two friends. 'Now he's going to give them a little talk.'

'He's as white as a sheet,' observed Lisa. 'Not a bit like M. Caffin. His fat face always seemed to have a grin on it . . . My little sister Rosie says that when she confesses she never dares tell this one anything.'

'That don't matter,' blurted 'Ginger'. 'He's not a bad sort. His illness has aged him, though, hasn't it. But it rather suits him. His eyes are bigger and there are lines at the corners of his mouth make him look more of a man . . . Before that fever, he was too girlish.'

'If you ask me,' said Babet, 'he's got a sorrow at heart. Anyone would think he was always playing a part. His face may look dead, but, Heavens! aren't his eyes bright! Perhaps you haven't seen him when all at once he closes them slowly, as if he was trying to put out that fire in them.'

Teuse brandished her broom. 'Shh!' she hissed, so violently that anyone might have thought it was a gust of wind breaking into the church.

The Reverend Mouret concentrated his thought, then, in scarcely audible tones, he began: 'My dear brother, my dear sister, now you are united in Jesus. The institution of marriage is the image of the sacred union of Jesus and his church. It is a bond which nothing can break, which God desires to be eternal, so man shall never separate what Heaven has joined. In making you bone of each other's bones, God teaches you that you have the duty to walk side by side, and be a faithful couple, according to the ways prepared by His universal might. And you should love each other in the very love of God. The least bitterness between you would be disobedience to the Creator, who made you both from one single body. Therefore, remain united for ever in the image of the Church which Jesus has espoused, giving us all His body and His blood.'

Fortuné and Rosalie, their noses upturned in curiosity, listened hard.

'What's that he says?' asked Lisa, who was a bit deaf.

'Lordy, just what they always say,' replied Rousse. 'He has a nimble tongue, like all parsons.'

All this time, the Vicar of Artaud was proceeding with his homily, his eyes vague, staring beyond the heads of the young couple into a far corner of the church. And little by little his voice took on a softer tone and he instilled some emotion into the words, which he had learned earlier, with the aid of a handbook specially written for young priests. Turning slightly towards Rosalie, when his memory failing him, he now began to add words full of emotion.

'My dear sister, be submissive to your husband, as the Church is submissive to Jesus. Never forget that you should abandon all things, to follow him, as his faithful servant. You will abandon your father and your mother and attach yourself to your husband, you will obey him, in order to obey God himself. And your yoke shall be a yoke of love and peace. Be his repose, his happiness, the sweet scene of his good works, the salvation of his moments of weakness. Let him always find you at his side, as his grace. Let him need but to hold out his hand, to find yours. Thus will you be able to walk together and never get lost and you shall find happiness in the accomplishment of divine law. Ah, my dear sister, my dear daughter, your humility is loaded with generous fruit and that will engender in your family bosom the virtues of the home, the joys of the family hearth, and that well-being which is the lot of

213

God-fearing homes. Be as affectionate towards your husband as Rachel, as wise as Rebecca, as faithful through the long years as Sarah. Tell yourself that a pure life leads to all good things. Every morning, pray God for the strength to live as a woman who respects her duties, for the punishment would be terrible, and you would lose your love. Think, living without love, tearing flesh from flesh, no longer belonging to the man who is half of yourself, suffering far from the once loved one. You would hold out your arms, but he would turn away from you. You would seek your joy, but find only shame in the depths of your heart. Hear me, my child, it is in yourself, in submissiveness, in purity, in love, that God has implanted the strength of your union.'

At this moment, there came a loud burst of laughter from the other end of the church. The baby had just wakened on the chair where Teuse had put it to sleep. But it was no longer irritable. It was guffawing all to itself, having pushed its nappy down, to wave its pink little feet in the air, and those funny feet made it laugh.

Bored with the Vicar's homily, Rosalie swiftly turned, to smile at her babe, but when she saw it wriggling about like that unattended, on an ordinary chair, she was seized with apprehension and shot Catherine a terrible look.

'All right, you can look. I'm not picking it up again, to have it crying once more,' muttered Catherine, hurrying well away, under the gallery, to peer at an ants' nest where one of the flags was cracked.

'M. Caffin never had such a lot of jaw,' said Rousse. 'When he married Miette all he did was just pat her cheeks and tell her now she'd better be a good girl.'

'My dear brother,' the Reverend Mouret continued, now half turning back to Fortuné, 'it is God who today vouchsafes you a companion in life, for he did not wish man to live alone. But even though he has laid down that she should be your servant, he requires of you to be a master full of gentleness and affection. You will love her, because she is your very flesh and blood. You will protect her, because God has granted you strong arms for the very purpose that in the hour of danger you may hold them over her head. Do not forget that she has been confided to your care. She is all submissiveness and weakness, of which you cannot abuse yourself without crime. Ah, my dear brother, what happy pride must be yours! From now on, you will no longer live in the egoism of solitude. You will always have an enviable duty. Nothing is better than loving, unless it is to protect those whom one loves. Your

214

heart will grow big in this, and your man's strength will grow a hundredfold. Ah yes, being the mainstay, having gentle love confided to you, seeing a young girl give up her whole being to you, saying: 'Take me, do with me what you will, I trust you ever to be true to me.' And may you be damned, if you ever abandon her. That would be the most cowardly desertion God ever had to punish. The moment she gave herself to you, she was yours, for ever. Carry her away without delay and do not set her down till you can ensure her safety. Abandon everything, my dear brother . . .'

But here Mouret's voice changed completely, and all that came from his lips was a confused mutter. He had closed his eyes completely, and was white as a sheet, speaking now with such sorrowful emotion that even Fortuné shed tears, without knowing why.

'He is not quite himself again yet, is he?' observed Lisa. 'It's wrong of him to tire himself so . . . I say, just look, Fortuné's crying.'

'Men are always softer than women,' muttered Babet.

'It was a very nice talk, all the same,' summed up Rousse. 'These parsons do bring out a lot of things nobody else would ever think of.'

'Sh!' cried Teuse, getting ready to put out the candles.

But the Vicar of Artaud was still stumbling on, trying to find the right words to conclude his homily.

'That is why, my dear brother, my dear sister,' he mumbled, 'you should live in the Catholic faith, which alone can ensure the peace of your hearth. Your parents certainly have taught you to love God and pray morning and night, and not just count on mercy being granted . . .'

But there was no proper end. Suddenly, he turned, snatched the chalice from the altar and, head bent, plunged into the sacristy. Vincent scurried off to get in front of him, nearly dropping the cruets and sprinkler as he did so, because his eye was at the bottom of the church, trying to see what Catherine was at.

'Oh, you heartless creature!' cried Rosalie to Catherine, leaving her husband where he was, to rush and take her child into her arms. The baby laughed. Rosalie kissed it and refastened its nappy. 'If he'd fallen off this chair, I wouldn't half have knocked it out of you,' Rosalie cried, shaking her fist at Catherine.

Fortuné joined her. He seemed a little unsteady on his feet. The three girls crowded round, making coy faces. 'Ain't he proud now,' whispered Babet to the other two. 'Now the rogue really has got the money which old Bambousse keeps under the haystack behind the

215

mill . . . I used to see him and Rosalie crawling round there, evenings, under the little wall.'

All three laughed maliciously, but Fortuné laughed louder still, pinching Rousse and howling with delight when Lisa called him 'a great gawk'. He certainly was a big lump of a fellow, and he took all life lightly. No wonder the Vicar had made him sick with all that pi-talk.

'Hi there, Mum!' he cried—he had the voice of a bull, but old Mother Brichet was busy at the sacristy door, wheedling something more out of the Vicar. There she stood, a scraggy, droopy figure, while Teuse slipped some eggs into her apron pockets. But Fortuné was not embarrassed. With a leering wink, he cried: 'My old Mum's a wily one, ain't she? And the hell, too, if the parson wants somebody to attend his services.'

Meanwhile, Rosalie had calmed down. Before leaving the church, she asked Fortuné if he had remembered to ask the Vicar to come round in the evening to bless their bedroom, according to local custom. And off went Fortuné, clumping up the aisle with great strides, to catch the Reverend Mouret before he left the sacristy. A moment later, there he was back, announcing in stentorian tones, yes, parson would come round. Teuse meanwhile was thoroughly shocked by the noise these people were all making, anyone would think they thought they were out in the highway, so, clapping her hands quietly, she shooed them towards the door.

'It's all over,' she cried, 'you can go now, off to your work.'

And she thought she had got rid of them all, then turned, to see Catherine, now joined by Vincent. The pair of them were bent down, intent over the ants' nest. Catherine had found a long straw and was poking about between the stones. Ants were swarming out, all over the stone floor. Vincent was saying that she needed to poke right to the very bottom, and get the queen out.

'Oh, you little wretches!' cried Teuse. 'What do you think you're doing there? Will you leave those poor creatures alone, this instant! That's Miss Désirée's ants' nest. She would be pleased, if she saw you.'

The two children made themselves scarce.

CHAPTER II

THE Reverend Mouret now came back to the altar, in cassock only, and bareheaded, and knelt there. Under the grey luminosity shed by the windows, his tonsure cut a very large, pallid patch in his hair and one might have thought that the faint trembling which ran over his bowed head and shoulders came because he felt the chill there. He prayed with great fervour, hands clasped, so lost in his supplication that he did not even hear Teuse's heavy tread as she stumped to and fro round him before she could bring herself to interrupt him. It seemed to hurt the good woman to see him so humbled there, so broken-kneed. For an instant she thought he was crying, and hid behind the altar to spy and see if it was so. Then she emerged again, quite decided now she could not leave him there in the church all alone. One evening she had found him there in a fainting fit, teeth tightly clenched, cheeks icy, like a dead man.

'Do please come here, Miss,' she cried to Désirée, who at this moment happened to peep in at the sacristy door. He's still here, and doing himself no good, either . . . You know you're the only one he will ever pay any attention to.'

Désirée smiled. 'Of course it's time for breakfast,' she murmured, 'I'm famished myself.' And, creeping up to her brother, she put her arm about his neck and kissed him.

'Morning, brother mine!' she cried. 'Do you really want me to die of hunger today?'

He looked up, so unhappy that she kissed him again, on both cheeks. He was still lost in his mortification. Then he saw who it was, and made a gentle effort to edge her away. But she held fast to one of his hands, and would not let go. She scarcely let him make the sign of the cross. She led him off.

'But I tell you, Serge dear, I'm famished. And so must you be.'

Teuse had laid breakfast at the bottom of the little garden, under the two mulberries, whose outspread branches provided a leafy canopy. The sun had at last conquered the stormy cloud banks of early morning and was warming the vegetable beds. The mulberries threw a large patch of shade over the rustic table set with two cups of milk and thick slabs of bread-and-butter.

'See,' cried Désirée, 'isn't it wonderful out here?'

She was already hacking off enormous mouthfuls and munching with wonderful appetite.

'And aren't you going to have anything?' she asked, since Teuse remained standing, facing them.

'In a minute,' replied the old domestic, 'I'm hotting up a bit of soup for myself.' Then, after a short silence, admiring that big child Désirée's magnificent champing, she ran on, addressing the Vicar: 'Yes, there's one enjoys her food . . . Doesn't it give you an appetite, Vicar? You should make yourself eat.'

217

Mouret looked at his sister, and smiled.

'Ah, there's nothing amiss with my sister, that's true,' he said. 'She puts on flesh daily.'

'But of course I do!' cried Désirée. 'Because I eat! You would, too, if only you'd eat. You'd get fat too ... Are you ill again, Serge, it was too awful, when they had to take you away, to get you better.'

'Your little sister's quite right, sir,' said Teuse, 'you're doing yourself no good, like that. That's no way for a man to live, that isn't, on two or three crumbs a day, like a dicky-bird. Why, Vicar, you don't eat anything to make yourself any blood, that's the truth of it, and that's what makes you so white. Aren't you ashamed, looking thinner than a rake, when we're both so comfortable, and we only womenfolk. Anyone might think we starved you.'

Thus the two women, both bursting with good health, scolded him affectionately. He smiled at them. His eyes were enormous, and so limpid that one might have thought that behind them was empty space.

'I am all right,' he said. 'I have nearly drunk my milk.'

He had in fact taken two little sups. His *tartines* he had not touched at all.

'Animals,' said Désirée, pensively, 'animals do better than people.'

'Hm, that's a fine discovery to make about us humans,' cried Teuse, with a coarse laugh.

The words, however, had been said with not a trace of malice.

'But of course,' Désirée insisted. 'Look at the hens, for instance, they don't worry their heads off, do they? And you can stuff rabbits as much as you like. And nobody's going to say my piggie ever looks miserable.' Then, turning to her brother, she cried rapturously: 'Did I tell you? I've christened him! Matthew! That's because he's so like our postman. He's such a fine pig now ... It isn't very nice of you, Serge, to refuse ever to see him. You will let me show you him one day, won't you?'

While she wheedled him, she took her brother's ration of bread-and-butter and with her lovely teeth munched away at that too. She had finished one piece and was just starting on the second, when Teuse saw what was happening.

'Now, now,' she cried, 'that's not yours! Look! Who's snatching food away from his mouth now?'

'That's all right,' said the Vicar, gently. 'I should not have touched it, anyway ... You eat it up! Eat away, my pet!'

For a moment, Désirée was embarrassed. She stared at the

218

tartine and by sheer force of will avoided bursting into tears. Then, with a cheerful laugh, she finished it, and ran on:

'And my cow hasn't got the blues, like you . . . You were away, when Uncle Pascal gave it me and made me promise to be good. Or you would have seen how she loved it when I first put my arms round her neck.'

She suddenly turned, to listen. From the farmyard came the cry of her cock-bird and then a rapidly growing uproar, wings fluttering, grunting, hens' raucous voices, a regular animal panic.

'Oh, and I didn't tell you, either, my heifer really must be full . . . I took her to the bull, you know. At Béage, eight miles away. It's rotten not having bulls in every place . . . But while she was there with him I stayed, to watch.'

Teuse's shoulders heaved anxiously, and she watched the Vicar with anxious eye.

'The best thing for you to do, Miss,' she said quickly, 'would be to go out and see what's frightening your hens . . .. There's murder going on in your yard.'

But Désirée stuck to her story.

'He mounted up on her, he got her tight in his front legs. How all the men laughed! But there's nothing to laugh at, it's quite natural, isn't it? Mother animals have to have babies, don't they? I say, do you think she will have a baby?'

Mouret made an indefinite gesture. He had lowered his eyes, unable to face the young girl's flawless glance.

'Here, here, hurry?' cried Teuse, 'they're killing each other!'

The farmyard quarrel had certainly become so violent now that Désirée rushed off with a great flurry of petticoats. But the priest called her back.

'Darling,' he said, 'I don't think you've finished your milk.'

She came back, and, despite Teuse's angry eyes, drank down the milk without question. Then off she rushed again, as madly as before, to her farmyard, where she could be heard restoring peace. Apparently, she had sat down amid all her creatures. She was humming softly to them, a sort of lullaby.

CHAPTER III

'AND now my soup's too hot,' grumbled Teuse, coming back from the kitchen with a bowl out of which stuck a wooden spoon.

She took up a stand facing the Vicar, taking cautious sips with the tip of her spoon. She hoped to enliven him and get him out of that crushed silence in which she saw him. Ever since his return from Paradou he insisted that he was quite well again, and never once complained. Indeed, his smile now was often so gentle, that the opinion of Artaud was that the illness had made him a more holy man than ever. Nevertheless, there were times when he was possessed by a fit of speechlessness, and then he seemed to be inwardly writhing in agonies to which he refused to admit. He was in fact then absolutely shattered by a silent inward pain which for hours on end made him senseless, the prey of some frightful internal struggle, the sole outward sign of which was the painful perspiration on his forehead. In such moments Teuse never left him. She would confuse him with a flood of talk till at last, as if master of the rebellion of the blood, he gradually resumed his more gentle mien. But this particular morning, the old housekeeper sensed the advent of a worse attack than any before, so while continuing to handle her scalding spoon with great prudence, she set her tongue wagging nineteen to the dozen.

'I tell you, one has to live in a back-of-beyond place like this to see such goings-on. Now, did you ever hear of folk in a decent village getting married on the sly at screech of dawn? That alone shows these Artaud folk are no cop. Why, back home, in my Normandy, I've seen weddings which lit up everybody for a good five miles round. There used to be three days uninterrupted eating and drinking, Parson and Mayor and all. Why, I remember, even the Fire Brigade came to the marriage of one of my cousins. And what goings-on too! But getting a Vicar up before sunrise when even the hens aren't properly up, to perform the ceremony, no, that's going a bit too far! If I'd been in your place, Vicar, I'd have put my foot down! Why, Vicar, dear, you didn't have a proper night's sleep, and you might have caught a chill in church. That's what's brought your trouble back, all right. And what's more, you'd have done better to join a couple of farmyard creatures in holy matrimony, than that hussy Rosalie and her good-for-nothing lout, and that bastard brat wetting on one of the church chairs, too . . . Listen to me, Vicar, you are very wrong not to tell me where you feel it . . . I could make you up something nice and warm . . . What about it, Vicar dear? . . . Will you please say yes or no!'

He replied weakly that he was all right, all he needed was a little fresh air. He had slumped against one of the mulberry trees. His breath was coming in short gasps.

'Very well then, be headstrong, if that's your will,' ran on

Teuse. 'Get away with you! Perform the rites of holy matrimony when you're not well enough for it and it's bound to make you ill! I had my misgivings about it, I told you so yesterday . . . And just the same, if only you would listen to me, you wouldn't stay where you are. You know the smell of that farmyard upsets you. It stinks frightful, today. It makes you wonder what Miss Désirée won't clean out next. But she's all right, she can sing like a canary all the time, a lot she worries about it, it all puts colour into her cheeks. And I was going to tell you, you don't know how hard I tried to prevent her staying away when her cow went to the bull, but she's just like you, so pigheaded, and it's her pleasure, all the animals and their young . . . Now do be sensible, Vicar dear. Let me take you to your room! So you can lie down and rest a little! . . . What, you won't? All right, then it serves you right if you do feel ill. But I tell you, it's no good brooding over your misfortunes till they choke you.'

She was now so worked up that at risk of scalding her gullet she gulped down a whole ladleful of soup. Then, banging the wooden handle on the bowl, she went on grumbling her thoughts out loud.

'If one ever saw such a man. He'd burst rather than open his mouth to speak . . . Well he may hold his tongue too. I know quite enough about it all! It's easy to guess the rest. Oh yes, well may he hold his tongue. Perhaps that's the best thing to do!'

Teuse was jealous. Doctor Pascal had had to have a real tussle with her to get his patient away from her when he came to the conclusion that if he stayed at the vicarage the young priest would not pull through. He had to drum into her head that the mere sound of the church bell aggravated Mouret's brain fever, that the holy images of which his room was full haunted him and gave him hallucinations, in short, that what he needed was complete oblivion, a complete change of environment, in which he could so to speak be born again in the tranquillity of a new existence. She had tossed her head indignantly at this, insisting that there was nowhere that 'the dear boy' could find a better nurse than she was. Yet in the end Teuse had acquiesced. She was even resigned to seeing him go to Paradou Park, though to the last she uttered her protests against the doctor's choice. And for all Doctor Pascal's arguments, she had retained a sturdy hatred of Paradou. But what hurt her most of all was the Reverend Mouret's never saying a word to her about the time he spent there. And today, beside herself with anxiety at his pallor and his stubbornness in suffering without saying a word, she finally began to wave her spoon about like a conductor's stick, and cried:

'The best thing you could do, Vicar, is to go back there, if you were so well off . . . I don't doubt there is a person at Paradou Park can look after you better than I can.'

It was the first time she had ventured a direct allusion. It was such a crude blow that the priest raised his agonised face and actually groaned, whereupon good-hearted Teuse was all regrets.

'Anyway,' she murmured, 'it's all your Uncle Pascal's fault. As if I didn't tell him so enough. But these scientific men are always so headstrong. They are capable of letting a patient die, just to be able to examine his body afterwards . . . It made me so mad I preferred not to say a word to anyone. Yes, dear Vicar, if nobody knew where you were, that was thanks to me, I found it all so hateful. When, Sundays, the Reverend Guyot of St. Eutrope, who acted for you, came to say mass, I told him all sorts of yarns, I swore you were in Switzerland, and I don't even know properly where Switzerland is . . . Far be it from my wishes to want to cause you pain, but it's certainly at that Park place that you got this new trouble of yours. A fine cure I call that. Far better have left you with me, it wouldn't ever to occur to me to turn your poor head.'

Serge Mouret made no effort to halt Teuse. He had bowed his head again. She had squatted on the ground, close to him, trying to catch his eye. Then, maternally, delighted to find him so ready to listen to her, she went on:

'You always refused to hear about M. Caffin. The moment I ever started to tell you, you shut me up . . . Well, the poor Reverend Caffin, in my home parts, you know, at Canteleu, well, he had a spot of trouble. That's what happened. And such a saintly man, he was, too, with a heart of gold. But, you see, he was a very dainty man, too, he was fond of fine things, and that's what did it. There was a young girl kept a-flitting round him. Daughter of a miller, she was. Her parents had sent her to a boarding school. To cut a long story short, the inevitable happened. You understand what I mean, don't you . . . Yes, it happened like that. And when it all came out, the whole district was wild with him, they could have stoned him. He got away to Rouen, and went to weep and confess it all to his Archbishop. And then they sent him here. It was enough punishment, I can tell you, for the poor man to live in this hole . . . Later, too, I had news of that girl. Married a cattle dealer, that's what she did, and lives in clover to this day.'

Delighted to have told him her story at last, Teuse found the Vicar's immobility encouraging. Drawing closer, she continued:

'Dear M. Caffin. He never was proud with me, he often used to tell me about his sin. And it doesn't mean he is not in Heaven, either, I can assure you. He can sleep in peace, just out there, under the grass, poor dear, he never did any man any harm . . . I can't see any sense in having such a down on a clergyman when he gets off the road a bit. It's all so natural. Not exactly nice, I'll agree, it's a dirty act, and it angers the Lord, and quite rightly too, but far better do that than go stealing. You can confess afterwards, can't you, and clear the slate? Isn't that right, dear Vicar, when anyone really repents, what they have done does not prevent their salvation?'

Slowly, the Reverend Mouret straightened his back. By a supreme effort he contrived to conquer his unrest. Still pale, he said firmly: 'One should not sin. Never, never!'

'Oh, come now, sir,' cried the old housekeeper, 'you mustn't have too high a standard. Pride's a nasty thing too, you know . . . If I were in your place I wouldn't be stiff-necked like that. The thing to do is talk about your misfortune, not chop up your heart all at once, why, talk about it, then you grow accustomed to separation. The pain gets smaller and smaller . . . Whereas you, why, you even avoid merely mentioning folk's names. You won't allow us even to talk about them, as if they were dead. Since you came back home, I haven't dared give you the least bit of news . . . Ah, but I'm going to talk now, and say all I know, because I can see that it's all this silence that's eating at your heart.'

He shot her a stern glance and raised his forefinger, to silence her.

'Oh yes,' she continued, 'I've had my news from Paradou all right, and quite frequently, too, and I'm going to give you it . . . First, the person in question is no happier than you are.'

'Will you be silent!' the Reverend Mouret cried out, loudly, and at last he found the strength to get to his feet and prepare to go out.

But Teuse too got up, and she barred the way with her enormous frame. She was getting quite angry. 'Sh! So you thought you'd got away, did you? . . . But you're going to listen to me first. You know I'm no lover of those Paradou folk, am I? If I mention them, it's for your good . . . People make out I am jealous. I should just think! Me, who contemplates taking you back there. You should be in my care, you would have no need to be afraid of doing anything wrong . . . Shall we go?'

With a gesture, he dismissed her. His countenance was calmer as he said:

'I neither want anything nor know anything. Tomorrow we have high mass. The altar needs doing.' Then, as he walked away, he added, with a smile: 'And please don't worry yourself, dear Teuse, I am stronger than you think. I shall recover all by myself.'

With this, he left her, in appearance quite robust, head upright, having won the day. His cassock rustled softly as it swept along the border where the thyme grew. Teuse, still planted where she had stood, gathered into her hands bowl and spoon. She was still gnashing her teeth and grumbling, and with many a fierce shrug of her ponderous shoulders she ran on:

'Showing off, are we, built different from other men, are we, just because we're a priest . . . The truth is, he's a very frigid man, is the Reverend Mouret. I've known men as didn't need so much tickling up. He's capable of crushing his own heart like he'd crush a flea. It's the Almighty he worships gives him the strength for it.'

And she was about to go into the kitchen, when her eye fell on the Vicar. He was standing at the gate into the farmyard. Désirée had intercepted him there, to insist on him judging the weight of a capon she had been feeding for some weeks back. He had said meekly that it was very heavy, and that had made the overgrown child roar with laughter.

Teuse was blind with rage.

'Capons,' she spluttered, 'capons! They're all of them capons, they'd crush their own hearts like they was fleas. But capons have got a reason for it . . . there's no honour in them living a clean life.'

CHAPTER IV

THE Reverend Serge passed all his time at the Vicarage, and avoided the long walks he had taken before his illness. The scorched-up Artaud countryside and the sultriness of all this valley, where only twisted vines grew, made him very restive. Twice, he had tried morning excursions, to read his breviary while walking the roads, but did not get past the village before he turned back, over-excited by the smell of it all, the sunlight and the vastness of the skyline. Only in the evening, in the freshness as night gathered, did he venture a few paces up and down in front of the church, on the level patch of ground which reached as far as the graveyard. In the afternoon, feeling a need for something to do without any

224

notion how to discover it, to pass the time he had started mending
the broken panes in the church windows by pasting them over with
paper. For a week, that kept him busy, up a ladder. He made
great efforts to make his paper panes a good fit, cutting them off
as if it were fine needlework he was doing, and laying on his adhesive
very carefully, so it should not drip. Teuse stood at the foot of the
ladder, while Désirée clamoured that they should not close all the
holes, or how would her sparrows get in. In the end he did leave
two or three open squares in each window. And when this repair
job was accomplished, he grew ambitious, got a desire to beautify
his church, without calling in mason or carpenter or decorator. He
would do it all himself. He maintained that this manual labour
both entertained him and restored his strength. Every time that
Uncle Pascal called, the doctor encouraged him, insisting that such
physical tiredness was better than any medicine bottle. From then
onwards, the Vicar of Artaud stopped up holes in his church wall
with handfuls of plaster, patched up his altars by much work with
the hammer, and pounded colours in a mortar, preparing to give
the pulpit and confessional a coat. It became quite an event in the
countryside, the talk for miles around. Peasants came, hands
behind their backs, to watch Monsieur le Curé at the work. A blue
apron tied at his waist, his hands all scratches, Mouret got completely absorbed in his rough task. And this was another excuse for
never going out. He lived out his days amid lumps of plaster, and
was now more at peace, almost a smiling man, indeed, forgetting
that world beyond the trees, forgetting the sunshine and the warm
winds, which only disturbed him.

'You've a free hand, Vicar, so long as it costs the parish nowt,'
sniggered old Bambousse, looking in every evening to see how the
work was getting on.

On those efforts the Vicar spent all he had saved in his college
years. It was, one must admit, ill done, so clumsily and in such
elementary fashion that it raised smiles. Moreover, the stonework
soon enough proved too much for him, so that he was satisfied to re-
point the church tower as high as he could reach. Teuse mixed the
mortar. Then she suggested he went on to repair the vicarage,
being, as she put it, that she was afraid of its crumbling about
their ears. He said that was more than he could cope with, they
would have to have a man in, which resulted in a frightful quarrel
between them, Teuse shouting that there was no commonsense in
doing so much lovely work on the church, which was nobody's
dwelling, when next door there were bedrooms in which one fine

H   225

morning they were certain to be found dead with the ceilings fallen in on them.

'Well, I know what it'll come to, and I shall be the first,' she nagged, 'I shall come and make up my bed here, behind the altar, I'm afraid at night in that house.'

But when the supply of plaster ran out, Teuse stopped talking about the vicarage. By now the sight of the Vicar's paint-work made her rapturous. She said it put the cap on the whole job. Having made good all the missing boards, the Vicar with great satisfaction plastered them with lovely yellow paint, laying it on thick. In those to and fro strokes of his brush, Mouret found something very soothing. It lulled him into a dreamy state. For hours on end he did not think of anything but those oily strokes his brush made. When all the woodwork—confessional, pulpit, altar footpace, even the clock casing—was yellow, he actually had a go at marbling, to brighten up the main altar. Gaining still more courage, he now repainted the whole of it. White, yellow and blue, it was superb. People who had not been to mass for fifty years queued up to have a peep at it.

Now the painting was all dry. All that remained to be done was to outline the panels in brown. So, immediately after lunch, he set to work, anxious to finish it all that day, the following day, as he had reminded Teuse, being set apart for high mass.

Teuse was waiting to do the altar. She had already stood the candlesticks and the silver cross out on the credence table, then the china vases with their artificial flowers and the lace-edged altar cloth which was always brought out for high days. But it was such a ticklish job doing those edging lines that the work dragged on till night fell, and it was almost dark when he completed the last panel.

'That's going to be too pretty,' suddenly came a rough voice from the grey dust of twilight now filling the church.

Teuse, who was on her knees to follow the passage of the outlining brush along the rule, shook with immediate apprehension.

'Oh, it's you, Friar Archangias,' she cried, swinging round, 'did you come in through the sacristy, then? How you do frighten me! I could have sworn your voice came from right under these flag-stones.'

Giving the Friar a curt nod of greeting, the Reverend Mouret resumed his work. Without a word, the Friar stood beside him, his massive hands clasped in front of him over his cassock. Then he shrugged his shoulders with scorn at the care the incumbent

of Artaud was taking to keep those fine lines of his straight, and
said again:

'That's going to be too pretty.'

Teuse, who was in a state of absolute bliss, started again.
'Lovely!' she cried. 'Do you know, I had already forgotten you
were there. You might at least give a cough before you speak so
suddenly. All at once, like that, you have a voice which grates
like a corpse's.'

Clambering to her feet and drawing back, to admire, she realised
what the Friar had said.

'And why too pretty?' she demanded. 'There be nothing too
pretty if it's for our dear Lord . . . If the Vicar had had gold leaf
he would have used that! So there!'

As at long last the Reverend Mouret completed the final stroke,
she hastened to change the altar cloth, taking care not to smudge
the bordering. Then she arranged cross, candlesticks and vases
symmetrically. The Vicar had gone beside the Friar, to lean
against the wooden bar which separated chancel from nave. Neither
spoke, they merely stared, both of them, at the silver cross which,
in those gathering shadows, preserved drops of light on the feet,
down the left thigh and on the right temple of the crucified man.
Completing her tasks, Teuse came forward, triumphant.

'Now, that's very nice, I call it, you'll just see what a crowd
you'll have at mass tomorrow! The heathen, they only visit their
God when they think he's in the money . . . And now, dear Vicar,
you'll have to do up the altar of the Virgin the same.'

'Waste of money,' growled the Friar.

At this, Teuse was really quite annoyed, and as the Vicar himself
still said nothing, she took both men by force to the altar of the
Virgin, half pushing them, half pulling at their cassocks.

'But just look!' she cried. 'That jars too much, now the main
altar is cleaned up. Nobody'd even think it had ever been painted.
I might as well not have dusted it this morning, the dust clings so
to that rough wood. It's all so dark and ugly . . . Have you really
given a thought to what folk'll be saying, Vicar? They'll say you
have no love for the Holy Virgin, upon my word they will!'

'And so?' demanded the Friar.

Teuse simply choked.

'And so?' she muttered. 'Goodness gracious, my dear man,
'twould be a sin, that's what . . . That altar is like one of those
neglected graves you see in churchyards. If it wasn't for me, it'd
be all spider's webs, and moss would be growing on it. From time

227

to time, when I can spare some flowers, I give them to the Virgin . . .
There was a time when all the flowers in our garden used to be
reserved for her.'

She had mounted the altar steps and now took down two faded
bunches of flowers from the gradines.

'See for yourselves,' she said, 'just like a graveyard,' and she
tossed the flowers at the Vicar's feet.

Mouret picked them up, without replying. It was already quite
dark. Friar Archangias lost his way among the chairs and,
nearly had a fall. He cursed, muttering obscure phrases in which
the words Jesus and Mary came frequently. When Teuse, who had
gone for a lamp, came back, she asked the Vicar if this meant she
was then to put the paint-pots and brushes away in the attic.

'Yes,' said Mouret. 'This is all that we're going to do. We can
think about the rest some time later.'

Without a word, she stumped out in front of them, bearing the
whole paraphernalia with her. She was afraid of saying too much.
Just as they were passing by the farmyard, noticing that the Reverend
Mouret was still holding those faded bunches of flowers, Friar
Archangias grunted: 'Come on, man, throw those away.'

Head bowed on his bosom, Mouret took a few more steps, then,
suddenly, tossed the flowers through the gateway, on to the manure-
heap.

CHAPTER V

HAVING eaten, himself, the Friar had turned his chair round and
was seated straddling it, waiting for the Vicar to have his supper.
Ever since Mouret's return to Artaud, the Friar had come in to
spend nearly every evening like this, at the vicarage. Never before
had he forced his entry so unceremoniously. His heavy boots would
grind on the tiled floor, and his voice would thunder, his fists banging
the furniture, while he recounted all the girls' bottoms he had
tanned that morning in school or summarised his outlook on life
in formulations as unbending as the stout stick he wielded. After
that, to pass the time, this evening he had proposed a game of cards
with Teuse.

Teuse and Friar Archangias played the old game of *Bataille* inter-
minably, because the dear old housekeeper had never been able to
master any other card game. While they flicked their opening
cards furiously down on to the table, Mouret smiled at their game,
but gradually he lost interest and sank into a deep meditation.

For hours he would forget himself like that and slip away elsewhere, with the Friar shooting at him glances of sheer defiance.

On this particular occasion, Teuse had been in the mood to say she was going to bed, the moment the table was cleared, but Friar Archangias had been set on a game. With pats on the shoulders he succeeded at last in getting her to sit down again, so violently indeed that her chair gave an ominous crack. Friar Archangias was already shuffling the cards. Désirée, who detested the man, had taken off her dessert, as she did most evenings, to eat in bed.

'I'll have the red cards,' said Teuse, and the battle was on. At the first go, Teuse took several of the Friar's good cards. Then, in the same instant, two aces fluttered to the table.

'Bataille!' cried Teuse, with extraordinary emotion. Then, to her own consternation, she played a nine. But as the Friar only played a seven, she gathered in the cards, in triumph. After half an hour, she once again had only two aces, and the balance was restored. And towards the third quarter of the hour, it was Teuse who lost an ace. The traffic in knaves, queens and kings was as savage as any massacre.

'Damn it, this is a fine game!' cried the Friar, turning to the Vicar of Artaud, but saw him to be so lost in thought, so far away, with so unconscious a smile on his lips, that he raised his voice, and with some violence cried:

'Here, what about it, Vicar, aren't you watching the game? That's hardly polite of you! . . . We're only playing for your benefit. We thought we'd entertain you . . . Come on, man, give a look to the game, that'll do you more good than brooding there. A penny for your thoughts!'

Mouret started violently, but made no reply, merely attempted to follow the game. His eyelids twitched. Play went on with great fury. Teuse got her ace back, then lost it again. Some evenings they would wrestle over the aces like that for four hours on end, and often enough they retired to bed at last with neither the victor.

'I knew I had something on my mind!' cried Teuse, suddenly— for she was terribly afraid of losing a game—'why, the Vicar has to go out this evening, he promised Fortuné and Rosalie Brichet to go and bless their bedroom, as the custom is . . . Quick, Vicar. Friar Archangias will go with you.'

Mouret was already on his feet, looking for his hat, but for the moment the Friar stuck to his cards. He was indeed rather put out.

'Oh, don't bother,' he objected. 'Surely that pig-sty doesn't call

229

for your blessing. As if they were going to do anything decent in their dirty bedroom . . . That's another custom you'll have to put an end to. It's not a priest's job sticking his nose between a young married couple's sheets . . . You stay home. Let's finish our game. That's far better.'

'No,' said the Vicar, 'I promised them. The good people might be hurt . . . You stay and go on with your game, and wait till I get back.'

Teuse was very upset by this, and stared at the Friar.

'As you like,' said he, 'I'll stay. It's really too silly.'

But the Vicar had not opened the door before the Friar had angrily thrown down his cards and got up to follow him. On the threshold he turned for a moment.

'I would have won,' he said. 'Leave the cards as they are . . . we'll finish it tomorrow.'

'Too late,' replied the old housekeeper, who had hastily shuffled the cards. 'They're all mixed now. You didn't think I was going to put your cards in a golden frame on the wall, did you? Besides, I might have won, I still had an ace.'

In a few paces, Father Archangias had caught up with the Vicar, who was striding rapidly down the narrow path which led to the village. The Friar had given himself the task of keeping an eye on Mouret, and he was going to carry it through. Throughout the day, he surrounded the Vicar in a net of espionage. When he could not manage it himself, he had him shadowed everywhere, if only by one of his school-pupils. With his terrible laugh, he said he was 'God's policeman.' And, true enough, the priest did seem now to be a guilty man caught in the black shadow of the Friar's cassock, a character to be mistrusted and adjudged weak enough to return to his sin the moment the watchful eye was off him. In this there was the spite of a jealous old maid and the niggling diligence of a gaoler who drives his duties as far as blocking out any patches of sky the condemned man may be able to glimpse through the peepholes of his cell. Friar Archangias was ever-present, ready to block off any sunshine of Mouret's, or prevent any outer fragrance entering his life, walling off the dungeon so thoroughly that nothing of the outer world should enter it. He ferreted out the Vicar's slightest foible, quick, by the limpidity of the priest's eyes, to detect any tender thought, and then swift with merciless language pitilessly to crush it, as if such thoughts were vermin. Mouret's silences, his smiles, his pallors, the palsy of any limb, were all Friar Archangias's. True, he avoided any overt mention of the Vicar's fundamental sin.

230

His mere presence was a constant reminder. The way he uttered certain phrases lent them the bite of a whip's lash. He could instil a mere gesture with all the filth which he spat out on the sin itself. Like those deceived husbands who with blood-drawing allusions subject their wives in a cruelty which only they can taste, he never referred to that scene in Paradou Park, but merely evoked it whenever he could, by selecting precisely the word which in any moment of emotion would abash the rebellious flesh. He felt that he too had been deceived by the priest. He had been sullied through and through by Mouret's divine adultery. He himself thereby became a traitor to his own vows, assuming for his own flesh prohibited caresses, the mere remote guessing of which were enough to inflame in him all the concupiscence of that randy old goat who had never once really satisfied body's needs.

It was nearly ten. The village slept, but on the far side, over towards the mill, there was a din coming from one of the squat houses, which was brilliantly lit. Here, old Bambousse had set aside a corner of the house for daughter and son-in-law—of course keeping the best part for himself—and now they were all having a last round of wine while they awaited the Vicar.

'They're all drunk,' growled the Friar. 'Can't you hear them at their wallowings?'

The Vicar of Artaud made no reply to this. It was a superb night, absolutely blue with a moonlight which transformed the distant valley into a slumbering lake. Feeling as it were bathed in well-being by that soft luminosity, he slackened pace. He even halted at some patches of light, feeling all that lovely thrill which one feels as one draws near fresh water. The Friar, however, continued his huge strides, nagging at him and urging him on.

'Come along there ... It's not healthy, running about the countryside at this hour of night. You would be better in bed.'

But, suddenly, as they entered the village, the Friar planted himself in mid-road and stared up the slopes, where the white lines of the ruts faded into the dark patches of the little patches of conifers, and he growled like a dog which scents danger.

'Who's that coming down there, so late?' he muttered.

Now it was the Vicar, neither hearing nor seeing anything, who wanted to press on.

'Get away with you,' cried Father Archangias, fiercely, 'there he is, just coming round the bend. Look, there's the moonlight on him. You can see him clearly, now ... A big fellow with a stick.'

231

Then, after a moment of silence, in tones choking with fury, 'It is him, it's that scoundrel . . . I could feel him.'

By now, the newcomer had reached the foot of the slope, and Mouret recognised Jeanbernat. Despite his eighty years, the old fellow trod so firmly that the heels of his heavy sabots struck sparks from the flints on the road. He walked as upright as an oak, without even using his stick, which he was carrying over his shoulder, like a gun.

'Oh, that hell-hound,' stammered the Friar, glued to the spot. 'May Satan heap all the coals of hell under his feet!'

Very worried, and losing hope of getting his companion to keep quiet, Mouret turned round, to continue on his way, still hoping that by hurrying to reach the Bambousse's he might avoid Jeanbernat. But he had not gone five steps when there was the old man's mocking voice, almost at his heels.

'Hallo there, Vicar, wait, are you afraid of me then?'

Mouret having halted, Jeanbernat came up with him.

'Damme!' cried Jeanbernat, 'those cassocks of yours aren't handy, are they, you can't run in 'em! Another thing, even in the night anyone can tell who you are . . . As I came over the hill, 'Heavens,' says I to myself, 'there's our little parson down there.' Yes sir, I can still see pretty well . . . What's the matter, you never come to see us now?'

'I have had so much on my hands,' muttered Mouret, but the blood left his cheeks.

'As you will, every man's his own master. I only mention it to show you I've nought against you because you're a parson. We needn't even discuss your fine God, it's all the same to me . . . But the kid there home thinks it's me keeps you away. 'Your parson's a beast,' I say to her, and that's what I think, too. Did I interfere with you at all, while you were ill? I didn't even once come to see you . . . Every man his own master.'

He spoke with his usual magnificent freedom of language, and as if he had not even noticed the presence of the Friar. But when that person uttered a more threatening growl, he had to speak.

'Well, Vicar,' he said, 'I see you take your pig out for walks with you.'

'Steady, you scoundrel!' shouted the Friar, clenching his fists.

Jeanbernat, stick poised on high, then pretended to recognize who it was.

'Oh, it's you, sky-pilot, is it? Down with those fists!' he barked. 'I ought to have recognized the stink of your hide. I once swore I'd

232

lop off your ears in front of your school, didn't I. That would amuse the kiddies you poison.'

Faced with that stick, the Friar fell back, belching insults, stammering, unable to find enough words.

'I'll put the police on your tracks, you murderer! You spat on the church wall, I saw you! You give folk a mortal pestilence merely passing their doors. At Saint-Eutrope you aborted a girl by making her chew up a consecrated host you had stolen. At Béage you exhumed some children and carried them away on your back for your abominations . . . Everybody knows that, you miscreant! You're the scandal of this country. The man who strangled you would go straight to paradise.'

The old man listened to all this with a snigger, whirling his stick round his head all the time. Then, slipping in a word between one and another insult pouring from the Friar's mouth, he said:

'Come on, cough it all up, you viper. In a minute, I'll lay this stick about you.'

Mouret tried to intervene, but Friar Archangias thrust him aside, shouting:

'You're on his side, you are! Did he not make you trample on the cross, deny it if you can!' Then, turning back to Jeanbernat: 'Yes, Satan, you must have had a good laugh when you had a priest in your hands! May Heaven punish those who aided that sacrilege! What did you do at night when this man slept? You came, didn't you, to wet his tonsure with your spittle, to make the hairs grow faster? You breathed on his chin and his cheeks to get a finger's growth overnight. You massaged your filthy charms into his body, you breathed your rabies into his mouth, it was you put him on heat . . . That is how you changed him into an animal, you Satan!'

'The man's a fool,' said Jeanbernat, letting his stick sink back to his shoulder. 'A tiresome fool.'

Emboldened, the Friar went up to Jeanbernat and held his two fists under his nose.

'And your trollop!' he shouted. 'It's you thrust her stark naked into the priest's bed!'

Then he uttered a howl and leapt back, for the old man had brought his stick down full crack on the Friar's back. He retreated farther still, rummaged in a pile of stones beside the road, got a flint as big as a man's two fists and hurled it at Jeanbernat's head. If Jeanbernat had not ducked, his forehead would have been split open. He ran to another stone-heap, took shelter, gathered stones,

233

and there began a terrific battle, a rain of flints between the two stone-heaps. The bright moonlight cast clear shadows.

'Yes, you thrust her into his bed,' the Friar repeated, beside himself. 'And you put a crucifix under the mattress so the filth would drip on Jesus . . . Ah, you are surprised I know all about it, are you? And now you expect a monster child from that rut, don't you. Every morning you make the thirteen signs of hell on that trollop's belly, so she shall give birth to anti-christ. You want an anti-christ, don't you, you scoundrel? . . . You wait, this stone'll blind you.'

'And may this one shut your dog-collar trap!' came Jeanbernat's reply. But all the same, the old man now grew very calm.

'What an idiot the creature is,' he said scornfully, 'with his ridiculous talk . . . Here, must I crack that skull of yours, to be able to go my way? Is it your catechism has turned your brain?'

'Catechism? Do you want to know the catechism which is taught the damned souls of your breed? Yes, I'll teach you to make the sign of the cross, I will . . . Here's one for the Father, and this for the Son, and—this for the Holy Ghost . . . What, still on your feet? Just you wait . . . You'll get it.' And he flung a handful of small stones, like grape-shot. One hit Jeanbernat on the shoulder, whereupon the veteran let go the stones he had picked up and went calmly up to the Friar, while that man took two more handfuls, muttering:

'I'll kill the creature, that's God's will, God is in my arms.'

'Will you shut up?' bellowed Jeanbernat, and seized the Friar by the nape of the neck.

There then followed a brusque wrestling match in the dust of the road in the bluish moonlight. Finding himself the weaker, the Friar tried to bite. The dried-up limbs of Jeanbernat were like bundles of whipcord, binding the Friar so tightly that he felt the knots enter his flesh. He was silent now, choking, wondering what dirty trick to play next.

When he had got his man down, Jeanbernat spoke again, mockingly:

'You make me want to break your arms for you, just to break your fine God . . . You can see for yourself, he is not the stronger, this God of yours. It's I who can do the killing if I want . . . But all I'm going to do is lop off your ears. You've tried my patience too much.'

Quite calmly, he drew a knife from his pocket. Now Mouret, who had already made a number of attempts to separate them,

234

protested so vigorously that Jeanbernat agreed that he might postpone the operation till a later day.

'It's quite wrong of you, parson, you know,' he muttered. 'This rascal needs a bit of bloodletting. But if it worries you, I'll wait. I shall come across him somewhere or other.' Hearing the Friar start groaning, he broke off to say: 'Now, don't you budge, or I'll whip 'em off in a jiffy.'

'But you're pressing too hard on his chest,' said the Vicar. 'Do let the man get a breath.'

'Not on your life, he would only start his folly over again. I'll let him go when I'm ready to go . . . I was saying, Vicar, when this villain came between us, you are always welcome at Paradou. The girl's the mistress, you know. I don't worry her any more than I worry my lettuces. It's all natural increase. It's only imbeciles like this see harm in it . . . What harm do you see, you rascal? It's you invented the harm. Dirty brute!'

He gave the Friar another good shaking.

'Do let him get up now,' begged Mouret.

'All in good time . . . The child has been very poorly for some time now,' he continued. 'I had noticed nothing, but she tells me about it, so I'm off to see Dr. Pascal, at Plassans. It's quiet, at night, nobody on the road . . . Yes, she's not at all well.'

The priest did not know what to say. Head sunk on his breast, he staggered slightly.

'She was so happy while she was looking after you,' the old boy continued. 'I used to sit puffing at my pipe, listening to her laughter. I couldn't have asked for more. Girls are like wild roses, when they bloom, they bloom profusely. Well, if the heart moves you, we shall be seeing you. It might cheer the child up a bit . . . Good-night, Parson.'

He slowly got to his feet, gripping the Friar's wrists firmly as he did so, wary of a treacherous move, and then, without once turning back, made off, with his usual long, heavy step. Without a word, the Friar crept to the stone-heap. He waited till Jeanbernat was some distance away, then, throwing with both hands, he began again, but the stones all fell short, on the dusty road, while Jeanbernat, not even deigning to turn, continued his way through the tranquil night, erect as a tree.

'Accursed man,' muttered Friar Archangias. 'Satan is behind him,' and he sent a last stone whirring through the air. 'A flick of the finger ought to finish off a man in his years. He's been baked in the fires of hell, he has. I felt his claws.' And his impotent rage trod the scattered stones. Whirling round suddenly to face the Reverend Mouret, he accused him: 'It's all your fault,' he cried. 'You should have helped me. Between us we could have throttled the life out of him.'

The din in the Bambousse's home on the far side of the village had meanwhile increased. They could distinctly hear the rhythmic beat of wine-glasses on the table. Mouret had proceeded on his way again, head still sunk on his chest, and he made for the broad bar of light pouring from a window like the bright glow of a bonfire of vine-cuttings. The Friar followed him, very grim, his cassock soiled with dust and one cheek bleeding where a pebble had caught it. After some silence, he suddenly demanded in his hard voice if Mouret really intended to go to Paradou. And as there was no reply, he continued:

'You mind your *p*'s and *q*'s, you are slipping back into sin . . . Merely that old bastard coming made you quiver all over. I could see you, in the moonlight, pale as a girl . . . You look out, do you hear? This time, God will not forgive you. You would go down into the worst possible filth . . . Oh, miserable filth, it's that carries you away.'

Only then did the young priest at last look up. Large tears were coursing down his cheeks. And, breaking his agonised silence, he said, with pitiful gentleness:

'Why do you speak to me so? You are always with me, you know what struggles I go through all the time. Don't doubt in me so, let me have the strength to conquer myself.'

These words, of utter simplicity, watered with silent tears, assumed such a note of sublime sorrow in the night that even Friar Archangias, for all his crudity, was moved. He did not say another word, merely shook his cassock to get the dust off it and wiped his bloodstained cheek. And, when at last outside the Bambousses', he refused to go in, but sat down on the upturned body of an old wheelbarrow, where he proceeded to wait with the patience of a dog.

'Here's the Vicar!' came the sudden roar from the combined families of the Bambousses and the Brichets. And all the glasses were at once topped up. Mouret of course had to take one too.

There had been no proper wedding-breakfast. All they had done was after dinner bring out a ten-gallon demijohn of wine, to be finished off before bed. There were ten of them, and the old man was already able to tip the enormous wicker-covered bottle with one hand and get only a thin red trickle out of it. Rosalie was well lit. She was dipping her baby's chin in her glass, while 'big Fortuné' was doing his parlour tricks, lifting chairs in his teeth.

They all trooped into the bedroom. Custom demanded that the Vicar should drain his dose of wine there, which is what they called blessing the bedroom, supposed to bring luck and prevent family fights. In M. Caffin's day they always had a jolly good time, because that grizzled priest loved his laugh. Indeed, he was quite famous for his skill at draining his glass without leaving a drop at the bottom, the more important since the womenfolk at Artaud maintained that every drop left in the glass meant one year less of love for the marriage partners. With the Reverend Mouret, the joking was a bit more subdued, but all the same, he quaffed his in one go, which apparently pleased old Bambousse, though Mother Brichet did not fail to peer grimly into the glass and find some drops left. A gamekeeper uncle who was standing right in front of the bed ventured a few rather hot wisecracks, at which Rosalie—whom by way of caress Fortuné had already pushed face downwards on to the mattress—roared with laughter. And when everybody had had his wisecrack at the expense of the newly-weds, they all went back to the living-room, where Vincent and Catherine had stayed by themselves, to find Vincent perched on a chair with the enormous demijohn in his arms, draining the last drops into Catherine's open mouth.

'Thank you, indeed, Vicar,' cried Bambousse, when he saw the Reverend Mouret off. 'Well, they're spliced now, eh, and you are satisfied. Ah, the rapscallions, and do you really think now they're going to spend much time saying *Paters* and *Aves* when they get to their room? Good-night, Vicar, pleasant dreams yourself!'

Brother Archangias had meanwhile slowly risen from the upturned wheelbarrow.

'May Satan,' he muttered, 'put shovelfuls of burning coke between their bodies and may they burst of it!'

He did not say another word, as he accompanied the Vicar back home, and waited till the vicarage door was firmly closed, before he started out for home. He even turned back twice, to make quite sure that Mouret had not come out again.

When the young priest reached his own bedroom, he flung himself fully dressed on the bed, his hands stopping his ears, his face buried in the pillow, to hear and see nothing more. Thus blotting himself out, he fell into a dead sleep of death.

CHAPTER VI

The following day was a Sunday. The Exhaltation of the Holy Cross this year thus falling on a day of high mass, the Reverend Mouret wished to observe the feast with especial brilliance. He had latterly been taken up with particular devotion to the Cross. In his room he had replaced the statuette of the Immaculate Conception by a large ebony crucifix, before which he passed long hours in adoration. And this exaltation of the Cross, planting it before him, setting it above all other things in glorification, the sole aim of his life, gave him the strength to bear his sorrow and to struggle. It was his dream to nail himself there in Jesus' place, to be crowned with thorns, to have his limbs pierced, his side gashed open. How poltroonly he was, indeed, to dare to complain of a false wound, when there his God bled from his whole body, yet still smiled the smile of Redemption. And, miserable though he was, he offered his own wounds as sacrifice, ending up in an ecstatic state with the conviction that blood really was pouring from forehead, limbs and breast. Those were moments of assuagement, when all his impurities were drained out from his wounds.

He drew his shoulders back, and with the heroic efforts of a martyr stressed his body, craving frightful torture, so he might bear it without a quiver of the flesh. Since crack of dawn he had been kneeling at the crucifix, but at last grace did come, grace as copious as the dew. He made no effort now, he had but to bend his knees for it to rain down upon his heart, soaking him through to the bone, in a fashion gloriously sweet. The evening before, he had had to endure agonies before grace thus came to him. Cursed as he was, he had had to wait a long time indeed before it responded to his lamentation. Often enough grace thus came to his succour when he could no longer do more than clasp his hands like a little child. But this particular morning, it was a blessing, absolute repose, complete faith, and the trials of the preceding days were forgotten. He gave everything to the triumphant joy of the Cross. Armour fortified his breast, armour so impenetrable that the world broke into mere foam against it. When he came downstairs, he was walking in an atmosphere of triumph and utter calm. Teuse was so struck with wonder that she went to find Désirée for him to kiss. Both clapping their hands, they cried that he had not looked so well for a good six months.

In church, during high mass, he completed his rediscovery of God. It was long since he had gone to the altar with such emotion. He had to hold himself in, not to burst into tears when he pressed his lips to the altar-cloth. They celebrated solemn high mass. Rosalie's gamekeeper uncle sang such a diapason of a bass that the deep vibrations filled the low vaulting with the glorious rippling of organ pipes. Vincent, decked out in a surplice which had belonged to M. Caffin, and was too large, with much delight in the tinkle of its little chains swung an old silver thurible, swishing it up extra high to make as much smoke as he could, all the time peeping behind him to see how many people he was making cough. The little church was nearly full. Folk wanted to see the parson's painting. The women were all beaming with pleasure, because it smelt so lovely, while at the west end, under the gallery, the men tossed their heads scornfully every time the cantor failed more clumsily than usual to reach his proper note. The full sunlight of mid-morning was pouring in through the windows. The new paper panes softened it, spreading it wide over the freshly-painted walls in cheerful pools of colour, and the women's bonnets cast fluttering shadows just like butterflies. Even the artificial flowers on the altar gradines had the moist delight of freshly picked flowers. When the priest turned to give the benediction, he felt more moved than ever, seeing his church so clean and so full, so drenched in music, incense and light.

After the offertory, a whisper ran through the womenfolk. Peering up in curiosity, Vincent all but tipped the hot coals of his thurible over the Vicar's chasuble. When the Reverend Mouret shot him a stern glance, the boy apologetically whispered :

'It's your uncle, sir, he's just come in.'

It was quite true. At the west end, standing by one of the slender wooden columns which supported the gallery, the Reverend Mouret did indeed now see Dr. Pascal. But today his uncle was not his usual kindly, smiling self, with that slightly teasing light in his eyes. Standing there, hat in hand, he seemed grave and angry, and as the service dragged on made no effort to hide his impatience. The sight of the priest at the altar, with all that pious concentration, with those drawn-out gestures, with that perfect serenity of countenance, seemed to irritate Doctor Pascal more and more. Indeed, he was unable to wait till the service was over, and suddenly went outside again, to fidget about round his horse and trap. He had tied the animal to one of the vicarage shutters.

'Look here, isn't that fine fellow of ours ever going to finish smoking himself with incense?' he asked Teuse, when all at once she emerged from the sacristy.

'It's all over,' she replied. 'Will you go into the drawing-room, sir . . . The Vicar is disrobing. He knows you are here.'

'I should think so, indeed, unless he's blind,' muttered the doctor, following her into the chilly room with hard furniture which she had dignified with the name of drawing-room. For some minutes Pascal strode up and down. This room, with all its grey gloom, augmented his ill humour. As he stamped about the room he kept whacking the worn horsehair of the chairs with his stick. He might have been cracking stones by the wayside. Then, feeling tired, he took up a stand at last, facing the fireplace, where the usual place of a clock was occupied by a large abominably coloured St. Joseph.

'Hm,' he grunted, 'and time too!' when he caught the sound of the door. Going up to his nephew, he began: 'Do you know you made me swallow half a mass? It's a long time since that happened to me . . . But I simply had to see you. I've something I must have a talk with you about.'

He broke off, staring at the priest in some surprise. Then, after a moment of silence, 'Are you feeling well?' he asked, suddenly, in rather a different tone.

'Oh yes,' said the Reverend Mouret, with a smile, 'I am better now. I did not expect you till Thursday. Sunday's not your day . . . You have something to tell me?'

To this, Uncle Pascal did not reply at once. He went on quizzing the young man. Mouret was still soaked in the hot-house air of the church. In his hair he bore the odour of incense. Deep in his eyes was the joy of the Cross. Faced by this triumphant serenity, the elder man shook his head.

'I've come straight here from Paradou,' he said, brusquely. 'Last night Jeanbernat came out for me . . . I have been to see Albine. I am worried about her. She needs a lot of care.'

While he spoke, he continually studied the priest. But Mouret's eyes did not even blink once.

'To cut a long story short,' he went on, more bluntly, 'she looked after you. Without her, my boy, at this moment you might well be in a padded cell at Tulettes with a straight-jacket on you . . . Well, and I've promised you would go to see her. I will take you. To say good-bye. She wants to go away.'

'I can but pray for the person of whom you speak,' said the Reverend Mouret, very gently.

240

And, seeing the doctor lose his temper and bring his stick swishing down on the sofa, he added, quite simply, but in very firm tones:

'I am a priest, I have only prayers to give.'

'Damnation, and you are right,' cried Doctor Pascal, and he flopped into an armchair. His legs had suddenly failed him. 'I am an old idiot!' he said, angrily. 'But let me tell you, I cried all the way here, all by myself, like a child . . . That's the result of living in a world of books. You get very clever, then you do shabby things. As if I ever suspected that it was all going to turn out so badly.'

Very agitated, he got up and began pacing the room.

'Yes,' he said, 'yes, I ought to have had the sense to see it. Everything pointed that way. Of course, it all went rotten in you, you are not a man like other men . . . At the same time, don't forget, I'm not joking, you were a lost man. Only the climate that girl created round you could have saved you from going right off your head. But of course, you know that, I have no need to tell you what a state you were in. And it's been one of my finest cures, too. And I am not at all proud of it either, mind you, because now as a result, that poor child is dying.'

The Reverend Mouret was still utterly impassive. He stood there with all the tranquil radiance of a martyr whom nothing human can ever again overcome.

'God will be merciful to her,' he said.

'God! God!' muttered the doctor, in a hollow voice. 'He would do much better if He would kindly avoid tripping us up. We could manage things ourselves.' Then, more loudly, he went on: 'I had worked it all out so nicely, too. That's the worst of it. Oh, what an idiot I was . . . You would spend a month, convalescing. The shady park, the fresh breath of that delightful child, all that youthfulness of hers would set you right again. At the same time, she would lose her wildness, you would civilise her, I thought, between us we should turn her into a sweet young thing who then would easily find a husband somewhere round the country . . . A perfect scheme!
. . . But how on earth was I to imagine that that old philosopher, Jeanbernat, would leave you two utterly to yourselves. True, I am just as much to blame, all that time I never once left my lab. But I had some experiments on . . . That means it was all my fault . . . I have behaved very shabbily.'

Choking with mortification, he would have left the room, but he could not find his hat. All the time, it was on his head.

'Good-bye,' he stammered, at last. 'I will be going . . . So you

241

refuse to come to Paradou, is that it? I am asking you to come, if only for my sake. Can't you see what I am going through? I swear that she will go away from this district at once, after. That is all agreed ... The gig's at the door. You'll be back in an hour. Come, please do come!'

The priest made a vast gesture, one of those gestures which the doctor had seen him making before the altar.

'No,' he said, 'I cannot.' And, going out with his uncle, he added: 'Tell her to kneel and pray earnestly to our Lord, and he will hear her as he has heard me. He will assuage her as he has assuaged me. There is no other salvation.'

The doctor gaped at him. Then his whole body heaved, and he shrugged his shoulders desperately.

'Good-bye,' he said, finally. 'You are all right. You don't need me any more.'

But as Doctor Pascal was untying his horse, Désirée, who had just caught the sound of his voice, came racing up. She adored her uncle. When she was smaller, he used to listen for hours to her childish babble, and never tired of it. He still spoiled her, even today, taking an interest in her animals, ready to spend a whole afternoon with her among her hens and ducks, his keen scientist's eyes smiling down on her. He would call her his 'big animal,' in a tone of fond admiration. He seemed to place her above other girls. So, in a burst of affection, she flung her arms round his neck. 'Are you staying? she cried, 'Are you lunching with us?'

But, kissing her, he refused, and rather gruffly unlaced her arms from round his neck. With peals of laughter, she embraced him again.

'You are very mistaken,' she cried, 'I have some eggs still warm from the nest, I've just been looking at my hens, they've laid fourteen, this morning ... And we could have roasted a pullet, that white one which pecks the others. Why, you were here on Thursday when she pecked out that speckly's eye!'

Uncle Pascal was much put out. That delightful bridle knotted round his neck, which he could not undo, exasperated him. Then Désirée began dancing round him, clapping her hands, chanting softly in her flute-like voice:

'Yes, yes, of course you're staying ... We'll cook that white pullet, we'll cook that white pullet.'

His anger could not hold out. He looked up suddenly, and smiled. She was too healthy, too vital, too genuine. Her lightness of heart was too expansive, as natural and frank as the flood of sunlight like gold on her skin.

242

'What a lovely creature of nature!' he muttered. He was enchanted by her. Then, taking her by the fists, while she went on bounding about, he said firmly:

'Listen to me, my dear, not today. I have to go to see a poor girl, who is ill. But I shall come round another morning . . . That is a promise.'

'When? Thursday?' she insisted. 'The heifer's in calf, you know. The last two days she has seemed a bit poorly. You are a doctor. Perhaps you can give her something.'

The Vicar of Artaud, who was still standing passively by, could not restrain a little laugh. Doctor Pascal now leapt quite cheerfully up into his trap.

'Right,' he cried, 'I'll treat your heifer . . . Now come here, my dear, and let me kiss you, you big beastie! How good you do smell, you smell of health. You are worth more than all the world. If the rest of them were like my big beastie, it would be too lovely on earth.'

He gave his horse a click of the tongue, and as the trap went down the hill, went on, to himself: 'Yes, just brute creatures, that's what we should have, then it would be fine, cheerful, strong. Oh, what a dream! How well life has turned out for that girl, she is as happy as her heifer! And how badly for the boy, going through hell in his cassock! Just a bit more blood, and a bit better nerves, and what a time he'd have! Like this, he just misses life . . . Real Rougon and Macquart, those two are, the tail-end of the band, the final degeneration.' And, urging on his horse, he bowled off down the slopes towards Paradou.

CHAPTER VII

SUNDAY was a very busy day for the Reverend Mouret. He had vespers, usually with an empty church, even Mother Brichet not driving her devotion so far as to go back for afternoon service. Then, at four, Friar Archangias brought the kids of his school for the Vicar to give them their catechism lesson. That sometimes went on till rather late. When the children were too unruly, Teuse would be called in and she put the fear of God into them with her broom.

This Sunday, towards four o'clock, Désirée was alone at the vicarage. Finding time long, she went out to gather feed for her rabbits in the churchyard, where there were some magnificent poppies which the animals adored, and she was crawling about among the graves on hands and knees, to bring home apronfuls of juicy herbage, which her pets attacked ravenously.

'Oh, what lovely plantains!' she murmured, crouching down at the Reverend Caffin's tombstone, delighted by her discovery.

There were indeed magnificent specimens, spreading their broad leaves from crevices among the stones. She had just filled her apron, when she thought she heard a strange sound. Then came a rustle of foliage and slithering of loose shingle came up from the chasm which ran along one side of the graveyard, below which flowed the Mascle, the mountain river which flowed down from the high ground of Paradou. The cliff at this point was so steep and impassable that Désirée concluded it must be a lost dog, or perhaps somebody's goat loose. But when she rushed to the edge and leant over, in the thick of the brambles clambering up the rocks, making use of the slightest rugosity, she was amazed to see a girl.

'Let me give you my hand,' she cried down to her. 'You might break your neck.'

Seeing herself discovered, the stranger started with fear, and seemed about to go down again, but then raised her head and found the courage to take the hand offered her.

'Ah, I know who you are,' said Désirée, suddenly remembering, with delight, and she let go her apronful of leaves to take the other girl by the waist with all the natural affection of a child. 'You gave me some blackbirds, didn't you. Those poor little darlings died. I was terribly upset . . . Just a moment, I know your name too, I heard it once. Teuse often speaks of you when Serge isn't about. But she says I am never to mention it . . . But just a minute, and I'll remember.'

She made an effort of memory which left her quite grave. Then, getting back the missing word, she was all cheerfulness again. She played with the music of the name, repeating it again and again.

'Albine, Albine, that's it. It's a very sweet name. At first I thought Albine must be a kind of finch. I once had a finch I called something like that. But not exactly.'

Albine did not smile. She was very pale, and in her eyes was the glow of fever. There was blood on her hands. At last she got her breath back.

'No, it doesn't matter,' she said, 'you'll only dirty your hanky if you wipe it off. It's nothing, only a few scratches. I didn't want to come by the road. I should have been seen. I preferred to come this way . . . Is Serge home?'

The fact that Albine used her brother's name so familiarly, and with such grim intentness, did not in the least shock Désirée. Yes, she said, he was there. He was in the church, with his catechism class.

'We musn't talk loud,' she added, putting a finger to her lips. 'Serge says I must never talk aloud when he is doing catechism. If we do, he'll come out and scold us ... We'll go into the stable, shall we? It's nice there, we can talk.'

'I want to see Serge,' Albine insisted, single-mindedly.

The grown-up child lowered her voice still more. Casting furtive glances at the church, she whispered.

'All right ... We shall have him caught properly. Come with me. We'll hide. We shan't make a sound. Oh, what fun!'

She gathered up the leaves she had dropped and with infinite precautions made her way back to the vicarage, enjoining Albine to follow close behind her and keep low. Just as they took refuge and raced across the churchyard, they saw Teuse crossing through the sacristy, but without seeing them, so it seemed.

'Sh!' cried Désirée, beside herself with delight when they were both huddled at the back of the stable. 'Now nobody will find us. Here's some straw. We can lie down here.' And Albine had to seat herself on a bale of straw.

'And Serge?' she asked, single-minded.

'Why, can't you hear his voice? When he claps his hands, that's the end, the little ones will go then ... Listen, he's telling them a story now.'

It was so, they could just hear the Reverend Mouret's voice. It came through the sacristy door, which Teuse must have opened. It was like a whiff of church air, a low mumble in which the word Jesus stood out two or three times. With a shiver, Albine rose to her feet. Her instinct was to run to the voice she so loved, the caress of which she knew so well, but the next instant, the sound seemed to be wafted away once more, damped down as the door was closed. She sat down again, hands pressed together, all expectation, completely absorbed in the thought which burned deep in her limpid eyes. Désirée nestled at her feet and stared at her with naive wonder.

'Aren't you lovely,' she whispered. 'You are just like the statuette which Serge used to have in his bedroom. She was all white, just like you, with great locks of hair tumbling on to her shoulders, and just where I can feel your heart thumping she showed hers. All red it was ... You are not listening to what I say, you are

245

unhappy. Let's play, shall we?' Then she broke off, to cry out in a desperate whisper: 'The hussies! They will give us away.'

She still had her apronful of leaves, and the animals were attacking it. A flock of hens had run up, clucking away, calling one to another, pecking at green blades which stuck out. And the goat slyly thrust her head under Désirée's arm, to crop large leaves. Even the heifer, which was tied to the wall, tugged at her rope and stretched out her muzzle, snuffling the air and snorting with hot breath.

'Oh, aren't they awful robbers!' Désirée ran on. 'Why, this was to be for the rabbits! ... Will you let me be! You'll get a clout, you will! And if I catch you again, I'll turn up your tail for you! ... Wretched things, they would rather eat my hands.'

She shooed away the goat, scattered the hens with a few hearty kicks and drove off the heifer by punching its nose as hard as she could. But they all only shook themselves and came back, greedier than ever, leaping at her, surrounding her and tugging at her apron. Then, screwing up her face with delight, she whispered to Albine—as if the animals might have heard her—'Aren't they funny, the loves? Wait, you shall see them eat.'

All this, Albine watched solemnly.

'Now, behave yourselves,' cried Désirée. 'You shall all of you get something, but each in turn... First, big Liza. Ah, don't you love plantain, old thing?'

Big Liza was the heifer. Slowly she began munching a fistful of juicy leaves which had grown on the Reverend Caffin's grave. From her muzzle dangled a thin thread of spittle. Her big brown eyes gleamed with greedy gentleness.

'Now you,' Désirée continued, turning to the goat. 'Oh, I know you want some poppies, and you prefer the blooms, don't you, you like buds popping all juicy between your teeth like chops done in paper ... Ah, there's some beauties. They're from the corner over to the left, where they dug last year's graves.'

As she chattered away, she offered the goat a bunch of bloodstained blossoms, which the animal chewed eagerly. When nothing was left but the stems, she thrust those between its teeth. Behind her, the angry hens were pecking at her skirts. She threw them wild chicory and dandelion which she had gathered round the old flagstones along the church wall. The hens fought most fiercely over the dandelions, and so voraciously, with such beating of wings and use of spurs that the remainder of the farmyard heard, and then it was a real invasion. First came the big, savage cock,

Alexander. He pecked at a dandelion, but only to cut it in two without picking up either part, then cackled, calling up the hens which were still outside, and drawing back to invite them to take it. And in came first a white hen, then a black one, then a whole column of them, pushing each other, mounting on each other, till it was all one mellay of angry feathers. Behind the hens came pigeons and ducks and geese, then turkeys. Surrounded by that flood of livestock, drowned in it Désirée laughed and laughed.

'It's just the same, every time I bring them fodder from the graveyard, they would murder one another to get a share ... It must taste specially good.'

With a struggle, she raised the last few handfuls over her head, to save them from the greedy beaks all upturned towards her. She had to keep some for her rabbits, she said, if they were so greedy, they would make her angry, she would put them all on dry crusts. But she was giving way. The geese tugged so fiercely at her apron that she nearly fell to her knees. The ducks gnawed at her ankles. Two pigeons flew on to her head. There were hens now on her shoulders. In this was all the ferocity of wild creatures scenting flesh, juicy plantains, blood-red poppies, sap-full dandelions, all imbued with the life of those buried where they had grown. Désirée was overcome with laughter, felt she would slip to the ground at any moment and have to let the last two handfuls go, when a frightful grunting put all the birds into a panic.

'Oh, it's you, my dear fatty,' she cried, in rapture, 'you eat it and save me!'

In came her pig, no longer a dainty piglet, pink as a newly painted toy, its hindquarters gay with a string of curly tail, but a monster porker, rotund as a church cantor's corporation, ready for the knife, its back thick with coarse silk which was simply oozing fat grease. Its belly was amber-coloured, from sleeping on the dung-heap. Its snout thrust well forward, it came tumbling in and charged the mixed flock, which enabled Désirée to slip away and give the rabbits the scrap of fresh fodder which she had managed to save for them.

When she returned, peace was restored, the geese's necks were swaying gently and they had their normal silly, blissful expression. The ducks and the turkeys were sidling along the walls, like lame old men. The hens were clucking softly, pecking out invisible grains of corn from the panned stable floor. And the pig, the goat and the big heifer just stood, blinking, as if overcome with sleep. Outside, a thunder shower had suddenly begun.

'And there's some rain,' said Désirée, re-seating herself on the straw, with a little shudder. 'You'd better stay here, darlings, if you don't want to be soaked.' And, turning to Albine, she added: 'Don't they look smug? They only wake up if there's anything to eat.'

All this time, Albine said nothing. The laughter of this handsome lass, wallowing about among all those greedy muzzles and beaks, kissing her and tickling her, seeming ready even to nibble at her flesh, had turned her quite pale. So much good cheer, health, life, made her miserable. She clutched her fevered arms to her, hugging empty space to breasts which drooped from neglect.

'But Serge?' she asked again, her voice precise, insistent.

'Sh!' whispered Désirée, 'I heard him a moment ago, but he hasn't finished yet. We were making a lot of noise just now. Teuse must be deaf, this evening . . . Let's be quiet, now. How nice to listen to the rain.'

The storm came in through the open door, lashing the threshold with its large drops. Worried hens, having ventured forward, had taken refuge at the back of the stable. The whole yard took shelter there, round the skirts of the two girls, all except three ducks, which were strolling undisturbed up and down in the rain. It was quite hot in the straw. Désirée pulled two more large bales across and stretched out on them at full length, as on cushions. She was absolutely comfortable, every bone of her enjoying it.

'Isn't it good!' she cried, 'isn't it good! You should lie down like me. I dig myself in, I feel it pressing me all round, and the straws tickle at my neck . . . If you rub yourself against it, you feel it run all up your legs, just as if little mice were creeping up under your frock.'

And indeed she did rub herself against the straw, laughing to herself, slapping at the bales, first here, then there, as if to defend herself against those little mice. Then, letting her head sink back and raising her knees high, she went on babbling.

'When you are home, do you tumble about in the straw? I can't think of anything nicer . . . Sometimes, I tickle the bottom of my feet. That's awfully funny too . . . I say, do you ever tickle yourself?'

But at this moment, the big brown cock, who had come solemnly forward, seeing her sprawling like that, leapt on to her bosom.

'Will you get off, Alexander!' she cried. 'Isn't he a silly creature? I can never lie down but he tries to get on to me . . . No, you can stay, darling, only be good, don't peck at my hair, will you?'

She took no more notice of the bird, and the cock stayed, firmly perched on her bodice, peering every now and then under her chin, eyes blazing. The other creatures came close to her petticoats. She wallowed again for a while, then fell back, relaxed, in a pose of utter abandon, her legs parted, her head sunk back. She babbled on:

'Oh, it's too lovely! But it always makes me feel tired. It makes you quite sleepy, doesn't it? Serge doesn't like doing it. Perhaps you don't either. Then what do you like doing? . . . Tell me, I'd like to know what you do.'

Slowly she relaxed into a drowsy state. For a few moments, she kept her large eyes wide open, as if in search of some pleasure of which she was ignorant, then her eyelids sank down over her eyes, and there was a peaceful smile on her face, as if she was completely satisfied. She seemed to doze, but after a few minutes suddenly opened her eyes and said: 'My heifer is going to have a baby . . . That's good too. I shall enjoy that more than anything.'

She then slipped into a deep sleep. In the end, her animals did climb on her, till she was lost under a flood of live plumage. The hens seemed to cover her feet. The geese lay their breasts down along her thighs. On the left, the pig warmed his loins against her, while on the other side was the goat, stretching its bearded head up under her armpit. There were pigeons all over her, in her open hands, in the hollow of her groin, behind her drooping shoulders. And as she slept she was all pink, caressed by the more powerful breathing of the heifer, choked by the weight of the cock crouching, now lower down, his wings outspread, his crest aflame, his dun belly burning her with fiery caress through her skirts.

Outside, the rain was not so heavy now. A patch of sunlight slipped out from under a cloud and gilded the dusty cloud of breeze-blown rain. Motionless, Albine watched this other girl sleep, this lovely body finding its satisfaction by wallowing in straw, and she longed herself to be able thus to be languid, in the drowth of love, and slumber sweet from an orgasm reached merely by a few straws tickling her neck. She was envious of those powerful arms, that firm bosom, that utterly fleshly life lapped in the fertile warmth of a flock of farmyard creatures, that purely animal blossoming which made of that plump child the passive sister of the big white and red heifer in calf. She dreamed of being loved herself by a brown cock-bird and of herself loving naturally, without shame, as any tree grows, merely opening all her veins to the ejaculation of life's sap. It was the earth itself that satisfied Désirée when she wallowed on her back.

Meanwhile, the rain had now entirely stopped. One after the other, the three household cats crossed the yard, along by the wall, taking infinite care not to wet their paws. The peered inquisitively into the stable, then came straight to the sleeping girl, purring away, and lay down beside her, their front paws just resting on her skin. Then Mumu, the big black one, lay against one of her cheeks and began slowly licking her chin.

'But Serge?' Albine whispered, mechanically.

What exactly was the obstacle? What prevented her satisfying herself thus happily in the heart of nature? Why did she not love and why was she not loved in the full sunlight, in liberty, as trees grew? She did not know, and felt herself for ever deserted, for ever desolate. Then again came a new surge of fierce purpose, a wild need to take her treasure in her arms and hide him away and have satisfaction from him again. With this, she rose to her feet. The sacristy door had opened once more. She caught the faint sound of a hand-clap, followed by the noise of the sabots of a troop of children clattering over the stone floor.

The catechism was over. She stole out of the stable, where she had been waiting now for an hour, with all the hot stench of the farmyard about her. As she slipped in and down the sacristy corridor, she caught a glimpse of Teuse, back in the kitchen. But the housekeeper's back was turned to the door, and she did not look round. Then, confident of not having been seen, Albine opened the door and carefully closed it noiselessly behind her. She was in the church.

CHAPTER VIII

AT first, there seemed to be nobody there. Outside, it was raining again, a persistent drizzle, and the church was wrapped in greyness. She went behind the main altar and down as far as the pulpit. In the nave there were only the benches which the children had left in disorderly lines. The clock pendulum rang hollow in the emptiness. She went farther down, to tap on the woodwork of the confessional at the far end. Then, as she passed the Chapel of the Departed, she found the Reverend Mouret prostrate before the big, blood-stained crucifix. He did not stir. He must have thought it was Teuse, putting the benches straight. Going up to him, Albine lay her hand on his shoulder.

'Serge,' she said, 'I have come to see you.'

The priest raised his head. He was very pale, and she saw that he was trembling. Remaining on his knees, he made the sign of the cross. His lips were still mumbling a prayer.

'I have been waiting,' she continued. 'Every morning, every evening, I have waited, but you never came. I counted the days. Then I stopped counting. Now it is weeks ago . . . Then, when I was sure you would never come, I decided to come to you. I said to myself: 'I will take him away.' Give me your hands, and let us go now.'

She held out her hands, as if to help him up. Again, he made the sign of the cross. He continued praying, his eyes all the time on her. But he had already subdued that first spasm which leapt into his flesh. From the grace in which he had been bathed all day as in a heavenly dew he drew superhuman strength.

'Your place is not here,' he said gravely. 'Go back . . . You are only aggravating your suffering.'

'I no longer suffer,' she said, with a smile. 'I am better, I am cured, now I see you . . . Let me tell you, I made myself out more ill than I was so they would come to fetch you. I make no secret about it, now. Just like that promise that I would go away and leave this district, once I saw you again, you surely never thought I would keep it . . . Oh, how much better had I carried you away then on my shoulders . . . Nobody else knows, but you do, you know I cannot live at all, but by your side.'

She was gaining heart now, and went up to him, caressing as any child of liberty, blind to the icy rigidity of the priest in him. Then, all eagerness, she clapped her hands with delight and cried:

'Come, Serge darling, make up your mind. You are only wasting our time, here. There's no need for so much reflection. I shall take you away, it's so easy . . . if you don't want anybody to see us, we can go up the Mascle. It isn't a good road, but I managed it all by myself, and when we are two, we can help each other . . . You know the way, don't you? We go across the graveyard, down the cliff to the river, and then all we have to do is follow that, it goes all the way up into the garden. And how secluded we shall be, deep in the park! Nobody there, don't fear, nothing but brushwood and lovely smooth rock. The stream is almost dry now. On the way here I said to myself: 'When Serge is with me, in a little while, we shall walk slowly home together, arms enlaced round each other's waists.' Come, let us make haste. I am waiting, Serge darling.'

The priest seemed no longer even to hear her. He had withdrawn again into his prayers, imploring Heaven for the courage of the saints. Before engaging in the ultimate battle, he was arming himself with the flaming swords of faith. For a moment, he had thought he might falter. He had needed the stout heart of a martyr, to keep his knees on the flag, hearing every word of Albine's appeal. His heart went out to her, all his blood rose up, casting him into her arms, with unbearable longing to kiss her hair. By the mere scent of her breath she had awakened and instantaneously filled him with memories of all the growth of their gentle love, of their huge garden, of those strolls under the trees and of the radiant delight of their union. But grace poured its dew over him in greater abundance. It was but the agony of an instant that drained his veins of blood, till all that was human was gone from him, and he was but the thing of God.

Albine had to lay her hand to his shoulder again. She was worried now, and gradually losing patience.

'Why don't you say anything? You cannot refuse, you are going to follow me . . . Bear in mind that if you refused, it would kill me. But no, you cannot possibly refuse. Wake up. We were once together, and never should have left one another. You gave yourself a score of times. You told me to take the whole of you, to take every limb of you and your breath and your life . . . It is surely not possible that I merely dreamt all this? There is not a spot of your body which you did not give over to me, not a single hair of your flesh of which I am not the mistress. That birthmark on your left shoulder I have kissed, and it is mine. Your hands are mine, I have held them in mine for days. And your countenance, your lips, your eyes, your forehead, it is all mine, I have done what I would with it, to lavish my caresses on it . . . Do you hear me, Serge?'

She stood fully erect and sovereign before him, holding out her hands. Then, more loudly, she said again: 'Do you hear me, Serge? You are mine.'

Now, slowly, the Reverend Mouret rose to his feet. With his back to the altar, he declared: 'No you are mistaken, I am God's.'

He was utterly tranquil. His hairless face was like that of a saint cut out of stone, troubled by no heat from human entrails. His cassock draped in rigid folds, like a black shroud, revealing no hint of his body. Albine started back suddenly, seeing this ghost of her love. Gone now was the free-flowing beard, gone the loose locks of his head, and now, amid hair cut short she saw a pale patch, the tonsure, which disturbed her as might an unknown disease, a malignant wound, eating its way there, larger and larger, till it

252

would consume all memory of the days of happiness. She did not even find the hands she had known before, hands so warm, so fondling, nor the fine line of the throat ringing with laughter, nor the sinewy feet whose gallop had borne her deep into green groves. Was it possible this was that young male powerful of muscle, whose loosened shirt collar had revealed the flue of a broad chest, the skin blossoming under the sunlight, the loins vibrant with life, in the embrace of which for an epoch of her life she had lived? At this moment he seemed to be utterly without flesh, his hair shamefully limp, his very virility dried away from him under those female garments which left him sexless.

'Ah!' she cried, in a soft gasp, 'how you frighten me ... Did you think I was dead, to put yourself in mourning so? Strip away this blackness, put on an ordinary shirt, roll up your sleeves, and we shall again angle for crayfish ... Your arms were as tanned as my own.'

She had placed her hand on the cassock, as if to rend the black cloth from him, but with a mere gesture, without even touching her, he repulsed her. He gazed at her, growing steadily stronger against temptation, his eyes constantly fending her off. To him she seemed to have matured. She was no longer the mere tomboy of the wild coppices, scattering gypsy laughter to the winds, nor the loving maiden in white skirts, her slim body lissom as she trod slowly and lovingly through woody glades. Now on her lips he saw an apricot bloom, her hips swayed loosely, her bosom billowed like a luscious flower. She was now a woman, with her long countenance, which lent her a tremendous atmosphere of fertility. Life slumbered in those spreading loins, and in the complexion of her cheeks he saw the growing richness of the lovely maturity of her body. And then, thus all enveloped in the love-enriched fragrance of her woman's maturity, the priest found a particular gall of delight in braving the caress of the red lips, the laughter of the eyes, the appeal of the bosom, the intoxication which at her least movement flowed from her, and he drove his temerity to the point of seeking out the very parts of her body which once he had so madly kissed, the corners of her eyes, the corner of her lips, the narrow temples, satin soft, the ambered neck, silky as velvet.

Never, even in Albine's embrace, had he tasted such delights as he tasted, martyrising himself, gazing boldly at this full love which he rejected. Then, suddenly, he feared he might succumb to some new snare of the flesh. Lowering his eyes, he said gently:

'I cannot listen to you here ... If you insist on adding to our

253

regrets, let us go outside . . . For us to be together in this place is sacrilegious. We are in God's house.'

'Whose house, God's?' cried Albine madly, again the young girl run wild in nature. 'I know nothing of him, this God of yours, and I do not want to know him, if he steals you from me, who never did him any harm. So my Uncle Jeanbernat is quite right, is he, when he says that your God is an invention of evil, a device to frighten people and make them weep! . . . You lie, you just don't love me any more, your God does not exist.'

'You are in his house,' the Reverend Mouret repeated, with emphasis. 'You blaspheme. With one breath he could reduce you to dust.'

She laughed, superbly. Raising her arms, she defied Heaven.

'So,' she cried, 'you prefer your God to me? You think he is stronger than I am. You think he will love you better than I would? Ah, what a child you are! Do stop talking such twaddle. What we are going to do is go back to the garden together, and love each other, be happy and free, for that is life.'

This time, she succeeded in slipping her arm about his waist, and began to draw him with her. But he broke free. He was shuddering all over. He went back to lean against the altar, but he forgot himself so far as to speak to her now in intimate words, as he once had done.

'Dearest Albine, go, do go,' he stammered his plea. 'If you still love me, dearest one, go away . . . Oh, Almighty God,' he murmured, quickly, 'pray forgive her, forgive her for defiling Thy dwelling. If I go out of this door behind her, I may follow her. Here, in Thy house, I am strong. Allow me to stay here, to defend Thee.'

For a moment, Albine did not speak. Then, more quietly, she said:

'Very well, then, let us stay here . . . I want to talk to you. You cannot be so bad as not to understand me. You will not let me go away by myself . . . No, do not defend yourself, I shall not take you again, if it hurts you. See, I am quite calm. We are merely going to talk gently to each other, just as we used to, when we lost our way and, merely to have longer to talk to each other, did not try to find it.'

She smiled, then continued:

'I really don't quite know . . . Uncle always said I was never to come to your church. He said: 'Stupid child, when you have a garden, what do you think you can do in a stuffy hovel?' And I grew up very happily. I looked in birds' nests without ever touching their eggs. I did not even pick flowers, for fear they would bleed to death. You know I never caught an insect to torture it . . . So whatever reason is there for God to be angry with me?'

'You need to know him, to pray to him, at all times render him the homage due him,' the priest replied.

'And then you would be satisfied, is that it?' she asked. 'You would forgive me and love me again? All right then, I agree to all you want. Tell me about God, I shall believe in him and worship him. Every word of yours will be a truth I shall listen to on bended knees. Have I ever had a thought other than yours? We shall resume our long walks, you will teach me, you shall do what you will with me. Oh, agree, do, please!'

The Reverend Mouret indicated his cassock.

'I cannot,' was all he said. 'I am a priest.'

'A priest,' she repeated, after him, and the smile left her face. 'Yes, Uncle makes out that priests have neither wife nor sister, nor even mother. So it is true, is it? But why did you ever come to Paradou? It is you who took me for your sister, then for wife.'

He raised his pale face, beaded with agonised sweat.

'I sinned,' he muttered.

'But you see,' she said, 'when I saw you so free, I thought you were no longer a priest. I thought that was all over, you would stay at Paradou for ever, for me, with me . . . But now what would you have me do, seeing that you have taken my life from me?'

'What I am doing,' he said. 'I would bring you to your knees, to die kneeling, and never rise again till God forgives you.'

'Then that means you are a coward,' she said now, her lips twisted with scorn, as anger took command again.

He staggered, but did not say a word. Frightful agony choked him, but he remained stronger than his pain. He held his head upright, almost smiling with the corners of his quivering lips. For a while Albine defied him, with unflinching stare. Then, in a fresh burst of anger:

'Come now,' she cried, 'answer me, accuse me, say it was I who went to Paradou to tempt you. That would be the limit . . . All right then, I will allow you to make excuses for yourself. You can strike me if you like. I would rather you struck me than stood stiff like a corpse. Is there no more blood in your veins? Do you not hear me charge you with cowardice? Yes, you are a coward, my dear, you should never have loved me at all, since you are incapable of being a man . . . Is it that black gown that hinders? Tear it off. If you were naked, you might perhaps remember.'

Slowly, the priest repeated exactly what he had said before. 'I sinned, I have no excuse. I am doing penance for my sin, with no hope of pardon. If I stripped off my vestments, my flesh would come with them, for I have given my whole being to God, with all my soul, all my bones. I am a priest.'

'And I? What am I?' cried Albine, again.

He held his head erect. 'May your sufferings be counted as so many crimes of mine! May I suffer eternal punishment for having to leave you alone! That will be justice . . . All unworthy though I be, I pray for you every evening.'

In a sudden access of terrible hopelessness, she shrugged her shoulders. Her anger was cooling. She was almost a prey to pity now.

'You are insane,' she murmured. 'Keep your prayers. It is you that I want . . . You will never understand. I had so much to tell you. Yet you stand there and all you can do is make me furious with your talk of some other world . . . Look here, Serge, let us be sensible, you and I, let us wait till we calm down more, and have another talk . . . I cannot just go away like this. I cannot leave you here. It is because you are here that you are like a dead man, your skin so cold that I dare not touch it . . . Let us stop talking now. Let us wait.'

She was silent. She took a few steps. She looked about her at the little church. The rain was still streaming ashen grey down the windows. A cold light, drenched with dampness, seemed to moisten the walls. Not a sound came from outside except the monotonous rustle of the shower. The sparrows must have been crouching under the eaves. Obscured by the dust of fine rain, the mountain-ash reared shapeless foliage. The clock struck five, each stroke torn harshly from the cavernous thorax of the works. Then the silence grew immense again, and duller, blinder, more desperate. Scarcely dry yet, the paintwork lent the main altar and the other woodwork a dismal cleanliness, the air of a convent chapel where the sun never shines. Lamentable throes of pain seeped into the nave, spattered with the blood flowing from the limbs of the large crucifix Christ, while along the walls the fourteen images of the Passion exhibited their frightful tragedy, a mass of yellow ochre and red, perspiring horror. It was life itself in death throes there, a last shudder of death, on these altars like tombs, amid this mortuary bareness. Everything was eloquent of night, terror, annihilation, nothingness, slaughter. A last breath of incense lingered. It was like a last miserable gasp of a dying woman, stifled under the heavy flagstones by a jealous God.

'Oh!' cried Albine, 'how lovely it was in the sun, don't you remember? One morning, over to the left of the garden, we were walking along by a hedge of lofty rose-bushes. I even remember the colour of the grass, like blue silk shot with green light. When we reached the end of that hedge, we made our way back, the sun there smelt so sweet. And that was all our walk, for a whole morning, twenty steps one way, twenty steps back, a corner of happiness from which you refused to emerge. Wild bees buzzed, a blue tit hovered fast by us, leaping from twig to twig, there were processions of wild creatures about their tasks all round us, and you whispered: 'How good life is!' Life was that grass, those trees, that water, the sky, the sunshine which illuminated us, turning our hair to gold.'

She dreamt again for some moments, then continued:

'Life was Paradou Park. We could never find the end of it. The greenery reached us in free waves murmuring to the horizon. And what blueness above our heads! We could grow up and fly aloft and be fleet as the clouds, and never meet worse obstacles than they were, for all the air was ours.'

She paused, then with a swift gesture indicated the squat church walls.

'And here,' she said, 'you are in a dungeon. You can never stretch your arms wide enough without barking your knuckles on these cramping stone walls. That vaulting hides the sky from you and robs you of your share in the sunlight. This box is so small that your limbs grow stiff in it, as if you had lain down alive in the grave.'

'No,' said the priest, 'my church is as vast as the world. All God is in it.'

Again she pointed, to the cross, to the dying Christs on the crucifixes, to the tortures of the Passion.

'And you live amid death. Everything, grass, trees, water, sunshine, sky, is in death throes here.'

'No, everything lives again, everything is purified, everything goes back to the source of all light.'

He had reared himself very erect, and there were flames in his eyes. He left the altar, for ever invincible, lapped in the glow of faith such that he scorned the dangers of temptation, and he took Albine's hand, speaking to her intimately, as to a sister, and led her up to the dismal pictures depicting the road of the Cross.

'But see,' he said, 'what my God suffered . . . *Jesus is scourged* . . . You see, his back is bare, his flesh is torn, his blood streams down his loins . . . *Jesus is crowned with thorns* . . . Bloodstained beads of sweat ooze from his pierced forehead . . . A great gash has opened his temples . . . *Jesus is insulted by the soldiers* . . . To scorn him his executioners fling a piece of purple cloth about his neck, and they cover his face with their spit, they hiss him and with blows of their rods they drive his crown of thorns into his forehead . . .'

Albine looked away, not to see those crudely coloured pictures where blotches of lacquer cut into the yellow ochre flesh of Jesus. Round his neck the cloak of purple looked like a strip of flayed skin.

'What good is there in this suffering, in this death?' she replied. 'Oh, dearest Serge, did you but remember . . . That day you told me you were tired. And I knew well that you were lying, because it was cool weather and we had not walked more than a quarter of an hour. But you wanted to sit down, to take me in your arms. You well know that at the far end of the orchard there was a cherry-tree planted on the bank of the river, which you could never pass without wanting to cover my hands with little kisses which fluttered all the way up my arms, to my shoulders, to my lips. The season of cherries was over, so you devoured my lips . . . The flowers when they faded made us weep . . . One day, when you found a little kid dead in the grass, you turned quite pale and pressed me to you, as if to prevent the earth taking me.'

The priest drew her on past the other stations of the cross.

'Silence, he cried, 'look again and listen again. You must bow low, from sorrow and pity . . . *Jesus faints under the weight of the cross* . . . The climb up Mt. Calvary is rough. He has fallen to his knees. He doesn't even wipe the sweat from his face, but gets to his feet and continues on his way . . . Yet again he succumbs under the weight of his cross. At every step he staggers. This time, he has fallen on his side, so badly that for a moment he has no breath. His torn hands have let the cross slip from them. His agonised feet leave a bloodstained trail behind them. Monstrous fatigue crushes him, for on his shoulders he bears the sins of the world . . .'

Albine looked at Jesus. Dressed in a blue petticoat, he was stretched out under a disproportionately large cross, the black colour of which had run, staining the gold of his halo. Then, not knowing where to look away from this, she murmured:

'Ah, those paths through the meads! Have you no memory left, Serge dear? Do you no longer know of those paths of fine grass across the meadows through the vast lakes of greenery? The afternoon of which I speak, we had only gone out to spend an hour. But we kept straight on, and on, so that when the stars came out we were still walking. It was so soft, that endless carpet, soft as silk. Our feet never came upon harsh stones. One might have thought it a green ocean whose mossy waters cradled us. And we knew quite well where those paths which in all their softness led nowhere were taking us. They led to our love, to the delight of living with arms round each other's waists, to the certainty of days of real bliss . . . When we returned, we felt no weariness. You were lighter than when we left for you had given me your caresses and I had not been able to give them all back to you.'

With hands shaking from his pain, the Reverend Mouret pointed to the last pictures. He stammered:

'And here is *Jesus on the cross* . . . Under the hammers, the nails pierce his open hands. One nail only is enough for each foot, and the bones snap. But while his flesh quivers, he smiles, his eyes on heaven . . . *Jesus is between two thieves* . . . The weight of his body enlarges his wounds frightfully. From his forehead and his limbs pours the blood-stained sweat. The two thieves insult him, passers-by mock, the soldiers squabble over his clothes. And dusk spreads over the scene, the sun is hidden. *Jesus dies on the cross* . . . He utters one terrible cry, he renders up his soul. Oh, frightful death! And the veil of the temple was rent in twain, from the top to the bottom; and the earth did quake, and the rocks rent; and the graves were opened . . .'

He fell to his knees, his voice broken by sobs, his eyes on the three crosses at Calvary, where the whitish bodies of the tortured men suffered their agony, bodies which the crude draughtsmanship had emaciated monstrously. Albine placed herself between the pictures and him so that he should see them no more.

'One evening,' she said, ' in a long-drawn-out twilight, I had lain my head on your knees. It was in the forest, at the end of that big avenue of chestnuts down which the setting sun sent its last rays. Oh, what a fond farewell! The sunlight lingered at our feet with a kind and friendly smile which bid us *au revoir*. The sky grew slowly paler. Laughing, I said to you that it was doffing its blue gown and donning a black one with gold flowerets, to go out to a party. And you peered into the shadow, impatient for us to be alone, without the sunshine, which embarrassed us. And it was not night which drew near, but a discretion of gentleness, a veiled tenderness, a moment of mystery like one of those very dark paths under the foliage in which one goes to hide for a moment, yet sure that at the far end one will again come into the joy of full daylight. This particular evening the twilight with its serene pallor brought the promise of a marvellous morning . . . That was when, seeing that the daylight was not waning fast enough to suit you, I pretended to fall asleep. Now I can tell you the truth. I was not asleep when you planted that kiss on my eyes. I was enjoying those kisses. I had to squeeze myself not to laugh. I breathed evenly, and you drank in my breath. Then, when it was really dark, it was all like a long lullaby. The trees, you see, slept no more than did we . . . That night, you remember, the flowers smelt stronger than usual.'

And as he remained kneeling, his cheeks streaming with tears, she seized his fists and drew him up, and with passion went on:

'Oh, if you only knew, you would tell me to take you away, you would knot your arms round my neck so that I could not go without you . . . Yesterday, I had a desire to see the garden again. It is larger now, deeper, more inscrutable. I found fresh scents there, scents so soft they made me cry. In the walks I came upon downpours of sunshine which soaked me in quivers of desire. The roses spoke of you. The bullfinches were so surprised to see me alone. The whole garden sighed . . . Oh, do come with me! Never did the greensward offer a softer bed. I have marked with a flower one deep, hidden corner to which I want to take you. It is deep in a thicket, a nook in the greenery like a large four-poster bed. And from it one can hear the garden's life-beat, all the trees, the waters and the sky. The very breath of the soil will be our lullaby. Oh, do come, we shall love each other in the love of the whole of life.'

But he repulsed her. He had come back to the Chapel of the Departed, facing the big painted pasteboard Christ. It was of the height of a boy of ten, depicted in agony with shocking verisimilitude. The nails really imitated iron, the wounds, frightful gashes, were wide-gaping.

'O Jesus, who died for us,' he cried, 'tell her what nothingness we are! Tell her we are mere dust, filth, damnation. But stay! First grant me to hide my head beneath a hair-shirt and lay it at your feet and remain thus, motionless, till death rots my flesh away. This earth will then exist no longer. The sun will be extinguished. I shall no longer see, nor feel, nor hear. Naught of this wretched world will then come to distract my soul from worship of Thyself.'

He became more and more ecstatic. His hands raised, he suddenly approached Albine.

'You are right, my dear,' he said, 'it is death who is here, it is death that I crave, the death which delivers and saves us from

260

all foulness . . . Do you hear me? I renounce life! I reject it, I spue it from me! Your flowers stink, your sun blinds me, your green-sward infects those who lie on it with a leprosy, your garden is a charnel house where the corpses of all things decay. The earth itself is an abomination. When you speak of love, of light, of a happy life deep in your palace of greenery, you lie. In your world there is but darkness. Your trees distil a poison which changes men into beasts. Your thickets are black with the venom of vipers. Your rivers sweep pestilence along under their blue waters. If I tore its belt of foliage and its petticoat of sunshine from that nature of yours, you would see it is hideous, a Megaera, and that goddess of vengeance has the loins of a skeleton, loins eaten away by vice . . . What is more, if you spoke the truth, if your hands were full of real delights, if you did carry me away on a bed of roses, even if you did bring me into your dreamed-of paradise, I should defend myself the more fiercely against your embrace. Between us there is war, century-old, war implacable. See, this church is very small. It is poor, it is ugly, it possesses a pitch-pine confessional and a pitch-pine pulpit, a concrete font, and altars made of four planks, painted by my own hand. What matter? It is greater than your garden, greater than the valley, greater than the whole world. It is an invincible fortress which none shall overthrow. In vain may winds and sun, forests and seas and all that lives assail it, it will remain standing, not even shaken. Yes, let those groves of yours grow, let them batter on these walls with their thorny arms and let the swarming insects emerge from every crack in the soil to eat at the stones of my church, yet, however damaged it may be, it will never be swept away by that over-abundance of life. It is death inexpugnable. And would you like to know what will happen some day? This little church will become so huge and will cast such a shadow that all your nature will be overthrown by it. Ah, indeed it will, in death, in the death of everything, the heavens opening wide to receive our souls, far above the abominable material debris of this world.'

He was shouting now, as he pushed Albine towards the door. Deathly pale, she fell back, step by step. When suddenly he was silent, with choking voice, gravely she said:

'So is this the end? Are you then driving me away? But yet I am your wife. It is you who made me as I am. Having allowed this love of ours to be, God can never punish us to such extent.'

She was at the threshold. There, she added:

'Listen, Serge, every day, when the sun goes down, I go to the

261

far end of the garden, where the wall is broken down, and there I await you!'

And she went away, and behind her the door of the sacristy closed with a choking sigh.

CHAPTER IX.

IT was silent in the church, save for the drumming of rain on the roof, harder now, filling the nave with an organ throbbing, and in this sudden calm the priest's rage left him, and he was overcome with emotion. It was now with tear-wet face and sob-shaken shoulders that he returned to fling himself on to his knees before the big crucifix. Avowals of burning gratitude broke from his lips.

'Oh, Gracious God, I thank you for the succour you have vouchsafed to send me. Without your grace I would have heard the voice of my flesh and returned to my miserable sin. Your grace girded my loins like a warrior's belt; your grace was my armour, my courage, the inner support which kept me upright, with no weakening. Dear God, you were in me, it was you who spoke in me, for I no longer found my animal cowardice, I felt myself strong enough to sever all the bonds of my heart. And here is my heart, all bleeding. It no longer belongs to any but yourself. For you, I have torn it from the world. But, dear God, do not think that I draw pride from this victory. I know that I am nothing without you. In my humility, I grovel at your feet.'

He had slumped down, half sitting now on the altar step, unable to find another word, his half-opened lips merely breathing forth his soul without words. The abundance of his grace bathed him in inexpressable ecstasy. He was all inturned, seeing Jesus Christ in the depths of his own being, in that sanctuary of love which he held in constant readiness to receive Jesus with all the honour due him. And Jesus, he felt, by reason of the astonishing gentleness which pervaded him, was indeed there. And thereupon he started one of those inward conversations with Jesus during which he was swept off this earth and spoke mouth with mouth with his God. He stammerered the verse of the Song of Songs:

> My beloved is mine, and I am his:
> He feedeth among the lilies.
> Until the day break, and the shadows flee away.

He mulled over the words of the *Imitation*: '*Knowing how to hold converse with Jesus is a great art and knowing how to keep him with one a great safeguard.*' There followed the most delightful familiarity. Jesus stooped to his level and for hours told him of his needs, his delights, his hopes. And two lovers meeting after separation and going aside to the seclusion of a lonely river have things less moving to say to one another than now, for in these moments of divine condescension Jesus deigned to be his best and most faithful friend, a friend who never could be disloyal, and for a mere moiety of affection gave him all the treasures of eternal life. And on this occasion more than any other, the priest longed to possess Jesus a long time. When six o'clock struck in the voiceless church he was still giving ear to him amid the silence of all living things.

It was confession of the whole person, free interchange of intimacy without the hindrance of language, the natural effusion of the heart rising as spirit before even thought itself. The Reverend Mouret told Jesus everything, speaking to him as to a God come close in the intimacy of his affection and able to hear all. He confessed no less than that he still loved Albine. He confessed that he was astonished to have been able to treat her ill, driving her away, without his bowels rising in revolt against him. He confessed that this fact astounded him. He gave a serene smile, as if suddenly seeing an act of miraculous strength performed by another. And Jesus replied that this should not astonish him, that the greatest saints were often unconscious instruments in the hands of God.

And now the Vicar expressed his great doubt. Had it not been less meritorious of him to take refuge at the foot of the altar and even in the passion of our Lord? Was his not still after all most puny courage, seeing that he dared not fight it out alone? And Jesus proved surprisingly tolerant, explaining that man's weakness is God's continual concern. He said he preferred suffering souls to those which know no suffering, and to these he came as to seat himself at the bedside of a friend. Was it a damnation to love Albine? No, it was not damnation, if the love went beyond the flesh, if to his desire for that other life he added hope. Then, how was he to love her? Was he to love her without a word, without taking a step towards her, letting affection of absolute purity exhale from him like a fine scent pleasing to heaven?

Here, Jesus gave a kindly little laugh, and he drew closer and encouraged this confession, to such point that the priest gradually grew bolder and rendered up details on Albine's loveliness. She had the fair hair of the angels. She was white. She had large, gentle eyes, like those of saints with haloes. Jesus said nothing, but still laughed. And how she had grown up! She was like a queen

263

now, with those rounded lines and magnificent shoulders. Ah! how wonderful to put his arm round her waist, were it but for a second, and feel those shoulders lean back as he held her! Then Jesus' laughter faded out, dying like a ray of the great sun on the skyline, and the Reverend Mouret found suddenly that he was talking only to himself. There was no gainsaying it, he said, he had been too hard; why if Heaven allowed one to love, why chase Albine away without a single kind word?

'I love her, I love her,' he cried, out loud, in a desperate voice which reverberated into every corner of the church.

He seemed still to see her there. She was holding out her arms to him. She was desirable enough to make him break all his vows. And without respect for the church he flung himself on to her bosom. He took her thighs in his grasp and under a rain of kisses, he possessed her. Then he knelt before her, begging for mercy, begging forgiveness for his brutalities. He explained that at moments there was a voice within him which was not his. Could he himself ever have treated her ill? It was only that stranger voice that had so spoken. That could not be himself, for he would have shuddered to think of laying a cruel hand on a single hair of her head. Yet he had certainly driven her away, the church was indubitably empty. Where was he to run to find her, to bring her back and fondle her, to wipe away her tears?

It was raining harder still now. The roads were pools of mud. He pictured her lashed by the storm, staggering up the ravine of the river, her petticoats sodden, clinging to her body. No, no, that was not himself, that was the other man, the jealous voice, the voice which had been so cruel as to will the death of his love.

'Oh, Jesus!' he cried, more desperately. 'Be kind and give her back to me.'

But Jesus was no longer there.

Then, awakening suddenly, the Reverend Mouret turned deathly pale, and he understood. He had been unable to keep Jesus with him. He had come to lose his friend, and was now defenceless against evil. Instead of that inner clarity with which he had been illumined and in which he had received his God, all he could find in himself was darkness, an evil smoke which irritated his skin. Withdrawing from him, Jesus had taken grace away with him. And, strong as he had been since morning by the aid of Heaven, he felt himself now suddenly utterly wretched, abandoned, as weak as a child. And how frightful the fall, how immense the bitterness. To have struggled heroically and not fallen, to have been invincible, implacable, while the temptation was there in the flesh, with rounded figure, marvellous bosom and the odour of a woman loving, then to succumb shamefully, gasping with loathsome lust, when the temptation had withdrawn, leaving behind it but a rustle of skirts and the fragrance wafted from a fair bosom! For now, with such memories, she came back invading the church, all-powerful.

'Jesus, Jesus!' for a last time, the priest cried out, 'return, enter into me again, speak to me once more!'

Jesus was deaf to these words. For a few moments, raising his arms desperately, the Reverend Mouret implored Heaven. His shoulder-blades cracked, with such fantastic force did he pray. But soon enough his arms fell to his sides, his hopes abashed. From heaven came one of those silences utterly void of hope known to the devout. He seated himself again on the foot-pace of the altar, crestfallen, his features ashen, and pressed in his elbows to his sides as if trying to make his very flesh shrink. Under the biting tooth of temptation, he was trying to make himself small.

'Dear God, you are abandoning me,' he murmured. 'Thy Will be done!'

Not another word did he utter. His breathing came hard, like that of a harried beast, rigid now with paralysis in its fear of the teeth which may kill. Since his descent into original sin, he had thus been the plaything of the whims of grace. When he craved it most fervently, it would refuse to come, while when he no longer dared hope to possess it till many years had gone by, it would suddenly come to him, unforeseen and full of enchantment. At first, deprived of grace, he had rebelled, using the language of the jilted lover, demanding the immediate return of that winsome comforter whose kiss made him strong. Then, after fruitless bouts of rage, he grasped that humility did him less hurt and alone could help him to bear this abandonment.

Then, for hours, for days, he abased himself, awaiting a relief which never came. It was vain to put himself again into God's hands, to grovel before him, repeating to satiety the most efficacious of prayers, for the fact was that he no longer felt God. Broken free, his body was swollen with desire. Prayers on his lips were embarrassed and turned into filthy mutterings. It was a drawn-out agony of temptation in which one by one the weapons of faith fell from his treacherous hands and he was no more than an inert thing in the grip of his passions, and he was a shocked onlooker at his own ignominy, without even the pluck to raise his little finger to chase sin away.

Such was now his life. He knew all the ruses of his sin. There was not a day when he was not tested. His sin took a thousand guises, it came in by his eyes, by his ears, it came straight at him and took him by the throat, it leapt slyly on to his shoulders and it tortured him even in the marrow of his bones. That root sin was always there, Albine's nakedness, dazzling as the sun itself, shedding its rays on the green groves of Paradou. It was only in those rare moments when grace deigned to seal his eyes with fresh caresses that he ceased to see this source of sin. And he hid his infirmity like a shameful disease, shutting himself in those ghastly silences into which nobody was able to break, those taciturn moods which drove Teuse beside herself, till behind his back she shook her fist at Heaven.

This time, he was alone, he could go through his hell without shame. His sin had struck him down with such a savage blow that he had not the strength to move from the altar step onto which he had fallen. He continued panting there, consumed by painful fires, and without a single tear flowing.

Oh, what peace, what confidence there had been when he first came to Artaud! Salvation then appeared to him a lovely road, and if anyone spoke of temptation, he laughed. He lived amid evil without either knowing it or fearing it, confident he could always be its master. He was then a perfect priest, so chaste, so innocent before God, that God led him by the hand like a little child. Now all that childlike state was gone. God came to him first thing in the morning and at once submitted him to temptation. Temptation became his very mode of his existence. Thus, grown older, and having sinned once, he was eternally rent apart by inward struggle. Could it be possible that God loved him more now this was so? The great saints had all left strips of their flesh on the thorns of the *via dolorosa*. In that conviction he tried to find solace. At every new laceration of his body, every fresh sound of a creaking bone, he promised himself extraordinary recompense. Heaven would never strike him enough. He actually came to despise his former serenity, that facile fervour which in the rapture of a young girl brought him to his knees without even the slightest sense of the hard ground wounding his knees. He became clever enough to find lush enjoyment in the throes of suffering, to make his bed in it, to sleep in it. But while he blessed Almighty God his teeth chattered with greater horror, and the voice of his rebellious blood cried out to him that all this was a falsehood, the only delight a man could wish for was to stretch out in Albine's arms under the shelter of a flowering thicket in Paradou.

Now, however, he had abandoned Mary for Jesus, sacrificing his heart to conquer his flesh, dreaming he could find a place in his faith for his virility. Mary upset him too much with the delicate ribbons of her brow, with those outstretched hands of hers, and her woman's smile. He could not kneel before her now without having to lower his eyes, for fear lest he caught sight of the edge of her skirts. Moreover, he charged her with having been too gentle to him in time past. She had held him so long within the folds of her gown that he had slipped too easily from her arms to those of this earthly woman, without even noticing that the caresses were those of another. And to his mind came the coarseness of Friar Archangias, the man's refusal to worship Mary, the mistrustful eyes with which the Friar seemed to supervise him. What slender hope he had of ever attaining that high level of crudity.

All he did was to turn away from the Virgin. He concealed all his images of her and deserted her altar. But she was still there, all the same, deep in his heart, ever present, like an unconfessed love. And by a sacrilege, the enormity of which left him aghast, sin actually made use of the Virgin now to tempt him. When from time to time, in moments of irrespressible emotion, he did call on her, it was Albine who came to his mind, Albine in a white veil, round her waist a blue scarf, and about her naked feet, roses of gold. All the Virgins, she with regal cloak of gold, she crowned with stars, she visited by the Angel of the Annunciation, and the Virgin serene between lily and distaff, with the smiling eyes, the sensitive lips, or the soft curve of cheek, all brought him fresh reminders of Albine. His sinning had destroyed the virginity in Mary. Therefore, by a supreme effort, he expelled the female sex from his religion and took his refuge in Jesus, though even his gentleness at times disturbed him. What he wanted was a jealous God, an implacable God, an Old Testament God, surrounded with thunder, never revealing himself but to punish the awe-stricken world.

It was an end to the saints, to the angels and to the Mother of God. Only God himself remained, omnipotent overlord who insisted that all should breathe but for him. The hand of that God he could feel crushing his loins, holding him at his mercy, in space and in time, as if he were a faulty atom. The *summum bonum* now was to be nothing, to be damned, to dream of hell, in sterility to wage that fight against the monsters of temptation. From Jesus all he could get was the cross. He was possessed now with that obsession for the cross in which so many lips have worn themselves away on crucifixes. He took up the cross and he followed Jesus. He made the cross heavy, overbearingly heavy, his greatest delight to succumb beneath the weight, to carry it shuffling along on his knees, broken-backed. In the cross alone he saw the strength of the soul, the delight of the spirit, the highest point of virtue, the perfection of holiness. In it was everything and everything led to death in it. Suffering and death, these were the words which ceaselessly rang in his ears as the ultimate human wisdom. And when he had fastened himself to the cross, he had the limitless consolation of the love of God. It was no longer Mary that he loved with filial affection and lover's fire. He loved merely the concept of loving, in an absolute of love. He loved God more than himself, above all else, deep in a great radiance of light. Thus he became like unto a torch, consumed by its very brightness. When he craved death, in his eyes it was only a great upsurge of love.

But whatever could be his shortcoming, to be subjected to such harsh tests? He wiped away the perspiration which poured from his temples. He reflected how only that same morning he had examined his conscience without finding in it any grave fault. Did he not live a life of austerity and self-mutilation? Did he not love God and only God, and blindly? Oh, what benediction he would have pronounced had God but held him sufficiently punished for his sinning and give him peace at last. But for all he knew his sinning would never be expiated.

And thus, in spite of himself, he came back yet again to Albine, to Paradou and its burning memories. At first, he sought excuses. One evening, he had collapsed on the floor of his bedroom, struck down by a brainstorm, and then for three weeks he had been in the grip of a crisis of the flesh, his blood furiously washing his veins, to the tips of his limbs, roaring through him with the din of a torrent unleashed. From skull to sole of the feet his body was cleansed, restored, in his illness so mentally belaboured that often in his delirium he heard the hammers of workmen rivetting his limbs together again.

Then, one morning, he had awakened, as if a new man. He was thus born a second time, freed of all that twenty-five years of life had accumulated in him. His childhood devotions, his seminary years, his young priest's faith, were then all gone, submerged, swept away, leaving a vacancy.

268

Unquestionably, hell had thus prepared him for sin, disarming him and transforming his bowels to a bed of softness into which evil could enter, to sleep. And all the time, as he let himself gradually make his way to his sinning, he had been unconscious of this. When at Paradou he had re-opened his eyes, he had felt as if bathed in new childhood, with neither memory of the past, or trace of religious discipline. When life thus began anew, his organs functioned gently in rapturous surprise, as if they had never known life before and now found the greatest delight in learning what it all meant. Oh, delightful apprenticeship! What enchanting world it was that he came upon, what precious discoveries he made!

Paradou had been immense happiness. Bringing him there, hell knew very well that he would be defenceless. Never, in his first youth, had he tasted such raptures of enjoyment, and if he recalled that first youth, it came to him entirely blank, as an existence slipped into utter remoteness from the sun, existence thankless, ghastly, and sickly. This being so, how he welcomed the sun, how he marvelled at the first tree, the first flower, the minutest insect he saw, the smallest stone he picked from the ground! The very rocks enchanted him. The horizon was an astounding miracle. His senses,—a morning clarity filling his sight, fragrance of jasmin wafted to his nostrils, the song of a skylark heard, caused him such violent emotion that he was as paralysed. Teaching himself life had been a long-drawn-out pleasure, to the slightest quiver. And that morning when Albine too was born at his side, amid the roses! He still laughed ecstatically at the memory of it. She rose up like an orb essential to the sunlight itself. She lighted everything, she made sense of everything. She completed him.

Then with her, he had begun to walk again, in the enclosed world of Paradou. He recalled the little hairs which broke free on the nape of her neck when she ran before him. She smelt so good. She had skirts which in their warmth swayed harmoniously and if they but touched him, it was a caress. When moreover she took him in her bare arms, supple as snakes, he expected to see her, so fragile was she, curl snug within him and sleep there, close to his skin. It was Albine who showed him the way through the garden. She led him by a side path, and on their way they lingered, not to arrive at the end too soon. She inspired him with passionate love of the soil, and by watching the love of the plants, he learned to love her, in all their delicate slow advance into delight, till at last, one evening, in the sap-exuding shade, Albine and he too came to the supreme delight under the giant tree.

There, they had reached the end of their road. Albine, on her back, her head lying loose amid her unknotted hair, held out her arms to him, and he took her in close embrace. Ah, that taking of Albine in love! Oh, if he could but take her so once again, once again thus possess her, once again feel her loins quiver with their fertility, and thus himself make new life, and be God!

Suddenly, the priest uttered a hollow moan. He reared up as if seized by invisible teeth, then fell back, to crouch on his knees again. He was tempted to tear at his own flesh with his teeth. Into whatever filth was this that memory in him had wandered? Did he not know that Satan was up to all the tricks and profited even by moments of self-questioning to glide his serpent head into a man's very soul? No, no, there was no excuse. Illness never justified sin. It was up to him to preserve himself and as soon as he emerged from the fever, to seek out God again. But he had done the contrary, he had sought out pleasure, wallowing in his own flesh. And how luridly that did reveal what loathsome desires there were within him! Why, he could not confess his sin without backsliding, despite himself, down into the compulsion to commit the same sin again in thought. Could he never compel that foulness within him to be silent? He dreamt of emptying his heart of all thought, so he should never reflect again, of opening his veins, so that his guilty blood should torment him no more. For a moment he hid his face in his hands, shivering as if with cold, hiding the smallest parts of his foul skin. It might have been wild beasts prowling about him that by their hot breath made his hair stand on end.

But yet, despite all, the blood thudded through his heart, still he turned these things over in his mind. Though he had sealed his eyes with his fists, he still saw the supple silhouette of Albine's body traced in flame against the darkness, her bosom bare, blinding as the sun. Every time, by pressing hard on his eyes he essayed to drive that vision from him, she merely became still more dazzling, standing out clearly, her loins straining back, her arms held out, and the sight wrung a hoarse cry of agony from the priest. Had God then completely abandoned him, was there no longer any refuge for him? Thus, the intenseness of his will, his sin, the old Adam within him, insisted on rising ever new in his heart and taking terrifyingly concrete form. All over again, he saw even the tiniest blades of grass, peeping by the edge of Albine's skirts, and caught in his hair he found a small thistle bloom against which he recalled having pricked his lips. He was even haunted by the

270

scent of the somewhat acrid sugars of the crushed grass stems. He heard the same distant sounds again and the regular cry of some bird. He heard the vast silence, broken only by the gasp of wonder which swept under the trees.

Why had not Heaven struck him down at once? He would have suffered less. For, with the carnal delight of a condemned soul, he now found satisfaction in his very abomination. Rage shook him when he heard the vile words he had uttered when he grovelled at Albine's feet. As they echoed now, they were a challenge to God himself. He had admitted this woman to be his sovereign. He had given himself in slavery to her, kissing her feet, dreaming of being the water which she drank, the bread she ate. Now he understood why he could not recover. God was abandoning him to woman. But he would fight with her, he would break her bones if otherwise she would not let him go. She it was who should be the slave, who was the unclean flesh, to which the Church should have refused to give a soul at all. He reared up, tense, raising his fists, to strike Albine. And his fists opened, his hands sliding in soft caress down from her shoulders, the lips which had been ready to spue insults, glued now to her unknotted hair, stammered words of adoration.

The Reverend Mouret opened his eyes. The fiery vision of Albine disappeared. Sudden, unhoped-for relief was there, and he could weep. Sluggish tears refreshed his cheeks. He kept his breathing slow and deep, afraid still to move, lest once again arms knot about his neck. He could still hear the voice of wild nature at his back. But it was so sweet no longer to suffer that he suddenly forgot himself, and was immersed in the enjoyment of bliss.

Outside, the rain had stopped. The sun was setting in a sky which glowed so red that it seemed to drape the windows with curtains of rose-hued satin, the church became warm and living with that last breath of sunlight, and the priest muttered vague gratitude to God for vouchsafing him this respite. A broad ray of gold dust shining through the nave lit up the depths of the church, clock, pulpit, main altar. Would this be grace returning to him on a pathway of light direct from Heaven? His eye was caught by the minute points of dust glittering and dancing down the ray at miracle speed, a crowd of urgent messengers ceaselessly bringing news from sun to earth. A thousand lighted candles could never have filled the church with such splendour. Behind the main altar hung curtains of gold. Down from the gradines streamed fine gold work. Candlesticks blazed out in sheaves of brilliance. There were thuribles in which the hot glowing coals were precious stones. Sacred vessels of the altar gradually grew in size, with comet-like radiance, the white air was a rain of luminous blossoms amid flying lace, bouquets, rose garlands, from which, as the buds opened, scattered clouds of stars.

Never had he hoped for such riches for his poor church. He smiled, dreamt of eternalising that glory and shaping it to his will. He would have preferred the gold curtains a little higher hung, and the altar cruets, to his taste, were carelessly placed. He gathered up flowers which fell, he refashioned bouquets, he bent garlands in easier curve. Yet what a marvel it was when all this splendour lay spread out! He had become the pontiff of a church of gold. The bishops, the princes and the women wore regal robes. Foreheads in the dust, there were pious crowds paying him homage, encamped in the valley, waiting for weeks at the door before they could get in. They kissed his feet, because they were of gold and they performed miracles. The gold rose as high as his knees. In his breast there beat a heart fashioned of gold and its sounds were so clear and musical that the crowds outside could hear them. Then immense pride took possession of him. He was idolised. The ray of sunlight rose still higher, the main altar was all aflame. The priest was now fully convinced himself that this was indubitably grace returning to him, he felt such inward delight and such satisfaction. The murmur of unbridled nature at his back became a soothing sound, and round his shoulders he felt nothing but a velvet hand, as if a cat caressed him.

He continued his reverie. Never before had he seen things in such dazzling light. Now, so strong did he feel himself, that everything became easy. Since Albine was awaiting him, he would go to join her. That was but natural. Had he not married big Fortuné to Rosalie that very morning? The Church did not prohibit marriage. He recalled how they had smiled and nudged each other under the hands which gave them the benediction, and, that evening, he had been shown their bed. Every one of the words he had spoken to them echoed louder in his ears. He had told Fortuné that God was sending him a companion, because God had not wanted man to live a solitary life. He had told Rosalie that she should cleave to her husband, never leaving him, his submissive servant. But those words were also spoken for himself and Albine. Was she not his partner, his submissive servant, given him by God so that his virility should not dry away in solitude? Besides, they were already united. He was astonished now not to have understood

272

this at the time, surprised that he had not gone with her as duty required. But now it was definitely decided. He would go to her at once, when day broke. In half an hour, he would be at her side. He would go straight through the village, he would take the road up the hillside. That was much the shortest way. He could do anything, he was the master, nobody would say a word to him. If anyone looked, with one gesture he would make them avert their eyes.

He would live thereafter with Albine. He would call her his wife. They would be very happy. The gold rose higher still, streaming through his fingers. He was back in a bath of gold. And he took the altar vessels to serve him for table ware. He lived in grand style, paying people with fragments of the chalice which without much effort he fragmented with his fingers. He lined his marriage bed with the cloth of gold of the altar. As jewellery, he gave his wife those gold hearts, those gold chaplets and gold crosses hanging now round the neck of the Virgin and the saints. If but an upper floor were added even the church could be turned into a palace for him and Albine. God would raise no objection, since God permitted loving. Besides, what did God matter? Now, was he himself not God, with his feet of gold that the crowd kissed and the miracles he performed? And the Reverend Mouret rose to his feet and made a vast, sweeping gesture just like Jeanbernat, a gesture of negation which took in the whole horizon.

'There is nothing, nothing,' he cried. 'God does not exist.'

A terrible shudder seemed to pass through the church. Frightened, again mortally pale, the priest listened. Whoever had now spoken. Who had blasphemed? Suddenly, that velvety caress which he felt on his neck became savage, claws lacerated his flesh, his blood flowed yet again. But he tried to stand out this attack. He mouthed insults to victorious sin sniggering at his temples, where all the hammers of evil were beginning to beat again. Did he not know those ruses? Did he not know that common trick of approaching on velvety paw, a moment later to thrust the hidden claws bone-deep into the victim's flesh?

His wrath grew great at the thought of having been taken in like a child by this trick. Would he always be thus supine, with sin triumphant straddling his breast? Here he was, actually denying God. It was the fatal downward slope. Fornication was destroying faith. Next, dogma crumbled. A mere doubt born of the flesh could argue by its foulness and sweep away all Heaven. Divine law exasperated him, the mysteries were ridiculous to him. Amid the ruins of religion one lay down to debate one's sacrilege till like a mere animal one hollowed out a bed in which to sleep off one's filth. Then came other temptations: gold, power, libertarian living, irrepressible craving for the accomplishment of sex, all leading to an extravagance of debauch wallowing in beds of riches and pride. And one turned thief and stole from God. One broke up the sacred monstrances, to string them on the impurity of a woman!

Clearly, he was damned. Nothing embarrassed him any more, sin could use him as mouthpiece and shriek out through him at the top of its voice. But it was good to struggle no more. The monsters which had clustered round his head now writhed in his bowels. He strained his loin muscles, the better to feel their teeth. He abandoned himself up to them with frightful delight. Rebellion made him shake his fists at the church. No, he believed no longer in the divinity of Jesus, he believed no more in the Holy Trinity, he believed only in himself, only in his own fibre and the appetite of his parts. He wanted to live. He needed to be a man, yes, to race through the open air, to be strong, to have no jealous master, to kill his enemies with stones and to take the girls upon whom he picked over his shoulder and carry them away. He would rise again from the tomb in which uncouth hands had laid him. He would reawaken his virility, for it must be but lulled to sleep. And might he die of shame, if he found that virility extinct! And might God be cursed, if he had withdrawn him from the world of ordinary being, touching him with his finger to keep him for his service alone!

Thus the priest stood in his church, lost in his hallucination, and imagined that at this reiteration of blasphemy the church was falling down. The sheet of sunlight flooding the main altar had slowly grown, lighting the walls with the lurid glow of a conflagration. Flickers of that light rose higher and higher, licking the ceiling, then died out again, to leave the bloodstained glow of hot coals. And all at once the church was in utter darkness, as if that sunset glow had broken the roof in, splitting the walls and opening gaping breaches for an attack from without. The grim carcase of the building shuddered as it awaited the formidable attack. Night fell rapidly, and from far off, the priest heard a murmur rising from the Artaud valley.

Previously he had never understood the perfervid language of that scorched earth where only the gnarled stumps of vines, fleshless almond trees, olives lurching gawkily on crippled limbs could grow, and he had passed through that realm of lust in all the

274

serenity of ignorance. But, today, knowing the meaning of the flesh, he was sensitive to the merest sigh of leaves in the sunlight, exhausted by their love-making. First, on the far horizon, the hills, still warm from the sunset farewell, started up and seemed to vibrate as under the heavy tread of an army on the march. Then the outcrops of rock, and the stones of the road, every pebble of the valley, rose up too and breathed and moved, as if urged forward by imperative need to go on. Next, the expanses of red soil, those rare fields won by toil with the mattock, began to flow and to mutter like rivers breaking their banks, in the torrent of their bloom sweeping on with them the adumbration of new seed, the shape of new roots, the copulation of their vegetation.

Soon everything was in movement. The trunks of the vines reared like giant insects, the meagre wheats, the dry grasses, formed battalions armed with tall lances, the trees mounted each other for the race, massaging their limbs like wrestlers before the contest. The fallen leaves surged on and the dust of the roads advanced, all a multitude which at every step recruited new forces, human beings in their rut whose hard breathing drew closer, tornadoes of life in furnace breath, sweeping all before them into the maelstrom of one immense confinement of new life. Suddenly, there came the attack. From the far edge of the skyline the whole countryside hills, rocks, earth, trees, rushed at the church. Under the first shock, the edifice cracked, the walls split asunder, tiles flew. Only the large crucifix, though shaken, did not fall.

There was a brief respite. Outside, voices sounded, more angry now, and the priest suddenly made out human sounds. It was Artaud, that band of bastards spawned on these rocks, stubborn as brambles, now they in their turn, breathing out a giant breath heavy with the pullulation of life, Artaud fornicating on the soil of Artaud, planting there a forest of men, trunk to trunk, absorbing all free space, rising up the slopes towards the church, breaking down the door with one thrust, threatening to block the whole nave with the invasion of the branches of their kind. Behind them, in the confusion of undergrowth, ran the wild animals, cattle trying to bring down the walls with their horns, asses, goats, sheep, in their herds, like living waves, trampling the church to ruins, ant-heaps of woodlice, flocks of locusts, attacking the foundations, powdering them away with their saw-like teeth. And on the other side, there was also Désirée's farmyard, the manure-heap of which poured out its stifling stink, the giant cock Alexander sounding his trumpet call, the hens loosening the very stones with their beaks, the rabbits hollowing their burrows right under the altars, till they fell in disorder, the pig, so fat he could not move, grunting and waiting till the sacred ornaments were reduced to a handful of warm ash, to wallow his belly in their remains. Then came the rumble of a frightful thundering, and there was a second attack. Village, animals and all this flood of life overflowing swallowed up the church for an instant under a storm of bodies which bent the rafters low. In the confusion the females released from their entrails a continuous birth of new warriors. This time, a large section of the church wall came crashing down, the ceiling shuddered, the window frames were swept away, the mist of twilight, darker and darker, came in through the frightful gaps. And on his cross the big Christ now held only by the nail through his left hand.

The collapse of that section of wall was greeted by a great din. But despite its wounds the church still stood solid, savagely stubborn now, silent, grim, clinging to the smallest stone of its foundations, as if to remain erect this ruin needed no more than the slightest of pillars, by a miracle of balance to bear the cracked roof aloft. Then the Reverend Mouret saw the coarse vegetation of the plain start work, menacing growth toughened in dry rocks, stems like snakes knotted, of hard wood all lumpy with sinew. Rust-hued lichens like enflamed leprosity first consumed the flaking plaster. Thyme thrust its roots in like crowbars between the bricks, lavenders slipped their long, hooky fingers under each piece of loosened masonry, drawing it to them, tearing it out by the slow force of attrition. The junipers, the rosemaries, the thorny hops climbed higher with irrepressible upthrust. Even the grasses whose sear blades had crept under the main door took part, turning to lances of steel, cutting the door asunder, advancing into the nave, raising the flags with their powerful pincers.

It was a victorious riot, revolutionary nature raising up the overturned altars to make barricades of them and demolishing the church which for centuries had cast too much shade over them. And the other warriors gave this herbage its scope—thyme, lavender, lichen,—all this corrosion of small things, more destructive than the sledge-hammer blows of the big growth, crumbling away the foundations till at last their silent labour would bring down the whole structure.

Then, all at once, it was the end. The mountain-ash, whose high branches in under the vaulting had already thrust through the broken windows, came bursting inside in a formidable jet of greenery and took its stand in the centre of the nave. There, it grew enormously, its trunk becoming monstrously large, till the church about it burst like a belt become too small. On all sides, the branches stretched out huge knots, each of which carried away a section of wall, a strip of roofing, and these branches continued to multiply, each ramifying infinitely, from each knot a new tree growing with such fury of growth that the debris of the church was holed like a sieve and burst asunder, to fly afar through the skies like finest ash.

Now, the giant tree had reached its fingers to the stars, its forest of branches was a forest of legs, arms, trunks, swollen bellies, exuding a sweat of sap. The hair of females hung loose, the bark budded and burst noisily, expanding into men's laughing heads, while high up above were lovers at their coupling, couples exhausted from love, sprawling in abandon on the edge of their hotbeds, filling the air with the music of their orgasmic breath and the scent of their semen.

A final breath of the storm which rushed at the church swept its last dust away, turning pulpit and confessional to dust, carrying off the torn sacred pictures, the smashed altar cruets, the rubble in which pecked greedily those sparrows which had once lived under the tiles. Torn from his cross, the big Christ dangled for a moment, caught in the loose hair of a woman, then crashed with resounding clatter. The tree of life had split Heaven open, and grown beyond the stars.

Like a damned soul, at this vision, the Reverend Mouret applauded wildly. The church was defeated at last! God had no longer any house. God could get in his way no longer. He could rejoin Albine, for she had won. And so he laughed at the man who an hour before this had asserted that the church would consume the whole world with its shadow. The earth had taken its revenge, eating up the church. Then, all at once, his own mad laughter shook him out of his hallucination. Stupidly, he stared into the nave, now slowly sinking into the dusk. Through the windows he saw patches of sky, pricked out with stars, and he reached out his arms, thinking to feel those walls, when there came Désirée's voice from the corridor which led from the sacristy to the house, calling him.

'Serge, are you there? But do speak out, Serge, I have been looking for you for the last half-hour!'

She entered the church, a lamp in her hand. Then the priest saw that the church was still standing. Now he no longer understood anything, but was beset with terrible uncertainty, caught between invincible church, risen again from its ashes, and all-powerful Albine, who merely by one breath could overthrow God.

CHAPTER X

DÉSIRÉE came towards him, noisily cheerful as ever.

'Why, that's where you are!' she cried. 'My word, what do you think you're at? Playing hide and seek? I've been yelling at the top of my voice, I called you a dozen times . . . I began to think you had gone out.'

Her glance peered inquisitively into the depths of shadow. She even went down to the confessional, creeping up to it as if preparing to surprise anybody who might be hiding in it. But she was disappointed. She came back to him.

'So you're all alone?' she said. 'Were you asleep then. Whatever fun is there here when it's quite dark? Come along with you, do, we are going to have supper.'

He drew his fevered hands across his forehead, to wipe away the thoughts that the whole world surely must be able to read. Mechanically, he tried to re-button his cassock. He felt it must be undone, torn open, in shameless disorder. Then he followed his sister, his features stern, not a trace of emotion on them, rigid with that will of the priest concealing the agony of his body under the dignity of his ritual. Désirée did not even notice how upset he was, but, as they entered the dining-room, merely babbled: 'I had a lovely sleep. You've been talking too much, you're quite pale.'

After dinner, Friar Archangias came in to have his tussle with Teuse. He was overflowing with high spirits this evening, and when he was high-spirited he would dig his fists into Teuse's plump sides till she boxed his ears soundly, when they would both laugh so uproariously that the rafters rang, or he would resort to the most outrageous of tricks, such as with his nose trying to crack plates laid flat on the table, or betting he could break the dining-room door in merely by banging it with his rump, or he would tip his tobacco-pouch out into the old housekeeper's coffee or bring in a handful of pebbles and tuck them right down her bosom, making sure they lodged round her waist. Such outbursts of horseplay would suddenly develop for no apparent cause, with the Friar as morose as usual at one moment and monkeying about the next. Sometimes a trifle which amused nobody else would provoke a noisy outburst in him and he would hold his sides and twirl about and dance in a frenzy of hilarity.

'So you just won't tell me what makes you so cheerful?' demanded Teuse, this evening.

He did not even answer. Instead, without a word he sat himself down, straddling backwards on a dining-room chair and hobby-horsed himself round the table.

'All right, act the zany, act away,' cried Teuse. 'Heavens, what a loony you are! If our dear Lord only saw you, I'll bet he'd be pleased!'

The Friar now let himself tip right over backwards, and lay there on the floor, legs kicking in the air. Without attempting to get up, he said solemnly:

'Our dear Lord does see me, and, what is more, he is pleased. The Almighty in particular wants me to be cheerful ... When he vouchsafes to send me a little amusement, he rings a bell in this old carcase of mine, and all Paradise guffaws.'

He crawled on his back as far as the wall, then his weight poised on his shoulders, he trod higher and higher up the wall, up as far as he could lift his feet. His cassock fell back, revealing black trousers patched with green squares of cloth at the knees.

'I say, Vicar,' he called across the room, 'just look where I've got now, I'll bet you can't do that ... Come on, have a laugh, man, better drag along on one's back than crave to sleep on a trollop's hide. Get me? Yes? You just let yourself go, be an animal for a few seconds, give your own hide a good scratch, de-louse yourself a bit, it's a refreshing change. When I scratch my behind like that, I imagine I'm God's lap-dog, that's what makes me say all Paradise runs to the window, and laughs at the sight of me ... You might as well join in, Vicar. It's for the benefit of the saints, yourself included. Look, here's an arse-over-head for Saint Joseph, here's another for St. John, another for St. Michael, one for Mark, one for Matthew ...'

On he jabbered, stringing a whole rosary of saints, as he somer-saulted all round the room. The Reverend Mouret said not a word, but, sitting there, fists on the table, in the end he did give a smile. Usually the Friar's cavorting just worried him. But now, as the Friar came within reach of Teuse, she gave him a good kick.

'Come on there,' she cried, 'having a game, are we?'

Friar Archangias replied by grunts. He got on to all fours and like that made straight for Teuse, pretending to be a wolf, and when he reached her, he stuck his head in under her skirts and gave her right knee a good hard bite.

'Will you let me alone!' she shrieked. 'What are you thinking of now, you shameful, lewd old man,'

'Me?' gasped the Friar, so tickled by the notion of lewdness that he was transfixed and simply could not get up. 'Why, look, one taste of your knee has quackled me. Too salty it is, Teuse . . . Whenever I bite a woman, I spit it out quickly, you see. Look-ee!' he cried, intimately, to her, and actually spat on to her skirts. He got to his feet and stood panting a moment, rubbing his sides. Gulps of wild laughter still convulsed his belly, as if he were draining a leather bottle. At last, suddenly solemn again, he thundered:

'And let's have our game of *Bataille* . . . If I laugh, that's my business. No need for you to know what for, my good Teuse.'

They began their game, a terrible tussle, the Friar simply slamming his cards down, and when he yelled '*Bataille*' the windows rattled. Teuse was winning, too. She had had three aces for some time and her gleaming eyes were on the look out for a fourth. And now Friar Archangias suddenly began his horseplay again. He heaved up the table with his knees, at great risk of tipping over the oil lamp, and he also began to cheat openly, brazening it out with the most outrageous lies, all 'just for fun,' as he claimed. Then all at once he began intoning *Vespers* in a regular choirman's bass, and carried right on, verse after verse, with most unseemly snorting, beating time with his cards against his left hand. Whenever Friar Archangias's tomfoolery reached its climax and he could think of nothing else to relieve his feelings, he would sing the evening service like that endlessly. Teuse, knowing him well, suddenly leant forward and, raising her voice above the bellowing, which filled the dining-room with its reverberations, chanted: 'Do shut up, it's unbearable . . . You're going too far this evening.'

The Friar then struck up *Compline*. The Reverend Mouret, meanwhile, had gone to the window to sit. He did not seem either to see or to hear what was going on close to him. During dinner, he had eaten as well as usual, and even contrived to answer Désirée's eternal questioning. Now he had given way to his exhaustion and slumped into his chair, all out, absolutely broken by the infuriated dispute still going on within him without truce. He lacked even the resoluteness necessary to go to his bedroom. He began to be afraid lest, if he turned his face towards the lamp, they saw the tears which he could no longer hold back. He pressed his forehead against the window-pane and peered into the darkness outside, and in this position he gradually slipped into a half-sleep, a nightmare state of stupefaction.

Still intoning away, Friar Archangias suddenly nodded in his direction.

280

'What is it?' demanded Teuse.

The Friar nodded yet more pointedly.

'You can jerk your neck out of joint as much as you choose,' said the housekeeper, 'but if only you'll say what you want to tell me, perhaps I'll understand ... Ah, a king is it! Right! Then I'll have your queen!'

Putting his cards down for a moment and leaning forward, till he was puffing straight in her face, the Friar spoke up:

'That trollop's been here,' he said hoarsely.

'I know,' she said, 'I saw her in the farmyard, with Miss Désirée.'

With a terrible glance, the Friar brandished his fists at her.

'You say you saw her? You let her in here? You should have sent for me! We could have strung her up head down in your kitchen.'

But for some reason, Teuse was angry. Keeping her voice down just enough not to waken the Vicar, she stammered:

'It's all very well, that sort of talk, a fine sort of goodness, yours is, talking of hanging people up in my kitchen! Of course, I saw the girl. And what's more, when she went to find the Vicar in the church, after catechism class, I turned a blind eye, I may tell you. In there, they could do whatever they pleased, as far as I was concerned. I had my beans to see to ... If you want to know, I detest that girl, but the moment the Vicar's health is in question ... she can come here any time in the twenty-four hours she wants, and if they want, I'll keep watch at their door.'

'If you were to do such a thing, Teuse, cried the Friar, icy with anger, 'I would choke the life out of you!'

But Teuse talked to him as if he were a mere urchin.

'Stop talking nonsense,' she cried, ' such childish talk! You know very well you yourself have no more need of a woman than a donkey has of the *Lord's Prayer*. But you just try choking the life out of me, any time you like, and see what you get. Here, don't be such an old fool, finish the game, come on with you! Oho, another king!'

Obediently, the Friar raised his own card to play. But not without continuing to grumble:

'She must have got here by some road only Satan knows, to escape me today. I spend every afternoon now up there by Paradou, on the look-out. And if I ever catch them together again, I'll teach the little hussy with a good dogwood stick which I've cut special for her ... Now it seems I shall have to keep a watch on the church too.'

He played his next card, just throwing away his knave to Teuse. Then tipped back in his chair, and that great laugh came over him again. He simply could not stay really angry, this evening.

'No matter,' he said, cheerfully, 'even if she did not see him, she came up against something . . . And I'll tell you all about it, Teuse, if you like. You remember, it was raining. I was at the school door when I saw her coming away from the church. She was holding herself very straight, in that cocky way of hers, though it was pouring cats and dogs, but when she got to the road, all at once she came a cropper, full-length too, on account of the road being so slippery. Oh, how I laughed, how I laughed! I clapped my hands, I can tell you . . . When she got up, there was blood on one of her hands. That put me in a good mood for a week. I can't even think of her sprawling on the ground, without feeling such a tickling in my throat and my belly I want to roar a-laughing.'

Puffing out his cheeks, he resumed his horseplay and now proceeded to sing the *De Profundis*. They went on playing, but even when he had lost, he went on singing, now, for his better enjoyment, sometimes swelling his voice into such a crescendo that the sound was deafening. Indeed, it was his crazy singing that lost him the game, though today he was not in the least put out by that. When, after wakening the Reverend Mouret, Teuse at last had shut the door on him, together the priest and his housekeeper heard him. The Friar's voice receded into the night, in tones of unusual jubilation repeating the last verse of the psalm: *Et ipse redimet Israel ex omnibus iniquitabus ejus.*

CHAPTER XI

THE Reverend Mouret slept like a log. When he opened his eyes, later than usual, he found his cheeks and hands wet with tears. He had cried all night, in his sleep. This morning, he missed out morning mass. In spite of his long sleep, he was still so exhausted from the previous evening that he stayed upstairs till midday. A stupor which increasingly took possession of him now robbed him even of the feeling of suffering. He was conscious only of a great gulf and of the immense relief of the sense of amputation, of being utterly crushed. It needed a supreme effort to read his breviary. The Latin of the prayers seemed to him now a barbarian tongue, the mere mouthing of the words of which eluded him. Then, throwing the book down on his bed, he spent a long time simply staring out of the window across country. He had not even the energy necessary to raise his arms and rest his elbows on the sill. In the distance, he could see a thin white line running along the crest of the hills, broken by the dark blotches of little coppices of pines— the white wall of Paradou. Over to the left, behind one of those small woods, was that breach in the wall. He could not see it, but he knew it was there. He recalled every single trailer of bramble among the fallen stones.

As recently as yesterday he would never have dared thus raise his eyes to look out at that awesome skyline, but now he was completely absorbed in tracing out the continuation of the broken line of the wall beyond each patch of conifers. The broken line of white clung to the green mass of living like the lace edging round the hem of a skirt. But even this did not make his heart beat more strongly. As if scorning the impoverishment of his blood, temptation had abandoned his timorous flesh, and this left him incapable of any effort, devoid of divine grace but also without even the urge to sin. The result was that all which the day before he had so vigorously rejected, he was now inanely prepared to accept.

Once he caught himself talking aloud. As there was still that gap in the wall, when the sun went down he would go back to Albine. This decision left an undercurrent of uneasiness in him, but he felt there was nothing else he could do, for she was waiting for him there, and she was his wife. Yet, when he tried to evoke her image, it came to him only very pale, at a great distance. Moreover, he was now beginning to get worried about the material details of their life together. It would not be easy for them to stay in these parts. They would have to conceal this from everybody; they would have to run away. But even when they had found conceal- ment somewhere, they would need a lot of money, to be happy. He now made a score of attempts to establish some sort of plan for their elopement, some way of organising their life so that they could share each other's love in happiness, but he could think of nothing. Now that he was no longer mad with longing, the practical aspect of it all left him aghast, and he found himself weak-kneed before an undertaking so complex, one in which he was ignorant even of the first step to be taken. Where would they get horses for their elopement? But, if they went on foot, would they not be taken in charge as vagabonds? Further, was he capable of any job, could he hope to discover any occupation by which he could support a wife? Such things he had never been taught. He knew nothing of life. When he raked through his memory, all he could find were scraps of prayer, details of ritual, odd pages of Bouvier's *Theological Handbook* which he had once learned by heart at the seminary.

Even trifles now began to worry him greatly. In the street, would he dare offer his wife his arm? He doubted very much whether he would even be physically capable of walking with a woman on his arm. He would look so awkward that people would turn and stare. They would at once guess that he was a priest. Then they would insult Albine. In vain he strove to cleanse himself of things ecclesiastical. He would never get rid of that mournful pallor, that reek of incense. And if some day he had children ... This unexpected thought made him tremble. He felt a strange repugnance. It seemed to him that he would have no affection for them. In his thought they increased to two, a boy and a girl. But he edged them away from his knees. He felt ill at ease when they lay their hands on his clothing. He felt nothing of the delight of other fathers at dandling them on his knee. Above all it was the little girl who worried him. He could not get used to such flesh of his flesh, which he still felt exuded his own male impurity. Yes, above all the little girl made him uneasy, with her large eyes, in the depths of which there already glowed the emotional warmth of her womanhood.

But of course not, he would have no offspring, he would see that he was relieved of the loathing which came to him at the mere thought of seeing the parts of his body renewed in the eternal renovation of life. And after the realisation, the hope that he might be impotent became a sweet one. For no doubt during his long-drawn-out adolescence, his essential virility had vanished from him. And that made up his mind for him: yes, when evening came, he would elope with Albine.

When evening came, however, the Reverend Mouret felt too fatigued, and he put off his departure to the following day. And when that day came, he gave himself another excuse: he could not simply run off and leave his sister alone with Teuse. Then he thought he would leave a letter providing for her to be taken to Uncle Pascal. For three days he kept telling himself he would write that letter: up in his room, paper, pen and ink were laid out in readiness on the table. Then, suddenly, he took his hat and set out for Paradou, foolishly driven, obsessed, unthinking, by the idea, resigned to it, taking himself there as if performing a task from which he had found no means of escaping. The actual image of Albine had faded still further. He could no longer picture her at all. He

284

was moving solely in response to a volition established in him previously and which, though not really dead in him, was, in the great vacancy of his being, still endowed with lingering momentum.

Outside, he took no precaution at all about concealing his movements. At the far side of the village, indeed, he paused for a few moments to talk to Rosalie. She told him that her baby had had convulsions. Nevertheless, she still had that laugh of hers lurking at the corner of her lips. Then Mouret plunged up into the rise of rocky ground and made straight for the breach in the wall. By sheer habit he had taken his breviary with him, and as the road was long to him, and tedious, he opened the little prayer-book and began to read the prayers laid down for that day. And by the time he had concluded them, and tucked the book back under his arm, he had forgotten all about Paradou. His thoughts were now on the new chasuble which he rather wanted to buy, to replace the gold-cloth one, which was certainly beginning to crumble to dust. For some time he had been putting a franc by now and then, and he reckoned that in seven months he would have sufficient. But while his thoughts played with this, he kept on plodding the way he had taken.

He had reached the top of the rise when the distant song of a peasant reminded him of a canticle he once sang, years back, as a seminarist. And he tried to remember the first verses, but could not get at them, and was annoyed to find himself becoming so forgetful. But when at last he did recall the lines, it was a very sweet pleasure indeed to half sing, half hum them, as one by one he recovered them. They were the lines of a hymn in praise of Mary. He smiled now as if a fresh breeze from his youth had touched his cheeks. How happy he used to be in those days! He could indeed be happy once again, had he not grown up, for all he craved was that same happiness, that unruffled peace, a corner in a chapel where his knees could leave their imprint, a life of seclusion with the lovely childish things of boyhood to give it zest. Little by little, he raised his voice, and he was singing that canticle with the loud and clear voice of a flute, when all at once, there before his face was the gap in the wall!

For a moment, it seemed to surprise him. Then, the smile quitting his cheeks, he murmured naively to himself: 'Albine must be waiting for me, the sun is already sinking.'

But as he clambered up the rubble, to move aside some of the stones and get through, he was startled by a monstrous heaving of a man's hoarse breath. The next instant, he had to jump back from his

285

foothold, for he had all but planted a foot full in Friar Archangias's face. The Friar lay there, sprawling on the ground, against the stones, snoring sonorously. No doubt sleep had overcome him during his task of guarding this entrance to Paradou. He lay at full length right across the opening, his legs outstraddled in a posture almost indecent. In his right hand, flung back behind his head, he tenaciously clutched that dog-wood cudgel, as if he were brandishing it in his sleep, like a flaming sword. Thus he snored on, amid the brambles, his face full in the sun, though his leather-tanned physiognomy was not a bit troubled by that. Fat flies were swarming in the air round him and clustering about his gaping mouth.

For quite a time the Reverend Mouret stared at the Friar. He was envious of such saintlike slumber, in the dust. He was tempted to wave away the flies, but they were persistent, and came back at once, clinging to the Friar's purple lips, which were quite indifferent to them. Then the Vicar of Artaud stepped over the slumbering hulk, and entered Paradou Park.

CHAPTER XII

On the inside of the wall, only a few feet from the gap, was Albine, seated on a grassy bank. When she saw Serge, she rose to her feet.

'There you are!' she cried, quivering from head to foot.

'Yes, he said, calmly, 'I have come.'

She flung her arms round his neck. But she did not kiss him. The beads of his canonical bands had come up against her bare arm, and she had felt their chill. Already uneasy, she looked closely at him.

'What is the matter?' she asked. 'You give me no kisses on my cheeks as you used to, remember, when your lips sang . . . No matter, if you are ill, I shall cure you once more. Now you are here, we can begin our happiness again. There is to be no more sadness . . . See, Serge darling, I am smiling, and you must smile too.'

Then, seeing that he remained grim, she went on:

'You can be sure that I have had a lot of grief too. I am still very pale, am I not? For a week I have lived out here, on this grassy patch, where now you have found me. There was only one thing that I wanted, and that was to see you come in through that gap in the wall. At every sound I have got up and run to meet you. But it was never you, only leaves borne by the wind . . . Yet I knew so well that you would come. I would have waited for years.'

Then she asked him: 'Do you still love me?'

'Yes,' he replied, 'I still love you.'

They stayed looking at each other, rather embarrassed. A profound silence had fallen between them. Serge, serene, had no desire to break it. Twice Albine opened her lips, but, surprised by what came to the tip of her tongue, closed them again. The only words that came to her now were words of bitterness. She felt tears moisten her eyes. What was it she was going through now, not to be happy when her love had come back?

'Listen,' she said at last, 'We must not stay here. It is the hole in the wall that chills us . . . Let us go to our own corner. Give me your hand.'

And they plunged deep into Paradou. Autumn was coming, and the trees with their sear summits from which, one by one, the leaves were falling, were care-ridden. The paths were already beds of dead verdure, sodden with damp, where their footsteps seemed to stifle the sighs. On the far edge of the lawns floated a haze, cloaking the bluish distance with weaving mists. And the whole garden was silent, breathing only melancholic breaths which brushed them by like shivers of cold.

But when they entered the avenue of the big trees, Serge began to shiver with cold. In a whisper, he was forced to cry:

'How chill it is, in here.'

And her reply came in sad undertone:

'Yes, you are cold,' she said. 'And my hand can no longer warm you. Shall I wrap a fold of my gown round you? . . . Come, dearest, we shall revive all our old loving caresses for each other.'

She led him to the sunken garden. The rose shrubbery was still fragrant, but these last roses had a bitter tang to their scent. The foliage had overgrown, and hid the soil under its drowsy cascade. He felt such repugnance now against entering those thickets that they stayed outside them, peering to see the walks down which in the Springtide they had strolled. She reminded him of every little corner, pointed out the cave where the marble woman slept, the loose-flowing hair of the honeysuckles and clematis, the fields of violets, the fountain gushing its red carnations, the broad steps smothered under cascades of wild wallflowers, the ruined colonnade in the centre of which the lilies had built their white lodge. There it was, in the sunlight, that they had both known their birth. And she told him again of the tiniest details of that first day: how they had walked, and how the air in the shade had been fragrant with scents. And he had seemed to be listening to her when, by a clumsy question, he made it clear that he had not taken a thing in, and

287

the faint shivering which drained the blood from his cheeks now did not leave him.

She would have taken him to the orchard, but they could not even get near it, for the river was swollen now, and Serge did not even suggest he should carry her across, in three bounds to reach the far bank. Yet, on the far side, the apple and pear trees were laden still with fruit, and the vine, its leaves nearly all fallen, was bent under the weight of its amber grapes, each grain of which was tinged with red where the sun fell. What games they had then had in the lavish shade of those fine old trees! But then, they themselves had been but children, and Albine was forced to smile when she thought of the outrageous way she had shown her legs when the branches broke under her. Did Serge not at least recall those plums they had eaten? To everything he replied with nods.

He already seemed tired. The orchard, with its dark green masses, its confusion of mossy stems, like a forest of wind-swept, ruined scaffolding, disturbed him. It made him think of damp places where snakes and nettles flourished.

She took him to the water meads. There, he had to wade some way through deep grass. It came to his shoulders, now, and seemed like so many wiry arms trying to bind him, to trip him, to drown him, deep in an endless ocean of green. And he begged Albine not to go any further. Walking in front, at first she would not stop. Then, seeing that he was in real discomfort, she came to his side. Gradually gloom descended on her too. She became a victim of shivering apprehension. But in spite of this, she went on talking, with generous gesture pointing to the streams, to the rows of willows, to the sheets of rich herbage reaching out to the very end of the horizon. Once, all this had been theirs. They had spent whole days in it. Over there, where three willows stood, they had played at being lovers. And in those moments they had wanted the grasses to be taller than they were themselves, so they might lose themselves in the oncoming flood of fragrant green and be even more alone, from everything remote, like skylarks dizzily aloft above a wheat-field. Why then did they shudder so today, merely at the thought that only their toes might sink into the lush marsh pasture.

She took him to the forest. The trees frightened him still more. He did not know them now that their black trunks were so grave. Here more than elsewhere, amid these stern, tall giants, where daylight freely fell, the past seemed dead to him. In the sand of the rides the first rains had effaced their footprints and the winds had carried away all trace of them amid the low-sprung branches

288

of the undergrowth. Yet from every thicket the warmth they had left as they brushed their way through was wafted up into his face again, and all the time, her eyes all supplication, she continued her effort to stir memory in him. Down this path they had walked without a word. They had been very moved, too frightened far to admit to one another that they loved each other. Here, in this very clearing, they had forgotten themselves, one evening, lingering very late, watching the stars floating down upon them, luscious as summer heat drops. Farther on, under this oak, they had exchanged their first kiss. The oak still cherished the perfume of that kiss and even the mosses had never ceased to whisper about it. It was false to say that the forest was becoming silent and bare. But he turned aside, to avoid her eyes, for they wearied him now.

She took him to the big rocks. Perhaps there he would not shudder in that fragile way which so worried her. These alone, these rocks, so late, were still warm from the rubicund glow of the setting sun. They still kept their tragic love, and their hot beds of shingle, where lush plants undulated in their monstrous coition. And here, without speaking, even without turning to look at him, Albine led Serge along the rough rise of ground, intending to take him higher and higher, beyond the springs, till they both came out again together into the sunlight. There they would find again that cedar under which they had known the pang of their first love's desire. They would lie down on the hot rock face and let the love heat of mother earth encroach on their being. But, only too soon, Serge's feet stumbled cruelly, and he could go no farther, and for the first time he fell to his knees. With a supreme effort, Albine got him to his feet and carried him along a little way, but again he fell and then lay, still, utterly defeated, in the middle of the path. Below him, under his gaze, stretched the vast park.

'You told a lie,' cried Albine. 'You don't love me any more.'

And as she stood at his side she wept, feeling utterly incapable of carrying him any higher. She was no longer indignant, all she did was tell their troubled love story in tears. He was utterly broken.

'The garden is dead,' he said. 'I feel cold all the time.'

She took his head in her hands, and pointed to the park.

'But look, do look, Serge! Oh, dearest one, it is your eyes which are dead, your ears, your limbs, your whole body, which fail. You have passed through all our delights without seeing them or hearing them or feeling them. All you could do was slump to the ground like this. You came back to Paradou, merely to fall, sick with weariness, dying from lack of interest. You do not love me any more.'

He protested gently, but without heat. It was then that for the first time, she became angry.

'Silence!' she cried. 'As if our garden could ever die! During the coming winter, it will sleep. But in May it will waken again and bring us back all the tender love we confided to it before. Our kisses will bloom again in its borders, our avowals will once more grow together with its plants and its trees. If only you could see it and hear it, it is deeply moved. It loves in a more gently poignant way in this autumn season while in all its fertility it sinks to its seasonal sleep . . . But you no longer love me, you can no longer know of this.'

He looked up at her, imploring her not to be angry. His features were pinched and white with childlike fear. The sudden sound of her voice even made him tremble. At last he persuaded her to rest a while beside him, but only half-way to their lovers' goal. He said they would talk quietly to each other and so, without even the tips of their fingers touching, and all Paradou spread out before them, these two again spoke of their love.

'I love you, I do,' he said in a dull voice. 'If I did not love you, I should not have come . . . True, I am worn out. I do not know why. I thought here to find that lovely warmth, the mere memory of which was a caress. And I am cold, the garden seems black, I find nothing that I left here. But that is not my fault. I am trying hard to be like you, I would like to make you happy.'

'You love me no more,' Albine still repeated.

'Yes I do. I suffered frightfully the other day, after sending you away . . . Yet let me tell you I loved you so wildly that if you had then come to throw yourself into my arms, I should have crushed you to death in my embrace. Never had I desired you so wildly as then. For hours you were living before me, tearing at my flesh with your lissom fingers. But it was when I closed my eyes that you lit up like the sunlight and wrapped me in your flames . . . Then I trod on everything and came.' He paused for a moment, thinking, then continued: 'And now my arms are broken arms. If I wished to press you to me, I could not hold you, I should let you fall . . . But wait till this attack leaves me. You will give me your hands again and once more I shall kiss them. Be kind, do not look so angrily at me. Help me to get back my heart.'

His sadness was so genuine and his desire to restore their bonds of love so obvious, that Albine was touched, and for a moment she was very gentle again. With great concern she questioned him.

'Where do you feel it?' she asked. 'Where does it hurt you?'

'I cannot tell,' he replied. 'I feel as if all the blood were draining

290

from my veins . . . Just now, as we came here, it was just as if somebody wrapped a cloak of ice about me, which clung to my skin from head to foot and turned my flesh to stone . . . I already felt the ice paralysing my shoulders . . . then all was a blank.'

'You are a child,' she laughed, chiding him with warm affection in her voice, 'you must have caught a slight chill, that is all. Tell me, I at least do not frighten you, do I? In the winter we shall not live far away but here deep in the country, like wild creatures. We shall go away wherever you like, to some big town. And with other folk warm all about us, we shall live as tranquilly as we loved here in summer amid these trees. And you will see that I am not just a tomboy who knows how to birdsnest and walk for hours . . . When I was little, I wore embroidered petticoats, net stockings, all lace and furbelows. Perhaps you did not know that?'

He was not really listening. He did all at once gasp faintly: 'Ah, now I remember!' But when she asked him what he remembered, he would not say.

He had suddenly recalled what that feeling was—the seminary chapel chill about his shoulders. That was the icy cloak which had turned his body to stone. And with this realisation, he was ineluctably the prisoner again of his priestly past. Those vague memories which on his way to Paradou from Artaud had been stirring in him had now become sharper, forcing themselves on him with sovereign authority, and while Albine went on talking to him of the happy life they would lead together, he was hearing only the bell being wrung for the elevation of the host, seeing only the thuribles tracing crosses of fire over vast, kneeling congregations.

'And so,' she said, 'for your sake I shall go back to the dress of a town lady . . . I want to be happy. We shall find all sorts of things to entertain you. Perhaps you will love me more when you see me pretty, dressed like a lady. I shall no longer wear my hair down my back with only a comb stuck in it. I shall stop rolling up my sleeves. I shall fasten my gown to the neck, so you will not see my shoulders. And I still know how to curtsey and walk with drawing-room dignity, chin daintily nicking the air. Don't you fear, you shall have a pretty wife on your arm when we go out walking in town.'

'I wonder,' he said, half-whispering, as if continuing despite himself, continuing out loud the reverie which had prevented him from listening to her, 'perhaps when you were little you even went to church. I myself could never go past one without going in. The moment the door closed silently behind me, I used to feel I was in paradise itself, with the voices of angels whispering in my ears

291

tales of gentle things, and the breath of the saints caressing my body from head to foot . . . Yes, I wanted to live there, for ever, lost in the heart of such bliss.'

She looked quickly round at him, then stared, while from out of the tenderness of her glance suddenly flared a point of fire. But, still holding herself in, she tried again :

'I shall fit in with your every whim. In the old days, I used to study music. I was rather a clever girl, brought up with all the graces . . . I shall go back to school, I shall study my music again. If you want to hear some piece that you love, you will merely have to tell me it. I shall work at it for months, till at last, one evening, in our home, in a snug little room, when we have drawn all the curtains, I can play it to you perfectly. And all you will need to give me in return as reward is one single kiss . . . Agreed? A kiss on the lips which will give you back your love. You will take me and then you can break me in your arms.'

'Yes, yes,' he murmured, as if to answer her, though in fact merely replying to his own thoughts. 'My first great pleasures were to light candles in church, to prepare the altar vessels, to bring the missal, hands crossed on my breast. Later, the slow progress to God was my great pleasure, and I thought I would die of that love . . . I have no other memories. I am a blank. When I rise in the morning, I rise for a benediction. When I thrust out my lips, it is for a kiss to be given to the altar. When I try now to find my heart, it is no longer to be found. In those past days I offered it to God, and God has taken it from me.'

She turned very pale, her eyes burned. With uncertain voice, she persisted:

'And I never want my daughter to leave my side. When you think the time ripe, you may send the boy away to school if you like, but my fair-headed girlie I shall keep beside me, and it is I who shall teach her to read her letters. Ah, it will all come back to me, and if not, I can take tutors . . . We shall live with our little world round us, and you will be happy, won't you? Tell me, say, you will be warm, you will smile, won't you? You will not regret the past?'

'I have often thought,' he said, in a very low voice, 'of those stone saints incensed for centuries in their niches. In course of so much time, they must be permeated with it, through and through . . . Well, I am like one of them, I am soaked in incense, to the innermost fold of my entrails. It is that embalming which makes this calm of mine, this serene death of my body, the peace I enjoy by my not-living . . . Oh, may nothing ever disturb me in my immobility! I shall ever be cold, rigid, an everlasting smile on my lips of stone, incapable of descending to the level of ordinary men. That is my only desire.'

She rose to her feet, exasperated and menacing. She shook him and cried:

'What is that you say? What dreams are those you mutter out loud? Am I not your wife? Have you not come here to be my husband?'

Shivering more violently, he fell away from her.

'No, let me be,' he stammered, 'I am afraid.'

'And that life of ours together, our happiness, our children?'

'No, no, I am afraid.' And then he uttered the overpowering cry: 'I cannot, I cannot.'

For some moments she was speechless, facing this unhappy man shivering at her feet. Fire darted from her countenance. She made as if to open her arms, and embrace him, hug him to her in a fierce upsurge of desire. Then she seemed to think better of it, and merely took his hand in hers. She made him stand up. 'Come,' she said. And she led him under the giant tree, to the very place where she had given herself to him and he had entered into her. They found the same felicitous shade, the same trunk like a great bosom breathing, the same branches like protecting arms far outstretched. The tree was still kind, robust, powerful, fertile. As on that day of their union, there was the languorousness of a secret alcove, the glow as of a summer night dying on the bare shoulders of a loving woman, a whisper of love scarce audible, issue of a grand orgasm, all lingered in that glade, drenched in greenish clarity. And then, despite the first shudder of autumn, far below them Paradou Park too re-found its whispers of passion and aided and abetted. From the sunken garden, from the orchard, from the meadows, from the forest, from the great rocks, from the vast heavens once again came the joyous laughter of body's enjoyment, a glorious breath which as it swept through them, shed its fecundating pollen. Never even in the warmest nights of spring had the garden known such profound tenderness as these last lovely days during which all vegetation bade its lingering farewell shrinking slowly back into its annual slumber. And through the thinning verdure the effusion of the ripened seed bore to them an intoxication of desire.

'Hearest thou, dearest?' whispered Albine, in Serge's ear. She had let him sink to the greensward at the foot of the tree. He was weeping. 'Canst not see that Paradou is not dead? Paradou cries out that we should love! Paradou still wants our marriage! Ah, forget not, Serge dearest, but take me to your bosom, and let us again be but one flesh!'

But he wept.

Not another word did she speak, but took him herself in savage embrace, glued her lips to the corpse, to kiss back life into it. But still all that Serge Mouret could do was weep.

There was a long silence. Then Albine spoke again. She had risen to her feet and stood staring down at him in utter scorn. She was resolved at last.

'Out of here!' she hissed, her voice scarcely audible.

With an effort he staggered to his feet. His breviary had fallen to the ground. He picked it up. Then he went.

'Out of here!' she cried, louder and louder now, following him, chasing him before her, and thus urged him on from thicket to thicket, all the way to the gap in the wall. On either side reared the tall trees, motionless in their gravity. And when at this point, his head sunk on breast, he hesitated, she cried out in a very loud voice:

'Out of here! Out of here!'

Then, slowly, without looking back, she withdrew into the garden. Night was falling. Paradou was but a vast coffin of shadow.

CHAPTER XIII

FRIAR ARCHANGIAS had awakened and was standing over the gap, lashing at the stones and swearing horribly.

'May Satan break their bones! May he stick them together like a dog and its bitch! May he drag them by the feet with their noses in their own ordure!'

But when he saw Albine chasing the priest out, for a moment he was astounded. Then he lashed the stones more furiously than ever and laughed a terrible laugh.

'Goodbye to 'ee, trollop! And good riddance! Now go and fornicate with the wolves ... A saint wasn't enough for you! You want stronger thighs than he's got, don't you, you want an oak tree up you! Want a dose of my stick? Here you are, sleep with that, that's the lad'll satisfy you!' he yelled, and with all his force flung the cudgel into the dusk after her. Then, looking Mouret up and down, he turned to upbraiding him.

'I knew you were in there. The stones had been moved. Now

you listen to me, Vicar, this latest sin of yours has made me your superior, and through my lips God tells you that hell has not torment terrible enough for priests so sunk into the flesh as you. And, if God ever forgives you, it will be too kind of him, and to the detriment of justice.'

The two men slowly made their way back towards Artaud. The priest did not utter a single word. Gradually, he raised his head higher, and at last his trembling ceased. When, afar off, against the lilac-coloured sky, he saw the black rod of the solitary cypress rear itself and the red patch of the church roof, he smiled feebly. An immense serenity was beginning to flood into his clear eyes.

All this time the Friar from time to time had kicked at stones on the road. Now he turned and harangued the Vicar of Artaud.

'Well, is it all over now? When I was your age, I was possessed too, I had a devil gnawing at my guts. Then at last he got tired of it and left me. Now I have no guts any more, and I live quiet. Yes, Vicar, I knew very well you'd go there. I've been keeping my eye on you for these three weeks. I peeped into the garden through that gap. I should have liked to chop those trees down. I often threw stones in, and whenever one broke a branch, I was happy. Tell me, is what you enjoy in there so extraordinary?'

He had halted the Reverend Mouret in the middle of the road and was sizing him up with eyes which glowed with frightful jealousy. The delights of Paradou which he had glimpsed had tortured the Friar. For weeks he had hovered on the brink of that place, sniffing those accursed enjoyments from afar. But as Mouret made no reply, the Friar resumed his way, sniggering and muttering double-talk. Then, raising his voice again, he continued:

'What you've got to see is that when a priest does what you have been doing, he upsets all the others ... Why, I could not feel chaste myself, walking side by side with you. You poison our sex, you see ... Now you are sensible again. Get away with you man, you needn't confess. I know what a whacking you've taken. Heaven has made your loins ache like all the rest of us. Serve you right, serve you right!'

He clapped his hands in triumph. Mouret did not pay any attention to him. He was lost in his own meditation. But his smile had gained in strength, and when the Friar had left him at the vicarage door, he went round the house and straight into the church. It was sunk in greyness, just as on that terrible rainy day when temptation had shaken him so. But it was now merely poor and indrawn. There was no gold today pouring over it, no agonising breath coming in from the countryside around. It was sunk in grave silence. Solely a breath of mercy seemed to hover there, and fill it.

On his knees before the large crucifix of coloured pasteboard, weeping tears which he let stream freely down his cheeks like rivers of delight, the priest murmured:

'Oh, beloved God, it is not true that Thou art without pity. I feel that Thou hast already forgiven me ... I feel this from Thy grace which, for some time now, has been coming down on me again, drop by drop, bringing me salvation slowly but surely ... Oh, dear God, it was in the moment when I deserted Thee that Thou didst protect me most surely. Thou hidst Thyself from me, to salvage me from evil. Thou didst let my flesh run away with me, so I might be foundered by its impotence. And now, dear God, I see that Thou hast ever marked me with Thy seal, that awesome seal, so replete with joys, which places a man outside the world of men, and the imprint of which is so ineffaceable that sooner or later it reasserts itself even on those parts of the body which are guilty of sin. In sin and temptation hast Thou broken me. With Thy flames hast Thou devastated me. Thou hast willed that in me there shall be but ruins, that I may move among them in safety. I am now an empty house in which Thou canst dwell. Blessed by Thee, oh my God.'

He prostrated himself, babbling into the dust. The church was victorious, the church was still standing, erect above the head of the priest, the church with its altars, its confessional, its pulpit, its crucifixes, its holy images. The world did not exist. Like any material conflagration, temptation was extinguished. It was no longer necessary for the purification of his flesh. He was entering into a peace which was above man, and he uttered this supreme cry:

'Outside of life, outside of all living things, outside everything, I am Thine, oh dear God, Thine alone, for ever and ever, Amen!'

CHAPTER XIV

ALL this time Albine was wandering wildly about the great park like a wild creature with cruel, bleeding wound. Her tears had dried. Her face was bloodless, her forehead knit by a deep furrow. Whyever should she have to suffer by all this death? What sin had she committed for the garden thus to fail her in the promise she had known since early childhood? On and on she trod, blind to the woodland glades down which she passed, where the shadows now were flowing fast, and she asked herself those questions. For she had never run counter to those trees and could not remember ever wilfully destroying a single flower, but had always been the beloved child of all that growth and obeyed it all with utter submission, yielding her whole self to nature, full of faith in the delights which it reserved for her. When, on that final day, Paradou had cried to her that she should lie down under the giant tree, she had lain down and opened her embrace, repeating the lesson whispered to her by the smallest herbs. That being so, so that she could find nothing to reproach herself with, it must be the garden which had been false to her and tortured her, for the sheer pleasure of seeing her suffer.

She stood still and looked about her. The sombre towering masses of the greenery were pensive and silent. The rides, where black walls now rose, became impenetrable darkness. The far-off stretches of greensward breathed slumber into the winds which stirred them. Desperate, she stretched out her arms, with a protesting cry. It surely could not end like this.

But the silent trees stifled her voice. Three times she begged Paradou to answer her, and the lofty summits gave no explanation, not one single leaf took pity on her, and when she began to walk on again, she realised that she was moving on into the doom of winter. And now that she no longer questioned the soil rebelliously, she caught a low-pitched voice which crept at ground level, the farewell voice of that vegetation, wishing her a happy death. Imbibing the sunshine for the whole of a season, living throughout amid all one's fellow flowers, breathing out one's own constant fragrance, then at the first throe having to depart, in the hope of growing again somewhere—was that not long enough, a life well filled, which persistent clinging to mere existence could only spoil? Ah, how happy one should be in death, with only endless night before one, dream-state of the brief day lived, its fugitive delights eternalised.

She halted again, but not to protest, amid the immense contemplation of Paradou. She thought that now she understood. It was beyond doubt for her that her garden, as supreme satisfaction, provided death for her, and it was to her death that it had so delicately led her. After love there could be only death, and never had the garden loved her so. She would be ungrateful, indeed, were she to accuse it of anything, and she remained its most beloved child. The silent foliage, the paths with their barricades of darkness, the lawns where the winds sank to rest, all were silent now solely to invite her to the delight of a long silence. They pleaded with her for this, in the great repose of cold, their dream to bear her away enwrapped in dead leaves, her eyes frozen like the water-pools at the springs, her limbs stiff like the bare branches, her blood sleeping the sleep of all sap. She would live their life to the very end, even unto their death. Perhaps they had already determined that when the next season came, she would be a rose of the garden, a golden-glowing willow of the spring meadows, a graceful young birch of the forest. This was the great law of life. And she was now going to die.

For a last time now she passed through the whole garden, seeking death. Which scented plant needed her hair to augment the perfume of its leaves? Which flower sought the gift of her satin skin, the impeccable white of her arms, the delicate lacquer of her bosom? To which young shrub should she offer her blood? She would have liked to serve the plants which grew along the paths, killing herself there, so that greenery should sprout from her body, superb, lush greenery, full of May birds, warmly cherished by the sun.

But Paradou remained silent a long time yet, still unresolved to confide to her in which last kiss it would bear her away. She had to visit every corner, yet once again making the pilgrimage of the walks she had used to take. Night had now almost completely engulfed the earth and she had the impression that she herself was gradually being swallowed into the soil. She climbed up the large rocks, questioning them, asking them if it was on their stony bed that she was to die. She went through the forest, full of expectancy, with a longing which slowed her every step, hoping a veteran oak would suddenly come crashing down and bury her in the majesty of its fall. She went along by the rivers through the meads, leaning over at nearly every step, peering into the depths of the waters, wondering whether her bed were not prepared there among the water-lilies. But nowhere did death call to her, nowhere did it hold out refreshing hands. And yet she was not mistaken. It was unquestionably Paradou that was to teach her to die, as it had taught her to love. Once again she beat her path through the dense undergrowth, hungrier now even than she had been those warm mornings when she sought love there. And all at once, just as she reached the sunken garden, she discovered death, among the evening perfumes, and raced towards it, with sensuous laugh. She was to die amid flowers.

First, she ran to the thickets of roses. Here in the last glimmer of the twilight, she thrust into the thick masses of them, culling all the blooms drooping there on the outskirts of winter. Careless of the thorns, she stripped the briars of their blossoms to the very ground. She gathered those at arm level, she gathered those high up, reaching on tiptoe and bending the branches down. Such haste urged her on that she broke off whole sprays, she who had such respect for the merest twig of growing things. Soon her arms were full of roses, a burden under which she staggered. With them, she went back to the lodge. She had plucked the whole rose garden, bearing away even the fallen petals, and when she had dropped her load of roses on the floor of the blue-ceilinged room, she went back into the garden.

Next, she looked for violets. Of these she made enormous bunches which she clutched one against the other to her breast. Then she sought carnations, cutting even the buds, tying huge bunches of them, white as jugs of milk and giant red like jugs of blood. Then she sought out stocks, evening primroses, heliotropes and lilies, gathering handfuls of the last stalks of the stocks, pitilessly crushing their satin ruffs, robbing the beds of evening primroses, scarce opened yet, mowing the patch of heliotropes, piling the blossoms in a heap, and tucking bundles of lilies under her arms, like bundles of reeds. When she had gathered this load, she went back to the lodge to fling violets, carnations, stocks, evening primroses, heliotropes and lilies down beside the roses. Then, without pausing for breath, she went back yet again.

This time, she went to the dismal corner which was like the sunken garden cemetery. Here, burning autumn had brought forth a second flowering of springtime flowers. Above all she attacked borders of tuberoses and hyacinths, kneeling among the flowers, harvesting like a miser. In the tuberoses she saw precious flowers, which drop by drop should distil gold, and richness of unheard-of good things. The hyacinths, their little bells like beads, were necklaces, each grain of which brought her delight no man should ever know. And although the armfuls of hyacinths and tuberoses which she had plucked completely covered her, she went farther, to play havoc in a field of poppies and then a field of marigolds as well, and marigolds and poppies were piled up over the tuberoses and the hyacinths, and then, anxious lest the wind steal even a single pistil, she raced back to unload all these in the blue-ceilinged room. And back she went again.

What was she to gather now? She had harvested the whole

sunken garden. When she stood on tip-toe, she could see only this lifeless little world in the still grey shadows. And, without the gentle eyes of its roses, the red laughter of its carnations, the perfumed hair of its heliotropes, it was quite dead. But she was not going to go back empty-handed, and she now attacked the grass and the green leaves, crawling, her bosom on the ground, as if in a supreme orgasmic embrace she would carry away the very soil. It was now a harvest of aromatic plants, citronella, peppermint, verbena, which filled her skirt. She came upon a border of balsams and did not leave a single leaf. She even took two large fennels, which like two trees she slung over her shoulder. If she could have gripped it in her teeth and carried it thus, she would have dragged at her heels the whole greensward of the sunken garden. On the threshold of the lodge, she turned back and cast her eyes over Paradou. It was all black. Night had completely fallen and cast its black cloth at her face. And she went indoors, never to come out again.

Soon the large room was decorated. On the chest of drawers she put a lighted lamp. She shredded off the petals of the piled up blooms and of them made plump cushions for all the corners. She arranged the lilies on the chest of drawers, behind the lamp, piled up lace, the white purity of which made the lamp-light gentle with soft emotion. Then she took handfuls of carnations and stocks to the old settee, the century-old faded upholstery of which already had its own red bouquets, and the worn cloth now vanished and in its stead, against the wall, there was a mass of stocks, topped with carnations.

She then placed the four armchairs facing the alcove. The first she filled with marigolds, the second with poppies, the third with evening primroses, the fourth with heliotropes, till only the arms of the chairs could be seen and the furniture was like a wall of flowers.

Finally, her thought turned to the bed. She moved a small table close to the pillows, and here built a tremendous mound of violets. Then in huge armfuls she covered the bed itself from top to toe with all the hyacinths and tuberoses that she had brought. The cushion of them was so thick that it overflowed at the foot and at the head against the wall, with streams of blooms trailing to the floor, the whole bed one single huge blossoming. Now the roses alone remained, and these she scattered everywhere, without regard to where they fell, on the chest of drawers, on the settee. The arm-chairs all got some and one corner of the bed was covered. For some minutes it rained roses in heavy downpour, blossoms splashing

300

down like thunder showers of colour, and in the holes in the flooring the petals made brilliant puddles. But as the heap she had brought in was still hardly touched, she ended by weaving garlands of them, to hang on the walls, and the plaster cupids at their rogueries over the alcove now had real roses on their necks and arms and round their middles, till their naked bellies and buttocks were clothed with them. The blue ceiling, the oval panels with their framing knots of flesh-coloured ribbon and the erotic pictures which time had faded were now hung with rose cloaks and rose drapery, and the large room was all decorated and ready. Now, she could die there.

For a little while she stood, looking about her, peering and wondering if death were already there. Then she gathered the aromatic leafage, the citronellas, the peppermints, the verbenas, the balsams and the fennels, tore them in shreds and crushed them, to make material with which to seal the least crevice at window or door. After this, she drew the white calico curtains with their big stitching close, and, speechless, without even a sigh, lay down on this bed, under the profusion of hyacinths and tuberoses.

This was her final act of sensuous enjoyment. Her large eyes wide-open, she smiled at the room. How ardently she had loved, in this chamber! She was happy now to be dying there! In these moments no impurity from the plaster cupids reached her, for all that the naked legs of a sprawling woman could be seen, and there was nothing in the paintings which could any longer trouble her. Under the blue ceiling there was naught but the suffocating scent of flowers, and it seemed that this fragrance was nothing less than the fragrance of that long-departed love from which the alcove was still warm, a redolence which had grown now a hundredfold, becoming so powerful that it breathed asphyxiation. Perhaps it was the breath of the lady who had died there, a hundred years ago? Motionless, her hands clasped on her heart, Albine continued to smile, listening to those perfumes whispering inside her whirling brain, and they played her a strange music, a music of scents which with incomparable gentleness gradually lullabied her to sleep.

First came a merry, childlike prelude. It was her own fingers, which had torn those scented leaves, releasing the acridity of the macerated greenery, reminding her how as a girl she had been the tomboy playing in Paradou's wild beauty. Then the melody of a small flute was to be heard, tiny, musklike tones swelling out from the piles of violets on the chest of drawers by her head, and as it wove its air into the tranquil breath of the lilies which accompanied it on the chest, this flute sang the first enchantment of her love, the first avowal, and the first bliss in the thick wood.

But now her breath came shorter and harder, as with the sudden explosion of the peppery redolence of the carnations came the fires of passion, and for a third time that brassy note dominated all other sounds. Then she felt she would suffer pain from the unhealthy cadences of the marigolds and poppies, which recalled her torments and desires. But, all at once, after this there was peace, she breathed more freely, sliding into serene immensity, her lullaby the falling scale of the stocks, ever slower, sound fading out into the lovely chant of the heliotropes, whose vanilla-like breath told her that the wedding-hour was nigh, a nuptial music surmounted now and then by the discreet trill of the evening primroses. There was a dead pause. Then, languorously, the roses came in. Voices floated down from the ceiling, a vast distant assemblage of voices in chorus, at the first onset making her tremble faintly. And this chorus rose in volume till she herself throbbed through and through with the incredible sonority which was diapasoning all about her. The wedding trumpets were there, with fanfares of roses to announce the awesome moment.

There Albine lay, panting, exhausted by love, her hands clutched closer and closer to her heart, breathing her last. She parted her lips, seeking the kiss which should obliterate her, and then the hyacinths and tuberoses exhaled their incense, wrapping her in a final sigh, so profound that it drowned the chorus of roses, and in this culminating gasp of blossom, Albine was dead.

CHAPTER XV

THE following day, towards three o'clock, Teuse and Friar Archangias were chatting on the vicarage steps, when they saw Doctor Pascal's gig race through the village at full canter, with the doctor's whip cracking out from under the raised awning.

'Wherever can he be hurrying to like that?' said the old house-keeper. 'He'll be breaking his neck.'

When the trap had come round under the mound on which the church was built, the horse reared, pulled up violently. A moment later, the doctor's white head appeared, his hair streaming in the wind.

'Is Serge there?' he shouted, wildly. Teuse hurried down to him. 'The vicar is indoors,' said Teuse, 'upstairs, reading his breviary,

I expect . . . Is there any message for him? Or shall I call him?'

Uncle Pascal looked terribly upset. Savagely, he lashed out at the air with his whip. Leaning from his gig at risk of tumbling out.

'What?' he cried, 'Reading his breviary? . . . No, don't get him out,' he ran on, angrily, 'I'd only wring his neck, and that won't do any good . . . I only have news for him . . . Albine is dead! Understand? Tell him she is dead! That's all. Tell him that from me!'

And he was gone, with such a fierce lash of the whip that his horse started off at full gallop. But, after twenty yards, he reined in, stuck out his head again, and shouted back:

'And you can also tell him from me that she was pregnant! That should certainly delight him.'

With menacing jolts the gig resumed its mad race up the stony slope which led to Paradou.

There was a lump in Teuse's throat. She could not speak at once. The Friar leered at her and sniggered, with a savage glint in his eyes. Suddenly, she gave him so violent a shove, that she nearly pushed him headlong down the steps.

'You clear out of here,' the old woman spluttered. Now it was her turn to be angry, and she vented her fury on him. 'I shall end up by hating you . . . What sort of way do you think that is, rejoicing when you hear people are dead? Not that I ever liked the girl, but dying at her age is nothing to be jubilant about . . . Go away from here, will you, and stop that wicked leer, or you'll get my scissors in your ugly mug!'

It was not till one o'clock that a peasant, going down to Plassans with vegetables, had informed the doctor that Albine had passed away, and Jeanbernat wanted to see him, and the message which he had left for his nephew as he passed the church had somewhat relieved the doctor's feelings. He had come the long way round solely for the satisfaction of bringing Serge Mouret that piece of news. All the same, Doctor Pascal took the young woman's death sorely to heart, as if he himself was terribly responsible. All the way to Paradou he heaped foul words on himself. He constantly had to wipe the tears from his eyes, to see where he was going. Once, he drove straight over a heap of stones, as if subconsciously desiring to break a limb, to punish himself. When at last he had reached the sunken road round the endless park wall, a flicker of hope stirred in him. Perhaps it had been no more than a bad fainting-fit? Oh, if only he could get out there in time, if only he could save her, and he lashed at his horse as he would have liked to lash himself.

It was a marvellous day. Just as in the height of summer, the lodge was bathed with sunshine. But where the ivy reached the roof it was already touched with rust and the wild bees no longer hovered round the wallflowers growing in the stone crevices. Swiftly, he tied up his horse and opened the wicket gate.

There was the usual intense silence, in which he expected to find Jeanbernat smoking his pipe as usual. But the old man was not on his bench. 'Jeanbernat,' he called. Nobody answered. Entering the hall, he saw something he had never seen before. At the far end of the corridor, under the stairs, a door which led straight into the park was wide open. Paradou's immense garden there unfolded its yellowed foliage in the pale sunshine, offering an expanse of autumn melancholy. Doctor Pascal crossed the threshold of this door and took a few steps across the damp grass.

'Ah, it's you, doctor,' came Jeanbernat's calm voice.

With tremendous strokes of a spade, the old man was digging a hole at the foot of a mulberry tree. Hearing steps, he straightened his back. Then, with one heave bringing up a huge spit of good clay soil, he resumed his task.

'What on earth do you think you are doing?' the doctor demanded.

Again Jeanbernat straightened his back. With his sleeve he wiped the sweat from his forehead.

'Digging a hole,' he said bluntly. 'She always loved this garden. It is a good place for her to sleep in.'

Doctor Pascal felt his feelings get the better of him. He stood for a moment by that grave, choking, unable to utter a word, just gaping at Jeanbernat lustily wielding his spade.

'Where is she?' he asked, at last.

'Up there, in the bedroom. I left her on the bed. I want you to sound her before I put her in there . . . I've tried to hear her heart beat, but I cannot.'

The doctor mounted the steps and went inside. The room had not been touched, only one window opened. Faded now, choked by their own scents, the emanation of the flowers which filled the room was now only that of the stale odour of their own dead flesh, though in the depth of the inner alcove still clung a suffocating warmth, which seemed to flow out into the room and thence escape in fine coils of smoke.

Very white, her hands on her heart, Albine was sleeping, a smile on her face, amid her hyacinths and tuberoses. And she was happy, too, for she was quite dead.

The doctor stood by her bed for a long time, gazing at her with that intentness of the clever men who try to resurrect the dead. But in the end he decided not even to disturb her clasped hands. He planted a kiss on her forehead, in the spot which her pregnancy had faintly marked with shadow.

Down below, in the garden, with regular, heavy, regular strokes, Jeanbernat's spade was delving deeper and deeper.

After another quarter of an hour, the old man entered the house, his task complete. He found the doctor seated by the bedside, so deep in thought that he did not even seem to notice the large tears trickling one after another down his cheeks.

The two men exchanged only one glance. After a brief silence, Jeanbernat spoke.

'Don't fret so, Doctor,' he said. He made his usual sweeping gesture. 'I was right. There is nothing, nothing, nothing ... All that is twaddle.'

He remained standing, then picked up the roses which had fallen from the bed and tossed them, one by one, on to Albine's skirts.

At last, he spoke again. 'Lovely flowers only last a day,' he said. 'But rotten old nettles like me wear out the very stones they grow on ... Now it's goodnight, I can conk out. My last little patch of sunlight is gone. It's a rum go, life is.'

Then he too sat down. His eyes remained quite dry, he showed only that desperate grief as of a mechanical thing whose mainspring was broken. Mechanically, he reached out and took a book off the little table deep in violets. It was one of the old volumes from the attic, coverless, a work of Holbach's, which, while he watched over Albine's body, he had been reading since morning. Seeing the doctor still so upset that he could not speak, Jeanbernat began to read again. Then, suddenly, he thought of something.

'If you were to give me a hand,' he said, 'we could get her downstairs between us right away and bury her with all these flowers.'

A shudder shook the doctor from head to foot. He explained to Jeanbernat that it was against the law to bury people like that.

'What? Against the law?' the old man cried. 'Well, then I'll give myself a permit ... Is she not mine? Do you think I'm going to let the parsons get her? Well let them try, if they want a dose of buckshot.'

He stood up and brandished his book furiously. The doctor took his hands and held them firmly, begging him to be calm. Then he talked to Jeanbernat for a long time, telling him all that was on his mind, charging himself, stripping confession from his own flesh, then vaguely coming back to those who had killed Albine.

305

'Do listen to me,' he said at last. 'She is no longer yours, you must let them have her.'

Jeanbernat shook his head in refusal. All the same, he was less convinced in his pigheadedness, and at last he said:

'Very well, then. Let them take her and may she break their arms. May she rise from her grave to kill them all with fright . . . But it suits me all right, I've a little reckoning to settle down in that village . . . I'll see about it all tomorrow. Good-bye now, Doctor. That hole will serve for myself.'

And when the doctor had left, he sat down again beside the dead girl's bed and gravely resumed the reading of his book.

CHAPTER XVI

THIS morning there was a great upheaval in the vicarage farmyard. The Artaud butcher came to slaughter Matthew the pig, in the outhouse. Désirée was all excitement. She herself held Matthew's feet while they bled him. She kept kissing the pig's bony back to make him feel the knife less, telling him that of course he really had got to be killed now he was so fat. There was, it may be said, none the equal of Désirée at lopping off a goose's head at the first strike of the hatchet or slitting a hen's throat with a pair of scissors. Her passion for her animals never flinched a bit from the slaughter in which they all ended. It was, she said, a necessary thing, it made room for the little ones to grow up, and she was most cheerful about Matthew's demise.

'Miss,' grumbled Teuse time and again, 'you'll do yourself harm. There's no sense in it, getting so excited just because a pig is being killed, you're as red in the face as if you'd been up all night dancing.'

But still Désirée clapped her hands and whirled busily about, whereas poor Teuse felt her legs would sink right into her body. Since six that morning she had been trundling her great bulk to and fro between kitchen and yard, for it was her job to make the black pudding. She had already whipped up the blood, and two large crocks pink with it stood in the bright sunshine, but she would never be finished, because Miss Désirée would keep calling her, for such trifles too. One should add that while the butcher was bleeding Matthew, Désirée had a great new excitement. She went into the stable, and when she got there, what should she see but Liza, her heifer, calving! Then she really was beside herself and quite lost her head.

It was eleven o'clock. From time to time the sound of singing came from the church, with a muddled muttering of gloomy voices, mumbling a prayer out of which in loud tones would suddenly emerge shreds of Latin.

'But do come!' pleaded Désirée, for the twentieth time.

'I've got to go and ring the bell,' muttered the old housekeeper. 'Oh, I shall never be through today . . . Now what else is it you want, Missie?'

But she did not await the reply. She flung herself at a flock of hens greedily drinking her blood in the crocks. She furiously sent them packing with vigorous kicks. Then she covered up her crocks.

'I must say,' she said, 'instead of worrying me like you do, you might keep an eye on these vermin . . . If you let them have their way you'll have no black pudding, understand?'

Désirée laughed. What harm would it do, if the hens drank a little blood? That would fatten them nicely. Besides, what she wanted was to show Teuse her heifer. It was kicking about.

'I tell you, I've got to go and toll the bell,' said Teuse. 'They'll be bringing the coffin out any minute now. Do understand!'

At this very moment, the voices in the church swelled loud, then dragged out a dying note, and a very distinct sound of footsteps was to be heard.

'No, you come and look,' insisted Désirée, pushing her towards the stable. 'Tell me what to do.'

Sprawling on the litter, the heifer turned to stare at them with its big eyes. Désirée was convinced that it needed something. Perhaps you could help it, so it suffered less? Teuse shrugged her shoulders. Did not the animals know how to manage their business themselves? One should never worry them, and that was all, and she definitely made off towards the sacristy. But as she passed the penthouse, she cried out again:

'Just look,' she cried, brandishing her fist, 'Oh, the wretched thing!'

Under the penthouse, trotters in the air, Matthew was stretched out, waiting to be singed. The knife-hole in his throat was quite fresh, and there were drops of blood still oozing. And there was a little white hen, a dainty little thing if ever there was one, pecking those drops one by one, as they appeared.

'Silly,' was all that Désirée said, 'she's having a lovely time.' And bending down, she patted the swollen belly of the pig, and added: 'Isn't she fatty? Eh? You ate their soup often enough, didn't you, so they might have a bit of your old neck now, eh?'

307

Swiftly, Teuse slipped off her apron and wrapped it round the the pig's throat. Then she hurried off, to vanish into the church. The hinges of the main door had just groaned open, and a cloud of chanting burst into the open air and serene sunlight. Then all at once, the bell began to jangle regularly. Désirée, still kneeling at her pig, still patting his belly, raised her head and listened, but the smile did not leave her cheeks. Then, realising she was alone, she looked craftily on either side, then slipped into the stable, shutting the door after her. She would help her heifer.

The little iron gate of the churchyard, which they tried to open wide, to get the coffin through, now hung half off its hinges against the wall. In the empty enclosure on the sear grasses lay the drowsy sunlight. The procession entered, chanting the last verse of the *Miserere*. Then there was silence.

'*Requiem ae ternam dona ei, Domine*,' the Reverend Mouret resumed, gravely.

'*Et lux perpetua luceat ei*,' added Friar Archangias, in his bellowing cantor's voice.

First came Vincent, in surplice, bearing the cross, a large silvered copper one, now largely bare of the brighter metal. He carried it very high, clutched in both hands. Then came the Vicar, very pale, in black chasuble. He bore his head erect and intoned without a quiver of the voice, his eyes fixed in the far distance. The lighted candle which he bore hardly added a single drop of warmth to the open air and light. Then, two paces from him, almost touching him, came Albine's coffin, borne by four peasants on a black-painted bier. Badly draped with a cloth which was too short, the foot end of the coffin revealed its fresh deal planking, the heads of the nails like bright sparks of iron. In the middle of the covering were scattered flowers, handfuls of white roses, hyacinths and tuberoses, all taken from the dead woman's bed.

'Look out there!' cried Friar Archangias to the peasants, when they tipped the bier a little, to get through the gateway without catching on the wicket. 'You'll upset the whole thing.'

And with his massive hand he steadied the coffin. As there was no other officiant, he carried the holy water stoup. He also took the place of the gamekeeper who was cantor, but had been unable to come.

'Come on, you others,' he said, turning back.

This was a second funeral procession, that of Rosalie's little boy, who had died the previous day in another fit of convulsions. This group included the mother and father, old Mother Brichet, Catherine and two girls, Carroty Rousse and Lisa. The latter two were carrying the baby's coffin, one at each end.

All at once, the voices died down, and there was another silence. Without hurrying, the bell went on tolling, a mournful sound. The procession passed right through the graveyard to the corner formed by the church and the farmyard wall. Swarms of grasshoppers leapt, lizards flicked swiftly into their holes. A sultry heat bore down on this patch of rich soil. The faint rustle of the grass crunched under the mourners' feet sounded like stifled sobs.

'Now, you stop there,' said the Friar, barring the way to the two grown-up girls carrying the baby. 'Wait your turn. There's no need to get into other people's way.'

The girls lay the little coffin on the ground. Rosalie, Fortuné, and Mother Brichet halted in the middle of the churchyard. But Catherine slipped slyly after Friar Archangias.

Albine's grave had been dug to the left of M. Caffin's, the white gravestone of which seemed in the sunlight to be sown with flecks of silver. Freshly dug that morning, the hole gaped amid tremendous tufty growth of herbage. On the edges, tall plants, half cut through, dangled their wilting stems. A flower had dropped to the bottom, staining the black of the soil with its red petals. When the Reverend Mouret came forward, the soft earth gave way under him and he had to jump back, not to tumble into the trench.

'*Ego sum . . .*' he began to intone in a rich voice, overpowering the lamentation of the tolling bell.

During the antiphon, those present instinctively glanced furtively down into the pit, which was still empty. Vincent, planting the cross at the foot of the grave, opposite the priest, kept pushing little streams of soil over the edge with his foot and watching them rain down, and that made Catherine laugh, for she was leaning from behind him to get a better view. The bearers had put the coffin down on the grass. They stretched their cramped arms, while Friar Archangias got the thurible ready.

'Here, Voriau!' cried Fortuné.

The big black dog, which had gone to sniff at the coffin, came sullenly to heel.

'What did you have to bring the dog for?' snapped Rosalie.

'Why, silly, he just followed us,' replied Liza, who was secretly amused.

Everybody was talking in a whisper round the baby's coffin. Every now and then the parents forgot themselves, then, realising what was there, at their feet, were suddenly silent again.

'So Father Bambousse refused to come, did he?' asked Rousse.

Old Mother Brichet raised her eyes to Heaven.

'Yesterday, when the babe passed away, he said he would smash the place up,' she murmured. 'No, he is not a good man, and I say it to your face, Rosalie . . . Did he not nearly strangle me, he said he had been robbed, he would have given a field of wheat for the babe to have died three days before the wedding, he said.'

'We weren't to know,' said Fortuné, slyly.

'What do I care if the old man's wild,' added Rosalie. 'We two's married all right, now.'

They grinned across the little coffin, their eyes gleaming, and Liza and Rousse nudged each other. Then they were all solemn again. Fortuné took a clod of earth to drive off Voriau, who was prowling among the graves.

'Ah, now we shall get it over at last,' whispered Rosalie, suddenly.

At the other grave, the Reverend Mouret was just finishing the *De profundis*. Then, at measured pace, he went up to the coffin, drew himself straight, and looked at it for a few moments without batting an eyelid. He seemed taller, and there was peace in his expression which quite transfigured him. Then he stooped down and took a handful of soil which he scattered on the coffin in the form of a cross. In a voice so clear that not a syllable was lost he declaimed:

'*Revertitur in terram suam unde erat, et spiritus redit ad Deum qui dedit illum.*'

A shudder ran through those present. With a sudden frown, Liza said :

'It ain't cheerful, anyway, when you come to think of it, we all end up the same.'

Friar Archangias had passed the thurible to the priest, and the Reverend Mouret shook it several times over the body, murmuring:

'*Requiescat in pace.*'

'*Amen,*' replied Vincent and the Friar together, the voice of the one so squeaky and that of the other so profound that Catherine had to stuff her fist into her mouth not to burst out laughing.

'No, it certainly ain't cheerful,' Liza ran on . . . 'No mourners at all for this one. Without us, the churchyard would be empty.'

'They do say she killed herself,' said Mother Brichet.

'Yes, I know,' interrupted Rousse. 'Friar Archangias was against having her buried beside Christians, but the Vicar insisted that eternity is for everybody. I was there . . . All the same, the old Philosopher might have come.'

Then Rosalie shut them all up, murmuring:

'But there he is, look!'

It was true. Jeanbernat came into the churchyard at that moment, and went straight to the group about the grave. He walked with his usual rakish gait, and so nimbly that his footsteps made no noise at all. When he got there, he stood immediately behind the Friar, whom for some moments he seemed to be measuring from head to toe. Then, as the Reverend Mouret came to the end of his prayers, Jeanbernat calmly drew a knife from his pocket, bent forward, and slashed off the Friar's right ear.

Nobody had time to intervene. The Friar uttered a frightful bellow.

'I'll leave the left-hand one for another time,' said Jeanbernat, calmly, tossing the severed ear down. And left them.

Everybody was so staggered that there was not even any attempt to pursue him. Friar Archangias just sank down on to the upturned ground beside the grave. He had formed his handkerchief into a pad, and pressed it to the wound. One of the four bearers would have taken him home, but with a gesture he rejected their aid. He stayed there, bitter to the end, merely with his own eyes to see Albine lowered into the grave.

'Our turn at last,' said Rosalie, with a faint sigh.

But the Reverend Mouret still lingered beside the grave, watching the bearers slipping ropes under Albine's coffin, to lower her down. The bell was still tolling, but Teuse must be getting tired, for the strokes were uneven, as if the bell was irritated by the length of the ceremony. The sun was gaining heat. The shadow of *le Solitaire* crept slowly over the greensward, swollen here and there by the graves. When the Reverend Mouret was obliged to step back, not to be in the way, his eyes lit on the marble gravestone of the Reverend Caffin, the priest who had loved and now slept there, so peaceful, under the wild flowers.

Then, suddenly, just as the coffin was going down, on the ropes, the knots of which caused the boards to groan, there arose a tremendous din from the farmyard, just over the wall. The goat started bleating. The ducks, geese, and turkeys flapped their wings and made a hullabaloo. All together, the hens cackled. Wild Alexander, the cock, uttered his clarion cry. One could even hear the rabbits leaping about, shaking the boards of their hutches. And over and above that din of this small nation of animals, rang a tremendous laugh. With a great rustle of petticoats, Désirée suddenly appeared, her hands over the coping of the wall. She was bare-

311

headed, arms bare to the elbows, face scarlet with triumph. She must have climbed on top of the manure-heap.

'Serge, Serge!' she yelled.

At this very instant, Albine's coffin had reached the bottom of the grave, and the men drew out the ropes. One of the peasants tossed in the first shovelfull of earth.

'Serge, Serge!' she yelled, louder still, clapping her hands, 'the heifer has made a new calf!'